THE LAST STRATIOTE

Also by LeAnn Neal Reilly

The Mermaid's Pendant

An Ordinary Drowning (The Mermaid's Pendant #1)

Grounding Magic (The Mermaid's Pendant #2)

Saint Sebastian's Head

The Last Stratiote

LeAnn Neal Reilly

Zephon Books

Reviews of The Last Stratiote

"*The Last Stratiote* contains the relentless pace of James Patterson's novels; the political intrigue and pragmatic characters found in Daniel Silva's and Jeffery Archer's books; and the historicity, philosophy, and theology of Anne Rice's work. The novel is a reinvention of the vampire mythos, bringing new blood to the tired trope. It is infused with intensity and intelligence that does not emphasize vampirism."—Lee Gooden, 5-star *Clarion Foreword Review*

"In this urban fantasy tale, the author digs into the bloody history and language of the Balkans, and Albania in particular, to create the mercenary Elira. [Neal] Reilly's deep knowledge of the Balkans' history of oppression and her use of native languages give the narrative a keen authenticity."—*Kirkus Reviews*

"This novel has a lot going for it. [Neal] Reilly's writing skills are top-notch; she handles language very well in bringing out the exact effects that she wants, and she knows the perfect way to handle scenes that in lesser hands could be a challenge."—Werner Lind, author of *LifeBlood*

First published in the United States by Zephon Books in 2013.

Hardcover Edition ISBN: 978-1-7351318-5-6

Print Edition ISBN: 979-8-9850781-0-7

Digital Edition October 2021 ISBN: 978-1-7351318-6-3

Cover design by Volodymyr Stadnyk

SECOND EDITION

It was the best of times, it was the worst of times, it was the age of wisdom, it was the age of foolishness, it was the epoch of belief, it was the epoch of incredulity, it was the season of Light, it was the season of Darkness, it was the spring of hope, it was the winter of despair, we had everything before us, we had nothing before us, we were all going direct to Heaven, we were all going direct the other way—in short, the period was so far like the present period, that some of its noisiest authorities insisted on its being received, for good or for evil, in the superlative degree of comparison only.
—Charles Dickens, **A Tale of Two Cities**

Lord! We know what we are but know not what we may be.
—Ophelia, **Hamlet**, Act 4, Scene 5

One

"SHARP SCENT OF HOT BLOOD," Elira breathed, pressing into the shadows against the rough brick wall at her back, "blooms beneath"—here she risked a glance at the roofline above her—"darkening skies."

She grinned and ran her tongue along the edge of her front teeth, grateful for the rush of adrenaline clarifying her hazy thoughts. It was always a sign of impending success when she composed blood haiku as she tracked her enemies. She pulled the tiny earphones out, but the heavy beat of the club music she'd been listening to as she raced through downtown Boston remained in the rhythm of her veins. As long as that rhythm played, she'd be an avenging angel, a true stratiote as in the old days. Clutching the pouch holding Branilo's finger bone where it lay on her chest, she squinted toward the street. Any second now, the three men she stalked would walk past the alley's mouth. And then she'd appease her bloodlust. For another day, anyway.

The first sloping shoulder slid into view. Moonlight gleamed on the dark metal of a gun barrel.

"*Pidhi budalla,*" said a rough voice. *Stupid cunt.*

Elira felt her grin turn wild as she eased away from her hiding place. She finished the three-line poem: "Justice rends March night."

Another burly man followed behind the first, his gait awkward. Elira scented perfume, and her eyes narrowed as she studied his oddly formed outline. He wasn't alone. They'd already snatched a victim. He tugged the stumbling woman along between him and the third man, a tall, nervous-looking fellow whose head bobbed as he scanned the sidewalk around them. In his jerky dance, Elira recognized the twitchiness of the drug addict, not nervousness about her. These *derra—pigs*—never suspected that she hunted them until it was too late.

Bending down, she pulled her dagger from her boot, its heavy carved grip making her heart sing. All too soon its weight only echoed against her palm. The tall man grunted and lurched, a frantic bony hand reaching for the blade embedded in his left shoulder. A second later, he dropped to the pavement, and Elira faded behind a dumpster. She really didn't need surprise, but cold fear from her prey always added to the flavor of her kills. And she'd left it too long, her blood duty. She didn't have the strength now to finish them off in hand-to-hand combat. She'd had to follow them like a thief.

Yet another debt she owed to Dr. Aconcio.

The two remaining miscreants whirled, the second dragging the woman so hard she fell to her knees before he pulled her upright again. She never cried out, but Elira's grin disappeared as her vision darkened. No matter. She only needed her nose to know where the *derra* were.

The first man, more than a head taller than Elira, crouched over their fallen comrade. Elira listened to his bastardized Albanian, a sound that caused her lips to peel back against her teeth and her nostrils to flare. He clearly recognized the symbols on the grip of her knife. The symbols that told him just exactly what kind of death came for them. Bitter saliva coated her mouth, whetting her appetite and forcing her to swallow.

As she edged along the dumpster's side, she mouthed one of her favorite lines from Macbeth to refocus her attention: "'Blood will have blood.'"

She'd reached the end of the dumpster closest to the group, a garrote wrapped around her hands, when she lost all control of the situation.

An air current penetrated her awareness, distracting her as she stepped out into the open. Across from the dim figures just beyond the reach of the nearest streetlamp, a red-hot shadow wavered against a wall. *Mut! Shit!* Who the hell was that? Male by his smell. A compatriot for these assholes? Certainly not the average unaware pedestrian. Should she abandon her duty? Abandon the woman being struck by the vicious animal gripping her so tight that Elira felt the pain in her own arm?

Even as the instinctive hard-driving beat she'd been moving to stuttered and lost its rhythm, the gun-toting bastard caught a glimpse of her. Shouting his triumph, he whipped his hand around and fired. Elira managed to throw herself backward, launching herself off the ground before palming the top edge of the dumpster into a wobbly back handspring. A tearing burn in her thigh confirmed the hit. She dropped behind the dumpster out of sight, her left hand pressed against the wound.

"Biri i një derr mut-ngrënie!" Son of a shit-eating pig. The hoarseness of her whisper infuriated her.

"Unë dyshoj se ai ka qenë në një fermë kohët e fundit." I doubt he's been on a farm lately. The answering whisper came from her right.

Elira jumped into a crouch at this new threat, her thigh screaming as she turned to face him. The stranger she'd sensed across the street leaned against the end of the dumpster, a finger against his mouth. The *derr* sneaking along the street had no idea he was there—her enemies knew that she fought alone. She didn't recognize her surprise visitor, but his American accent and furtive actions told her a lot. She'd use him to best these bastards, and then she'd see what else he'd be good for.

Elira grinned again, the heavy beat returning to orchestrate her movements and drown out the agony burning her leg. Nodding at the stranger, she fell onto her ass and began dragging her injured leg, whimpering as she hadn't since the first time she'd been wounded in battle. Hadn't she learned then how the enemy saw a wounded woman? As she came out into the streetlight, time slowed along with her breath. She dragged her head up, her hair hiding the hungry light that she knew shone in her eyes.

The gunman's own eyes gleamed as he took in Elira's blood slicking the pavement. He straightened and began to walk toward her, his gun held down at his side.

"Jo aq e tmerrshme." Not so terrifying. His disdain ratcheted Elira's fury to an icy implacability.

Behind him, the third man had already started dragging the woman away, no longer watching to see his colleague kill Elira.

"Stupid fuckers," she said in English.

Even as his eyelids flickered at her virulent tone, he began raising his gun hand. At the same time, the stranger kicked the gun away, following his kick with a tackle. Elira didn't wait to see if the American could take the gunman down. He clearly knew how to handle himself.

Instead, she leveraged her fury to spur her waning strength, pushing to her feet before taking after the final man. She snatched up her dagger from the dead man before hitting full speed, its weight against her palm more than enough to gird her resolve.

The third man heard her boots pounding behind him and whirled. He held a knife to the woman's throat. "*Ndalur, lugat! Ose unë do të prerë fytin e saj.*" *Stop, specter! Or I'll cut her throat.*

Elira halted on the pavement and grasped the dagger along its blunt edge, balancing its weight. The pain in her thigh had grown excruciating, but she ignored it to smile at the *derr mut-ngrënie.* She ran a deliberate tongue across her upper teeth and took a long breath through her nose. His rank fear increased her excitement. When he did nothing but blink, wide eyed, she laughed.

"*Shkoni përpara. Unë jam duke pritur, derr.*" *Go ahead. I'm waiting, pig.*

She saw when he realized that she meant it, saw when he concluded that he'd throw the woman to her as some sort of bloody bone as if she were a growling dog who'd foolishly choose to let him escape. She felt her triumph at his arrogant ignorance, felt her heart slow and calm in preparation for the final spring when she'd land on him and gut him from crotch to gullet, spraying that hot blood for which she'd waxed so poetic.

In less than a heartbeat, everything she cared about, everything she was and would always be—everything that made the world spin on its axis—disappeared.

"Mirjeta!" The anguished voice of the American tore through the evening air.

Elira glanced over and her gaze riveted on his, which was focused on the other woman. He stood, vividly revealed, within the phosphorescent halo of a streetlight.

His eyes. They were the color of the Adriatic as seen from the coast below her beloved Lezhë.

Dizziness returned. The internal driving beat that always underlay her fighting shifted into something else, something long unfamiliar but just as powerful.

The dizziness passed, and Elira knew what she must do.

She dropped her dagger and stepped forward. "*Zgjidhni mua në vend të saj.*" *Take me for her.*

As if to underscore what she gave her enemy, she wobbled in sudden overwhelming fatigue. Her increasingly incoherent thoughts latched onto the final chance of killing him before she lost consciousness.

The kidnapper blinked, the sweat slicking his brow. His gaze darted between Elira and the American, and he clutched his victim against his side as if suspicious of Elira's change of heart.

"*Shansi i fundit, derr.*" *Last chance, pig.* Elira snorted, wavering. She felt her life force throbbing out of her leg.

Before Elira finished another breath, the man shoved the woman toward the American, who caught her as she fell. Elira felt the Albanian's meaty hand on her shoulder as he pulled her onto his knife, but she let the fiery pain clarify her thoughts.

With her last strength, she gripped his neck and looked into his heartless black eyes. "*Një pickim për një pickim.*" *A bite for a bite.*

Then she bit down on his carotid with all her furious soul. As the darkness descended, she sighed at the hot saltiness coating her face and tongue.

WHILE LIFTING MIRJETA'S SAGGING form, James saw the strange, fierce woman follow the sex trafficker to the pavement, blood trailing from her in a grotesque arc. He heard her last words, followed by a sharp scream and a terrible thrashing, but despite the other man's efforts to dislodge his attacker, she clung to him, just as Mirjeta clutched at James, trembling. His own heart racing, James ran careful hands up and down Mirjeta's back, searching for any obvious wounds as much as trying to soothe. The entire time he murmured endearments in Albanian and wondered what the hell had just happened.

Rapid footsteps sounded from the direction he'd come. Hugging Mirjeta, he turned, his Walther PPK rising to meet the intruder.

"Andrew!" Relief shook his voice, but his hand stayed steady as he dropped his arm.

His partner, Andrew Cruncher, his suit still neat despite blocks spent racing after their group, stopped ten feet away.

“I called for an ambulance, but the guy who was knifed is dead.” He looked toward the two bodies on the sidewalk just beyond them. “A bloody night, eh?”

James shook himself. “Yeah.” He pulled away to look at the woman in his arms. “Mirjeta? I need to take a look at them.”

Mirjeta, her dark eyes wide, nodded and let her arms drop. Crouching, James held his PPK at the ready while reaching a cautious hand to feel at the woman’s neck. Her pulse, weak and tachycardic, confirmed his fears. Under her, the man who’d held a knife to Mirjeta’s throat only moments before stared through the woman’s wild mane but didn’t blink. Whatever she’d done, she’d managed to take him out, and he didn’t feel the least sorry. Holstering his weapon, he turned the woman over and saw the blood covering her face all the way down her torso where the wicked handle of a knife protruded. Beneath the blood, her skin was cold and pale.

In the distance, sirens shrilled.

“Thank God,” he breathed.

“What? That one gonna make it?”

James looked up at Cruncher. “It’ll be a close one. She’s lost a lot of blood.” As he spoke, he pulled off his belt to stop the bleeding from her thigh wound, but there was no way he’d remove the knife before the ambulance got there.

“What’s that tattoo on the back of her right hand? Some sort of gang insignia?”

James studied the back of the woman's limp hand where the design of a circle with rays on it stood out in stark contrast against her skin. Inside the circle was something like a cross.

"Doesn't look like anything I've seen on gang members." He frowned and pushed up the sleeve of her leather jacket where a second cross had been tattooed. "It does look familiar though."

Mirjeta, who'd stood nearby during James's examination, spoke now. "They're traditional Albanian Gheg tattoos. I've seen them in history books and on some old peasant women."

"She looks like you." Cruncher crouched down next to the unconscious woman before looking up at Mirjeta. "Except for the crazy hair, piercings, blue face paint, tats, and oh, yeah, that vicious scar on her upper lip, you two could be sisters."

James frowned. It was true, he supposed. This stranger who'd nearly ruined his mission—and in some ways had totally fucked it up given that there were now two dead Albanians he had to explain—had the same hair color and build as Mirjeta. She was dressed in a short, pleated skirt, floral leggings, and steel-toed boots. Studying her features, he found himself agreeing that she had almost the same cheekbones, the same jaw line. Even her delicate eyebrows curved in the same manner. He guessed she looked liked Mirjeta, if Mirjeta was a pale, twisted hip-hop pixie whose face held a certain feral glint even in repose.

"Who the hell is she?" James asked, muttering to himself, and began looking through her pockets for ID.

Mirjeta answered. "He called her 'lugat.' That's a term reserved for a really wicked person. Or a bloodsucking ghost."

She shivered and her teeth clattered together. The movement startled James, who looked up to see something wing across her features. Her gaze darted to the street around them, and she took a step closer to Cruncher, who'd dragged the dead sex trafficker away from the unconscious woman.

Cruncher laughed. "You mean a vampire? We got us a vampire here? I thought they all came from Transylvania. I know that's not too far from your neck of the woods but still." He paused and then, right on cue, said, "Neck. Get it? Hah! Neck? Vampires suck blood from the neck."

James groaned and wished the ambulance and local badges would arrive. Mirjeta appeared to be in shock and the woman on the ground was on the verge of bleeding out. He found a leather wallet in her jacket pocket and pulled out a driver's license.

"Elira Dukagjini."

"The Kanun of Lekë," said Mirjeta, her voice distracted and her gaze watching the shadows around them.

James recalled the set of Albanian laws written by a medieval prince often cited by northern Albanians to explain their blood feuds. How it related to this mysterious woman he didn't know, but he'd ask Mirjeta later.

Taking his jacket off, he laid it across the figure, smoothing her wild black hair from her face. As fierce as she'd been—and he'd only ever seen that level of vicious intent on the faces of The Ones when one of their own needed to be avenged—there was something vulnerable, almost adolescent, in her profile.

That's when he realized that she had more blood around her mouth. Cruncher's lame-ass joke about vampires echoed in his thoughts. Just as he found himself leaning forward to pull her upper lip away from her incisors, the ambulance and a squad car screeched to a halt in the street. Doors slammed, and voices filled the night, dominated by Cruncher's deep timbre as he flashed a badge and explained to the guys in blue who everyone was.

Everyone, that is, except the mysterious woman.

James shook his head and let his hand drop before standing up to meet and greet the new arrivals, making sure that the EMTs ignored the dead guy to take care of Mirjeta and the other woman.

After Cruncher's hasty sitrep, the cops ran up the block to collar the trafficker that James had left unconscious behind the dumpster. He turned back to the EMT who was tending the stabbing victim.

"She's in a bad way," said the EMT as he threaded an IV needle into her arm. He'd already replaced James's belt with a tourniquet, started her on oxygen, and taped the knife in her chest to secure it. "I can do my best to reconstitute her, but if we don't get out of here pronto, she'll be as stiff as the other one."

"How far's the ER?"

"ETA ten minutes to Mass General, give or take a couple." The EMT never ceased moving, his actions efficient and skilled. "But that's about all we've got. This one's as dry as I've ever seen, even taking both wounds into account. Her BP's through the floor and her heart sounds like a chipmunk's."

The other EMT joined him, and together they lifted the stranger onto a gurney, strapped her in, and hustled to the waiting ambulance. James was right behind.

When the EMTs flashed him a look, he said, "I'm riding in the back with you," and jumped up.

Cruncher helped Mirjeta up after him. Other than enough bruises to make James want to dismantle something as well as a cut on her forearm, she had no serious injuries. Before disappearing inside the ambulance, she paused and searched the surrounding shadows again. Something in her wide eyes made the hairs on the back of James's neck stand on end, but she said nothing and turned to go inside where she sat, zombie faced, on a bench. James sat next to her before putting his arm around her shoulders.

"You're safe, Mirjeta." She trembled at his words but said nothing. "We busted their ring earlier this evening. That's how we knew those *derra* had snatched you."

Mirjeta's gaze flickered toward the motionless woman on the gurney.

James's gaze followed. The EMT had cleaned the blood and blue face paint from the woman's face. Dark purple shadowed her lids and hollowed the soft skin under her eyes.

"Why? Why did they snatch me? And who is she?"

James found that he couldn't look at Mirjeta. "Everything points to Imam Xhemajl Krasniqi." Despite his care, fury clenched his jaw and tightened his voice.

When he glanced up, he caught the look of anguish on her face, her pallor. He took her hand."I'm not going to let anything happen to you. This is the United States. Krasniqi has no power here."

Mirjeta shivered and tried to pull her hand away. When he wouldn't let her, she laughed a little. "I don't suppose you found my violin?"

James shoved his fury about Krasniqi aside. It was an ancient burn that he'd long ago learned to ignore even as its subtle presence directed everything he did. "Lucky for you, sex traffickers don't value expensive and rare violins. It's safe."

Her fingers twitched inside his and her right hand curled, almost as if she imagined holding her beloved bow. "Thank you."

She looked up at him, and what he saw in her gaze more than repaid his fear and worry, but embarrassment slid over her features, displacing it.

She looked away. "You seem to appear just when I need you. Like a superhero or something."

Heat flared on the back of his neck. He cleared his throat. "I hardly qualify as Captain America."

"Then no one does." She turned back, and this time her gaze was somber. "How's your dad? I saw you two this afternoon."

Now it was his turn to look away. "Yeah, uh well. Pop always did like hearing you play."

"And you? Do you like hearing me play?" Her soft voice pinned him to the hard vinyl of the ambulance bench.

The EMT began swearing.

James's attention leapt to the other man, who had a stethoscope against the wounded woman's chest, and then moved to the Lifepak monitor. Her BP had fallen to 78 over 40, and her heart rate was a rapid 115 beats per minute. He watched as the other man administered epinephrine once, twice, three times to support her blood pressure, but her vital signs continued to deteriorate. The red Kool-Aid in her veins just wasn't enough to keep her going.

"She ain't gonna make it—she's going into cardiac arrest." The EMT looked up and called out to the driver, "Murph, tell 'em we need an immediate transfusion and a team standing by for emergency thoracotomy."

He began to intubate her.

"Cardiac tamponade?" James stood up and leaned over the gurney. "You need to drain her. Let me help."

The EMT turned startled eyes on him. "You got some EMS training?"

"The best in the world," James said. "Iraq and Afghanistan."

The man's sharp gaze traveled over James in the time it took him to exhale. "All right. I'm not certified, and I've only ever seen an ER doc do it once. Show me what you can do. But if anything happens, your bosses better make good with mine."

James nodded and got to work. It had been almost four years since he'd been in country—Afghanistan was his last tour—but he still dreamed in blood and guts. As the unknown woman's breathing became shallow and labored, his slowed and deepened. It was a trick his father had taught him to keep from letting the inherent terror of imminent death and his own pathetic efforts to stave it off win. Instead, he focused on minute actions: donning gloves, pulling the blanket down from her chest, bare except for the bandaged knife, and swabbing her skin. He observed her bone-white complexion and her small, almost pubescent breasts with their ashy-purple nipples. Compelling his mind to stay blank, he noted the image before shoving it aside.

"Blade?"

The EMT handed him a scalpel. Without hesitating, James sliced through the skin over her left breast, over what he'd been taught was the second intercostal space in the mid-clavicular line and through the pericardial membrane.

"14 gauge?' the EMT asked, holding a cannula out.

"Perfect."

James took the thin tube and inserted its tip into his incision. Dark blood, trapped in the sac around her heart, gushed out, but he knew there was more. A lot more.

"Give me a chest tube."

Working together, he and the EMT placed the flexible plastic tube in her chest, releasing copious amounts of once life-giving liquid.

"I estimate about three liters," he told the EMT. They so needed to be at the ER five minutes ago.

"Shit!"

The driver hit the brakes, nearly sending James and the EMT sprawling. Behind him, he heard a thump followed by Mirjeta's hoarse cry.

As he turned to find her rubbing her shoulder, the driver said, "What the fuck!"

"Murph, talk to me," the EMT yelled to his partner as he swiped up the blood that had sloshed from the basin that he held.

"Friggin' Bruins fans," the driver said.

He disappeared from view, but his next words suggested that he leaned out of the driver's window as he yelled. "Get out of the street, idiots! Can't you hear the siren?"

He leaned back even as the ambulance rolled forward what must have been only a couple of feet. "We ain't gettin' out of here anytime soon, bro'. The Bruins just beat the Devils for the division title."

The rock song Dirty Water—traditional victory song for all of Boston's professional sports teams—and loud laughter, voices, and even whoops filtered to them around the siren, upon which Murphy played a symphony of frustration in a futile effort to alert the milling and ecstatic hockey fans. Every ten seconds or so, he yelled again and took his foot off the brake, letting the ambulance creep forward to herd the fans.

The EMT next to James closed his eyes, pinching the bridge of his nose. His shoulders hunched, in what James guessed from long experience was a searing mix of hopeless rage, impotence, and despair.

"I'm O-neg," James said, his voice pitched to reach the EMT.

The EMT's head snapped up, and his gaze snagged onto James's. He didn't move.

"*Now,*" said James using his captain's voice and keeping his own gaze hard.

Without waiting for the man's nod, he urged Mirjeta into the EMT's seat and then lay down on the bench, rolling up his right sleeve.

The EMT pushed the gurney closer to James, who gave the other man pointers in how to transfuse his blood directly to the wounded woman.

Together, they watched the woman's vital signs stabilize, but James knew that they'd only delayed the inevitable: if they didn't get her into surgery in the next thirty minutes to stop the internal bleeding from the stab wound, she'd bleed out despite the transfusion.

"What's that?" Mirjeta gestured to James's exposed upper arm where a tattoo blackened his bicep. "I recognize the winged staff entwined by two serpents. It's used by doctors, right?"

"And paramedics. I was a paramedic in the Army."

The EMT looked away from the Lifepak monitor to the caduceus nestled among two overlapping arrows. "Dr. Hearst at Mass General has a tat like that. The A-One-Five is a Special Forces group assigned to the Mideast."

"The Silent Ones," Mirjeta read from James's tattoo. She looked at him, a question in her eyes.

James kept his gaze level but didn't answer.

Murphy's triumphant roar broke the silence. "Thank the ever-lovin' Lord! Boston's finest have arrived, and we can get out of this mess."

In moments the ambulance picked up speed, and James's instincts told him that they'd get to Mass General without losing the stabbing victim.

After swiveling his head to study her, he laughed as he recalled Cruncher's comments at the crime scene. "I suppose she looks like the undead."

The EMT started to take out the transfusion needle. "Well, she's certainly been staked."

Mirjeta's glance darted toward the motionless woman, whose dark hair stood out against the stark white sheets encasing her.

She laughed too, a slight wild edge to the sound. "She won't die. A *lugat* can't be killed except by wolves."

Then she shook her head, looked at James, and laughed again. When she spoke, she sounded sheepish. "I'm sorry. I'm being ridiculous, aren't I? It's been a very surreal night."

"Understood." James grinned at her.

What James couldn't know and Mirjeta wouldn't tell him was that at the moment she'd looked toward her savior, Elira Dukagjini's eerily pale eyes, wide open and fixed on her, had pierced her with their utter hate.

Back on the now-deserted sidewalk where Elira had killed the last of the three men, a silent figure crouched over the blood congealing on the pavement. An ornately carved walking stick lay on the ground near his right foot. He drew a cell phone from his coat pocket and dialed.

"I am afraid your men failed to acquire Mirjeta," he said in Albanian, a language that sang from his tongue as easily as the native Italian of the creature that he had subsumed. "She is untouchable for the moment. Federal agents have her in custody along with the only survivor of your hand-picked team."

He listened a moment. "No, I told you. I do not interfere. I just advise. When I have more information about the survivor, I will contact you."

The irate voice on the other end rattled the serenity of the night when it responded. He scowled and glanced down. Exhaling, he dipped a gentle fingertip into the cool blood and lifted it to his lips before touching a tentative tongue to the thickening liquid. A soft groan escaped him before he could suppress it.

"Please," he said, cutting the speaker off.

"Please," he said again, and a chill wind whipped down the street and around him. A thin cloud scurried across the moon. "Say no more. It will have blood. I am committed."

He swiped the bloody fingertip across his smartphone, ending the call. A grin widened his features as he placed his palms flat on the sidewalk and lowered his head to lap at the blood.

Two

THE LAST TIME SOMEONE HAD TRIED TO PRY HER HEART FROM HER CHEST, Elira had latched her teeth into his forearm and then wrapped her thighs around his neck and squeezed until his eyes had bugged out and he'd choked on his tongue.

Her fury at having to smell his stink—a combination of sweat, tobacco, and the dead man's favorite Turkish za'atar paste—after he'd collapsed onto her, pinning her to the ground, had blotted out the fiery pain between her ribs. It had also kept her from losing consciousness. To this day, she couldn't smell thyme, oregano, and marjoram blended with sumac and toasted sesame seeds without becoming simultaneously enraged and nauseous.

Poor Elira, she thought, paraphrasing the Bard while ignoring the present ache crushing her chest, *that eats the swimming frog, the toad, the todpole, the wall-newt and the water; that in the fury of her heart, when the foul fiend rages, eats cow-dung for sallets, swallows the old rat and the ditch-dog, drinks the green mantle of the standing pool—here she recalled the many times she'd knelt beside the foulest puddle and dipped her mouth to its brackish water—who hath had a horse to ride, and weapon to wear, but mice and rats, and such small deer, have been Elira's food for seven long year.*

She tried to laugh, but it came out a groan as deep as a growl, which pulled at the stitches in her chest and left her panting.

After her breathing returned to normal, she became aware that she lay on her back, her arms at her sides, and a coarse cotton sheet draped her from breasts to toes. The air felt cool on her exposed skin, raising gooseflesh. She shivered as unease filled her. When was the last time she'd been cold? And for all her marrow-deep aching and extensively bruised flesh, she hadn't felt so well so deep down for longer than she could remember.

A beep came from near her left shoulder, its sound muffled against something less solid than a wall, most likely a curtain. She tested her surroundings. The pungent scent of ammonia bit the tender inside of her nostrils, not quite stifling a familiar spicy cologne. The beeping sped up.

"It is not like you, my dear, to let your quarry bleed you so well. Or let anyone take you somewhere you did not intend to go, especially unconscious."

Now she did laugh. It was the special sputtering cough that she reserved for her law partner. It didn't hurt her chest because it stayed in her throat.

"How do you know I didn't have this little adventure in mind all along?" She hated how hoarse and strained her voice sounded. She told herself that was why she kept her eyes closed.

"Did you? Even for Mirjeta Gjakova, the daughter of the granddaughter of the great-granddaughter of your enemy? How curious." His whisper, poisonous as an asp, insinuated itself into her ear, and she flinched against her will.

Only Dr. Aconcio could approach without her hearing. She felt his fingertip slip under her hospital gown and trace over her breast. Fresh tenderness and taut skin met his delicate touch.

She wrenched her eyelids up and pinned her gaze on him. His pointy chin hovered inches from her face.

“It is also not like you to lose possession of your most precious relics.”

His eyes glittered. She wanted to spit into them. She wanted to dull their avarice and deny him any of the sustenance that he drew from her addiction.

Then she understood the meaning of his words. Her hand flew to her chest, to the empty hollow between her breasts where Branilo’s finger bone had lain curled like an embryo inside a black leather pouch. She’d worn it almost continuously since she’d stolen back to his grave against her cousin’s warning—three days after Branilo had died from blood plague, five days after falling in battle. Without conscious intent, her upper lip lifted from her teeth. She snapped at Dr. Aconcio, but he’d pulled his face away and looked at her.

Sinking back, she shrugged. “You should see what the others lost. Although I’m not sure. Is a carotid precious?” Even to her ears the quip rang hollow.

Dr. Aconcio ignored her. After a moment, he pulled the sheet down and opened the neck of her gown to touch the tender spot again. This time he pressed a fingernail into the incision there. Elira glared at him but didn’t cry out.

“Odd, isn’t it, my dear, that the American agent happened to be a former Army medic?”

He began digging at the stitches, pulling at them, watching her face as he did so. Elira felt the blood well to fill the tiny tears, felt the burning of her skin and the pulsing of her heart.

"How fortunate that he knew how to drain the blood from your chest. He inserted his cannula right here, almost exactly where your scar is. The one Branilo gave you, isn't that right?"

Elira tried again to deflect. "Astute observation as always, Doctor."

She narrowed her eyes. If she'd had her knife, he wouldn't have dared continue after her silent warning, but he knew the authorities had confiscated it. Still, she felt stronger than she'd felt in a long time.

"You'll have to bring it up again at Jink & Diddle after I get out of here."

Again, he ignored her, but his next words showed how well he read her. As usual.

"Ah, what a potent young man he must be, don't you think, my dear? I bet you feel his strength coursing through your veins even now. Perhaps you even feel ready to insist on a delay, hm?"

He laughed. It sounded as richly mellow as merlot, cultivated and easy. Only her familiar ears picked up the sting in the sibilant consonants.

Elira waited until he lowered his chin, shifting his gaze to focus on her chest as he tore another stitch free. As he lifted the bloody thread, she clamped her hand onto his wrist. The cold skin had the texture of leathery onionskin, not so much fragile as trivial—a bare attempt to lend some depth and volume to his lean frame. It covered bone as durable as steel.

"I do insist."

Dr. Aconcio's stare sharpened at her quiet tone, but he never looked at the fingers gripping him. Elira sensed the shift in him, the excitement that widened his eyes and increased his breathing.

"Just think: the blood of the righteous! He lay down next to you in the ambulance, rolled up his sleeve and told the EMT to transfuse his blood into you."

His free hand whipped around and caught the wrist of the hand gripping him. Under the fluorescent lights, the shadows under his eyes had darkened. Even his voice had deepened and hollowed.

Elira shivered.

"It was not simply a matter of permission, Elira. No, this brave, noble Homeland Security agent ordered the EMT to save your life by taking his blood. How delightful! How rare! We certainly do not experience that willingness every day, now do we?"

When she said nothing, he compressed her wrist until her fingers grew numb and icy, forcing Elira to realize just how warm and feeling they'd been. She held on, however, rising up to strike at him, sinking her teeth into the back of his spotted hand.

Dr. Aconcio chuckled and pulled his other hand free from her now-lax fingers before stroking it through the tangled mass of her hair.

"I know no reason to complain about such a precious gift, do you?" As he spoke, he slid his palm to the back of her head and pushed her mouth harder against his hand.

Elira gagged at the foul taste of him, the bitter, lifeless poison that leeched from his lacerated flesh. She struggled against his hold, her lips and teeth rolling against finger bones, her tongue pushing at the loose skin that had slipped into her mouth. He groaned.

Sitting upright, Elira punched him. Her hand, still slightly numb, crashed rock-like against his cheek.

"Enough!"

For a moment, she wasn't sure who had spoken. And then Dr. Aconcio raised his hand and, using a delicate forefinger and thumb, wiped the blood from the corners of his mouth.

"It is not enough. It will never be enough as you well know, my dear." His whisper only emphasized the finality of his statement.

Darting a look at the curtain, Elira licked her dry lips.

He answered her unspoken question. "No one is due to check you for another twenty minutes." And then he lunged.

They wrestled on her narrow hospital bed, silently, swiftly, and with the utmost compressed violence. It was a losing battle, no matter how resilient she felt. Even when he'd yanked both hands over her head, she bucked and writhed until he'd crawled up between her thighs, pinning her within the entangling sheets and hospital gown. He trembled, and he panted, letting out sour, cold puffs of breath. Unlike the countless enemies that she'd grappled whose heavy warm bodies gave her something to push against, something to sink fang and claw into, struggling against Dr. Aconcio was like being flailed with barbed wire wrapped around two-by-fours.

Almost as soon as they'd begun, it was over. He touched her forehead just between her brows, and she stilled.

"Mine," he said, leaning back and looking into her eyes.

Then he trailed his lips, as rough as parchment, across her cheek, down her throat, and over her chest, nudging the hospital gown open. Elira felt the last thread give way. Tears pricked her eyes. Furious, she turned her head to study the shadows on the other side of the opaque white curtain.

As Aconcio's icy lips parted over her breast, Elira bit the inside of her mouth, letting the metallic tang of blood mask the salt of her tears. She let go of rational thought and drifted into the memory of one of her favorite Scottish pipe tunes, *Farewell to Nigg*. Its haunting drone tapped into other memories, bringing up the scents of wood smoke, heather, and damp earth. In a heartbeat, Duncan was with her. He laughed at her, its rough, knowing sound conveying how easily he'd recognized her fierce love of Scottish music—one that she'd nurtured as much because the music never failed to bring Duncan back to her as because it called to the roots of her soul.

"Lass, ye've a way of takin' what ye find for yer own even as ye insist ye've got the best there is."

In this lucid dream, she had the power to call up Duncan's words from the first time that she'd brought out a *gajde*, the Albanian bagpipe that had made him chortle so long that he'd gotten dizzy.

"What happened? Ye've only got one pipe! Did ye take it away from its mother too soon?"

She'd hit him, of course, but not too hard. Just enough for his grin to fade and his dancing eyes to grow intent as he leaned in to kiss her. They'd made love, *gajde* and grownup Highland bagpipes forgotten.

Closing her eyes, she could almost summon up Duncan's shadowy features and the weight of his muscular torso, glistening in firelight as he drove into her, whispering endearments and enchantments in Gaelic.

When they'd been together, she'd almost forgotten Branilo. That had been the only time she'd removed the pouch with his finger bone from around her neck, carefully placing it in a carved box. It had lain there a long time, and for once in her life she'd been free. Free from Dr. Aconcio's toxic presence. Without her relic, he could never find her. It had drawn him to her all those years ago when her loss was still raw.

She might have been free forever, Branilo and her own Albanian heritage abandoned, if Duncan had lived longer.

"Come lass," Duncan said, no longer a vivid presence but a whisper in her ear. "Come with me. Let it go. I'm waitin' for ye."

Then the lucid dream faded along with the strains of *Farewell to Nigg*. Her wet cheeks burned.

Dr. Aconcio levered himself up onto his forearms. His gently flushed face gave him the look of a merry tippler. A dangerous illusion. "Better, my dear?"

Elira, drained, lifted her dull gaze to his before looking away.

A smirk twisted the corners of his mouth. "Good."

He pushed up to stand, straightened his blazer, smoothing it down and buttoning the bottom button, and snatched up his walking stick from where it lay against a chair.

"You know, I do wonder what would have happened if that brave agent hadn't managed to drain the blood threatening to drown your heart? Would I have found you in the morgue then?"

He chuckled as if at some private joke. "That would have been a shame, wouldn't it? I would never have discovered such a noble soul working for the U.S. government."

Elira, who'd been studiously ignoring the good doctor, turned sharp eyes on him—as she knew he'd intended with that last comment. "What could possibly interest you in a noble soul?"

He chuckled again at the knife edge to her tone. "What could possibly interest me in a noble soul except his burning desire for revenge, making him a perfect candidate for my law practice?"

Elira watched him as closely as one of the eponymous hawks of her homeland's mountains.

Dr. Aconcio smiled at her. "But I suspect that you knew that and thought to keep it from me."

Elira said nothing, just waited for the warning.

Dr. Aconcio twirled his walking stick, took two steps, and then paused at the curtain's edge to look back at her. "You know what I am going to say, so I will not, eh? We are partners in law, after all, so there can and will be no secrets between us."

Elira stared at him, black despair streaking through her.

And then Duncan's spirit touched her, dissipating it. "As Viktor Frankl said about the Nazis, you'll never own what's inside me. There I'm always free."

Her partner narrowed his eyes. In the clinical light, he appeared to grow taller and more menacing, the walking stick becoming a weapon.

He laughed, soft and assured. "Herr Doctor Frankl. What a confused soul. Even though his heart told him the truth, his mind kept him tied to the Old Law. It really is too bad that his heart was what mattered in the end or he might have joined us."

He paused, for effect she knew.

"Let us not dissemble, Elira. You could be free, if you chose to be. Heed my advice and do not mention it again. My patience extends only so far."

Silence stretched between them.

"Ah, well, I must be going. Business calls, but this has been a delightful interlude for me. Not that all our interludes are not delightful, but this one was particularly sweet."

He gestured with a magnanimous arm.

"I have left a bag with a change of clothes and another of those music players just inside the door. You will want to return to your apartment and shower, of course, but then you will want to retrieve your dagger and pouch from James Goodman, the ICE agent. His address is also in the bag. Perhaps, with persuasion, he will give you access to the last sex trafficker before the impatient imam negotiates his release from jail. Either way, I am sure you need a fix or you will soon suffer withdrawal, yes?"

And then he'd gone, leaving a cloud of cologne and a sense of deafness like the aftermath of a detonation.

Elira let out a long breath and raised her arms overhead, stretching. Dr. Aconcio was right as usual. Her body—that stranger she'd awoken to find—had started to recover its familiar hot itchiness. If she didn't get a fix in the next twelve hours, the nausea, vomiting, diarrhea, and muscle cramps would begin. Not to mention the general weakness and depression.

She pushed the sheet down and kicked it from her feet. No matter. She'd lived with the withdrawal symptoms so long that they didn't send her into a panic. There were ways to mitigate them. In fact, it had become a game to see how long she could go before she gave in to her craving. She'd see what she could do to take the edge off before visiting James Goodman. She didn't need an address for him, however. She didn't understand why it would be so, but his blood coursing through her veins bound her to him in a way that she'd never felt before. His every heartbeat echoed in her chest.

A vivid image of Adriatic blue clobbered her halfway to the bag. Then a slow smile released her. The good doctor had been right about the agent's potency—and what means she'd use to persuade him to take her to the last *derr*.

As Iago might say, she grinned to herself, *there's nothing like making the beast with two backs*.

Elira pulled on her clothes, but she no longer shivered. Her body temperature had dropped to match that of the air.

JAMES NEVER SAW OR heard Elira Dukagjini before she appeared behind him as he unlocked his apartment door. Between the astounding news Emil had given him that afternoon and the unmitigated mess his Albanian sex trafficking case had become—not to mention his inability to keep Mirjeta out of his thoughts—he didn't have his head in the game. Not even close. If the young woman had been an assassin, she couldn't have picked a better time to ambush him.

One moment he was alone, the next she was on top of him. "Did you know Shakespeare never used the word 'fuck'?"

James started at Elira's velvet whisper. He felt her press herself against him, a hand running up under his jacket to caress his flank. A scent of something leafy and floral drifted around him.

"He preferred instead to tease his audience with myriad puns. Verbal wanking so to speak. And they loved it, from lowborn to high."

James let out a breath, but his heart raced. He wanted to move but felt strangely immobile. A tremor raced down his spine as her firm nipples drilled into the base of his shoulder blades. *Christ!* He'd swear neither of them wore anything the way his skin burned.

"Ms. Dukagjini." *Great.* He sounded strangled.

"Puns like 'hit it,' 'go to it,' 'do,' 'jump,' 'lay it,' 'blow' and 'finger.'" She enunciated each word, the soft, accented syllables twining around his thoughts as a fingertip traced the outer rim of his ear.

“For the romantics, he used ‘dance’ and ‘kiss.’” She rose onto her toes to press a kiss above his collar. “For the less romantic, furtive fucks became ‘trunk-work,’ ‘stair work,’ and ‘behind-door-work.’”

She slid down his back, before planting her hands at either side of his waist. “I’m afraid he didn’t use ‘outside-front-door-work’ though.”

James closed his eyes, his key clutched between thumb and forefinger. Breathing in her scent had made him dizzy.

“You disappeared from Mass General without a release. The hospital notified the police, who notified me.”

She ignored him. “Taste, take, tumble, assail, assault, besiege, ransack—you’d think sex was war, wouldn’t you? Or how about ‘tup’? That’s sheep fucking.”

He cleared his throat and focused on speaking. “Dr. Hearst showed me your file. He’s never seen anyone who came so close to bleeding out from a heart laceration walk away in less than a week.”

Just as he said this, she pinched his nipples, causing him to suck in a ragged breath and arch his back. “Stop that!”

“Perhaps you’d rather talk about nothing.” She laughed and rubbed against him; it was a throaty sound that brought an involuntary tingle to his groin.

“Yes, of course you would. ‘Nothing’ meant ‘cunt’ or ‘fucking.’ Said as two separate words, it meant both. And cock as well. So ‘Much Ado About Nothing’ is really about doing the nasty. Clever wordplay, yes?”

James found himself panting, which made him simultaneously exasperated and excited. This woman, whoever she was, was playing him like the most cherry Fucking New Guy ever to wear a uniform. He swallowed hard.

"Listen to me! You've got to return to Mass General. They found some anomalies, especially in your blood."

The she-demon clinging to his back clearly heard him. She paused, but then her hands slipped into his pockets. He jerked at her touch.

"Blood and fucking. My favorite wordplay." Here she let her fingers grip the inside of his thighs. "Shakespeare spoke of 'blood desire,' a 'distempered blood,' and 'hot blood.' His characters 'bite,' 'exchange blood,' and 'mingle bloods.' Sounds like a teenage girl's wet dream."

James gritted his teeth and spun away, pushing Elira against the wall next to his door. Beneath his talon grip, she stood still and gazed at him, unblinking. James, who'd been about to speak, found himself tongue-tied with a sudden stinging in his chest.

They stood there while his heartbeat slowed, and his thoughts cleared. Elira waited while he studied her, her scarred and pierced features lambent and haunting—she reminded him of a will o' the wisp, that dangerous fairy light that leads unwary travelers to their watery doom in Celtic folklore.

"If I hadn't seen you take out those *derra*, I'd think you were a teenage girl yourself," he said, a trace of hoarseness belying the hardness in his voice. "And if you hadn't saved a woman's life, I would arrest you right now just for the problems you've caused me."

Something flickered across her eyes. "Not just any woman."

James hesitated, but for reasons he didn't understand, he confirmed what she'd implied. "Not just any woman."

They stood locked there, tension crackling between them until she tilted her chin.

"She means nothing to me," she hissed. Her light eyes intensified in luminosity, almost obscuring the darker ring around their irises. "Justice means everything."

"Does 'justice' have anything to do with the uterine scarring Dr. Hearst found?" He didn't mention the blunt trauma that had caused it. Or the fact that she could never conceive because of it despite ovulating normally.

Elira looked away from him but said nothing.

"You've been tortured, haven't you?" James gentled his fingers along with his voice. When she didn't answer, he decided to leave it. "You've got to go back. Your appendix is swollen—it's five or six inches long, about twice as large as normal. You've also got elevated antibodies and a high white blood count. Your red blood count is high, too."

Her gaze speared him. "So?"

"So, you need more tests. Something's got your immune system revved up. The antibody level almost doubled just while you were in the ICU."

She laughed, but this time her laugh sounded hollow and stony edged. "Nothing can kill me," she said in a flat voice.

James almost believed her certainty.

“I don’t need any doctor to tell me about my blood. I’m from the mountains, for one thing.”

“Which means you’d naturally have a higher red blood count.”

“Maybe I’m allergic to your blood.” She looked at him from under her eyelashes. “You gave me blood, didn’t you?”

“I’m type O negative and you’re type AB.”

“The universal donor giving to the universal recipient. It couldn’t have worked out better.”

“Look, I’m clean—I didn’t pass anything on to you. If anything, my blood may have jumpstarted your immune system. You can’t know what’s going on unless you return. It may be nothing serious, but it may signal a serious infection. Or cancer.” James narrowed his eyes. “How did you find me?”

She shrugged. “A reliable source.”

“Did this source tell you how to track those pieces of shit the other night?”

She said nothing, meeting his glare with her own.

James made a sudden decision. Holding onto her upper arm, he unlocked his door and shoved her inside before pointing to his sofa. “Sit.”

Elira smirked at him and half sat on the sofa’s back as he made his way around the room turning on lights. He stopped when he reached her. As on their first meeting, she wore leggings and a short skirt, its dull green-and-blue plaid making him think of a kilt. Despite the freezing March night, nothing covered her muscular arms except tattoos, lettering on her right shoulder and something winged on her left. A cotton bustier with thick straps revealed even more milky-blue skin at breast and midriff and another tattoo that disappeared into the waistband of her skirt. Heavy Mary Janes and a wide black ribbon around her slender neck made her look like a perverse schoolgirl.

Every exposed inch of skin glowed as if lit from within—every inch except the raised and thickened scar over her left breast, reminding him just how close she'd come to dying.

He crossed his arms over his chest. "Maybe I should just take you in right now for murder."

She grinned. "Think you can?"

Reacting to the challenge, James lunged for her, only to find himself falling over the back of the sofa and Elira above him.

"Sorry, *luftëtar të forte*." He heard the laughter in her voice as she called him mighty warrior. "No one takes me without my consent. *Kuptoni?*"

Understand? He understood all right. He understood that this little wench was a pain in his ass.

He levered himself to his feet, shaking his head and turning away from her. Sighing, he shrugged out of his jacket and dropped it onto a nearby chair before heading to his galley kitchen. He kept his shoulder holster on.

"Coffee? I can make it Greek if you prefer."

A gleam came over her expression. "Yes. Make it sweet. Very sweet."

"Why are you here?" he asked over his shoulder as he began pulling out the necessary items.

"You have something of mine. Two things, in fact."

"Ah, I see now. Feel naked without your wicked little blade?"

For the second time that evening, she ambushed him. This time, to his chagrin, the garrote around his neck told him she'd tired of her earlier seduction.

He froze.

"Not especially," she said in silken tones. She let the garrote slide free and dangled it before him. It was the wide black ribbon she'd been wearing. "Even when I'm naked, I'm not."

He felt her cool lips on his neck, and then the edge of her front teeth scraped toward his collar. Unbidden, the image from the ME's report of the second Albanian, his throat ripped open, flashed across James's inner eye. He shivered, wondering what he'd brought into his home.

And then her weight lifted from his back, and she slipped off him.

When he looked over his shoulder, Elira sat at his combination dining table and desk. She gestured at the stack of mail and case files, the dirty cereal bowl, the half-empty bottle of fish food sitting next to the 12-gallon tank filled with scummy water, the dock holding his digital music player, and a myriad other bits of detritus he'd let build up.

"Get visitors much? You might want to clean up a bit before inviting her here."

James turned a deliberate back on her and began making Greek coffee.

"Okay, I get it. You're one bad Albanian princess with a huge chip on her shoulder. But don't push it, Ms. Dukagjini. Messing with a federal agent, especially after what you did two days ago to Krasniqi's men, is a sure way to get your Albanian ass hauled to prison."

"Might be fun. I could form my own gang. I always wanted my own gang." A trace of mock wistfulness colored her words.

James poured the *glykos* into two espresso cups and carried them to the table before sitting across from her. In the light from the hanging lamp, he could see the blue veins running under the thin skin over her breast.

"What else?"

She didn't pretend to misunderstand the question. "The bag you cut off my neck." The humor had been wrung from her voice.

"Uh huh. The one with the human bone in it? Friend or family?" He picked up his Greek coffee and sipped. "Little creepy, don't you think? Even for a certified Albanian whack-job such as yourself."

She made a gesture with her lips that bore little resemblance to smiling. "My betrothed." Then she sipped her *glykos*.

"Sorry to hear that." James felt a twinge but pushed it aside. "And the dagger? It's got some pretty carving all over it. My expert says it's a medieval Turkish ear dagger. Very rare. Very valuable. Don't tell me. It's an old family heirloom."

Now her lips did curve into the feral grin she'd worn during the attack on Krasniqi's men. "No. That I took off my first kill. After I took his head off his shoulders."

"He the one who raped you?"

"No, they died much more slowly. And painfully." She sipped again. "He's the traitorous Venetian who let them inside our defenses."

James wasn't surprised to hear that the Italians had insinuated themselves into the Albanian mafia, but he didn't know the Venetian connection.

Nodding, he finished his coffee, letting the bitter grinds sludge his cup's bottom. "You're to be commended. Throwing an ear dagger and killing someone takes a lot of skill. I doubt I could do it."

"What? They don't teach Special Forces how to throw with long, unbalanced blades? Tsk, tsk."

James blinked at her taunt. *Who* was *she?* "The ear dagger is evidence, Ms. Dukagjini. It must remain in federal hands until we finish prosecuting the remaining man." He paused to let that sink in, noting her scowl—followed by a look of calculation.

Taking it as his cue, he added, "You cooperate and testify against Duka, we'll make sure you get your belongings back. That's how we do it here in the U.S. We have courts and judges, not blood feuds."

Elira picked up a book from among the debris on the table. "Let's see. What do federal agents read before bed? The Everlasting Man by G. K. Chesterton."

She set it down and picked up another. "*Averroes, Maimonides, and Aquinas: Aristotle's Heirs*. What a nerdy tongue twister. You're a versatile verbal wanker, aren't you, fuckchop?" She grinned as she used the Army slang for a screwup. "A Moor, a Jew, and a Catholic. Now there's the beginning of a *terrible* joke."

James grabbed her wrist. Although she didn't have any goose bumps, she felt cold. And strong.

"I don't know how you found out about Ms. Gjakova's kidnapping. I don't know how you know so much about me. But you're obviously no innocent bystander, no matter what my preliminary report claims. I'd like to keep this case simple, but I'm not above moving you to my list of suspects. *Kuptoni?*"

She glanced at his hand. He dropped it, angry at himself for letting her bravado goad him into physical persuasion. When she looked at him again, the temperature of his apartment dropped thirty degrees, chilling him to the marrow. She stood up and walked toward the door leading to the hall, her movements as graceful and deadly as a panther. As she turned, he read the name *MacNeil* below a circular design on her upper arm. Along her upper back ran the Albanian words *Të shpejtë për shpirtin, të vrasin për nder* in blood-red lettering. *Fast for the soul, kill for honor.*

Albanians made the worst enemies.

She stopped at the door but didn't look back at him. When she spoke, her low voice rang in the stillness.

"You do what you have to do, Agent Goodman. But know this: Elira of the Dukagjini knows her duty. These *derrat mafia*, they dishonor Albania before the world. They dishonor their blood through their drug dealing, their selling of women and children, their stealing and killing and violence. I don't need your laws or your justice to deal with them."

She paused, turning to look at him over her shoulder. "Some say Shakespeare had only three basic themes: sex, murder, and magic. What say you? Which one do you think draws me?"

Before he could answer, she'd slipped out the door, letting it click shut behind her.

After she'd left, James sat, lost in thought for almost fifteen minutes. Then he moved a stack of case files and some mail to reveal a small leather pouch. He reached behind the fish tank and snagged the tip of a dagger, pulling it out to lie next to the pouch.

James hefted the double-sided triangular blade. His expert at the Museum of Modern Art in New York had nearly wet her pants when she'd handled Elira's dagger. According to Dr. Julianne Greaves, he held a 15th-century Nasrid weapon, probably from North Africa and definitely worth millions.

Called ear daggers because of their unique round pommel design and once worn by great nobles throughout Europe (Dr. Greaves showed him a Windsor portrait of young Edward VI wearing one), the blade and grip strap of this particular example had been overlaid with hunting scenes in gold. Arabic and Latin inscribed the ears. Although Dr. Greaves couldn't be sure without examining Elira's dagger more closely, her gut told her that the same hand had made two others like it, one in the Bargello Museum in Florence and the other in the Ambrosian Library in Milan.

James didn't care whether the dagger had been made by the same Moorish smith or an obsessive geek who spent his days at Society for Creative Anachronism gatherings. He didn't care if there were two more like it under lock and key in Italian museums. That's not what intrigued him.

What really tweaked his nose was this: How did a young Albanian immigrant come to know its weight so well she could throw it with deadly accuracy at a man twenty-five feet away?

THREE

MIRJETA, HER HOURS INCREASINGLY HAUNTED by memories of pale eyes, boarded the T one sweltering July afternoon for the necessary, and inevitable, meeting with the woman who had rescued her from Krasniqi's henchmen. Despite firm attempts to squelch an exquisite gothic sensibility, she shivered as she stepped out of the Porter Square station, rubbed her bare arms with clammy palms, and swallowed around the ice cube wedged at the base of her throat. Crossing Somerville Avenue, she headed toward her doom behind the Porter Square Shopping Center. She didn't expect to find a slightly decrepit two-family Victorian, its porch sagging a little and the storm door on the left entrance missing its lower pane.

Nor had she imagination enough, despite her gothic sensibility, to anticipate what she found on the right half of the two-story house. Above the worn red paint of the entrance hung a sign with the rather cryptic words *Jink & Diddle* lettered in a kind of Middle Earth font. Below them, she read *Café, Bookstore, and Seisúns*.

"*Idiot i pa kuptim.*" *Silly idiot.*

Shaking her head, she stepped up onto the porch, her thudding steps reassuringly ordinary. The front door to the bookstore creaked open at that moment, the overhead bell jangling, and a white-haired gentleman wearing a tailored pinstriped suit and carrying a walking stick stepped out. Mirjeta began to move out of his way, but his head swiveled at her movement, and he held the door for her.

"Thank you," she said, glancing toward his face with a smile that froze as her gaze met his. In that brief encounter, something slithered through her.

Later, anxiety would clutch her as she tried to describe what she'd felt to James. "His eyes weren't natural. I know I must be remembering wrong, but every time I recall them, I imagine they were all pupil, you know, all black in the center. Now I know what you Americans mean when you say 'somebody just walked over my grave.'"

Shuddering, she would continue, "He said good day to me in the most cultured voice I've ever heard. It reminded me a bit of that actor, the Mexican one. Ricardo Montalbán. Only his accent wasn't quite the same."

Today that benevolent association failed to occur to her. Instead, his sharp features and ginger-tinged hair called to mind a fox, one hanging around the door of a henhouse. Mirjeta stood rooted until, with a slight smile on his thin lips, the old man tilted his head a fraction. She tore her gaze away and darted into the shop, shivers undulating through her. During her brief flight, she was transported to her eight-year-old self, huddled under thin covers between her mother and the bedroom wall, certain that a *shtriga*, a witch who fed off children, waited just outside their window. As she scurried across the shop, heartbeats pounding like cold rain against her ribcage, the old man's shadow loomed behind her. Yet when she forced her chin back over her shoulder, she saw nothing except the closed front door.

Mirjeta lurched to a stop, sucked in a slow breath, and let it out even more slowly, rubbing her cold hands up and down her arms until she began to feel warmer. As she stood blinking in the dim interior, details of the dusty, cluttered area came into focus. Around her, hulking shadows resolved into low bookshelves lined with a mix of paperbacks and hard covers. Sunlight filtered in through a window on the far side of the shop in what must have been a dining room in the original home.

In the background a woman's soulful contralto sang "make you feel my love" accompanied by a piano. Her lush voice, both soothing and aching with honest emotion, brought Mirjeta up short to listen. Whoever the artist was, she wove a mesmerizing cocoon perfect for browsing among the stacks, a latte in hand. The more she listened, the more at ease she felt.

"Adele. I discovered her on a trip to London last year." The silky low words caught Mirjeta off guard, pulling her around to face the owner of this eclectic bookstore, who stood so close that she felt compelled to step back.

Elira grinned and then turned away only to circle around the shelves and approach Mirjeta from the other side. "She keeps me company when customers are scarce."

Mirjeta opened her mouth. Then she closed it again.

She'd dreamt about this stranger, recalled her uncanny eyes even on the brightest, most ordinary days until the vision had taken on the urgency of a compulsion. Will she, nil she, Mirjeta had to confront the woman who'd offered herself to save her. Yet before the reality of that hard gaze, words failed her.

As if reading Mirjeta's thoughts, Elira narrowed her eyes and gestured toward the back of the shop. "*Mirëdita. Pu lutem, merrni bukë, kripë, dhe zemra ime.*" *Good afternoon. Please, take bread, salt, and my heart.* She spoke the traditional host's invitation with a slight accent, one that Mirjeta failed to recognize, and a stiff formality.

"*Ju faleminderit. Unë do të.*" *Thank you. I will.* She answered as custom required, following as Elira turned and headed toward a wide, arched doorway into another room where small café tables displaced shelves to the perimeter. Brilliant sunlight washed over them from a bay window along the back wall.

Elira headed toward what appeared to be an authentic Italian coffee bar in the corner. "Cappuccino? Or Greek coffee?"

"Cappuccino," Mirjeta murmured, half unaware of what she did as she sat on a stool, and Elira set a demitasse cup filled with *lëvozhgë portokalli i ruan*, orange-peel preserves, in front of her along with a jar of toothpicks. When she looked up, tears pricking her, Elira shrugged and rolled her eyes in the familiar Albanian manner.

"An old family recipe." She snagged a pick and stabbed a peel, popping it into her mouth. She followed this with a chocolate from a tray on the counter before swinging around to make Mirjeta's cappuccino.

"And how is the health of your family?" Mirjeta found herself asking the customary question more sincerely than she could have imagined only fifteen minutes ago.

Elira's shoulders stiffened, but she said nothing while she finished. Mirjeta studied her. Andrew Cruncher had said on that fateful March night that they looked alike. Was it true? Elira Dukagjini and she were about the same height, just under average for American women, and slight. Given her own weight and Elira's more obvious muscles, she'd hazard that the other woman weighed around one twenty. Beyond their size and dark hair, Mirjeta saw little that they had in common. Her skin had a warm brown tone that Elira's—tattooed and copiously revealed in a red-plaid bustier—lacked. She wore only simple silver or gold jewelry, and her thick hair she kept tamed in a long bob whose ends had been razor cut. Elira's hair resembled a bird's nest. It was less a style than a lack of grooming. Even to Mirjeta, she exuded a feral sexuality along with her potent, musky perfume.

Like a flash of lightning against a black sky, Mirjeta saw that Elira was her negative, the path not taken when she'd left Albania a decade ago, sixteen, alone, and pursued. Now that her past had caught up with her, what did it mean that she'd met this darker half of herself?

The subject of her study turned with a small gilt-rimmed cup and set it before her. "Ever compose haiku? I have a sudden urge to take Hamlet's words about Ophelia and set them into haiku. 'I will speak daggers to her but use none.'"

Elira picked up another chocolate, took a delicate nip, eyes thoughtful, the sight of her scarred upper lip drawing gooseflesh on Mirjeta's arms.

"Let's start: 'I will speak daggers.' Now you add the next bit. Seven syllables, though there's no need to be too rigid about that."

A cold trickle slid down Mirjeta's spine. She took a hasty sip of her cappuccino and cleared her throat. "I'm not a word person."

"That's all right. I have a way with words myself."

The other woman paused, considering. Mirjeta suspected that Elira knew exactly what she planned to say. "'But use none save my desire.' That's good. Sounds like the Bard penned it himself."

"I'm better with notes," Mirjeta said, her moist palms sliding on the cup. "I'm a violinist. You know? Dvorák. Csárdás. Bartok and Debussy." Her voice trembled a little.

Elira finished her chocolate, pushing the last bit into her mouth and licking her fingertip. She turned back to the cappuccino machine. As she did, Mirjeta recognized the Albanian double-headed eagle on her left shoulder.

"I think I'll wait to see if the last line occurs to me while we talk." Mirjeta couldn't explain the relief she felt—which disappeared when Elira continued. "So *motër të vogël,*"—Mirjeta shivered at the endearment *little sister*—"a Krasniqi hunts you. Why?"

Even though Elira's back was turned to her, Mirjeta looked down to shield her face as she struggled to compose her thoughts—though why she tried yet again to order them, to subdue her roiling, irrational anger and fear, she didn't know, except that the struggle kept her from becoming one of them. Blinking, she looked up to find Elira's face inches from her own, her breath cool and smelling of chocolate. The inscrutable gray eyes shone.

"The Krasniqi are a mountain clan who turned Turk."

Mirjeta laughed at the outdated description. It had been a long time since anyone had described a Muslim Albanian as one who had "turned Turk"—probably not since the Albanians had kicked the Ottomans out of their country in 1912 after five hundred years. Perhaps that explained Elira's accent and old-fashioned hospitality: she'd been sequestered in a mountain cave since birth.

But then she caught sight of Elira's expression and her amusement dissipated. Unbidden, the word *lugat* whispered through her thoughts. She flicked it away.

Elira turned back to spoon sugar into her coffee. Mirjeta counted a dozen tiny scoops.

"Are the Gjakova in blood with Krasniqi?" Elira turned around, pinning Mirjeta with her stare. "Are they, little sister?"

Mirjeta swallowed around a dry lump. As much as she'd like to laugh at that description for being outdated, she couldn't—her mother's life had gone toward paying the Gjakova blood debt.

"Yes." She looked away. "Because of me."

"The Gjakova owe allegiance to the Dukagjini, but I'm sure you know that."

Something flared in her. She whirled to glare at Elira, who'd tipped up her coffee and drained it. "Why do you talk as if we're from the old country? The old country of 1905?"

"Because we are. We're Albanian, little sister. Did you think you could run to America and start fresh, take on a new identity, and leave all the blood behind? Pretend the old law doesn't exist anymore? Eh? How'd that turn out for you?"

Mirjeta banged her cup on the bar and stood. "I came to say thank you for saving my life." Despite frustration at Elira's attempt to shove her into a blood-soaked Albanian box, she knew that this terrifying stranger had kept her from a short, brutal life as a sex slave somewhere in the Mideast. "I didn't come here to take an oath of loyalty."

Elira's lips retreated in an approximate grin. "She shows some spirit. Nice."

Plucking another chocolate, she tossed it into her mouth. Then her hand struck, capturing Mirjeta's wrist in an icy steel band. She leaned across the bar to press her lips against the outer rim of Mirjeta's ear before tracing a delicate tongue around it. Mirjeta squeezed her eyes tight, waiting.

Elira's velvety whisper scalded the well of her ear. "Like it or not, your blood feud has followed you to this land of milk and honey. You can't escape who and what you are: my *gjakova*." *My blood kin*. She kissed Mirjeta's cheek and then pushed her away without letting go of her.

Mirjeta sank down on the stool, her wrist growing numb in Elira's grasp. "I won't become one of them. *I won't*. I won't fight fire with fire."

Dropping her arm, Elira vaulted onto the bar next to her. "Are you sure you're Albanian? Or is life in Shkodra too cultured and genteel for the rough frontier law of the mountain clans?"

Mirjeta pulled her frozen hand against her chest where her fingers burned against her skin.

"You have no idea what kind of life I've lived." She didn't look at Elira as she let the quiet words filter into the air between them. "Or what kind of life I've escaped from. I spent my earliest childhood in Kosova hiding from Serbs who bullied children, beat old men, and raped any woman foolish enough to walk alone. When I was eight, my mother and I fled to the Accursed Mountains where the clans shoot at each other from behind rocks at twilight."

Now she did raise her eyes, did let her bitterness color her tone. “They’re *all* alike in their rough frontier law, Albanian and Serb, Christian and Muslim.”

The room darkened as the sun went behind a cloud. Elira’s eerie eyes gleamed with such hunger that Mirjeta half believed that her simulacrum’s appetite had sucked the light from around them.

Even as she leaned away, heart thudding, she heard James describing Elira’s evident sexual torture. In the stillness between one extenuated heartbeat and the next, Mirjeta saw through Elira’s eyes, saw the world in shades of red, white, and black, starved for the blood of her enemies. And then she saw Imam Krasniqi’s bearded face, the grooves alongside his mouth, the dark eyes that had fixated on her until his regard had burrowed through her oblivious innocence, and her creeping unease had grown into furious dread.

“Why don’t you tell me then, little sister? Your blood feud is my blood feud. Are you sure you trust yourself to the tender mercies of the Americans? Perhaps one specific American who looks like Achilles reborn with eyes the color of the Adriatic?”

Closing her eyes, Elira flattened her palms on her bare thighs and slid them up under the hem of her skirt, stopping short of revealing her panties. She moaned a little. “A warrior.”

A nearly visible cloud of musk exuded from her, potent and predatory.

And like that, Mirjeta’s vision snapped back into her own head. *Who the hell did Elira think she was?*

“I trust Homeland Security and law enforcement officers in general, not just my boyfriend. And I’m not your little sister.”

Elira studied her for more than a minute, her eyes narrowed and her nostrils flaring. Under her silent scrutiny, Mirjeta refused to flinch or blink, although her heartbeat tripped against her ribcage. She watched fleeting emotions cross Elira's face. Then Elira did something odd. She pressed her fingertips against the scarred skin over her breast before turning away.

"Ah, cherish what you have." An edge roughened her voice.

Mirjeta laid her hand on Elira's shoulder, unsure what to say. Elira brought her gaze back, and whatever emotion Mirjeta thought she'd seen had disappeared, replaced with the familiar cynical ferocity.

"You still haven't said why Krasniqi hunts you." Elira waved a careless hand. "It doesn't matter. Two bloods are owed for you."

"Why? Because I'm a Gjakova?" *And if so, what would Elira do if she learned that wasn't Mirjeta's father's last name?*

Elira's upper lip pulled back and something flared in her eyes. "I'm sworn to defend the blood of all Albanian women." Graceful as a panther, she hopped down from the bar and began walking away from Mirjeta, clearly finished with their talk.

Mirjeta got up and hastened after her. "That's only one blood. You said you had two."

Elira spun on one heel and caught her in a penetrating stare. "James Goodman's blood runs in my veins."

Before Mirjeta could ask why that mattered, Elira had stridden through the archway and the other room. As her heavy boots thudded on the stairs, the sun came out from behind the clouds, and the room brightened.

ELIRA HEARD THE BELL over the front door of Jink & Diddle as she reached the *seisún* space on the second floor, but she held her shoulders back and her head up until she reached the dilapidated sofa in the far corner. It had been too long since she'd pandered to her primal addiction and so had to satisfice her needs, but in doing so she'd begun to feel stretched too thin—not the fearsome state that she'd long cultivated, and in fact needed.

She plopped down, scrabbling between the seat cushion and arm until she found her bag of heaven dust. As soon as her shaking hands could open it, she inhaled a large pinch and sighed. Almost at once her heartbeat steadied and slowed. She drifted away.

When she awoke, the slant of the sun's rays told her it was late afternoon. Although she no longer felt anxious and drained, restlessness overtook her. Mirjeta's delicate features and polished appearance tortured her memory. Mirjeta, who'd studied at the Academy of Arts in Tirana and played classical violin like an angel.

Pushing upright, she went to get her fiddle from its case. Its familiar weight on her shoulder and the way her chin fit against the smooth rest comforted her in a way she couldn't express.

Closing her eyes, she brought up the image of her first sight of this fiddle, Duncan's fiddle. She'd found a place by his campfire, the lone *stratiote* in Linz, her status as a woman hidden inside men's clothes. Duncan, streaked with the blood and grime of battle, had pulled the fiddle from his pack as the other Scots mercenaries leaned on their weary arms and watched. He'd played a slow air, something haunting and sad, and without being told Elira had understood it was a lament for the dead. As she'd watched, he'd strolled around the fire toward the far side where its leaping flames highlighted his glistening bow arm while throwing the rest of him in shadow.

She'd never heard anything like it, although she'd been introduced to the Scots war pipes years before; every army populated with Scots had at least one piper. In fact, her initial view of the fiercely wild Scots among her comrades had stunned her. Outside of her native Balkans, she'd never seen men wearing *fustanellët*, which the Scots called kilts, and *çorape*, knee-high socks with tassels. For the first time after her cousin Progon's death, Elira had identified with other mercenaries who tramped throughout Europe fighting under a multitude of banners. Yet it wasn't until she'd allowed herself to join Duncan's camp that she'd found another home since leaving Albania.

But that was all years ago. Pressing her fingertips against the fingerboard and drawing her bow along the strings, she recalled Duncan's sensitive, passionate playing with an intensity that only one who'd watched him to the exclusion of all else could summon. Following that original encounter, he'd become her lodestone, her north star. After every daily march, she'd found his campfire, settling down just outside the reach of its light. And then she'd begun to ride behind him until at last she'd summoned the courage to ride beside him.

He'd said nothing, hardly acknowledged her presence at all except to guide his horse to give her leeway on the trail, but on the second day after she'd ridden at his side, he'd begun to sing, his voice rich and deep.

As her memory replayed his singing, Elira played along in perfect harmony, each grace note, each glide of the bow, each throbbing vibrato an echo of those he'd taught her. Every tune she'd ever learned had been learned this way.

From the very beginning, when Duncan had begun demonstrating how to play while speaking as if to no one in particular, she'd concentrated on watching his fingers and his bow arm. She'd heard nothing but his gentle voice as he instructed how to hold a bow as he drew it across the strings slowly. Each night for two months he'd taught the same tune, never looking at her even as he repeated musical phrases and rather madly described ornaments, Scotch snaps, and bow shakes. When at last he'd scooted close to her, he'd done so with a distracted air, stopping only when his thigh brushed hers.

And then he'd looked at her for the first time, a question in his eyes, before leaning in to set his fiddle under her chin. Her left hand had come up to grip its neck, and she'd accepted the bow, all without a word between them. The tune she'd played, shaky at best, was that first slow air, *The Flowers of the Forest*, a lament for the army of James IV, slain with their king in 1513. After many weeks of determined playing, when she'd mastered the tune, Duncan had joined her on the pipes.

She hadn't realized that she'd been crying until afterwards when he'd leaned over and brushed the tears from her cheeks.

"I see you," he'd said, only making her cry harder.

"Laments always make me cry, but I guess that's what they're for, right?"

Elira started at the sweet, lilting voice that ripped her from her blessed reverie. Opening her eyes, she groaned at the sight of the White Goth girl named Zophiel who'd plagued her since the end of March, appearing in Jink & Diddle when Elira could least tolerate her. Outside of Dr. Aconcio, this frail child-woman with the narrow frame and *manga*-girl eyes was the only person capable of sneaking up on Elira. The frilly, white dresses that she wore with their layers of lace flounces at cuff and hem, the saggy ruffled neckline over a meager bust, the patterned black hose, and the precarious heels all made Elira's skin crawl, not least of which because she had no idea why the adolescent kept dogging her.

"Don't you have somewhere else to go? The mall?"

Zophiel ignored her to twirl, her hands grasping her skirt. She tottered over to Elira, who swung her violin to safety as the girl reached for her pendant. "Oooh! Awesome! A real medieval crucifix! I'd love to have one of these."

She stroked her fingers over it until Elira, irritated, stepped away. "Don't you think it would look loverly with my dress? It doesn't really belong over that nasty red scar on your chest, you know."

"It belongs wherever I put it." Elira turned to put her violin back into its velvet-lined case, letting her fingers stroke its glossy surface.

When she stood up to face the intruder, it was to find her blowing bubbles and then twisting the pink gum around and around her index finger.

Zophiel stuck the gum back into her mouth, pushing the wad into her cheek with a deft tongue. "Not really, no, it doesn't."

She skipped over to the bookcase that shelved the sheet music that Elira kept for the local musicians who liked to drop in during the evenings. "Everyone just thinks they can do whatever they want with my father's gift, but they can't."

Elira had no patience for this nonsense. She doubted Little Miss Muffet would stick around if a big black spider sat down beside her and showed its fangs. Sidling over to the *ingénue*, she reached out to grasp her upper arm, intending to lean in and run her tongue along the girl's neck. Instead, when she touched the soft cotton sleeve, a strong current raced up her arm and down her spine, pinning her to the floor. Her teeth clinched, her heart sped and then slowed to a heavy thudding, and an excruciating pain vibrated through her skin and organs while causing her bones to ache.

Zophiel glanced over her shoulder and made a *tsking* sound. Shrugging, she released Elira's grip, turned all the way around and tapped Elira on the head with a book of sheet music.

"Naughty, aren't you? I like challenges. It's been centuries and centuries since I've had to look after someone like you."

"What do you want, Zophiel?" Elira rubbed her temples with trembling thumbs. How much longer would she have to listen to this inane chatter? "I've got errands to run before the *seisún*."

Zophiel rolled her eyes and popped her gum. "Zophie. I told you my friends call me Zophie." Her radiant smile stopped Elira's pacing cold.

Then her face grew serious.

"Why do you let that creepy old monkey-man boss you around? He's not your pimp, you know." She giggled at this, increasing

Elira's suspicion that she was very young for her age, whatever it was. "Do you know, he waited outside and watched your friend as she walked back to the T? You'd think he didn't get enough out of you, he's so greedy."

Elira circled her slowly. Frustrated, she hissed, "My friend? I have no friends, *Zophiel*, least of all a busy-body little girl who staggers around in her mother's high heels."

She turned away, intending to leave, when Zophiel's next words halted her, compelling her to face the young demon spawn.

"There's no need to be jealous of her. He'll just use it against you." Zophiel's bright, almond-shaped eyes brooked no disagreement.

Elira, unable and unwilling to leave, recalled that Dr. Aconcio had quizzed her about her missing relics, wondering aloud whether she'd grown attached to her handsome rescuer. What would he think if he saw her with Mirjeta?

The bell over the front door tinkled. Moments later, she heard the sound of steps on the stairs interspersed with the rhythmic *thunk* of a cane. Zophiel raised a finger to her lips, her eyes sparkling, and leaned against the bookcase. Winking, she blew Elira a kiss. The door to the hall opened, and Dr. Aconcio came in.

Ignoring the teen girl who lounged, grinning, in the corner, he came to stand only a foot from Elira. He reached a bony finger toward her cheek.

She refused to cringe, especially in front of that ignorant child. "Sorry, old man. You'll have to come back."

“Ah, my dear Elira. You have had the most fortunate visit, yes?” The mock sincerity in his voice caused her to snap at his finger. He laughed as he plucked it away.

“Why is Duka still in jail?” Elira watched him, her features tight.

“The young woman seems to have recalled you to your blood oath, despite your missing relic.”

“I don’t need it.” She turned away, considering whether to return to her stash. Out of the corner of her eye, she caught the wagging of Zophiel’s index finger.

She swiveled her head to look at Dr. Aconcio, restlessness sending her pacing around the perimeter of the room. “Or you. Vermin like Duka have multiplied in so many dark corners I will never run out of blood to recoup. So why should I wait for your machinations?”

“You appreciate a fine wine, do you not?” His wolfish smile suggested a private joke. “You yourself are—how did you put it? Oh, yes, ‘reeling’ in the American agent. Though the details are different, the need for persistence is much the same, yes? Besides, you have your *heaven dust*”—his disdain gave his smile a merry edge— “and your junior law associates. Surely your needs are being met for the time being?”

Elira scowled. It wasn’t at all like Dr. Aconcio to speak so freely in front of one who hadn’t been inducted into their law practice.

Watching his dark glittering eyes, she stopped within six inches of him and leaned so close that she could see the ravaged landscape of his face, its sagging gullies and porous earth. His fetid breath stank of the grave.

"Are you telling me the truth, old man? About the woman? Did she descend from a traitorous Albanian or not?"

Before he could answer, she touched the tip of her tongue against his loose jowl. He moaned even as she whispered her warning. "Because, senior partner or not, I'll take blood for her if I find you lie to use me."

Dr. Aconcio placed his palm against her cheek and drew her face up where she could judge the truth in his gaze. "Mirjeta Gjakova is the daughter of a man whose clan long ago turned Turk. You would be within your rights to claim blood from her."

The lupine humor returned. "And Imam Krasniqi would be thwarted in his desire to whore her among others of his religion."

Elira nodded, satisfied. Yet her restlessness increased. She pushed away from him and walked toward the window that looked over the backyard. Silence filled the room for long seconds, and then she felt a bit of paper against her palm. She clutched it but didn't turn as he spoke.

"You do need me, dear girl. Who else would give you the vermin on a silver platter? I think you'll find this particular specimen quite exceptional."

As soon as she heard his cane on the stairs, she crumpled it, aware as she did so that after the *seisún* and half a bottle of 14-year-old Oban that she'd smooth it out. She turned to shoo the fluttering White-Goth moth out of Jink & Diddle no matter how much pain to her psyche or her body the effort caused when she realized that she was alone. Zophiel had disappeared. Shaking her head and muttering, Elira went to the cabinet where she kept a fine selection of single-malt Scotch. After pouring a generous tumbler, she toasted the twin spirits of her own purgatory, letting herself imagine Dr. Aconcio on one shoulder and Zophiel on the other. Chuckling, she sipped the whisky and returned to the sofa to flatten his intelligence.

She stared so long at the paper that the sun slid below the horizon and dusk deepened the shadows in the room. Downstairs, the bell rang again as the first musicians began to arrive. She raised the tumbler to her mouth, tilted her head, and drained its contents in a manner that would irritate a connoisseur.

"I will speak daggers but use none save my desire," she whispered.

She looked toward the window, open to the sounds of nightlife and traffic from nearby Porter Square. Footsteps echoed on the stairs. "Blood streaks sunset sky."

Four

DESPITE MONTHS OF EXHAUSTING WORK running down leads in the tight-lipped Albanian communities in Boston and New York, James had little evidence to connect Ismail Duka, an American citizen, to Imam Xhemajl Krasniqi in Kosovo or the Krasniqi mafia, run by the imam's relatives in northern Albania. But he had more than enough experience to convince him that Duka had earned a lifetime behind bars for the forced prostitution and sex slavery the Krasniqis specialized in. As the situation stood, Duka would be convicted only of attempted kidnapping and get 10 to 15 years in prison, an outcome not even close to satisfying. The Krasniqi mafia would continue to snatch vulnerable women in the Balkans, sending them to their local representatives in Western Europe, the U.S., and the Middle East to sell to buyers and pimps. Yet if James could help the federal prosecutor build a solid case against Duka, not only would Duka live the rest of his life behind bars, but the U.S. would extradite Krasniqi and other members of the Krasniqi mafia for prosecution under the Trafficking Victims Protection Act. Proving that the imam had ordered Mirjeta's kidnapping would provide the linchpin to the case.

Unfortunately, modern Albanian organized crime employed all the raw violence and rigid family loyalty that once characterized the early 20th century Italian mob, refusing to admit outsiders into its close-knit clans and punishing infidelity swiftly, cruelly, and absolutely. Already, two cousins whom James had tried to groom as informants had come to bloody ends: one had been found in a Dorchester dumpster, his hands bound behind his back and his severed penis in his mouth. The other's charred remains at the wheel of a smoking Cadillac Escalade in Roxbury had to be identified from dental records.

The longer he went without driving a wedge into the opening that Duka's arrest offered, the more likely that the Krasniqis would either exploit some legal loophole to spring Duka or sacrifice him to a ludicrously short prison term. Either way, the Krasniqi operation would continue unabated, Mirjeta would live looking over her shoulder, and his father would go unavenged. To keep that from happening, he had to find a certain she-demon and convince her to work with him. Elira Dukagjini, despite being an outsider to the Krasniqi clan, had found a way to penetrate the airtight world of the Albanian mafia, apparently to pursue her own private vendetta. Trouble was she didn't exist. At least not as far as Albania or any U.S. government agency was concerned. Not only was her driver's license fake, but she didn't have a record anywhere outside of her visit to Mass General in March. She might as well be a *lugat*, the blood-sucking ghost that haunted Mirjeta.

And that's why, in the first week of August, James stood outside the nondescript red steel door to the Underground at The Garage, once a bar and now a small arts theater just off Brattle Square in Cambridge, touched his Walther PPK in its holster, and entered Elira's metaphoric lair. That is, he hoped that he'd find her watching Urban Shakespeare rehearsing for its upcoming production of *Othello*. He didn't know how many more of these rehearsals that he could tolerate. He'd already dropped in on five other Shakespeare productions and was starting to understand what he saw.

The door clanged shut behind him, shutting out the bright afternoon sun and rushing sounds of traffic, leaving him on a dusty landing to a steep staircase lined with rubber treads and red walls covered with graffiti and playbills.

As he descended into the shadows, the air cooled and the dust cleared. On the left-hand side, a large window revealed five rows of largely empty seats in a darkened room. At the bottom landing, an easel displayed a placard with the cast's photos, and on the solid entrance door a handwritten flyer invited the public inside for the open rehearsal at two.

James checked his watch. *2:35*. He eased the door ajar three or four inches, listening for the actors and any indication that his entrance would garner notice. He heard several voices in chaotic, unscripted conversation and laughter that gave way to an authoritative woman declaring a need for repeating the current scene.

Slipping inside the theater, James released the door so that it didn't bang, searching the seats for a familiar profile. He almost overlooked Elira in a seat at the far edge of the back row to the right side of the entrance, where the depth of the darkness obscured her slouching form.

In fact, he'd begun to turn away when a small movement brought his gaze back, and he recognized the outline of her hair. Frowning at the odd angle of her head on the seatback and its restless sideways movement, he began to edge behind the last row. Her eyes, too, were closed. A grin replaced the frown. This time, he would sneak up on her.

Yet just as James halted a foot from her, Elira fastened her luminous, if decidedly glazed, stare on him. That's when he realized that her feet rested on the seat in front of her, enclosing a shadowy figure kneeling between her thighs. A sly smile widened her mouth before her eyelids fluttered, and she tilted her head back again, the tip of her tongue darting out between her lips.

James strained nearer, his suddenly shallow breathing adding to the rustles and low moans. A flash-flood of heat swept over him, leaving a sweaty trail under his arms, down his spine, and across his forehead. Some small, rational voice warned him to whirl and beat feet back to the entrance and safety, but it had no power over him. Instead, he stood, pinned like a specimen to a lab tray, grossly aware of his body and the two women before him. No matter what he told himself later, for those five minutes, he participated in the writhing dance of tongue, the grip on hips, the subsonic humming that built and built and built until its pressure exploded.

And then the rest of the world slammed back into his awareness: the stuffy heat of the poorly air-conditioned theater, the hubbub of actors twenty feet away, the bright lights of the performance space.

Wrenching himself back, James returned to the entryway and looked toward the actors, some of whom were seated at a table. Behind these stood two men holding pikes at attention; clearly guards of some sort. Othello and two other men stood before the table. Five feet to their side, an elderly man gestured towards Othello while speaking to the seated group, one of whom was a middle-aged woman dressed in rich robes and wearing a haughty expression.

"Desdemona's father is bringing his complaint before the Duke of Venice," said Elira in his ear. "Or Duchess in this case. Urban Shakespeare likes to shake things up. Ol' Will would appreciate their gender games."

Ignoring her, James kept his eyes on the scene, rapt at Brabantio's anguished antics as the old man pulled at his hair and pivoted on his heel, declaiming loudly that his daughter had been abused, stolen, and corrupted through the use of magic.

"'For nature so preposterously to err, being not deficient, blind, or lame of sense, sans witchcraft could not.'" Elira delivered these lines in unison with the distraught father. James looked at her. Her smug smile reminded James of a cat that had dipped a paw in someone's bowl of cream. "A dutiful daughter would never run away with the wrong suitor."

Tightness replaced the fleeting smile. Her eyes narrowed as she watched the scene. "If he'd been an Albanian father, he might have suspected that Desdemona had been stolen. Muslim clansmen used to prefer snatching Christian virgins. Any blood they owed was well worth making Christian girls marry Muslim husbands."

"Surely that no longer happens?"

She lifted her shoulder in a prototypical Albanian gesture. "Who knows? In the mountains, probably." Then she gave him a wicked smile. "On the other hand, I think the only virgins left are goats."

James turned to watch Othello deny using a love potion, instead recounting how he'd wooed Desdemona with tales of his heroic exploits in battle. Like Othello's young and innocent Venetian bride, Mirjeta had responded to his own stories from Iraq and Afghanistan with tears and sighs. Keeping his eyes on the stage as Iago fetched Desdemona to confront her angry father in front of the Duchess and her council, he asked, "What do you think, Ms. Dukagjini? Has Desdemona gone against nature in marrying a dark-skinned Moor?"

When she didn't respond, he looked over to see her pull something from a small black bag slung across her body. She unwrapped whatever it was, popped it into her mouth, and returned to watching the rehearsal. The scent of chocolate filled the air.

James was about to repeat his question when she looked at him out of the corner of her eye and asked, "Why would it be against her nature to lust after a warrior? A national hero hosted and feted in her father's home?"

Her sly, knowing expression made James wonder if she'd read his earlier thoughts. She shifted closer, bringing with her the scent of previous arousal and the sweet, heady aroma of summer grass and wildflowers.

"Tall, muscular, exotic. Dangerous. Deadly." Her slow, deliberate gaze traveled down from his face to his feet, assessing, undressing, inciting.

Nostrils flaring, James struggled to focus. "Lust after yes, but marry in secret without her father's approval? Isn't it in our nature to remain loyal to our family? As an Albanian, surely you agree human nature is tribal."

Elira tilted her head and appeared to study the beautiful woman playing Desdemona, whose emphatic speech had turned the elderly man's face a convincing red. "Shakespeare was very generous to make Desdemona a modern woman and let her speak of her seduction as though she were Othello's equal."

"Albanians aren't so generous. In their eyes, only Othello owes blood for dishonoring Brabantio."

Her mouth quirked, but she remained serious. “Ah. Someone’s been reading my cousin Lekë’s *Kanun*. Or quizzing his girlfriend. No, Albanian women are not equal to men. They are too easily led astray, like sheep.“ She smirked and shook her head. “They can’t owe blood.”

She turned back to the action onstage. “Othello clearly owes blood, but the Duchess tells Brabantio to let it go: ‘What cannot be preserved when fortune takes, patience her injury a mockery makes.’ Brabantio doesn’t agree. Did you catch what he said?”

“No.” James let his annoyance and impatience color that one short word, but he squelched the surprising trace of fear that her use of the word *girlfriend* had elicited. How did she know that he and Mirjeta were dating? “But I’m sure you can tell me what it was.”

She laughed; it was the first genuine sound of humor that he’d heard from her. “Clever boy! Yes, I can tell you. Brabantio says, ‘So let the Turk of Cyprus us beguile; we lose it not, so long as we can smile.’ But he wisely tells the Duchess to proceed to the affairs of state. You see how highly the insult of a stolen daughter rates when compared to the imminent theft of an island?”

“I thought adultery and abduction created a huge blood debt, so huge most men don’t bother. Aren’t two bloods owed when a man steals a bride? One to her father and one to her fiancé?”

“Ah, but we were talking about the Venetians in *Othello*”—here Elira gestured with her chin toward the stage—“which is to say the English of Shakespeare’s day, who are pragmatic. They valued land ownership more highly than an insult to their honor. Albanians on the other hand never forget or forgive blood debt.”

"And how do you explain that, Ms. Dukagjini? Lekë's *Kanun* doesn't require blood vengeance. In fact, the only punishments it prescribes are fines or burning a man's house."

"The *Kanu*n also forbids killing women," she hissed, her eyes flashing in the darkened theater. "But that doesn't stop a husband whose wife has fucked another man from killing her too. His honor has been insulted too deeply. Just like Othello." The bitterness in her voice made James take a step back.

"Are you saying Othello murders Desdemona as an honor killing?"

"He's an Arab Moor, isn't he? Albeit one who has converted to Christianity and fights as the Venetians' most celebrated general." Her sharp eyes glittered as she looked toward the black actor. "Though no one seems to know what Othello's race is because Elizabethans used 'Moor' to describe dark-skinned people from Africa, Arabia, and even India. Anyone swarthy, in fact. It's only been since the 1830s that a black actor has played him on the stage."

"It's not a fit of passion? Jealous rage and hurt that lashes out?"

"Hardly." Elira folded her arms over her chest and stared. "Watch and see. Iago eggs him on, telling him he can be just one of millions of husbands whose wives cheat on them. In fact, Iago mocks Othello for grieving over his wife. *Be a man!* he jabs, over and over. Othello's pride can't handle it. When Iago insists that he strangle her in their bed, Othello will say, 'Good, good: the justice of it pleases: very good.' It's plotted and planned, all for honor. Too bad Othello got it wrong."

She broke off to step forward and shake her fist at the actors. "No, stupid girl!"

Desdemona, a look of wary recognition sliding across her features, glanced at Elira but continued to speak. James was impressed at her discipline.

"What?"

"She's just condemned herself. 'And to his honor and his valiant parts did I my soul and fortunes consecrate.' The Duchess will allow her to travel with Othello to Cyprus." She grinned, startling him. "No matter how many times I see this play, I always want to warn Desdemona not to go. Kinda like when you yell at the stupid teen in the slasher movie not to open the door to the crazy guy with the knife."

James knew that he needed to get down to business, but his curiosity compelled him to ask something that he'd wondered ever since Emil had described Elira's scars and infertility. "So if women can't owe blood, can they claim blood?"

The glittering hardness returned to Elira's odd pale eyes. Again, he was reminded of a will o' the wisp, a seductive fairy light hovering over treacherous, boggy ground.

"How do I justify my right to take blood you mean? As an Albanian woman?"

He nodded.

"Come. Buy me a drink. I've seen enough today." She didn't wait for his answer but instead pushed open the theater door and disappeared up the stairs.

Throwing a last glance over his shoulder at the actors—and catching a fleeting sense of relief in their silent observation of his and Elira's departure—James followed her up and out to the sidewalk.

Without looking to see if he followed, she strode away, her pale skin glowing in the late afternoon light.

Above the bodice of her corset and between her shoulder blades, the blood-red tattoo *Të shpejtë për shpirtin, të vrasin për nder* warned him. *Fast for the soul, kill for honor.* A thrill ran down his spine despite the sultry August heat.

He hurried to reach her side, matching her stride as he did so.

"Albanian women have long been warriors, even if our men forget that fact." He could see nothing of her strange eyes behind the dark glasses that she wore when she turned to him. "Queen Teuta of the Illyrians, our ancestors, led her people against the Greeks and made the city of Epirus a subject state. You know Epirus, right? Where Alexander the Great's mother was a princess? Not exactly a city of effete bootlickers."

Suddenly, she clutched his arm and stopped short.

"Shit! How does that *vajzë e vogël* find me?"

"'Little girl'?" James surveyed the street around them. "What's she look like?"

Elira leaned in and spoke in a low voice. "The mad whack *vajzë e vogël* across from us. The one dressed in that ridiculous frothy white dress like some Victorian angel."

James saw no one that fit that description. He lifted Elira's sunglasses with a thumb and studied her dilated eyes. "Perhaps you should stop taking whatever it is that's made you high. Then angels won't stalk you on the streets of Cambridge."

She hissed and pulled away, shoving her glasses down.

"Nora. Nora of Kelmendi. Heard of her, agent man? She lived in the early 1600s, so not long after Shakespeare's Desdemona. Her father dropped her off at an orphanage because he needed a son to fight the Turks. Nora's aunt rescued her but raised her as a son, knowing her brother would be tempted to train the disguised girl as a warrior."

They'd reached an Irish pub, one of those dark-windowed places with pseudo-wooden façades and pan-Celtic lettering. Elira entered without asking whether he wanted to follow her inside or not. Dropping her sunglasses on the bar, she told the bartender to bring them two pints of Murphy's Irish Stout and waved off James's quiet insistence that he was on duty. Turning on her stool, she propped her elbows behind her, which thrust her chest forward, and smirked at him. For the first time, he realized that she wore an ornate, jeweled crucifix. Its twisted, suffering figure nestled between her breasts, tarnished silver against her translucent skin. He cleared his throat and sat down, keeping his gaze on the polished counter between his forearms.

"Nora wasn't just an Albanian Brunhilde, though. She's often called the Helen of Albania."

"That beautiful?"

James, despite his usual devotion to regulations, sipped at the stout the bartender put in front of him and resisted the urge to lean closer to Elira. The effort made him feel a little dizzy.

"Don't tell me. She started a war with the Turks. Launched a thousand horses and all that."

"Pretty much. A pasha fell in love with her and demanded that she become his wife. Her father told him no. The petty tyrant then threatened to burn the Greater Highlands if he didn't get Nora."

"Obviously, she didn't marry the pasha. Where would the fun be in that?" He watched her as he joked.

Elira studied him over her shoulder before lifting her stout. James watched, riveted to the undulations of her throat muscles as she swallowed. Below the white column of her slender throat and partly hidden by the crucifix, the raised pink scar on her chest reminded him that she was unwell, that she needed to see a specialist.

That she'd nearly died after saving Mirjeta.

Wiping the foam from her lips, she said, "In 500 years of occupation, the northern highlanders never bowed to the Turks, their laws, their taxes, their religion, or their culture. So, no, Nora didn't marry the pasha. She killed him in a duel, some say with a magic dagger."

James whistled and eyed her. "Is she your role model?"

Elira shifted closer, laying her hand on his inner thigh and running it up toward his groin. She stopped short of his cock. The air crackled around them, its temperature seeming to drop twenty degrees in twenty seconds. Her lips pulled back in the feral grin he recalled from the night she hunted Krasniqi's men. She stared at him for several excruciating heartbeats.

When she spoke, her hiss seemed to come from the four corners of the bar. "Get this CFB, Captain Jack." Startled, James blinked at the familiar Army slang for the phrase *clear as a fucking bell*. "*All*

Albanian warriors are my role model. We clear? Diocletian and Constantine. Skanderbeg and Yanitza. Branilo, my betrothed, and Progon, my cousin. We're a nation of warriors."

She slid away and motioned toward the bartender, ordering a shot of Jameson Irish Whiskey when he came. She knocked the whiskey back, slammed the tumbler on the bar, and nodded for another before turning to look at James.

"You've seen so many Shakespeare rehearsals by now, you should audition for a troupe."

"You're a hard woman to find."

She leaned over again, her voice silky and her breasts pressed into his upper arm. "Only those I want to find me do."

James shut his eyes briefly, praying for strength. Then he looked at Elira. "Does that mean you're willing to help me put Duka away?"

She sat up and looked toward the rows of bottles behind the bar. "Do you know what happens to a sex slave?" She asked this so quietly that James wasn't sure that he'd heard her. Before he could answer, she went on. "My sister, Qendresa, was 14 when she was taken. I never found her."

She fingered the crucifix and looked away, but not before James caught the oddly disturbing brightness of unshed tears. "A virgin like her? With wavy hair falling to her knees and smooth cheeks? She had eyes the color of the sky over the mountains before the sun rises."

James touched her arm. When she looked at him, however, he found that he had to look away, his hand returning to grip his glass.

"I understand the need for revenge, Ms. Dukagjini. My father was held captive during the Kosovo War by rogue members of the Kosovo Liberation Army."

"Ah." James heard a world of meaning in that single syllable.

He turned back and saw speculation in her face—and something more. Something wolfish. "Tell me, am I correct in suspecting you've had some experience with the KLA? We know they recruited teens."

She swallowed the second shot before answering. "Do you know what the *stratioti* were?"

"No. It sounds Italian whatever it is." A note of impatience entered his voice, but Elira appeared not to hear it.

"It's Greek for soldier, specifically light cavalry from Albania and Greece." She toyed with the empty shot glass. "They were refugees from the Turks in the 15th and 16th centuries who fought using tactics Western knights in shining armor didn't know. Hit and run. Feints and ambushes.

"At first, Venetians hired *stratioti* to fight against the Turks, but then other countries offered them better pay and perks. So *stratioti* traveled all through Europe fighting in the wars between Catholics and Protestants."

"Mercenaries." James spat the word. He looked down at the tattoo for the Silent Ones, indistinct in the bar's dusky interior, and then raised his Murphy's and silently toasted his comrades, living and dead.

Elira's gaze hammered him. "After the Turks conquered Albania, the Dukagjini had two choices. They could hide in the Accursed

Mountains, where they would be princes who no longer ruled in their own land. Or they could escape to Venice where they'd earn money to feed their families by taking the blood of Turks. Seems like a no brainer, don't you think?"

"You see yourself as one of these *stratioti*, an heir to your clan's warrior bloodlines."

An odd expression flitted across her features. "You could say that."

She picked up her empty glass and waggled it at the bartender, a ruddy-faced man whose gaze adhered to her chest every time he came over.

James pursed his lips, his chin tilted as he studied her. Silently he pulled out the leather pouch containing her fiancé's finger bone and placed it on the bar between them.

"For good faith. If you help me nail Ismail Duka, I'll make sure you get your magic dagger back."

Elira sipped from her new stout, looking out of the corner of her eye at the offering. After a minute or so, she touched a fingertip to the soft, dark leather.

James waited.

"The *stratioti* weren't loyal to their paymasters," she warned. Then she looked at him, a sly gleam in her eye. "And they sometimes got distracted by the chance for booty and ransom."

She followed this up by letting her gaze travel the length of his body.

He shivered. "Duly warned."

"Hm." She swiveled on her stool and leaned her elbows on the bar. Again, James's eyes focused on the dagger-like crucifix thrust forward on the shelf of her breasts. The juxtaposition between the sacred and the carnal sent an uneasy thrill through his gut.

"Well, then. When do we start?"

LATER, AFTER ANOTHER SHOT of Irish whiskey and a pinch of heaven dust, Elira took the bartender in the back storeroom among the boxes of paper napkins and straws, the odor of cooking oil and sweat heavy around them. She rode him hard, gripping his shoulders and clasping his torso with her thighs. He rested his meaty hands on her buttocks, grunting and straining, his eyes squeezed tight and his mouth a grimace. He was nothing more than a means to an end. A living, breathing, heart-beating sex toy that was slick and pungent as new leather.

As she galloped along, eyes the color of the Adriatic floated through her hazy memory. She bent and ran her tongue up the cording along the bartender's neck. He tasted of salt and tobacco smoke, the fine hairs at the base of his neck giving way to the prickly stubble of his beard as she dragged her tongue toward his jaw. As she licked on his hot flesh, he moaned and dug his fingertips deeper into the twin muscles he palmed, driving her wild. Frantic.

She hurtled on so fiercely her knees banged on the concrete floor and her thighs ached. She felt herself, raw and vulnerable, conqueror and conquered. Beneath her, his striated abdominal muscles glided against her wetness, taunting her efforts to im-pale the empty hunger deep inside. Throwing her head back, she howled and increased her pace. The pouch containing Branilo's finger slipped free of her bustier, its top buttons undone to the bartender's urgent caresses, and bounced against the throbbing scar over her heart.

"Oh, God, yes, yes, yes. Ride me, ride me!"

The harsh, panted order filled her ears in the otherwise silent storeroom, increasing her desperation. She choked an angry sob.

The bartender pressed a hard palm against the back of her head, pushing her face toward his exposed chest. "Do it! Take me!"

She licked his pectorals, savoring the feel of smooth skin and taut muscle before she bit him. He purred and arched under her, rocking her harder against him. Her hunger sharpened until despair maddened her.

All at once, Beatrice's passionate declaration of impotent female rage from *Much Ado About Nothing* pealed in her thoughts: *O God, that I were a man! I would eat his heart in the marketplace!*

Her explosive release flooded them. The bartender shouted and bucked. As he did, she pressed her bloody lips against his chest, over his pinging heart.

Five

"FRANKLY, SHE SCARES THE SHIT OUT OF ME, CRUNCHER."

Cruncher, who'd been studying the white Victorian up the block from their parking spot, swiveled his head and eyed James. "What's to be scared about, Goodman? She just creeps up on you out of nowhere, flashing those damn spooky eyes of hers and quoting odd bits of Shakespeare and haiku—what did she say the other day? It sure wasn't all nature scenes, sunsets and birds on the wing."

James took a swig from his bottled soda, wishing as he did so that it was an ice-cold beer instead. That he sat at home in front of the TV watching a chick-flick with Mirjeta. "What makes you think I remember?"

"You remember. Maybe not the exact words, but you know what I'm talking about. Something like: 'There's savageness that draws teeth and blood.'" Cruncher shook his head. "No, that ain't it."

"'In unreclaimed blood, a savageness that draws teeth 'til fresh kill redeems.' It's a twist on something Polonius says in *Hamlet*."

James found himself recalling more of Polonius's words, words that might have been written for Elira: *the flash and outbreak of a fiery mind*. He'd taken to reading Shakespeare after seeing so many rehearsals.

"You might say you're scared shitless, but I'm pretty sure you'd still tap that."

James shot Cruncher a penetrating glance. "Ugh. She doesn't do it for me. At all."

Cruncher's gaze had returned to the Victorian, whose upper windows glowed alone among the dark houses in this street in suburban Natick. "Easy there, partner. Guess I'm guilty of a little projection." He paused. "How do you suppose she knows about the Krasniqis and their little immigration system? You think she was one of their girls?"

James shrugged even though Cruncher wasn't looking at him in the darkened car. "Who knows? Anything's possible. They've been running this game for a long time." He paused, mulling over the mystery of Elira Dukagjini.

"She told me her sister was snatched at 14, but she didn't say the Krasniqis did it."

They fell silent as a car drove past them and stopped, disgorging two giggling teen girls who ran into the house before which James had parked.

Cruncher snorted as he watched them, both clutching cell phones as their frantic thumbs danced across a micro keyboard.

"I should call the Natick PD and report the drivers for violating curfew. Wonder what their parents would think if they knew violent sex traffickers are running a holding pen up the street? Think they'd keep their pretty young things at home?"

"Doubt it. No one believes it could happen on their block."

James's phone buzzed in his pocket and he pulled it out. Mirjeta had sent him a text message. The row of hearts followed by a winking semi-colon made his heart ache. Using their private shorthand, he keyed in his plan to wake her after his shift before slipping the phone back into his jacket. The remaining hours loomed long, tedious, and likely wasted.

"I suspect she's ex-KLA."

Cruncher whistled. "Why's that?"

"She knows a lot about the military. Swears like a vet. I've been trying to discover which of our guys stationed in Kosovo a decade ago worked closely with KLA partisans, and if any of those included teen soldiers."

Cruncher grunted and reached into the family-size bag of sunflower seeds that he always brought on stakeout. "I got the feeling those guys just shoved an AK-47 into the hands of kids, showed 'em how to load, point, and shoot. The mysterious Ms. Dukagjini acts like a trained assassin, no gun required."

"She also knows too much about me. She ambushed me outside my apartment once."

James caught sight of dark figures on the sidewalk fifty feet north of the Victorian. He watched as an average-sized white male, his gait confident and his face forward, strode ahead of two well-built white males flanking him, their gazes scanning the nearby shadows and their arms hanging loose.

"Correct me if I'm wrong. That looks like Prek Krasniqi, the playboy. Wonder if Jak and Zamir know baby brother's making a stop here to inspect the goods?"

Cruncher huffed in rough humor and reached for his cell phone. "Yeah. We got a visual. We're gonna give him ten then follow him in. Make sure you're right behind us."

The next ten minutes took all the patience that James had, but they couldn't go in without backup. He'd just checked the clock on his cell phone for the fourth time when a figure winged by their car without warning and drummed a palm on the hood.

Stunned, they watched as a woman wearing heavy black boots and a plaid miniskirt sprinted up the street, her pale skin glowing moonlike beyond the reach of the few streetlamps. She vaulted the steps to the Victorian's front porch, paused to throw a mischievous grin toward them, and then disappeared inside.

"Shit!" James shouted at the same instant that Cruncher exclaimed, "What the hell!"

Both men bolted from the car, reaching for their handguns as soon as they'd achieved their feet, and ran in her wake. Just as they reached the sidewalk leading up to the porch steps, the front door slammed open and a man ran outside holding an automatic weapon. When he saw the agents, he threw it to the ground and raised his hands.

"Mos lejoni atë të më vrasin!" Don't let her take me! "Mos lejoni shijen e saj gjaku im!" Don't let her taste my blood!

James, recognizing abject terror when he saw it, halted but kept his Walther PPK trained on the babbling suspect. "S*a të tjerë janë brenda? Sa armë?*" he asked. *How many others are inside? How many guns?*

The man ignored him to jump from the porch and sprint toward the sidewalk. Before James or Cruncher could apprehend him, two more men staggered from the front door, followed by three pale and gasping women. One of the men clutched his throat with bloody fingers while leaning against the other man, who held a Glock with a silencer.

Trusting that Cruncher had the others covered, James swung his weapon around to the two men, whose dazed faces didn't seem to register the threat.

"*Unë jam një agjent federal! Hidhe poshtë arma juaj*!" *Federal agent! Throw down your weapon!*

The man holding the Glock ignored his command and they stumbled closer. James, adrenaline pounding through his heart and head, squeezed a round into the gunman's arm. Both men collapsed in a tangle of arms and legs.

Abandoning the sobbing women, Cruncher sprinted forward and grabbed the Glock from the ground. By the time that James reached the group, his partner had managed to separate the two men. He dropped to one knee, quaking so badly that he had to let the hand holding the gun fall to his side and hope that the wounded sex trafficker didn't notice.

"Good God! There's a garrote in this one's throat!" Cruncher's hoarse voice serrated the night.

Clenching his thighs to stop the tremors, James grabbed the wounded man by the shoulder and repeated his earlier questions. "*Sa të tjerë janë brenda? Sa armë?*"

The man, brawny in the manner of thugs who pumped iron without the concomitant aerobics, turned glazed eyes on him. “We're all dead men,” he said in accented English. “She has seen us. We're dead men.”

Cruncher looked away from the second man, whose damaged throat prevented him from doing little more than gasp and writhe. “They say a she-demon set them free after she killed two of their guards. That's all I can get out of their babble.”

James stood. “We've got to get in there before she kills anyone else. I want Prek alive.”

Suddenly automatic gunfire ripped through the quiet suburban neighborhood. The women screamed. Somewhere a dog began barking. Lights appeared in the houses on either side of the Victorian. Sirens wailed somewhere to the south in the center of town. The situation was rapidly deteriorating into a fucking bag of dicks as his old commander would say.

God, what he wouldn't give for Lieutenant Ralston's steely nerves right now.

“Upstairs,” James said, lifting his Walther PPK and wishing he had an M-16 instead.

His father, who'd given him the James Bond special when he'd finished ICE training, would understand. For a moment, despite the evidence of his senses, he was back in Iraq searching for insurgents through seemingly innocuous homes. Cold sweat beaded on his palms and under his arms.

“Cover the back? I'll take the front.”

Cruncher nodded once and took off at a run around the side of the house. James hopped up on the porch, his pulse racing and his breathing fast. He paused just outside the door and forced himself to count to ten before nudging it open. As he did so, he took several slow, deliberate breaths and scanned the interior of the house. The wails and sobbing faded into the background as he focused on the rooms just off the small foyer. In seconds, he'd assessed the situation for threats and, finding none in his line of sight, he stepped inside.

Cruncher peered out from a doorway fifteen feet down the center hallway, which ran beside a staircase.

Shaking his head, he said, “Male vic lying between kitchen and dining room.”

James edged toward the living room. Peering around the door-frame, he scanned the mess, most of which appeared endemic. Another male DB lay sprawled across the far end of a black leather couch, his head at an odd angle.

A slight movement caught James's attention. Behind the vic, a teen girl crouched, shaking, hands clutching the couch's arm as if her hold was the only thing keeping her from falling into a thousand pieces. Lowering the PPK, he maneuvered around the coffee table and its collection of dirty tumblers, ashtrays, and takeout cartons before dropping to one knee next to her.

“Let's get you out of here, okay?”

She turned blank eyes on him, so blank that James wondered if she were blind. He had to pry her fingers from the couch arm and catch her before she fell. Slipping his free arm around her waist, he stood and guided her back to the foyer where Cruncher and a Natick police officer met them. James had just eased the vic under the officer's arm and against her side when a heavy thump overhead alerted them to a falling body—a deadweight. It was followed by a bloodcurdling scream.

They ran up the unlit stairs, Cruncher following James's lead in the stifling darkness. James had made it halfway up before he saw the next woman, who sat curled in a ball against the wall. He paused and looked back at Cruncher, who dipped his head at the unspoken request. James sidestepped her only to be caught by another woman, a girl really, who launched herself at him from the shadows at the top of the stairs. James grabbed her, reflexively flinging out a hand to grip the banister to keep them from tumbling backwards. As he turned, he realized that Cruncher stood two steps below, having handed the second woman off to another Natick police officer. Cruncher pulled the girl into his arms and turned to take her downstairs, leaving James to continue alone.

As he crested the top of the stairs, he saw one of Prek's bodyguards lying crumpled against an open doorframe. Squatting, he crept forward and felt for the man's pulse at his neck. It was strong and steady. A hasty glance revealed no wounds.

An odd sound came from the room just beyond. It sounded like a dog lapping.

"I know you're in there, Elira. Come out with your hands behind your head." He waited thirty seconds, but nothing changed. The lapping continued. "Get your ass out here. You're in serious shit, you hear?"

A maniacal laugh answered him. Its pitch was too high for Elira's husky voice.

"Fuck!" James swore and shifted into the doorway, his PPK aimed into the room.

What greeted him twisted his guts and made the bile rise into his mouth.

Just inside the doorway the second guard lay prostrate, a hand clamped onto a Glock and a widening pool of blood beneath his head. A young woman, her dirty white blouse ripped open from neck to waist and completely naked below, knelt at the side of Prek Krasniqi, who lay on his back with his stomach and throat ripped wide and his slacks bunched around his expensive Italian loafers. She ignored James to swipe a delicate tongue along the ragged wound above his collar while her fingers rhythmically gripped the mess that constituted his abdomen.

Pivoting on his heel, James vomited against the wall.

As he braced his hands on his thighs and lifted his head, Cruncher held a mint under his nose, one of those pungent ones with real peppermint oil.

"Thanks," he croaked and popped it into his mouth before standing.

And he'd thought that Iraq and Afghanistan had inured him to everything.

"Where's Elira?" Cruncher asked as two Natick police officers stepped past him only to turn and race into the hall retching.

"Jesus, Mary, and Joseph! Stop that!" He stepped forward and grabbed the woman's arm to drag her away. She growled and snapped at him. He pulled her arms behind her back and handcuffed her, jerking her a bit as he did so. "I said stop it."

She growled again and struggled.

James surveyed the bare room, its only furnishings two bunk beds against opposing walls. "Unless she's cowering in that closet, she's not here."

Cruncher threw him a startled look. "We were right behind you. She didn't pass us on the stairs. Either she flew out the window"—he tilted his head toward the room's sole window—"or she wasn't here."

James squeezed his eyes shut, took a deep breath, and then held his partner's gaze. "You think she took out Prek and his bodyguards?"

He nodded at the woman, who thrashed and lurched in Cruncher's grip, determined to return to Prek's lifeless body. He ran his fingers through his hair and looked away from the lifeless body, but it was too late. He remembered his father walking out of the squalid hellhole that he'd been kept in for months, eyes blinking against the harsh sunlight. A sudden urge to kick the corpse surged through him, leaving him shaky.

Cruncher shook his head. "You know what they say. Whatever men can do, women can do better, backwards, and in high heels."

James laughed despite himself. "Right."

He shook his head too and stepped in to grab the woman's chin and force her to focus on his face.

"Where is she? Where's the *lugat?*"

She went still and studied him, her eyes dilated so wide that she looked drugged. Then she laughed. Its wild insanity sent chills down his spine.

"Not *lugat. Kukudh*. She's invincible, and now so am I."

She looked down at Prek and spat on him. Before Cruncher could anticipate her, she wrenched herself free, squatted over the grimacing corpse, and urinated on his exposed genitals.

Cruncher clamped his hand around her upper arm and dragged her up to stand before him. "Who killed him?"

She looked at Prek over her shoulder. Triumph blazed from her bloody face. "I did. I killed the *goxha djalë*."

Cruncher gazed on the dead man for half a minute, pity clouding his broad features. "Not such a pretty boy anymore."

Then he pulled off his jacket and draped it over the woman's shoulders. She seemed oblivious to his kindness and tried to kick Prek. He pulled her away again.

"Let's go now, sweetheart. The EMTs will be waiting to take you to the hospital." He nodded at James.

James watched his partner go before directing the Natick officers to secure the house until the crime-scene investigators and medical examiner arrived. Two dozen more women in various states of dress, intoxication, and abuse emerged from bedrooms and basement, but Elira had vanished as easily as morning mist. If it hadn't been for the multiple accounts from Krasniqi guards and the first women who'd staggered out of the house, James would have wondered whether he and Cruncher had actually seen her. As it was, he was beginning to entertain outrageous thoughts about bloodsucking ghosts. Sighing in frustration, he shoved the thoughts to the back of his mind, more than ever certain that he needed a cold beer and Mirjeta.

Mirjeta. He'd planned to make her breakfast in a few hours, watching her eat while she eagerly described her upcoming classes and how she planned to teach her most gifted violin student. Instead, he was forced to remain in Natick to coordinate victim transport and medical care, witness interviews, evidence collection, and arrests. He also had to explain, somehow, to the local district attorney as well as the federal prosecutor building the case against the Krasniqis how the situation had spiraled so out of control that a prime suspect had been brutally murdered.

When he stepped out onto the porch four hours later, dawn lightened the early September sky and traffic sounds filtered to him from the nearby downtown of this modest Boston suburb. Curious neighbors clutching coffee mugs and laptop bags glanced at the law-enforcement vehicles as they walked toward their cars or the train station a few blocks away. Stretching, James yawned before clearing the gathering sleep from the corners of his eyes. Then he pulled out his cell phone to call Mirjeta, letting her husky voice, rich with Albanian accents, soothe and anchor him. He no longer knew how he'd ever managed to face the roiling adrenaline, searing anger, and bloodshed that defined his life without her.

A young woman, crisp and alert at the start of her day, came up the sidewalk, handed him a hot coffee, and introduced herself as an assistant federal prosecutor. James eyed the aggressive angle of her jaw, the tightness of her fingers on her notepad, the tailoring of her charcoal-gray jacket.

"How did this happen, agent?" Her cool tone underscored the sharpness of her gaze.

Let the games begin, thought James. He returned her gaze and didn't blink. "Ma'am, that's a very good question."

When James arrived at Jink & Diddle later, his head ached from the hard forty-five-minute nap that he'd stolen in the break room along with the three large coffees that he'd consumed since 9 a.m. Needless to say, he was cranky. If he was going to feel strung out and hung over, he'd damn well better have enjoyed the benefits of overindulging first.

Stepping onto the Victorian's drooping porch, he surveyed the two entry doors and the dusty floorboards. Even though he stood alone in the warm dark of an early September evening, cold shivered down the back of his neck. As he fingered his Walther PPK and let his gaze linger on the cars lining the curb, he recalled what Mirjeta had said after meeting the elderly gentlemen outside the bookstore in July. She'd said that she finally understood the English idiom about someone walking over her grave.

A horn sounded a hundred yards away on Somerville Avenue, and a dog barked farther up the block, shattering the stillness around James and dissipating the disconcerting chill. Shaking his head, he grasped the handle to the bookstore's door and pushed. Inside, querulous voices tumbled one after another down the darkened stairwell along with the pungent scent of burnt pot and the clink of glasses. He was debating what to do when male laughter rumbled along the sidewalk behind him.

Turning, James saw Elira stumbling against the side of a bearded man whose arm draped across her shoulders. The unexpected sight made him lose his hold on the handle and stagger a step as the door swung inward.

Elira didn't look his way, but her partner turned keen eyes on James, who stood on the threshold waiting for them. In the minute it took for the couple to negotiate the steps, he noted the other man's bushy beard, his Buddy Holly frames, and his Amish-farmer suspenders over a button-down shirt.

As they emerged into the nimbus under the porch light, the stranger's dark hair flared auburn, and his eyes clarified into sharp brown. It was a startling effect.

When they stopped two feet away, Elira shifted bleary eyes toward James. "Look what the cat dragged in! A tasty morsel." She snapped her teeth, lurched, and laughed.

James felt unease grip him at her thick, blurred speech. Elira without her sharp enunciation and threatening tone knocked him surprisingly off balance.

"Never one to let a tasty morsel pass by, eh?" asked the Amish Buddy Holly.

James narrowed his eyes at the man's mocking tone but said nothing.

The stranger turned to him. "Hey, dude. Here for my lecture?"

James's fingers itched, but he kept them from straying to the butt of his gun. "I'm here to speak with Elira, but she doesn't look up to a talk."

"James," she slurred. "I'm always willing ... to talk. Are you *up* for it?" She sniggered.

Her partner rolled his eyes and removed his arm from her shoulders, forcing her to clutch at his waist as her balance shifted. He thrust his hand toward James. "Jacob Stryver, founder and senior lecturer of the world's first and only anarchic school, Acephela College."

James accepted the other man's hand, whose strange leathery warmth repelled him. He kept his face impassive, however. "Anarchic school?"

"No diplomas. No accreditation. Anyone can attend our floating campus—we meet in homes, bars, parks and bookstores." He gestured toward Jink & Diddle.

"Anyone can earn stripes and ranks, all the way up to guru. Everyone's a student. Everyone teaches."

He grinned, showing pointy canine teeth in a narrow jaw. "We're a mix between a gang, a quilting bee, a cult, and a book club. We're the wave of the future, man."

James laughed. "Not sure a school named 'headless' would top my list. What's tonight's lecture on? And what's your expertise?"

"You mean, why should you listen to me declaim? Good question. For those who care about such things, I can wave around a piece of paper that says 'Harvard School of Divinity' and 'master's degree.' I've got other pieces of paper from other institutions of higher learning if that's not enough. I've studied theology and hermetics, but my interests include black magic and the occult, radical ecology and environmental philosophy, and William S. Burroughs."

At this point, Elira inserted herself into the conversation. "James reads books with titles like *Averroes, Maimonides, and Aquinas: Aristotle's Heirs* and *The Everlasting Man.*"

Even through her clumsy speech, James heard pride in her voice as she listed the same books that she'd mocked during her visit to his apartment—at least until she spoke again. "He's probably got his own little piece of paper to wave around, Stryver."

James studied Elira. Her pupils had nearly swallowed her irises, leaving an odd double ring with a light gray center.

Resisting the urge to snatch her away to the nearest diner for a cup of strong black coffee, he turned and then shrugged when Stryver eyed him. "I got a master's in philosophy from Brandeis."

A spark flared in Stryver's gaze. "Ah, a fellow lover of wisdom. Though I'm not a fan of Chesterton."

When James made an impatient sound and started to step aside, Stryver put his hand on his shoulder and said, "Stay, stay. I'm beginning a series of talks on what I call Blood Law Theology.

"Tonight's opening talk is titled *The Original Vampire: It Ain't Dracula*. How can you resist? Everyone loves vampires. They're the romantic heroes *du jour*." His feral bark of laughter spiked a chill at the base of James's spine.

James felt Elira go still but didn't look at her.

When she spoke, sharpness edged her words. "James isn't interested in vampires. He wants to talk to me."

Stryver turned to her and for a moment James thought the porch light dimmed and Stryver loomed larger. "What are you afraid of, my love? That I'll steal him away from you by appealing to his intellectual curiosity?"

Even though he didn't want to listen to this sneering academic pontificate, James found the subject strangely compelling. And, he told himself, if he played his cards right, he could maneuver Elira out of the bookstore afterwards, sober her up, and then find out what the hell had happened in Natick earlier.

"Sure. Why not? I don't have any other plans right now."

Holding the door for them, he watched as Elira dragged her feet, her gaze straying to him even as Stryver slipped his arm around her waist and pulled her inside.

"Get yourself some espresso and don't come up until you can make the stairs." Stryver thrust Elira toward the darkened bookstore. "Wouldn't want you to break your neck."

"I'll go with her." James looked back as he followed and caught the sly smile that darted across Stryver's face.

Elira said nothing as she fumbled with the espresso machine in the café at the back of the store, but when James tried to help, she jerked away from him.

He waited until she'd brewed a double and tossed it back, but when she started to make another, he spoke. "Don't tell me. He seduced you by quoting Shakespeare."

She shot him a startled look which quickly turned to cynicism. "Of course. That's what he does. Figures out where your jugular is, then goes straight for it."

"Doesn't sound like a healthy relationship."

"It's not. And if you know what's good for you, you'll get the hell out of here and never come back or he'll trap you too."

"Listen, I'm not leaving until you tell me what happened at the Krasniqi house. If I have to listen to an effete bookworm first, then that's what I'll do."

She started to say something when a young man, his brown hair in dreadlocks and wearing a dirty t-shirt, called to them from the doorway to announce that Stryver had started lecturing. James followed, aware that Elira dawdled behind him.

Upstairs, a dozen men and women ranging in age from mid-twenties to early forties sat on a dilapidated couch, floor, and folding chairs in a large room carpeted in dull tan. Along the far wall, a dark wood cabinet stood next to a violin case. When Stryver saw him, he grinned and motioned James to a spot on the sofa directly in front of where he sat in lotus position. Then he looked around at the students of his anarchic college, touching each face with his gaze as possessively as any lover.

"Over the course of this lecture series, prepare to be enlightened, angered, titillated, castigated, provoked, and moved. I'm about to lay out for you my theology, my theory for what makes the human race tick. And when I finish, I'll leave you my plan to redeem it. After all, you can't expect to throw off your mental shackles until you know the nature of the beast you're dealing with."

He paused, again looking at each student in the Acephela class. "Blood, children. Blood. That's what it's all about." He smirked at Elira, who'd appeared in the doorway. "As Dracula says, 'the blood is the life.' Without blood, we cannot live."

He paused again, staring pointedly at her. "Without blood, vampires cannot live. As the undead, they must feed off the living to get it. They are parasites."

Elira leaned against the doorframe with her arms folded across her chest. Under the harsh fluorescent light, James could see that she was shockingly pale, almost as white as she'd been the night that she'd been stabbed in the chest. Her pupils, though large, no longer overwhelmed her irises. She watched him and Stryver with eagle eyes, the spirit of Albanian heroism incarnate.

"Monsters who consume the flesh and blood of the living have existed since ancient times, but vampires as we know them are peculiar to the Balkans post Christianity. Their lore has leeched"—here Stryver smiled at his own pun—"into Western culture and our popular imagination, beginning with Stoker's *Dracula*.

"Stoker, of course, took liberties with Dracula, playing on the Victorian gothic sensibility. Capes, estates, nobility, even Dracula's gender are all permutations of the peasant folklore, wouldn't you say, my love? After all, most of them were very old or very young women, poor and mistreated."

Elira shrugged, narrowing her eyes, but said nothing. Stryver, indifferent to her response, or perhaps encouraged by it as James suspected, continued speaking.

James let his gaze travel the group. Stryver's audience appeared enthralled by him. Then Stryver began speaking again, and his melodious voice drew James's attention like a lodestone.

"But Dracula and his Balkan brethren are hardly the beginning of vampirism. Just as Christianity is hardly the beginning of our fascination with drinking blood, divine or otherwise. There's a much older source. A source that goes all the way back to the beginning of human history.

"That early, and history is mythology. And mythology is populated with gods. Gods, like the Hebrew Yahweh, who demand blood sacrifice. It was a token payment for the miracle of human life. That's what blood law is, children. The primordial rule binding God and humanity.

"Blood law is the heart of the Old Testament. It's no coincidence that Stoker had his cultured count paraphrase Leviticus 17:11, which begins 'For the life of the flesh is in the blood.' So we must look for the ancient one who first broke the law to find the primeval vampire."

Stryver stopped to take a drink from a pint glass next to him, stretching his neck afterwards. A young woman wearing a khaki-green peasant skirt and sporting unshaven legs and armpits knelt beside him and began to rub his feet. Catching James's eye, he winked and let a small smile flit across his lips.

"Some say the first vampire is Lilith, the wife Adam rejected because she refused to assume a subordinate sexual position. What does that make you, Elira?"

Elira's hiss swelled into the corners of the stunned, suddenly frigid room. The other Acephela students shifted and muttered.

"Nice try, old man. But you said the original vampire was the first to break the blood law. Preferring to ride Adam like a horse didn't make Lilith a vampire. My money is on a man. God knows men always try to pass their faults onto women."

"It's Cain."

All eyes turned to James, expectant.

"He's the one who brought God the first fruits of his harvest, but God rejected his proud sacrifice. On the other hand, Abel his younger brother slaughtered a lamb from his flock and that pleased God."

Stryver nodded, his smile not reaching the eyes that studied James, who had the unsettling feeling that the other man was sizing him up much as a fox appraised an unsuspecting rabbit.

"Very good, James. You know your Old Testament history. Cain, the firstborn human, tried to weasel out of his blood debt to God. Then he compounded his error by killing Abel. If you ask me, that's when the primordial rule, the original blood law, was subverted.

"Almost from the very start, humanity in the person of Cain usurped God's role as the creator of life and therefore the owner of blood debt. Ever since then, people have claimed blood for themselves, heaping blood sin on top of Adam's original sin."

"'It hath the primal eldest curse upon't, a brother's murder!'" Elira quoted in a deadly soft voice, startling James, who'd forgotten everyone else as Stryver spoke.

She'd moved from the threshold to stand beside them, her hands clenched at her sides. When he tore his gaze away to look at her, he noticed the small leather pouch containing her fiancé's finger bone lying entwined with the medieval crucifix on her chest.

"So how did Cain become a vampire then? He didn't drink Abel's blood."

"No, he didn't."

Stryver stood up as if he faced an accuser. James didn't understand the currents running between them, but he couldn't turn his eyes away.

Without looking at him, Stryver asked, "What does blood do after it's shed, James?"

Mesmerized, James answered as if compelled. "It cries out to God, who avenges it."

"That's right. God marked Cain, some say with Abel's innocent blood, and sent Cain wandering, forever cut off from Him."

"Undead and feeding on the blood of the living." Elira's angry statement sounded like a thunderclap. "As you say, a parasite."

Stryver stepped close to her, wrapping his hands about her waist. She stood stiffly but didn't resist him when he nuzzled her neck.

"Ah, my love, that's Cain's punishment. To be the scourge of humanity. To claim blood from those who would steal it from God."

At his murmured words, a pall dimmed the fluorescent light and muffled the icy room. James's thoughts turned fuzzy, and angry buzzing filled his ears. Struggling to clear his head, he shook it. "Abel prefigures Christ...."

Stryver laughed, dissipating the darkness, and stepped back from Elira. He kept his hands at her waist, however, as he addressed the others. "Of course, this is all arrogant theologizing on the part of a divinity-school grad. Anthropologists see the Cain and Abel story as an ancient metaphor for the death of hunter-gatherer societies at thc hands of agriculture."

Turning a triumphant smile toward James, he asked, "And yet, the story has a certain elegant logic to explain human history, eh?"

He moved his hands to Elira's shoulders and looked down in what appeared to be genuine fondness. "It explains the arrogance, the hubris, the thievery. Paying lip service to God while slaking illicit blood thirst in the name of honor."

He rubbed affectionate thumbs along her collarbones before lifting the leather pouch from her breast. "The kind of honor *stratioti* pursued."

Elira, nostrils pinched in her white face, shrugged off his hands, swaying a little as she did. "What do you know of honor?"

"I know *stratioti*, those ragtag Albanian drifters who claimed the Turks owed them blood yet modeled their dress and their fighting after them, all the while stealing from their Venetian bosses. I know Skanderbeg, the Dragon of Albania, killed thousands of his own countrymen as a janissary before flipping sides and killing his former Ottoman friends. Where's the honor in that? Perhaps that's why history forgot them."

The dreadlocked young man, who sat next to James on the sofa, shook his head and muttered. "He's always baiting her."

James stood up, stepping toward them. Unease stirred in him at the sight of Elira, who looked strangely defenseless and as though the contents of her stomach had risen to her throat. He knew how it felt to have his heroes unmasked—even if Stryver made a good point. Honor, personal integrity and dignity, was earned, not conferred. And not stolen or abused. Only given away or lost.

"Elira looks like she's not up for debating her ancestors with you, Stryver."

She shot him a look, one so filled with venom and pain that James stepped back and lifted an involuntary hand. "Stryver knows that better than anyone."

She glared at the other man.

Then she gave a stiff, mocking bow and spun on her heel. The tattooed Albanian words *Fast for the soul, kill for honor* sinuated across her upper back as she strode away, their blood-red gothic lettering startling against her pallor. At the threshold, she stumbled but caught herself on the doorframe.

As her boots sounded on the carpeted stairs, Stryver began speaking, running his gaze around the room as he did.

"My Blood Law Theology builds on early human belief in blood as the essence of life and the subsequent need to elevate it to the sacred, to create divine laws to avenge its shedding. My theory will examine how Cain stands as the archetype for the competing human need to act, to claim authority for human justice in the real world.

"Next up on the agenda: 'Larry, Moe, and Curly: God's Three Stooges.' We'll return to the Fertile Crescent, cradle of civilization and end point of a bloody fault line running from the Mideast through the Balkans and north into Eastern Europe, where vampires and blood feuds are a central truth of everyday life."

He paused and then grinned. His pointy little teeth made him look dangerously wild.

"Now it's time for the real meat of Acephela: the salon. Elira usually brings us trays of cappuccino, but I'll have to show Althea here how to make them. Among other things."

He winked at James and slipped his arm around the hirsute young woman. "Let's go to the café and see what else Elira stocks that stimulates intellectual conversation."

James hung back while the others crowded toward the doorway, thinking. When he saw the dreadlocked young man, he motioned for him to remain, waiting until they were alone to speak. "Have you been attending these Acephela lectures?"

The young man nodded. "Stryver posted flyers around Cambridge last spring. I've been coming all summer."

"What you said earlier ... they're always like this?" James lifted his chin to indicate the previous interaction between Stryver and Elira.

The young man shrugged and then looked over his shoulder at the stairwell, warily thought James. "Yeah, I guess so. She doesn't much seem to like him, but she's always here. Hell, this is her place. He's got some kind of hold over her. Sometimes it even feels like they're competing for the same student, you know, some sort of kinky sex game. I get the feeling he usually wins."

James nodded, considering this tidbit, and then looked straight at the young man. "Ever compete over you?"

The other man looked uncomfortable. "No, not my thing. In fact, I'm thinking about dropping out."

"That's too bad. I'm intrigued about Stryver's Blood Law Theology. I thought I might come back for the next talk. Do you know when it is?"

The young man swept his gaze over James, assessing. "First Friday of October." After James nodded, he went on. "Might be worth it to return just to see them fight over you."

James, his eyes narrowed, watched the young man leave. Unaccountably, that had sounded like a threat.

Six

MIRJETA STOOD IN FRONT OF THE PICTURE WINDOW in her living room, her ethereal image on its darkened surface backlit by a golden glow from a single table lamp. She was incomplete, transparent, all dark hollows and indistinct edges that faded into the blackness of evening beyond the glass. Behind her, solid objects gave mass and volume to her apartment while outside the rustling leaves and indirect fluorescence of a nearby streetlamp whispered a promise of society, of communion with others. Despite the music playing on her stereo, a hush swaddled her.

James had proposed last week.

She picked up her violin from where it lay in its open case and settled it onto her shoulder. Its familiar sweet weight anchored her. It had always anchored her. Or perhaps more rightly, it tied her to another dimension where she could escape from memories of Imam Krasniqi, of the harrowing journey from Kosova to the Accursed Mountains, of finding her mother's broken and used body in their tiny Shkodra apartment. Whether she married James or not, she would always have her violin and the music that she had learned to create with it.

Breathing softly, she listened with her whole body to the haunting melody of *Nothing Else Matters* before skimming her bow over the strings in unison.

She knew the violinist, knew his playing almost as well as her own. She'd met David at Julliard, a virtuoso matched only by his intense personality and his smoldering German looks. When they'd dated, he'd worn his hair short and been clean shaven, reminding her of a younger Ralph Fiennes.

Now he styled himself a rock violinist and cultivated an image to match, bleaching his dark hair and wearing it shoulder length, looking purposefully scruffy in a day's stubble and jeans. Although she'd been the one to end it, stoically withstanding his desperate attempt to convince her otherwise, she'd known even then that she would never fit into his life, that he'd fling her off in a petulant fit or turn cruel when he discovered how unworthy of his charisma and talent she proved to be.

Today, she taught at the New England Conservatory of Music; David had just released his fourth album, his first in the U.S. Looking like a doppelganger for Kurt Cobain, he sported tattoos and modeled, filling stadiums for his concerts. Naturally he dated models. The only thing that she had in common with them was her dark eyes and hair.

Still, David had been her first love. He'd been the first peer who shared her passion for the violin, a stranger in the U.S. like her. They'd hung out at her tiny apartment, watching American TV, listening to American rock and pop music, and eating American junk food.

Closing her eyes, she drifted as she plied her bow, caressing and pressing the strings with her left hand, feeling their vibration through the pads of her fingers and along her forearms. As she swayed to their combined music, memories of his gentle lovemaking filled her until hot tears sheeted her cheeks, and she gasped.

She cried for her mother. She cried for the innocent that she'd still been when she'd met David. She cried in a thunderstorm of grief and gratitude and wonder, her emotions crescendoing with the music. Why had God spared her? Would He spare her again?

Tonight, the man who'd been like a father to her would learn that his son wanted to marry her. But she owed Dr. Goodman the truth—she owed them both the truth—before she could say yes.

She'd met James and his father along with their friend Jeremy Loring on the airplane to Boston ten years ago, fleeing from Albania and Imam Krasniqi. Nearly catatonic with terror and fatigue, stumbling from her first flight into the Rome airport, she'd grown frantic when she couldn't find the right gate for her connecting flight. Her broken English hadn't helped her. So she'd sat down in the middle of the concourse and started to sob.

And then James had crouched down and asked her in Albanian if he could help, and she'd answered without thinking. When she asked how he knew that she was Albanian, he'd said that he'd seen her address on her violin case. Then, he'd helped her to her feet, shouldered her backpack and introduced her first to his father, who'd just been rescued after six months in captivity, and then to Mr. Loring.

Together, they'd shepherded her onto the Alitalia flight, requested that her seat be changed so that she sat near them, and got her through American customs. Despite Dr. Goodman's frail health, he'd insisted that she stay with them until her Julliard audition, to which they'd driven her. And while she was at Julliard, they'd become her family.

Tonight, she might lose that family forever.

Would Dr. Goodman have it within him to forgive? Would James?

The final strains of *Nothing Else Matters* brought her weeping to a halt. She let her bow arm glide to her side. As she did, a cool breath rustled the hairs on the back of her neck, sending a shiver down her spine. Her eyelids winged up only to reveal her specter on the polished glass overlooking the street below. She was alone in a second-floor apartment. An abrupt image of Elira transposed itself over hers. She blinked, and it vanished. It had been nearly three months since she'd visited Jink & Diddle, yet the other woman's face and voice kept resurrecting in her thoughts, taking on a strength unexplained by their meeting. She kept remembering that Elira had called her *little sister*. Oddly, the memory made her feel safe, wanted.

A knock sounded, and she jumped. Forcing a laugh, she wiped her sleeve over her cheeks. She set her violin in its case and hurried to the door. The sense of being watched evaporated as she peered through the peephole and glimpsed James's broad shoulder and firm jaw. Trembling, she flipped the deadlock, yanked the door open, and, catching her breath to calm herself, offered a stiff smile to her guests.

James turned to her, his own smile broad and his eyes warm.

"Hey," he said and stepped forward to kiss her.

Mirjeta turned her face so that his lips brushed hers instead of lingering as it seemed he intended. A slight frown clouded his gaze and then disappeared. He slid his arm around her waist and turned to his father, who stood behind him in the hallway.

"Well, Pop, here she is, more beautiful than ever."

Mirjeta ignored James, slipping from his embrace to step back and open her door wide. "Dr. Goodman, please come in."

Afraid that her welcome would fall flat, she nevertheless offered them the traditional Albanian host's greeting. "*Pu lutem, merrni bukë, kripë, dhe zemra ime.*" *Please, take bread, salt, and my heart.* She wondered if he heard the tremor in her voice, the sincerity.

She needn't have worried.

Dr. Goodman, who remained as gracious as she remembered, nodded and responded in Albanian. "*Ju faleminderit. Ne do.*" *Thank you. We will.*

He leaned in to grasp her free hand before kissing her on the cheek. "Indeed, you are lovelier than I remember. It has been far too long." Releasing her hand, he entered her apartment with James close behind.

A creeping sensation crawled down Mirjeta again, but she saw nothing in the empty hall when she peeked around the open door. Shaking her head, she shut it.

She ushered the men to her living room and asked them whether they'd like red wine or beer before dinner. James followed her into the kitchen, ostensibly to help, but as soon as they'd disappeared inside, he drew her into his arms and kissed her.

"What's wrong?" he whispered when she didn't relax against him. "He can't see us."

"I know." She turned away.

"Nerves?" He tugged her around as she reached for the cabinet where she stored wine glasses. "This isn't the old country, *e dashur*."

Despite her growing anxiety, Mirjeta smiled at the endearment and touched her fingertips to his face. Then she took a small breath and said, "But it's important that I speak to your father before I give you my answer. It's not a formality."

He narrowed his eyes. "Okay."

She could tell that he didn't understand her reluctance. When she turned back to the cabinet, however, he didn't stop her.

They brought the drinks and a wedge of brie with crackers to the coffee table. Dr. Goodman smiled as he accepted his wine from his seat by the window.

"Who's this we're listening to?" He cocked his head to indicate the music.

She shrugged and sat down. "No one special."

James looked intrigued. "Really? You don't waste your time playing with 'no one special.' We heard you playing from the hall. Pop insisted we wait until you were done to knock."

"You sounded heartbreaking." Dr. Goodman held his wine to his nose and sniffed. "Mm. Cabernet."

She tittered and refused to meet James's gaze. "Hard to imagine anything by Metallica is heartbreaking."

James, who'd remained standing, picked up the CD case before shooting her an incredulous glare.

"Whoever he is, he's very talented." Dr. Goodman sipped his wine and sighed. "Although I can't say I recognize this piece either. Something modern?"

"Yeah, you could say that since it's by the rock group Queen." The sarcasm in James's voice sent a wave of heat down her neck and chest.

"I'm sorry it bothers you. Turn it off."

"No, that's okay." James took a drink from his beer, keeping his gaze on her. "If a virtuoso can play rock on his violin, I can listen to it." He raised his bottle.

Mirjeta saw the silent challenge in his eyes and flinched.

He'd confessed, quite simply, to having loved her since the moment he'd spotted her slumped in the middle of the Roman concourse while dozens of travelers parted around her like water flowing around a boulder, her battered violin case slung over her shoulder and her black wool coat threadbare at the elbows. His subsequent visits and invitations to spend the holidays with him and his father, comforting as they had been, had been motivated by more than simple friendship.

That last time six years ago, when he'd dropped in unannounced while on leave from the Army Rangers, he'd finally convinced himself to ask her out. By then, she'd been dating David for nine months, and James had found them celebrating her acceptance into the master's program at Julliard. The look on James's face and the massive bouquet of calla lilies he'd clutched had sent a bolt through Mirjeta. When he'd declined to stay, instead shaking David's hand and congratulating her, she'd known that she wouldn't see him again. She'd broken up with David the next day.

Mirjeta lifted her wineglass and sipped, inhaling as she swallowed. The spicy flavor of cloves hit her palate first, followed by caramel and chocolate, and finally black currant and cherry. She let her eyelids drift shut and sighed almost soundlessly. It was going to be a long evening. When she opened her eyes, she found James watching her with a slight frown.

"How was your drive down?" she asked, turning to his father.

Dr. Goodman lived almost five hours away in Castine, Maine, where he taught biology at the Maine Maritime Academy and reviewed pathology books for Thieme Medical Publishers.

"Uneventful, except when I hit 95. I keep forgetting what it's like to drive in real traffic."

Mirjeta shot a look at James and licked her lips. "We're really grateful you drove down. I'm sure your teaching load keeps you busy."

"Nonsense. I haven't seen James since June. And isn't it about time I spent some time with both of you? After all, he tells me you two have been seeing each other since the spring." He beamed at her. "Besides, I dropped in on an old friend this afternoon to consult on a case, so I'm mixing a little business with my pleasure."

"Good. That's good." Mirjeta sent up a silent prayer of thanks and sipped her wine.

"We"—she glanced at James again, who watched her with a set mouth and narrowed eyes—"I have a lot to share with you since we last saw one another."

THEY'D PLANNED TO DINE out, but in the end, Mirjeta called a nearby Pakistani restaurant for takeout before sending James to pick their food up. She could have taken that opportunity to confess who she was to Dr. Goodman while they were alone together, but her courage failed her. James had already arranged for Andrew to call around nine so that he'd have an excuse to step out onto her balcony, and she saw no reason to risk spoiling what promised to be a pleasant meal.

It might be the last time she enjoyed the company of two men who meant everything to her.

"Anything breaking for you on the Duka case?" Dr. Goodman asked as James poured him more cabernet. "I know how frustrating it can be to build a case, but you don't want to leave any stone unturned with people like these."

James paused to look at him, briefly covering his father's hand where it rested on the table. "I'm nothing if not patient, Pop." He glanced over at Mirjeta. "If I were Albanian, I'd say the Krasniqis owed two bloods, one for you and one for Mirjeta. But I'm not Albanian, thank God. I'm going to nail Duka and the Krasniqis in an American court of law."

"Does that mean you've tied Duka to the Krasniqis?" Dr. Goodman had set his flatware down and clutched his wineglass.

"Circumstantial evidence, but yes. Duka's mother owned the Natick house we raided last month, and the accountants and other paper chasers are toiling along a chain of bank accounts and property deeds. Sooner or later, we're going to find something that ties the money used to purchase the house to the Krasniqi smuggling operation. It's always the same: follow the money."

"How did you find this house?" Dr. Goodman studied him with hawk's eyes. "Are you sure it was a Krasniqi way station? They're notoriously difficult to link to anything."

James nodded, a smile stretching his cheeks but not touching his eyes. "Oh, it was a Krasniqi house all right. Prek Krasniqi showed up."

"Elira told you, didn't she?" Mirjeta watched James. He'd grown obsessed with her strange "sister," adding to her unease about the whole case.

He turned to his father. "Remember the Albanian woman who almost died preventing the Krasniqis from kidnapping Mirjeta?"

At his father's nod, he went on. "Well, she's got some vendetta going against them. I'm just glad she didn't cut us out of the loop and told us how to find the Duka house."

Dr. Goodman pursed his lips, swirling his wine. After a long moment in which James ate the last of his kebab, he said, "Did she show up at this raid?"

James swallowed some wine. "That's the funny thing, Pop. Cruncher and I both saw Elira right after Prek and his goons showed up. We thought she'd blown our operation and chased after her. The Krasniqi men and vics at the house all ID'ed her, but she was nowhere inside."

His father nodded, although he looked puzzled. "That's odd. Any evidence she was there?"

"The techs did find some stray blood drops in the room where I found Prek's body, but none of the markers from the PCR analysis matched anyone else's DNA. I suspect the blood is Elira's, but I have no reason to get a warrant for a sample from her."

Mirjeta felt faint. "Prek's body?"

James glanced at her, looked away, and then brought his gaze back to rest on her. He grabbed her hand and rubbed it. "Oh, sweet lord! I'm sorry, love. I forgot you're not used to this kind of talk at the dinner table."

"You mean you think this Elira killed Prek?" Dr. Goodman seemed oblivious to Mirjeta's discomfort. "How? Is she some sort of assassin? And who would take on the Krasniqi mob? They're so vicious the Italians are scared shitless of them."

James kept Mirjeta's hand but continued. "I saw her that night when she saved Mirjeta. She's definitely not just some crazy Albanian chasing the Krasniqis. I think she might be ex-KLA with some Special Forces training thrown in."

A look passed between James and his father. A look that Mirjeta knew didn't bode well for her and her future.

"Whatever she is, I owe her for more than Mirjeta's life. I owe her for what may be our big break in this case, not to mention saving those women at the house. Someone's priming her, and my gut tells me that she's our best bet for getting to the imam."

"What if she murdered Prek?" Mirjeta asked. Her voice came out a whisper. She cleared her throat.

James had an odd look on his face. "I don't really want to know."

"But what if you could get a blood sample from her that matched the drops in the house? Would you try to link her to his murder?" she pressed.

He wouldn't look at her and raised his wineglass to his mouth instead. "No. He raped one of the victims just before he died."

Mirjeta wanted to protest that Elira still didn't have the right to take his life, that James had sworn to uphold the rule of law, and that he'd be condoning murder if he suspected that Elira had taken blood but did nothing to bring evidence against her in a court of law.

Before she could speak, however, Dr. Goodman did. "Who do you think is feeding her information? A rival Albanian crime family?"

"There's no evidence that she's hooked into the local Albanian community, right, Mirjeta?"

She looked at Dr. Goodman. "I wanted to find Elira to thank her for saving my life and"—she paused, choosing her words—"and because she haunts me. Still does, in fact."

She rushed on to finish when it looked as though he wanted to question her. "It took me weeks to track her down. She doesn't spend any time at traditional Albanian events or venues, such as the community center or church. I found her through a chance question to a young Albanian who recognized her from a club they both frequent downtown."

James took up the tale. "Lately, I've been attending these odd lectures at the bookstore she owns near Porter Square, trying to insinuate myself, dig up some leads. This Harvard Divinity grad named Jacob Stryver who gives off cult-leader vibes has started what he rather pretentiously stylizes an 'anarchic college.'

"Maybe it's because of his background, but he knows *a lot* about blood laws, has a whole theology based on them. He and Elira have a mutual antagonism, but they're a duo of some sort. Maybe he's her source."

"What's his motivation?" his father asked.

He'd finished eating, having pushed his plate to the side, and focused on James's investigation. Mirjeta wondered if he missed being part of that world after all.

"Not clear. He's not Albanian, for one thing. But he's got a hold on Elira. I think he's her supplier, of what and from whom, I don't know. One of the 'students' at this college says she always looks like death warmed over, weak and trembling and often vomiting in the bathroom whenever Stryver holds a lecture."

"Seriously?" Mirjeta couldn't picture Elira as anything but coldly terrifying.

"Yeah. I've seen it." He shook his head. "He's nervy and a tad brilliant, I'll give him that much. Last week, he made fun of the three Abrahamic religions, calling them God's Three Stooges. Heaven help him if any radical Muslims get wind of his sacrilege."

"What was the point of his talk?" asked Dr. Goodman. "Just stirring up trouble?"

"Probably. I get the feeling Stryver sees himself as an iconoclast, hence his 'anarchic' college with no degrees, credentials, tuition, etc. But the brilliant part, I think, is how he casts human history as a struggle between opposing blood laws.

"He began his lecture series telling us that Cain was the original vampire because he stole blood from God, first by trying to pay God off with his harvest instead of blood from an animal, and then by killing Abel."

Dr. Goodman appeared to lose interest and picked up his wine. "That doesn't seem so brilliant to me. It's dogma that early humans sacrificed to pay a blood debt to their gods."

Mirjeta recalled what James had told her about the Cain lecture. "But what's different, Dr. Goodman, is *why* Stryver says the first humans owed God blood. It's not only to atone for sin. It's because blood equals life. Those sacrifices are a token payment to God acknowledging that."

Something sparked in Dr. Goodman's eyes at her explanation. He smiled. "Ah, that *is* a new twist. I think I know where this is going but go on. Go on."

James pushed his plate away and poured everyone a new glass of wine. "Yes, so Stryver claims that human understanding of this transcendent meaning behind the sacrifice was perverted almost from the start when Cain killed Abel. Through Cain, humans have moved their eyes from the Creator to themselves."

"And claimed ownership of blood, an eye, a tooth. But tell me, James, how does this Stryver fellow explain Leviticus and the rest of the Old Testament laws? I assume Abraham is Moe."

"I'm getting to that." James paused and appeared to gather his thoughts. "The original covenant between God and humanity lets humans have a chance, like Cain, to pay their debt themselves. But, of course, we know that humans have the innate desire to wrench God's authority and take it for themselves."

"Yes, that's part of humanity's origin mythology. That and what happens to humans when they try to be godlike. Take Icarus, for example." Dr. Goodman bent over the table, tapping it with his index finger. "Cain took credit for his harvest, didn't he? Instead of accepting that he needed a lamb as a substitute for himself, he offered God some of what he'd grown as if he were responsible for its life."

James nodded. "So as time went on, the reasons for the sacrifice got obscured, and the terms of the original covenant didn't get met as people focused on revenge and justice for themselves."

Mirjeta twisted her fingers together. This conversation reminded her too much of her conversation with Elira, who'd insisted that she couldn't escape who and what she was. And, of course, she was right. Mirjeta couldn't escape the confession that she had to make tonight, not if she had any hope of starting a new life with James that had a chance of surviving.

"Leading to a new blood law, a new covenant whereby God pays Himself back." Dr. Goodman sat up, his face glowing. "Whether Stryver plays a significant role or not in your investigation, this topic is very relevant in dealing with the Albanian mafia."

"I'm sure it is. His next talk he's titled 'The Balkans: A Bloody Cauldron.'"

"How did he distinguish the blood law theology of Islam from Judaism? Despite coming after Christianity, Islam is very Old Testament in its legal views."

"Well, Moe and Curly are pretty much the same when it comes to poking out eyes and slapping heads. But the key to all of this is recognizing the tribal prerogative. Jews have an exclusive covenant with God, but anyone can become Muslim. In the Middle East, both still believe in and collect blood debt, though Muslims also assign collective guilt."

Dr. Goodman slapped the table. "Ah ha! That's it. Combine individual human arrogance with our family instincts, and you've got the 'us-versus-them' situation that blood laws create. Tribe against tribe."

"Very Albanian," murmured Mirjeta. She thought of her own little family, of her mother, who was born Catholic, and her father, who'd been Muslim. Never had it been anything but us-versus-them between them.

"Very human," said Dr. Goodman, smiling. He turned to look at James. "This must be pretty fascinating to you, philosopher. Stryver's set up an epic battle between man and God: who gets the blood?"

"The real question is," said James, lifting his wineglass and studying the deep-red liquid inside, "whether Stryver plans to reframe the question to cut out God. That is, is Cain really the *über*-hero of our tale because he was the first to reject God?"

TWO HOURS LATER, MIRJETA sat alone with Dr. Goodman, toying with her cloth napkin as he took another piece of *baklava* from a serving dish. James had taken his coffee cup and a plate of the honey-drizzled pastry to the balcony to talk to Andrew Cruncher. She chided herself for eating the heavily seasoned grilled chicken and the accompanying rice spiced with whole cloves, saffron, and cardamom. It remained a heavy, cold lump in her churning stomach and flavored the acid creeping into her throat. Ignoring the gooey dessert, she slid her coffee cup a fraction of an inch to the side.

Dr. Goodman sighed and leaned back. When Mirjeta looked at him, she saw deep contentment on his features. "Did James tell you he took me to your concert last March? The one at Berklee? It was fabulous. Just fabulous. You've really grown into a commanding presence on stage."

She slipped the napkin into her lap to continue assaulting it. Licking her lips, she looked at him. "I saw you two. I–I planned to call you later, but then everything happened and I forgot."

Chagrin chased the contentment on his face away. "Oh, dear Lord. I'd forgotten. I'm sorry to remind you."

"That's okay." She shivered, calling a lie to her brave disavowal. "I try to focus on the good that came of it, reconnecting with James being the most important."

He nodded, looking thoughtful. Mirjeta knew that it was time to tell him. As her intense gaze winged over his face, she tried to absorb everything that she saw. He'd aged little in the decade since they'd met, less certainly than she and James, who'd both been teenagers, had done. Dr. Goodman was a big, robust man, well over six feet tall, who seemed more suited to outdoor physical labor than the lab. Despite the fact that he'd gone bald in his early twenties and wore nondescript glasses, his booming laugh and intelligent brown eyes lent a force to his personality that made it impossible to overlook or dislike him. Or break him. She wondered now if that was why the KLA had kept him alive. Had it been fury at his indomitable spirit that drove them?

Thinking that, an image of Dr. Goodman in the Rome airport accosted her.

As numb and scared as she'd been, she'd still shied away from the pale, emaciated man who'd trailed after James. The skin of his gaunt face had hung loose, his shoulders had hunched, and he'd shuffled along, flinching continually at the swiftly passing travelers and intermittent announcements. He'd looked sick, perhaps terminally ill, and he'd kept his gaze on the floor. Yet when the customs agent had questioned the validity of her passport and her reasons for traveling, Dr. Goodman had come to stand by her and returned the man's gaze with such quiet ferocity that Mirjeta had felt safe for the first time in months.

"Is there something you want to tell me, Mirjeta? Something to do with James?" The gentleness in his voice penetrated her reverie, and she started.

"I love James," she blurted and looked at her lap as if she could puzzle out what her fingers were doing as they twisted and twisted the napkin there.

"I know."

She looked up at him, tears pricking her, and blinked hard. "I love you, too. I never said that before, but I knew it. I was just afraid."

"As you are now? Why? Do you think I won't love you in return?" He slipped his big, warm hand across the table and laid it against her cheek. "I already love you, my brave girl."

It was her turn to acknowledge what she already knew. It came out as a whisper. "I know."

"I know James wants to marry you. He's only ever wanted you. Is that what this is about? Are you worried that he doesn't know his own heart? That he'll regret never having another serious love affair?"

Mirjeta's mouth snapped shut. She hadn't known that. James had never told her about his dating, and she'd assumed that he'd had his fair share of girlfriends. She'd always thought that he was kind, funny, loyal, and sexy, and she didn't think that her judgment or taste lacked. Hadn't Elira salivated over him? What had she said? That he was 'Achilles reborn with eyes the color of the Adriatic'?

"No." The word tasted like dust. "Though maybe I should be worried now." She laughed a little and looked away. "I'm afraid that you'll both stop loving me once you know who I really am."

"Who you really are?" He looked and sounded confused, but then his face cleared. "Nothing can make us stop loving you."

"Perhaps not, but you may love me less. You may not want your son to marry me."

Dr. Goodman gave an exasperated sigh and shifted in his chair, letting his hand fall to the table. He said nothing, simply waited.

"You know me as Mirjeta Gjakova," she said at last. "Gjakova was my mother's maiden name. I go by it instead of my father's name." She paused and forced herself to look at him, raising her chin a fraction, hot tears burning her vision. "I am Mirjeta Krasniqi, niece to Imam Krasniqi."

"'EXCELLENT WRETCH! PERDITION CATCH my soul, but I do love thee! And when I love thee not, chaos is come again.'"

Elira started at the voice behind her before reaching for her missing dagger.

"Don't you think those lines say it all?"

Zophiel stood facing a faded Urban Shakespeare poster, her hands on her hips. "Othello actually knows what he's supposed to do, but does he?"

Rising slowly, Elira scowled. She *really* missed her dagger about now. "How'd you do that?"

Zophiel turned to look at her. Under the harsh streetlight, her large, kohl-rimmed eyes regarded Elira. "Do what? Quote Shakespeare? Really, Elira. You ask the stupidest questions."

"No." Exasperation constricted Elira's throat and clinched her teeth. "Sneak up on me."

Zophiel turned back to study the poster. "I don't sneak. You just aren't paying attention as usual."

"What do you want from me?" Elira let anger overwhelm her unease. This woman-child and her sudden appearances disturbed her more than she would ever show.

Zophiel cocked her head. "It's man trouble, isn't it? You don't have to pretend with me."

She stepped forward and grasped Elira's hands in hers, which were warm and soft, sending a veritable earthquake through Elira. "He loves someone else, right?"

Elira tugged on her hands but couldn't free them. Her heart pounded. "I don't know what you're talking about," she whispered.

But she did. She'd heard James, seen his face. He wanted to marry her.

"That's who you were following just now. Tall and handsome? With his father?"

Elira couldn't speak. She could only shift her chin down and up.

Zophiel shook her head. "Unlucky in love, huh? Perhaps you're looking in all the wrong places." She paused. "Do you think he's found his true love?"

Elira looked away toward the shadows farther along the sidewalk where James and his father had walked, deep in conversation, not five minutes ago.

Zophiel dropped Elira's hands and began rummaging in a small lace bag hanging from her shoulder. "Well, you know what Shakespeare has Lysander say. 'The course of true love never did run smooth.' Maybe he'll dump her for you, if you give him the right reason."

Elira turned back to stare at Zophiel, who gave a small cry of delight before pulling out a tube of lip gloss, which she proceeded to apply.

"Maybe." She darted a glance in the direction James had traveled, all the while rubbing her hands. "Maybe I'll unleash chaos if he dumps her."

Zophiel shrugged. "You'll never know unless you try." She gave Elira what could only be termed a sly look. "After all, chaos can be exciting."

Elira took a step forward, her hands fisted. *Perdition catch my soul* whispered Zophiel in a voice that seemed to surround her on all sides. Elira spun, heart hammering and goose pimples puckering her flesh in the sudden unnatural warmth. Zophiel had disappeared in the mist rising as the heated air met the cold pavement.

"But I do love thee," Elira finished in her own whisper and, turning, sprinted into the night.

WHEN JAMES DROPPED INTO Jink & Diddle two days later, he found Stryver sitting in the café reading *Black Lamb and Grey Falcon*, a thousand-page tome by British writer Rebecca West on her travels through Yugoslavia before World War II.

"Hey, man," Stryver said, looking up. "Ever read Dame West?" He waggled the book with both hands.

James shook his head. "I've heard it's supposed to be one of the best books of the twentieth century though."

Stryver nodded and leaned back in his chair. “Exceedingly sharp broad. You want to know anything about the Balkans, you need to read her.”

James crossed his arms. “I suppose. But I heard she also had a bias toward the Serbs to the exclusion of all the other ethnic groups.”

“True, true.” Stryver nodded again. “Even so, she understood how religion ruined the Balkans. She herself was something of a Manichaean.”

“Interesting word choice, ruined. A divinity degree doesn’t make you a believer, does it?”

Stryver cocked his head. “Are you?”

“Lapsed Catholic, so yes and no.” James studied Stryver. “Don’t you believe that someone can be educated and still have faith?”

“I think the most educated have a faith of some sort or another. Though most these days wouldn’t be caught dead believing in a religious sense, making my expertise useless.” He grinned. “The problem for those who do, like you, is the same one that Dame West had.” Here he tapped the cover of his book. “Reconciling faith with intellect. My job, as I see it, is to help those who are struggling to find a way through to a worldview that fits.”

“Would that have anything to do with anarchy?”

Stryver laughed. “Oh, no. Just because I promote a freer intellectual pursuit doesn’t mean I believe in chaos. Far from it. It’s just my method for bringing the confused to clarity.”

"Then I look forward to your next lecture." James scanned the café and nearby bookstore. "Where's Elira? I need to talk to her. I keep stopping by, but the bookstore is always closed."

"I haven't seen her in a while. I just let myself in to work on the lecture." Stryver shrugged. "She does this every now and again."

"Aren't you worried?"

"Nah. I can always find her if I want her, no matter where she runs to. You want me to sniff her out for you?"

A creepy sensation washed down James's spine at Stryver's unabashed certainty. "No. Just tell her I'm looking for her when she gets back."

"Sure. It won't be long." Stryver sighed. "We've been together for ages, but sometimes she thinks she wants something else, you know? Then she goes AWOL for a few days. I don't mind, though. She always comes back hungry for me because I give her exactly what she wants."

Seven

TWO WEEKS PASSED BEFORE ELIRA SENT JAMES A NOTE telling him to meet her at an open rehearsal for *Hamlet.* This time, the production was being staged in a former church in Boston not far from the Boston Center for the Arts, its gothic stone sanctuary a medieval cave. The set design incorporated the audience, who sat along the sides of the nave in three center-facing rows of red-cushioned pews. Tall wrought-iron stands displaying silkscreened heraldic tapestries flanked these ornately carved benches. Where the altar would have been, a long table stood draped in heavy red and gold brocade with massive chairs behind. Standing sentinel on either end of the table, thick unlit white tapers filled two candelabra that matched the tapestry stands. A wooden-walled loft ran around the perimeter, but whether it was a part of the stage or the audience was unclear.

As James stepped into the empty theater from the entrance hall, a presentiment overtook him. He resisted the urge to cross himself, sending a hasty, furtive glance around the empty space. Elira sat alone in the second row, her arms crossed and her heavy black boots propped on a seatback in the front row.

Although overhead lights lit the interior, inexplicable shadows darkened her profile, shifting and flickering as though otherworldly candles illumined her. Instead of her usual provocative bustier and ghostly luminous skin, she huddled in a faded denim jacket whose frayed cuffs and worn seams gave little evidence of warmth. He sank into the seat next to her, refraining from sliding his arm along her shoulders and drawing her into his side.

There really was no point. No matter how much heat he shared, Elira would never grow rosy-hued and warm. The only time since he'd met her that her skin had been pink was in the ER after they'd been unloaded from the ambulance, and even then, she'd been the delicate shade of cream left behind from a dish of strawberries. His instincts told him that she was a living heat sink whose own temperature never rose to normal.

She didn't look at him, keeping her pensive gaze on the table and murmuring. "'What a piece of work is a man, how noble in reason, how infinite in faculties, in form and moving, how express and admirable in action, how like an angel in apprehension, how like a god!'" It was a line by Hamlet.

For a moment they were silent, but before James could speak, she continued the monologue. "'The beauty of the world, the paragon of animals. And yet to me, what is this quintessence of dust? Man delights not me; no, nor woman neither.'"

She fingered the small pouch lying over her heart. He couldn't see the crucifix and wondered if she'd taken it off because it didn't lie well next to her fiancé's finger bone.

"Melancholy?" He leaned forward, forcing her to look at him. "You're scaring me, Elira."

"Do you think Hamlet trusted himself? Did he doubt whether he had a righteous claim to his uncle's blood, even if he believed his father's ghost?"

James sat back and let out a low whistle. "Holy shit. If anyone had asked me just two weeks ago whether Elira Dukagjini's faith in herself ever wavered, I would have said no. Now you're really scaring me. The rules on which reality is based have just been called into question."

Now she did look at him. Her eyes, so large and eerie with their washed-out gray rimmed in black, stared at him with an intensity that pierced him to the core.

"Stryver said you came by Jink and Diddle a couple of weeks ago."

He noted her odd use of her partner's last name whenever she referred to him. This was no romance that he'd seen before.

"Yeah, I did. I wanted to know if you had any information on a couple of violent murders from last May and June. Krasniqi cousins, not Jak and Zamir's favorites, apparently.

"If an outside family did them, there haven't been any retaliation hits. We haven't heard *anything*. In fact, we've come to a dead end investigating the murders."

Elira turned to watch the acting troupe shuffle along the nave toward the table. The group laughed and chatted, seemingly unaware of James and Elira until a young woman halted and looked over her shoulder. In the stillness of her stance and blankness of her gaze, James was reminded of a young doe scenting a predator. Elira ignored her and continued to play with the pouch, rolling its contents between her forefinger and thumb as though unaware of what she did.

"We Albanians are nothing if not loyal to our clan." He heard a tinge of sarcasm and wondered at it. She turned a laser-like gaze on him, her fingers still now as she clutched the pouch. "Why?"

He shifted, sighed. "The federal prosecutor plans to convene a special grand jury next week to investigate the Krasniqi mafia. We have enough to indict Ismail Duka on kidnapping and sex trafficking, but we need more to build a bigger case against Jak and Zamir."

The group of actors clustered with the director now, scripts loose in their hands as she plucked shapes from the air around her head. It looked like it would be some time before they began blocking the action.

Elira, her eyes shadowed, moved in her seat. "So you'll get justice for her then. A weak justice that doesn't satisfy."

She paused, and he was about to speak when she jabbed the air with her chin. "Do you think Hamlet should've gotten Horatio to investigate his uncle? How would that have worked out?"

"We're not in sixteenth-century Denmark, and Duka's not a guilty king." He stole a breath, trying to calm the spurt of anger her question had tapped. "Would you have me take blood for Mirjeta?"

She swiveled to stare at him, her eyes cold. "Duka deserves to die. If he'd succeeded in taking your precious fiancée to that same Krasniqi house I alerted you about, she'd have been the one Prek raped until she shit blood.

"Sending him to live in a concrete cell with steel bars for the next three decades doesn't even compare to the hell she would've lived through in three months as a sex slave!"

James leaned his forehead into his hand and focused on breathing out.

It didn't work.

Elira's words had bypassed his mental safeguards and dove right into the searing images of Prek's last rape victim, so battered her bowel had been perforated, and she'd developed life-threatening sepsis. She'd only just been released from the hospital.

Turning, he said, "You don't need to tell me anything about what happens to trafficking victims. But I've got bigger fish to fry than Duka. Bigger than Jak and Zamir."

"That would have to be Imam Krasniqi, hiding like Shelob in his compound in Kosova."

She leaned closer, stroking his forearm where it rested between them, her voice a silky purr. "Tell me, why do you burn for him?"

He made a dismissive sound, but she cut him off. "You burn blue-white at the core. I see it in your eyes. It's the same burning I saw when you told me about your father."

"Krasniqi led the group that held him captive."

Elira threw her head back and laughed. The actors gathered around the table stopped and stared before returning to their scripts, their wide-eyed gazes coming back again and again to flit around him and Elira. He let her laugh, his anger so viciously scalding he imagined steam rising from his pores, only to drift toward her bottomless heat sink. Somewhere in the back of his mind he thought it might be nice to lose himself in her numbing cold. She wiped her eyes with a thumb, a large black-enamel ring jammed above its knuckle.

Then she looked at him, the corners of her mouth curling but no humor in her gaze. "That's the best thing I've heard in years."

James, his hands clasped loosely between his knees, scowled and stared at his feet. He felt Elira's hand on his forearm, grounding him. "He wasn't an imam then, just a dirty little insurgent with wild eyes and an AK-47."

"I confess to burning curiosity about how your father got captured by the KLA. Was he among the NATO forces sent to Kosova? NATO and the KLA had a love-hate thing going on."

James shook his head. "No, my dad's no soldier. He's a pathologist, actually. He'd been working as the deputy coroner for Allegheny County when the World Health Organization approached him, said they needed someone to head this clandestine group, investigating abuse of medical ethics around the world.

"Bioweapons, illegal experimentation. That sort of thing. He was in the Balkans when the Kosovo War broke out. It wasn't long after that reports starting filtering in that there was a black-market operation selling organs.

"It was pretty clearly a KLA operation involving Serb prisoners, but word was that someone inside WHO was the conduit, getting the organs outside Kosovo. Pop worried it was someone on his own team, so he kept what he could to himself."

He paused, remembering.

"Let me guess." Elira's soft voice pulled him back to the present and lifted his face toward hers. "He was set up, but Krasniqi couldn't be sure his contact hadn't been compromised, so he didn't kill your father outright."

"You got it. And then it became important to keep him alive while the KLA brokered peace."

"Alive, yes. But whole?" Her fingers continued stroking him.

A shudder convulsed James, but he said nothing.

"Why does Krasniqi want your fiancée?" Her fingers stopped. "You didn't meet her for the first time in March, did you?" Her voice had flattened. "You met her in Kosova, didn't you?"

"No." He didn't know why, but he couldn't look at her. "No, Mirjeta hadn't lived in Kosovo since she was eight, long before my dad was there."

He shook his head before continuing. "I don't know why Krasniqi is after her except that she was running from someone when I met her, just after my dad was freed, and we were on our way home.

"She told me she'd been on her own for a while, so I figured some guy had targeted her. Maybe it was him, though that seems such a coincidence, huh?" His shaky laugh belied his attempt at levity.

Then Elira's words sunk in. "We're not engaged."

"No?" The huskiness in her voice surprised him, flattered him a little. Yet her knowing eyes scared him. "You did ask her?"

"You followed me." Even as he said the words, James recalled the prickling along the back of his neck, the chill that had enveloped him as he'd walked from Mirjeta's apartment, the strange fog that rose to muffle the streetlights along the block.

She shrugged and waited.

He sighed, closed his eyes, and reached metaphorical hands around in his chest searching for the containment chamber, the place where he stuffed his roiling feelings until he could sort them out later in private. Or let them sort themselves out.

“I don’t know why I’m telling you any of this.” He paused but went on after a few moments. “Pop hasn’t seen Mirjeta in years. She really wants to spend some time with him before we get engaged.”

Elira watched the actors, two of whom had taken up positions in front of the table, prop fencing swords in their hands. “She wants him to approve before he says yes.”

“That’s ridiculous! Of course, he approves.”

“Hm.” The shadows had returned to Elira’s face. “Is that what he said?”

Annoyed, James frowned. “He said I should put the question on ice until the Duka investigation is complete, that it’s only fair to Mirjeta.”

“How long is that?”

“Probably not for another six months, then it’s another year until the trial.”

“Ooh. Justice is swift and terrible here in the U.S.”

James struggled to recall why he played the game of innocent until proven guilty in a court of law. He dredged up the Catholic prohibition against capital punishment, reminding himself that he didn’t have the right to take another’s life. No one was beyond redemption.

"So your dirty little insurgent trafficked in organs a decade ago. He's been trafficking in women and children probably as long. But you knew that, didn't you?"

"Yes. It's one of the reasons I became an ICE agent."

"Why do you think your loved ones want you to wait? Do you suppose it's because she's kept something from you, something about her past she fears will make you even angrier? Perhaps she escaped from one of Krasniqi's Albanian holding pens."

Her words jolted James. He jerked in his seat, pulling his hand from hers and sitting upright. "She wouldn't keep that from me. My dad wouldn't keep that from me."

"Are you sure?" She took his hand again, lifting the palm to study it, her cool breath teasing him.

He stifled a groan.

"Would you be man enough to handle knowing that Krasniqi, the man who tortured your father, also fucked her?"

The low growl that tore from his throat at her question stunned him.

She studied him, her head cocked and a shrewd glint in her eyes that burned off her moodiness like the sun on morning mist. "Are you Hamlet, who has trouble avenging his murdered father?"

She leaned toward him. "Shakespeare's wimpy prince at least has doubts, ghosts not being reliable evidence."

He exploded, and it was a relief. "What the fuck! Weren't you the one just wondering whether he has the right to take blood?"

“Ah! I’ve stirred up a hornets’ nest, haven’t I? Your father isn’t a ghost, is he? Your woman is flesh and blood, isn’t she?” As she whispered this last into his ear, her lips caressed him. “And it’s not a philosophical question, is it?”

“What do you suggest I do, huh, mighty little assassin girl? Waltz into Krasniqi’s mosque like a demented Rambo with an M-16 in each hand?”

Elira laughed again, but this time it was a low, musical sound that burrowed into his ear and ran down his neck. The subtle scent of chocolate on her breath made his mouth water. “Of course not. He must be hunted with stealth and cunning.”

She slid her hand down between his knees. Untangling his hands, she twined her fingers with his and nuzzled his neck. “We’re alike then, James, aren’t we? We’re both driven by a deep desire for revenge for our loved ones.”

She pulled his hand closer to her, turning it over so that she could trace her forefinger, its nail polished black, along his palm. He felt its path all the way to his groin. “We both burn for Krasniqi blood.”

“Yes.” The clanging of swords counterpointed his anguished whisper.

“You would exact your own pound of flesh from him, then?”

“Yes.” He wrenched his head back from hers. “For Krasniqi, for the right provocation, I would abandon the rule of law.”

A cruel smile curved her mouth as she placed a palm along his cheek. “Not the rule of blood law. That’s the most primal law, encoded in our DNA.”

The scent of heather in rain permeated his senses. Dazed, James realized that Elira had shimmied into his lap. "I'm bound by honor to take blood from the Krasniqis."

She leaned forward and placed cool lips on his before pulling back and looking into his eyes, her own dilated so wide he saw nothing in their black pupils. "And I'm bound by blood. Your blood."

In the silence after she spoke, James's harsh breathing sawed the air between them. His heart battered its bone cage. "You'd protect her?"

"I *will* protect her." She studied him, her gaze dark and feral. "I'll take blood for both of them."

This time, he was the one to touch her face. Her smooth cheek was as cold as if she'd just come in from the November night.

After a moment, he spoke, his speech thick and stumbling. "Thank you."

Elira smiled, appearing satisfied. Her mouth descended again to his, rampaging from eager lips to jaw and down along throat. Beneath each lick and kiss, his pulse beat a rapid staccato. She consumed him as flames consume dry tinder.

Voices interrupted his reverie. Turning toward the rehearsal, James saw that it had continued despite his conviction that time had stopped while Elira sat in his lap. A young man in hose, a woman attired in queen's robes, and a gray-bearded king sprawled on the floor almost in front of them, while another young man draped over the table's edge, panting and shiny with sweat, a rapier dangling at his side. A third young man stood, anguish carved into his features, not far from his dying friend.

In the sudden space that opened up between their words, Hamlet looked at James and spoke to him. "You that look pale and tremble at this chance, that are but mutes or audience to this act, had I but time"—he gasped and slid a bit lower, catching the point of his rapier in the wooden floor of the old sanctuary—"as this fell sergeant, death, is strict in his arrest—"

Again, he halted, his chest heaving. The theater waited. A cold bead of sweat slithered down James's spine. Something flitted across the actor's features. Some odd trick of the light transformed them into an adolescent girl's even as wind and shadows alter clouds. When he spoke, the timbre of his voice matched the wavering illusion. Next to James, Elira gasped, a sound that he had trouble identifying until he shot a glance at her shocked face.

"O, I could tell you—but let it be."

Hamlet slipped all the way to the floor, his sword clattering and the image of the angelic teen rising from his form. James blinked and saw only a young man in hose. The director stepped forward, and pandemonium ensued as the actors began to babble.

"How'd she do that?" Elira's low mutter reached James.

"What?" He shook his head, dropping his hand and blinking.

"Nothing." The brooding flicker had returned to Elira's face, turning her into a punk jack-o'-lantern. "That wasn't the end of his speech. Hamlet goes on and on in good stage-death fashion."

Ignoring her surly comment, James lifted Elira onto the pew next to him, scooting away so that their thighs no longer touched.

He inhaled, long and deep. "Thank you for your offer, but I've got to tie Jak and Zamir to those murders. The bean counters are busy poring over accounts and receipts, linking them to Duka.

"Once I've got them, we'll follow the trail all the way back to Krasniqi. He's not too far for the long arm of U.S. law. I'll see him rot in prison."

Elira lurched upright. As the two sides of her denim jacket parted, he glimpsed the milky curve of her breasts above her camisole, the hard ridge of her collarbone, and the raw pink scar between them. He refused to acknowledge an almost compulsory desire to tongue that scar, to suck her breast into his mouth and press her to the floor. He would think about his impulse later, when it was safe to do so. When it would prompt revulsion as dry as sawdust in his throat.

"So be it, Agent Goodman." Her mocking voice suggested that she knew exactly what transpired in his thoughts.

"Jak and Zamir like to hang at the All Souls Club in East Boston. Zamir takes trophies of his kills. If you check your ME's reports on the dead cousins, you'll see that each man is missing something. An ear or a finger. Or a left nut." She laughed and shrugged. "No accounting for taste."

James squirmed, a sharp pain like a hangover between his eyes. Grimacing, he stood. "Thanks, Elira."

"Oh, don't thank me yet. The club is members only." She fingered the pouch between her breasts, laughing. "And I don't need an invitation to get inside. I'll give you a head start though. We'll see who brings them down first." She grinned and sauntered out of the converted church.

James wasn't sure whether he was exasperated with her challenge or relieved that her swagger had returned, righting the world on its axis at the same time.

Eight

AS SOON AS HER BOOTS HIT THE CONCRETE LANDING outside The Gothic Playhouse, Elira wiped the grin from her face and descended the steps to the sidewalk as if demons nipped at her heels. She wrenched the confining denim jacket from her shoulders and threw it into a dumpster after snatching her music player and a bag of heaven dust from its pocket. Cold air slapped her clammy skin, but it couldn't reach her where she most needed it: between her legs. Wet and swollen, she wanted to rip off her tights and shrivel her needy flesh. Instead, she slipped earbuds in before selecting a hip-hop song from her playlist.

As the hard-hitting bass line filtrated into her swagger, she pinched some of the dust, flipping her head back to inhale. She tried to lose herself in the nonsense lyrics, and the cocaine. For a handful of heartbeats, she did.

But she hadn't taken blood in more than two months or taken a junior law associate for two weeks. Thin as her blood was, the heaven dust didn't even register. A block from the theater, she crossed the corner and circled back. Ahead, within a warm nimbus of streetlight, James bent over the driver's side of a parked car, his muscular torso in sharp relief. Seeing him, Elira sucked in a sharp breath and bit her lip so hard it bled. The salty iron taste burned, but she licked her lip, pushing her tongue into the painful cut.

Even as the singer's voice groaned and gyrated, the grotesque image of Hamlet's final monologue filled her thoughts. Shuddering, she spun and rushed away, the song's pulse an angry buzzing and her surroundings a blur of concrete and glass. Pedestrians parted around her, avoiding eye contact with her and with each other. They stopped talking and hurried past.

Elira ignored them. When she came to the stop for the S15 bus, she caught its door before it closed and glared at the driver who clamped his mouth shut. Dropping into a seat at the back, she ripped the earphones out and stared at the street sliding by. She didn't know how much longer she could do this. She'd known, she'd felt it in her bones, the first time she'd looked at James's eyes. She couldn't do it again. She wouldn't.

Dr. Aconcio's laughter filled her ears.

He'd known. He'd known that she would put off tasting James, anticipating the first blood from his heart as only a true addict would. Meanwhile, he'd played his lawyer games, and Duka remained in jail, unable to make bail and safe from her. And all the time he masterminded their every move, herding her as much as he herded James.

Duncan rose wraithlike before her, smiling, teasing.

Elira raised her hand to the window, pressing her palm to his. "Why did you have to die?" she whispered, tears pricking her.

She got off at Essex Street and took the stairs down to the Orange Line at Chinatown, transferring at State Street to the Blue Line. When she heard the conductor call out the subway's last stop at Wonderland, she laughed, causing nearby passengers to shift away. She, of course, wasn't going to Wonderland.

She was going to All Souls.

She'd kept Jak and Zamir as a final treat, slowly working her way through their family, savoring the blood that she took to pay their debt for all the women and children that they'd enslaved, tortured, raped, and murdered.

Women and children who got no justice in this world. She wouldn't collect just yet. She'd sample them to tide her over, to remind her for what she hungered. Her lips curved. Her fingers curled around the pouch as she anticipated the rest of her evening, the satiation awaiting her.

"Why do ye wear it?" Duncan's voice came at her shoulder.

Startled, Elira looked around. Everyone else kept their eyes down or averted. She let her eyelids drop and the memory of his subtle interrogation wash over her.

She'd shrugged, though her heart had squeezed tight. "I wear it to remember what I've lost."

"And what was that, Elira, my love?"

He'd stood next to her on the ship's deck, the brisk wind fingering his shoulder-length hair. It was then that she'd realized that he knew what was inside her precious pouch.

"His name was Branilo Kastrioti, grandson to Gjergj Kastrioti."

"The legendary Dragon of Albania?"

"None other."

"Who was this Branilo to you?" His gentle voice whispered.

Elira's eyes popped open. No, she hadn't been transported back in time to the waters lapping at the small rocky island upon which Kisimul Castle, Duncan's family home, stood.

The train slowed to a stop at Suffolk Downs. Elira jumped up, scarcely allowing the doors to squeak open before pushing through the waiting riders on the platform. As she jogged up the stairs to the street, she screwed the earbuds back in and searched through her playlist for the Lament for the Death of Hugh Allan.

I see you.

Duncan had been the first person to see her in two hundred and forty years.

And the journey to Scotland had been her only effort to escape her partnership with Dr. Aconcio. As Elira had gazed on Kisimul Castle, she'd told Duncan about Branilo, her betrothed. About his blond hair and erect posture as he rode a spirited blood-red bay, the gleaming tip of his long spear held at a jaunty angle. She'd told Duncan how she'd run alongside, clinging to Branilo's boot, as he and her cousin Progon had set off in a company of 200 *stratioti* to fight against the Turks near Lezhë, where the Venetians sought to expand their foothold in Albania. They were to be married after this battle, after he'd been blooded and earned his ranks among the men.

Duncan had wrapped her in his arms as she'd sobbed while describing Branilo's broken body carried on a litter between the horses that Progon and Gjergj Kastrioti, Branilo's older brother and Skanderbeg's namesake, rode. He'd died five days later from a blood plague brought by the hated Turks. He was only eighteen.

Elira glided down the sidewalk. In the chill air, the pedestrians around her left a warm vapor trail of breath, which swirled around her. Above, the evening sky had darkened to a deep blue. Not for the first time did she think about the skies over her home in Lezhë, how vast they were, how many stars were flung like a flickering net over her head. At sixteen, she'd been filled with the fury and courage of her ancestors. Skanderbeg had kept the Turks out for twenty-five years with few men and fewer resources. It was a holy struggle between Christendom and the infidels, one that defined Albania and saved Western Europe from Ottoman occupation. He'd not only been the Dragon of Albania, but the *Athletae Christi* of the Holy Roman Empire.

When the Turks found Skanderbeg's grave, they'd stolen his bones for amulets. And perhaps they'd indeed stolen Skanderbeg's bravery and fighting skills for no one after him, least of all his children and their children, kept the Turks from taking Albania and transforming it into a *vilâyet* of their empire.

At All Souls, the bouncer nodded and waved her in ahead of a small crowd huddled on the sidewalk. Several young women complained at the preferential treatment, their whiny voices grating on Elira, who whipped her face toward them and hissed. The bouncer laughed when the women shrieked once together then fell silent. Elira placed a palm on his chest and leaned in to kiss him.

"Later, Eddie," she promised.

Inside, she caught the eye of the bartender and held up a finger. He grinned to acknowledge the pint of Guinness that she'd ordered.

She made her way to the booth in the far corner away from the crowd at the bar and around the dance floor. It was early still for Jak and Zamir and she intended to drink herself into a stupor.

Sinking into the leather, she twisted to reach her boots up to the table and surveyed the dark room, letting the patrons' hot breath and musky bodies envelope her. Her fingers moved to the scar, tracing its lumpy ridges.

"How'd ye get that nasty scar?" Duncan's whisper echoed around the booth, but Elira didn't flinch.

Scrubbing at it, she said, "You know."

Before Progon and Gjergj had returned, the Turks had found her hiding in Lezha Castle. Twenty Dukagjini clansmen and her beloved nurse Drita had died protecting Elira, Qendresa, and their younger cousins Odeta and Dafina. Elira had crouched, her nostrils filled with the stench of blood, shit, and ammonia, gripping her father's sword so tightly that her hands had gone numb. The janissaries, led by an Albanian named Getoar, had laughed at her—at least until she'd sliced the hand off the man who'd grabbed for Qendresa behind her. But there was never any hope for her, fierce warrior woman though she was. Getoar had raped her, followed by twenty others. They'd left her for dead.

She smiled as she fondled her scar. She'd killed Getoar right after she'd decapitated Lorenzo, the Venetian who'd let the Turks into the castle while the *stratioti* had been away.

By the time Progon and Gjergi returned with the thirty *stratioti* who'd survived the Turks, Qendresa, Odeta, and Dafina had disappeared like so much smoke, bound for the Sultan's seraglio. Elira, who'd watched their return from the castle walls, had collapsed, still bleeding inside and so battered and swollen that Progon had recognized only her filthy, torn clothing.

She raised the Guinness and drank half the pint before slamming the glass down and wiping her mouth. A few people glanced at her but then looked away again.

Her cousin knew what she'd done. He knew that she'd snuck out three days after Branilo's death to visit his grave. He'd warned her not to do it, but when she'd appeared wearing her relic, he'd said nothing. Progon had only nodded and gestured for her to join him and the other *stratioti*, a gift of compassion that she hadn't fully understood until long after his death. By not acknowledging the rapes, he'd given Elira the right to live as a sworn virgin, a *virgjineshtë*, a woman who dressed and lived as a man. By taking her into his warrior band, he'd given her the right to collect the blood owed her as a Dukagjini and as a woman.

So much blood that one lifetime wasn't enough.

Thinking this, Elira snorted the last of her heaven dust. The massive dose unleashed the memory of the night that she'd visited her betrothed's grave—a memory that she'd let surface one other time in her long life.

She lay in her bed, body aching, and fresh dirt caked under her fingernails. Outside her window, a dog barked. She heard the voices of the sentries up on the walls, the jingling of their swords and armor, and the faint crackling from a nearby torch. The fire burned low, leaving her chamber dim. She studied Branilo's index finger, which she held near her face, but the shadows obscured its elegant lines and carefully trimmed nail. Kissing it, she placed it on the pillow and let herself fall asleep, the loamy scent of the grave filling her nostrils. As her eyelids lowered, she heard a wolf howl, voicing her mad grief.

Sometime later she awoke. Her chamber had darkened as the fire died, and silence blanketed the castle and grounds.

"Who's there?" she called.

Nothing but the fire's low hissing and popping answered her. Turning, her cheek brushed Branilo's finger, now entangled in her unbound hair. Sighing, she reached for it.

A cold white hand caught her wrist. A hand missing its index finger.

"Elira, my love." She looked up into his intense, hungry gaze. "Let me love you."

"Yes," she breathed, holding her arms up as he lowered himself onto her.

He gripped the sides of her face. "Mine. You're mine."

Their coupling was sweetly savage, everything that they'd been denied and more. At the climax, he struck, his teeth piercing her breast just above her heart. He tongued her torn flesh, groaning and bucking. The pain and ecstasy drove her mad. She wrapped her arms around his head and pressed, twining her legs around his torso and locking her ankles.

"Mine. You're mine," she said. "I'll never let you go."

She awoke the next morning with a fever so hot that Progon sent for the physic and the priest. The blood plague ravaged her. Instead of confessing her sins and dying, she'd lived.

"Are your memories troubling you, my dear?"

Elira looked up, blinking, to see Dr. Aconcio standing before her booth.

Wiping moisture from her cheeks, she reached for her beer without responding. He watched her, enjoyment twinkling in his eyes. After she'd finished the pint, she studied him, and he smiled, his pointy little teeth glinting in the club's murky light. For the umpteenth time, she longed to quit this immutable law practice that he'd started.

There was no way out, only a way to delay the inevitable. She'd realized that to her regret when she'd hung Branilo's finger bone again around her neck, inviting Dr. Aconcio back into her life, her renewed thirst for blood more fiery and sharp edged than before.

Perhaps Mirjeta Gjakova was the key. Mirjeta was her kinswoman, after all. But what blood law had Dr. Aconcio broken? He was too old, too wily, to mistake his purpose. She'd feel it in her very marrow if he'd broken the primeval blood law again. God had probably made it impossible, in fact, for him to do it. In spite of everything he *was* the scourge of humanity.

Elira was mired in an endless Sisyphean tug-of-war between need for blood and longing for communion. Dropping her feet from the table, she scooted around the bench. Dr. Aconcio nodded and leaned his cane against the wall before sliding into a seat. He raised his hand, signaling the waitress, who rushed over to take his order for cognac.

Turning to Elira, he smirked. "Do you await the Krasniqi brothers?"

She shrugged, but there was no point in denying it.

Dr. Aconcio waited until his cognac had been delivered before continuing. "Are you so anxious then to sample their vintage?"

He clicked his tongue, shaking his head slightly.

“Not really.” She held up a finger and the waitress, although absorbed in taking orders from a small group near the dance floor, acknowledged her and scurried to the bar. No one in the knot grumbled or looked Elira’s direction.

He chuckled and sipped his cognac. “Ah, you are so transparent, my dear. Never mind. Your patience shall be rewarded at last. Ismail Duka will be transported next week to a medical facility. The Krasniqis have bought one of the guards where he is being detained, but he will be expected to make his own way once the guard has done his part.”

The waitress dropped off Elira’s beer and fled. Elira toasted Dr. Aconcio with her glass, letting the rich malty beer tease her palate and fill her nostrils.

“That is simple enough. Yet I find that I no longer trust your judgment in legal matters, Elira.”

Dr. Aconcio slipped a fingertip under her chin and turned her to face him. “You have, for instance, neglected to tell me that Agent Goodman desires revenge on Krasniqi for what his father suffered. Did I not warn you that there can never be secrets between us?”

Elira narrowed her eyes and hissed. Dr. Aconcio only laughed and pulled his finger away, slicing the tender skin along her jaw with his fingernail. She jerked away from him but refused to touch the stinging spot.

“Just because I didn’t tell you doesn’t mean I kept it secret. We’ve been partners long enough that I don’t need to check in every time I pursue a recruiting opportunity.”

"So that is what you have been doing?" He shook his head and sipped cognac. "Your dawdling gives an unfortunate impression. Your reluctance to collect blood from Mirjeta Gjakova only adds to my conviction that you have lost your edge."

He touched her relic. "If you take the blood that she owes you, you will enflame Agent Goodman further against the imam. And then, of course, there is the matter of eliminating your rival. That alone should compel you."

Elira leaned forward, her nose almost touching Dr. Aconcio's. "What blood debt does a Gjakova, a clan bound to Dukagjini, owe me?"

"Whatever blood a Krasniqi owes. Did not the Krasniqis turn Turk long ago?"

Elira sat up. "What the hell are you spouting now?"

"Gjakova is Mirjeta's mother's name. Her father was brother to that very same imam who has ordered her taken and brought to him. Did you never wonder why Krasniqi demanded her return to Albania when doing so is so dangerous and difficult? Why would he want her when there are so many easier and more profitable targets?"

Elira shook her head. Even as confusion buzzed around her skull, something struck her. "Wait! You accuse me of withholding information. But you alluded to her blood six months ago when you visited me in the hospital. You *knew* even then."

A wide, foxy smile split the sagging parchment of his cheeks. "Never forget that I am in charge of our partnership. I, *I* decide when and how much to tell you. You have not shown me the respect and trust due my place. What should I do about that, hm?"

Now it was Elira's turn to let a smile seize her features, but hers was bitter. She pushed herself upright, drained her pint glass, and then bent over to look at him. "Indeed, Dr. Aconcio. What *can* you do about it?"

She left All Souls then, but not before she overheard Dr. Aconcio murmur, "Just wait and see, my dear."

When James showed up at Jink & Diddle on Friday to attend Stryver's lecture, he found the other students drinking espresso and eating biscotti in the café. Stryver sat on a stool in front of the espresso bar, his elbows propping his back up.

"James, my man!" he crowed, delight making his dark eyes snap. "We're starting in the salon tonight. I've had a long week and needed a few shots to keep me alert. Want something? Elira would be more than happy to wait on you."

Stryer gestured over his shoulder with his thumb. Elira stood behind him, a blue fountain of hair sprouting at her temple like a rooster's comb. Looking sullen, she glared and turned a cold shoulder toward James.

"Nice to see you, too." She ignored him, but he called out anyway. "I'll take a cappuccino when you get around to it."

Then he looked at Stryver, whose grin had sharpened. He grinned back. "Where should I sit to experience your wisdom most fully?"

"Oh, right there in front works for me. Listen up, peeps," Stryer said, looking at the others, who quieted as soon as he spoke.

"Time to talk about that bloody cauldron, the Balkans. 'Like a hell-broth boil and bubble,' right, Elira?"

Stryer shot her a wicked glance, paused, and then announced dramatically, "The Balkans were made to be Muslim."

James heard the sharp intake of Elira's breath, but he kept his eyes on Stryver. He had to give credit to this young man in the hillbilly suspenders and crisp, striped oxford: he knew how to captivate.

"It's true. The Balkans had only a Christian veneer before the Ottoman Turks showed up. Even then, they couldn't agree on how to practice it. The Pope sent emissaries. The Byzantine Patriarch sent emissaries.

"Neither side in the theological debate could persuade everyone to their position. The Pope got the Croats, the Albanians, and the Hungarians while the Patriarch got the Romanians, the Serbs, the Bulgarians, and the Greeks.

"They were like two dogs fighting over a pile of carcasses, greedy and snarling. But the Balkans understood conquest and blood. Waves of barbarians had hacked their way from Central Asia for millennia.

"So that's what the Turks did. And, once conquered, the honest parts of the Balkans eagerly adopted a religion true to their innate blood law."

"Once conquered?" Now it was Elira's turn to capture everyone's attention as she vaulted the espresso bar to confront him. "You make it sound so easy, Stryver.

"What of Stefan of Moldavia? Vlad of Wallachia? Hunyadi of Hungary? Were they not all part of the *Antemurale Christianitatis*, the bulwark of Christianity against the Ottoman Empire?"

"Were they?" asked Stryver. "Or were they just bloodthirsty power seekers squabbling amongst themselves?

"Hunyadi killed Vlad's father, and his son Michael stole money earmarked for a crusade from the Pope and then blamed Vlad. Vlad's cousin, Stefan, had to hide in his court, at least one of the times Vlad actually *had* a court.

"Vlad hated everyone: his father, his younger brother, and the Turks. He hated his father for betraying his oath to the Order of the Dragon, the one he made to defend Christendom against the Turks.

"But maybe it was really because the elder Dracul bought the Turks off and then sent his two sons to the Sultan's court where Vlad was beaten.

"He hated his younger brother Radu the Handsome for converting and then becoming a powerful janissary. The reason he hated the Turks is pretty clear.

"In his noble fight to keep his lands Christian, he earned his nickname 'the Impaler' from the tens of thousands of people he butchered, making even Mehmet II sick to his stomach.

"What an admirable lot. Your beloved Skanderbeg fit right in, didn't he?"

Elira's nostrils flared, but she said nothing for a long moment. "Skanderbeg did what he had to do. He played the game with the hand he was dealt. The Turks took him at 18 because he was already a warrior. They could see that.

"Should he have died then, when it would have been pointless? No. He did what he had to do to fight them. He lived at the Sultan's court and pretended to convert even while his three brothers were all poisoned.

"He gained their admiration. It was the Sultan who named him 'Iskender' in homage of his warrior skills. More importantly, he gained experience and power, first as a military commander and then as a governor in his own Kastrioti lands."

She bent down and looked into Stryver's eyes. A hush descended as everyone stopped breathing.

"Skanderbeg bided his time, and when the Turks were busy fighting Hunyadi, he defected. From that moment, he abjured Islam, becoming the Christian sword of Europe. He never stole money. He never butchered anyone."

Stryver picked up his espresso cup, sipping it without taking his gaze from Elira's strained features. "Tell that to the 3,000 men he supposedly slew."

"On the battlefield." Elira stood up and forced her response through a clinched jaw. "As you say, the Turks came to conquer the Balkans. What were Christians supposed to do when thousands of battle-hardened Muslims marched and rode into their cities with guns and cannon aimed at their knights wielding swords?

"By the time Skanderbeg's father sent him to the Sultan, the only Byzantine city left was Constantinople, a city whose walls hadn't been breached in a thousand years until the Turks fired cannon at them. If Skanderbeg wanted power, why didn't he stay loyal to the Sultan?

"Skanderbeg *had* power as a janissary and *vali.* He didn't need to spend 25 years of guerilla warfare against a much stronger, much richer opponent while protecting his back against conniving Western rulers."

"Blood law explains that. Skanderbeg was first and foremost Albanian. The Turks owed Albania blood. They owed the Kastrioti blood. It was early nationalism, not a Christian struggle against Muslim conquest.

"In this, Skanderbeg and the other so-called 'Christian' defenders in the Balkans are fundamentally the same as the invading Ottomans. Even the Western defenders had more interest in their budding nationalism than in defending their Christian beliefs. Blood. It's all about blood."

Elira, her fists balled, turned from Stryver. James thought for a moment that she would punch the espresso bar, but she didn't.

Instead, she strode away before spinning to confront the gathering. "The infidels—Arabs, Moors, and Turks—were a plague of parasites. They didn't so much conquer as co-opt.

"From the Byzantines of Anatolia and Constantinople, they stole the very infrastructure of civilization: government, law, and culture. While Western Europe fell into the Dark Ages, the Arabs lived a golden one."

Stryver yawned and stretched. “Yeah. So perhaps the ‘infidels’ weren’t as bad as Western Christians. After all, by the time the Turks took Constantinople, it had already been sacked by the Fourth Crusaders in 1204, and the Byzantine Empire carved up into little kingdoms. Can’t blame the ‘infidels’ for taking advantage of the situation, eh?”

He paused, and his gaze intensified. James had the impression that Stryver gathered himself to spring on his frustrated sparring partner. “I stand by my original thesis that the blood law of the Balkans and Islam are mutually compatible.”

“Compatible?” she sputtered. “Compatible? They took Albanian sons, forced them to convert to Islam, indoctrinated them in religious fanaticism, trained them in modern warfare, and then sent them back to subdue and kill their fathers, brothers, uncles, and cousins.

“Afterwards the Turks enslaved thousands of Christians, many of them women, while the rest of the world abandoned us. It is our *blood* that kept Western Europe free.”

James found himself speaking before he considered what he said. “Funny then that Albania leads the world in human trafficking. It’s been almost a hundred years since your country kicked out the Ottomans. Stryver’s right.”

Elira looked at him, and the anguish on her face knifed him in the chest.

Stryver’s obvious glee drove it deeper. Before James could say anything, she walked over and slapped him. As the sound echoed in the silent café, he touched tentative fingers to his stinging cheek. She narrowed her eyes.

"Never think Stryver is right. Never." She shot a glance at her smirking partner that would have etched glass. "He's very clever at bending the truth to suit his ends.

"He'll brainwash you into believing what you want to believe, that you can leave blood law behind, adopt a modern bloodless—*life-less*—theory.

"But no one is ever free from blood law. *No one*. It's the fundamental law of creation."

Nine

"GIBBOUS MOON BULGES BRIGHT AGAINST NOVEMBER NIGHT." Elira paused, thinking. For an instant, it was March, and she waited on a sidewalk in Charlestown for Krasniqi goons to hustle a stolen woman by. And then she was back in the present, waiting this time for only one of those goons. Ismail Duka. Her jaws ached. Her chest ached. She rubbed at the scar, pushing the leather pouch aside to press her skin.

"Blood. Bloody. Hot, bloody ... *mallkonte të gjithë në ferr." Damn it all to hell.* "Bright and night. Bulges and bright. Ugh. Nothing but alliteration and cheap rhyme."

Tonight, Duka would be transferred from the Plymouth County Correctional Facility to the Federal Medical Center in Devens to enroll in its suicide prevention program.

Elira sneered at the conceit.

Ahead, the facility's back entrance disgorged a three-headed mass. The heads on the sides bobbed above padded black law-enforcement vests with block letters proclaiming their employing agency, one ICE, one U.S. Marshals. The middle head emerged from a thick gray sweatshirt swaddling a form rank with body odor and the fetid scent of rotting meat. That would be Duka, who had blood on his hands.

Elira's nostrils flared, and her lip pulled away from her upper teeth. "*I papastër*." *Unclean.*

The mass moved into the light shed by a spotlight on the building's corner. The ICE agent clarified into a stocky woman whose glossy dark hair had been tugged into a tight ponytail. Elira's nose twitched. Something wasn't right about her.

In fifteen seconds, she found out what.

The ICE agent let go of Duka's arm so that he and the marshal continued on without her. Duka shrugged off his handcuffs and reached for a knife tucked into his waistband in the same movement. Turning, he jabbed it into the marshal's face. The marshal, likely through some instinct honed over years of experience, managed to block the knife before it reached its destination, but the die was cast. Duka sliced and stabbed at the other man so quickly and so viciously that he'd nearly hacked his forearm off by the time the marshal fell writhing to the ground where Duka jumped on his torso, lifted his left arm, and drove the knife into the agent's unprotected underarm and into his heart.

The killing took one silent minute.

Elira's stomach clenched as the marshal's blood spread in an oily pool on the pavement.

Duka looked up at the ICE agent, who'd backed into the shadows at the corner of the building. Without seeing the other woman's face or reading her thoughts, Elira knew what she was thinking: the money that she'd taken to slip Duka a knife and unlock his cuffs had morphed into blood money. And Duka had no reason to let her live.

Before Elira could act, Duka sprang off his fresh kill and launched himself at the remaining agent. She went down with a yelp, a sound so pitiful that Elira winced. But there was nothing she could do for the other woman, who owed blood for betraying her partner and her oath as a federal agent.

Duka wiped the blade on the dead ICE agent's pants before he stood and tucked it back into his waistband. From her hiding spot behind a car in the parking lot across the street, Elira studied her prey, slowing her breathing and heart rate as she crouched. Duka shot a glance in her direction, his eyes wide and his chest rising and falling. He rubbed the back of his neck and shifted from foot to foot as he fingered the knife hilt.

Elira gathered herself to hunt once he moved away from the building and toward the car the Krasniqis would have left for him. Now was the time.

If you take the blood that she owes you, you will enflame Agent Goodman further against the imam. Dr. Aconcio's observation echoed in her memory.

Perhaps she should let Duka go. Perhaps she could satisfy some of the Krasniqi blood debt by letting Mirjeta be snatched by him. After all, it was tantamount to a death sentence.

And, most importantly, James would be drawn to a partnership with her. A win-win.

She eased into a higher stance, letting her focus slip. Duka responded at once as if released from his spot. Shrugging, he turned away and bent to pilfer wallets and guns from the two dead agents. She crept closer while he stripped off his sweatshirt and tossed it onto the bodies before scanning the lot in front of him. As he began to jog toward a nondescript gray sedan, the back door opened to emit another woman, this time wearing the insulated brown jacket of a sheriff's deputy. She looked at the two bodies on the sidewalk in front of her and then up again.

"Halt!" she yelled and began to run even as she pulled the flap covering her sidearm up.

Duka swung around, assessed the threat, and instead of running away, he sprinted toward her while reaching for his knife. Elira took off, covering the distance between them in seconds. The deputy managed to pull her pistol free before Elira came within striking range, but he knocked the other woman's arm up and slashed at her. The deputy ducked, and the knife skittered across her upper back, gashing cloth and flesh. As Duka's arm arced forward a second time, Elira launched herself, knocking the woman onto her ass and his knife to the pavement.

Grinning at the stunned look on his face, she gripped his wrist and squeezed so hard that purple tinged his white fingers. "Now, now. *Ju nuk keni nevojë të bëni këtë." You don't need to do that.*

She let him go with a shove. "Go on, get lost."

When he remained as if anchored, she shoved his chest harder, causing him to stumble, and hissed.

Duka flinched and backed five feet away, his flat eyes wide. She suspected that it was the closest that he'd been to a state of shock since he was a toddler.

"Boo!" She stomped her foot and waved her hands, laughing at his lumbering gait as he spun and again ran toward his getaway car.

Elira held her hips and watched to ensure that he drove away. She felt rather than saw the sheriff's deputy moving toward the knife. She pressed a steel-toed military boot onto the hilt and looked down at the injured woman, who trailed blood from where she'd fallen to Elira's foot.

"Lay still, *budalla*." *Fool.*

The woman must have recognized the affection in Elira's voice because she looked up at her, her pupils dilated in shock but unafraid.

"Why'd you stop him only to let him go?" Elira's sharp hearing caught the faint words. "Why'd you save me?"

Elira sighed and crouched down. "You're bleeding. I'll take you inside."

She rolled the other woman onto her back before lifting her in a dead-man's carry. Reaching for the entry door's handle, she tugged the door and held it open with her left foot until they were inside. The long, white-tiled hallway gleamed under antiseptic fluorescent lights.

From the weight of the injured woman's body, Elira knew that she'd fallen unconscious. Where should she leave her? Something made her look up. Cameras. She grinned. They would, of course, see a blurry dark form on their video, but identifying her would be impossible. Only those in law enforcement who'd felt the sting of her love bites—her junior associates—would recognize her. And James. James, who'd given her his blood thinking that he'd saved her life in return for her saving Mirjeta's.

Elira halted and slipped the deputy to the floor before propping her against a closed door. She froze. Bright red blood trailed down the dark-blue paint and onto the glossy linoleum. After a few breaths, she dipped a tentative finger in it and touched the tip of her tongue. The blood bit into her flesh, sending a sharp tingle through that muscular organ. She closed her eyes and inhaled. This was what the blood of the righteous tasted like. So pure it stung and swelled her tissues until she thought she might choke.

Coughing, she stood up and reached for her cell phone, dialing with the thumb of one hand while rubbing her scarred chest with the other. As she pushed the entry door open and stepped outside, James answered.

"Duka's loose. He's headed for Mirjeta."

TWO HOURS LATER, ELIRA took up position on the balcony railing above the back entrance of Mirjeta's brownstone and waited. Duka, she knew, had abandoned his car somewhere along Route 3, exchanging it for some other vehicle—probably another nondescript sedan or even minivan—which the Krasniqis would have left for him at a busy roadside restaurant. He'd have taken the time to shave and wax his eyebrows, change his clothes into the expensive Italian suits that the Krasniqis preferred, and slick his hair back into a Eurosexual ponytail. She didn't doubt that he sported a gold watch, rings, an earring, and a Type 67 Chinese handgun with an integrated silencer.

She snickered almost soundlessly as she scanned both sides of the alley. “It’s what all the best-dressed traffickers wear.”

Even in the blacker shadows where they melted against buildings, fences, and a dumpster, the figures of half a dozen ICE agents scattered up and down the alley glowed red-hot in Elira’s night vision. James’s distinctive profile snagged her attention as he waited behind a fence just outside Mirjeta’s back door. Without scouting the area around the brownstone, she knew that another half a dozen agents waited in front, including James’s partner, Andrew Cruncher. More agents waited in unmarked cars in a two-block radius. Duka didn’t have a chance; he had no reason to suspect the *lugat* who’d inexplicably intervened outside the correctional facility, though what rationale for her actions he gave himself she had no idea.

It didn’t need to be said that none of them knew that she was there.

Duka’s stench wafted down the alley before she heard the soft squeak of his Italian loafers. Elira shifted on her perch, gripping the support post at the corner of the balcony tier. Below her, James clutched his Walther PPK, his face luminous even in the dark. He too had heard Duka’s stealthy approach.

Elira tilted her head to locate him. That’s when she saw what none on the ground could see: the other two men trailing Duka at the end of the block, just out of reach of the streetlight. So, the Krasniqis were taking no chances that Duka would fail again. She wondered again what game Dr. Aconcio played.

Perhaps, like the Joker in the movie *The Dark Knight*, he was an agent of chaos. It was a role that suited him, especially as he would have taken it upon himself. Too bad for him that she too chose to be unpredictable.

Noiselessly she swung over the balcony onto the ground, her boots hitting the pavement so lightly that she might have been hovering. Thirty seconds later, she heard James knock Duka to the ground, and thick curses pummeled the air behind her, but she never looked back and never stopped. The two Krasniqi men stepped into the open, their guns flaring red and bullets whining around her ears. Elira didn't stop. Swerving, she sped up the brick wall on her left, throwing herself around to run parallel to the alley for the last hundred feet.

The traffickers traced her with their fire, but she laughed as the cold wind rushed through her hair. The triumphant sound ping-ponged off the brick around them, surging in volume like hollow wind through castle ruins on a lonely moor. The two men stopped firing for fifteen seconds, their mouths agape. It was their fatal mistake. Of course, their true mistake had been to come out tonight on Jak or Zamir's orders.

They began shooting again as Elira launched herself into a back handspring off the wall. Her trajectory took her behind one of the shooters. A bullet burned a line along her upper arm as she gripped his head, twisting it so hard his neck gave a sharp crack. She shoved him into his partner, who turned and blasted the corpse before it fell into him, knocking his gun to the ground. Elira was on him before he could push the body off. She wrapped a ribbon around his neck, yanking the ends across each other so hard that it got embedded permanently. That was kind of sad. She liked that ribbon.

"Halt! Federal agent! Put your hands in the air where I can see them! Slowly. Slowly."

Elira smirked. She should have known that James's partner would catch her. She raised her hands as the piercing light of an LED flashlight caught her in its beam.

"Elira, goddamn it, is that you?" Cruncher swore some more as she turned to grin at him.

Keeping her hands raised, she stood up. Slowly. And turned around slowly. "You're welcome, Agent Cruncher." She blew him a kiss.

Cruncher grabbed her hands and pulled cuffs from his waistband.

"I wouldn't if I were you." When he looked at her, she shrugged. "They never stay on. It's such a trial." She wiggled her fingers at him.

Sighing, he dropped her hands. "Will you come with me then?"

She shrugged and matched her stride to his as he swung around toward the group ahead of them in the alley.

"Did you leave them alive back there?"

"No."

"Ah." A moment of silence followed. Then: "It's too bad I never saw what happened to those guys. I was so distracted by the action up here."

"It's for the best, really." She waited a beat. "You might've gotten killed."

"True. Then again, they might still be alive and under arrest."

"Good thing you'll never know. Makes it easier to sleep at night."

Cruncher stopped short. "Is that what you tell yourself?"

She eyed him. "You mean you're not going to sleep well tonight? Knowing that Mirjeta's safe, Duka's back in custody, and two more Krasniqi *derra* are no longer desecrating the air you breathe?"

"Just because I'm grateful I don't have to find out doesn't mean I'll sleep well. Insomnia is my middle name."

"Then that's another thing we have in common, Agent Cruncher."

They'd reached James, who stood talking to a group of ICE agents. Duka stood off to the side, his arms pinioned behind him. When he saw Elira, his eyes widened.

"Hey, *i dashur*," she crooned in mock affection. *Sweetheart, my ass.* "Thought you'd pay a visit to your last snatch?" James's in-drawn breath whistled at the double *entendre*. "Can't you get it through your thick Albanian skull she just ain't that into you?"

Duka stepped back, but the stockade fence behind him prevented him from putting more distance between them. Elira laughed. He flinched.

"Elira, thank God."

As she turned at his exclamation, James clutched her to his chest. He was warm. Lord in heaven, he was *warm*. And he smelled like the ocean. An unexpected image of Duncan and Kisimul Castle wavered before her, making her knees wobbly.

"Hey, hey. Are you all right?" James pulled back to study her. "What the fuck's going on, Elira? First you doubt yourself, now this. How can a cold-blooded assassin look green around the gills?"

Elira wriggled out of his embrace and averted her face. She locked her knees and rubbed at her scar, only slightly aware of what she did. Then she forced her gaze to meet his.

"I'm green from smelling asshole, that's what, Agent Goodman. Have you checked on Mirjeta yet? Is she all right?"

James threw a look at Cruncher, who nodded, and pulled Elira fifty feet from the crowd. Unmarked cars had entered one end of the alley and inched toward them, tires popping and crunching on the asphalt. On the other end of the block, an unmarked car sat perpendicular to the mouth of the alley, its headlights illuminating the grotesque, sprawling bodies of the two Albanians that Elira had killed. Somewhere in the distance, perhaps a mile away, the sounds of multiple sirens announced local police and an ambulance hastening to the scene.

"She's at my place. I moved her there after you called about Duka. Christ, when's this going to end?"

He ran his hand through his hair, realized that he still held his handgun, and shoved it into his shoulder holster. Then he laughed, but there was no humor in it.

"You know why the Krasniqis are after her, don't you?"

"She's Krasniqi's niece." Her voice swelled to fill the air around them. "I didn't know until a few days ago." She looked at his profile. It was as vivid to her as if they stood in daylight. "When did you find out?"

"Last Friday, after that lecture on the Balkans Stryver gave." He fell silent. Tension displaced the sound of her voice between them.

"Mirjeta and I had a talk. Seems she told Pop last month. That's why she couldn't answer my proposal."

"Ah."

"Yup." He said nothing for a long moment.

She wanted to trace the line of his jaw but found her finger tracing her scar instead.

He spoke again. "So you were right. She wanted his approval. He thought about it for a while, and he gave it."

"No need to wait for the end of the Duka investigation?"

He snorted. "Duka just handed Jak and Zamir to us, thanks to your timely tip. But no, we don't need to wait for the end of the investigation."

Elira thought the world contracted in on itself and the stars dimmed. Or maybe it was just that she forgot to breathe for a moment.

"Congratulations are in order then."

"Thanks."

He turned to her, and his gaze snagged on something below her face. She watched as he found the track of blood on her upper arm, running through the MacNeil tattoo, obscuring the motto *buaidh no bas—conquer or die* in Scots Gaelic. She stood, frozen, as James dipped a fingertip in the blood. He lifted it to his mouth. An answering need flared brilliant and white hot in him, illuminating his features from within like a paper lantern. She shivered.

In the next breath, something hard and long hit her palm. It was still warm from its sheath inside his jacket. It was her precious ear dagger. She ran a finger over its beveled blade. Her blood sang. Her heart pricked.

"Why have you returned this to me?"

James squinted as though he looked into a bright light, blinking and gazing away again. "I don't believe we can keep her safe anymore. Mirjeta. She's not safe even here in the U.S. with me and dozens of ICE agents and the whole of our mighty civil law. If it hadn't been for you, she'd be gone even now on her way back to her radical uncle in the wilds of Kosovo."

He wrapped her palm around the ear dagger, and she understood a little more of Dr. Aconcio's plan. One part of her, the lesser part, rejoiced in its cunning.

He strode away, leaving her there alone. She watched as he approached Duka and grabbed his upper arm, hauling him away from the fence so forcefully that the other man stumbled and went down on one knee. James jerked him to his feet, causing Duka's head to heave on his neck as erratically as a child's balloon dances on a stiff breeze.

It was clear what she had to do.

Grasping the pouch with both hands, she ripped it off, relishing the sting as the leather cord cut the flesh on her neck. Dropping her gaze, she weighed the pouch in one hand and the dagger in the other. After a moment, she slit the pouch open and pulled Branilo's finger bone free. Then she slid the dagger into the familiar slot between the top of her boot and her calf, clenched her fingers around her former relic, and trotted off without looking behind.

As Elira disappeared into the night beyond the halo of the nearest streetlight, James thrust Ismail Duka into the unmarked car waiting to take him back to prison.

Ten

SHE WAITED IN THE DEEPEST SHADOWS, as dark and still as a panther. Woad blue covered her face but not the scar bisecting her upper lip or the black studs arcing around her eyebrow. Black clothing covered her bone-white skin. If he'd searched carefully, the primeval one standing on the porch above her might have caught a glimmer of the whites of her eyes. But he did not. Instead, he spoke into his smartphone, weaving his interminable web in his most seductive voice.

"It is time to act, old friend. Despite my best efforts, the grand-jury investigation has linked Jak and Zamir to the deaths of those traitors last summer. The American Duka remains loyal, however, and may prove useful to you at a future date."

A pause and a slight exhalation. The primeval one sounded annoyed.

"What does that mean? Surely you jest. This is the United States where, broken though it may be, the justice system cannot overlook evidence of what it defines as murder. It is not Kosova where your word rules in the hearts and minds of your people. The U.S. federal prosecutor has issued warrants for their arrest."

She listened, her sharp hearing taking in every nuance in his tone, every corresponding syllable of sound transmitted over his phone's tiny speakers.

"Perhaps you should abandon this quest. You have found other wives among the daughters of the *giaour*."

She stiffened at the Turkish word for Christian infidel. Her fury grew at the smile that widened the primeval one's face.

"As you wish. I will tell them to come home only when they are able to bring her with them."

She'd heard enough. She faded into the space between Jink & Diddle and the neighboring house.

The primeval one paused as he slid his smartphone into his suit pocket, sniffing the air and listening intently for several seconds.

But there was nothing at this hour of the night, not even the sound of traffic.

"CHRISTIANITY HIT THE WORLD like a nuclear bomb."

Stryver sat across from James in the espresso bar of Jink & Diddle, his dark eyes glittering. They were alone for this lecture, Stryver having told James that it was too challenging to speak freely about Christianity even in such an intellectual and progressive milieu as Cambridge.

"You can't forget that Boston was the famed 'City on the Hill,' the New Jerusalem of the Puritans who settled the Massachusetts Bay Colony," he warned. "That belief is bred in the bone. It doesn't just fade away or grow stale. It has to be seduced away from."

Now James, who'd expected something shocking out of Stryver's mouth, sat back and frowned. "Come again? Nuclear bomb. That doesn't sound too complimentary."

"Whoa, now. I thought you were a philosopher. A man who appreciates a clever cognitive construct. Don't tell me you're bothered by semantics?"

James shifted on the hard café stool before sipping his espresso, which Stryver had laced with cognac. "I'm not. Just tell me where this is going."

"Okay, let's set the stage first. How solid are you on classical antiquity?"

"Well, I was obsessed with the Romans when I was a kid. At least, I was obsessed with Julius Caesar. Or more precisely, with modeling the siege works of Alesia."

"Caesar's decisive victory over the rebellious Gauls where a million died and a million more were sold into slavery."

At James's nod, Stryver went on, "Then you have some idea what the 'civilized world' felt like for the average person."

"To borrow a quote from Hobbes, it was 'solitary, poor, nasty, brutish, and short,'" said James.

“Quite. And Hobbes described life in a Christian West after the Renaissance. Can you imagine what it was like in ancient Rome or Athens? Especially if you weren’t Greek or a Roman citizen.”

“Yeah, I saw that HBO series on Rome.” James stopped, considering. “But the Egyptians, Greeks, and Romans all had gods. Lots of them. Gods who were capricious and meddling—“

”—and vain and jealous, who toyed with people or scarcely noticed them. Pretty much humans with superpowers, wouldn’t you say? Same with their monsters. Projections of the human ego, so *ipso facto* powerful archetypes.”

“I assume you’re working your way up to Christ?” asked James.

“Indeed I am. He was born into a Roman world, a fact that most people don’t really understand even though they read about Caesar Augustus’s census, Pilate the Roman governor of the Roman province of Judea, and centurions dicing for Christ’s belongings at His crucifixion.” Stryver paused and then went on.

“They don’t really get the reality of the ancient Roman world. They don’t know that Crassus crucified 6,000 rebellious slaves along the Appian Way into Rome or that he forced his legionaries to beat to death every tenth of their comrades after they fled the battlefield—possibly up to 4,000 men—thirty years before Christ was even born.”

“Nasty, brutish, and short,” murmured James.

Stryver poured cognac into their cups, now empty of espresso. “The Romans themselves were pragmatic people, even in spiritual matters. They began as simple animists who believed that everyone had a *numina*, or spirit. They had some rites and festivals but no temples or statues. What was important was pleasing these unknowable spirits with correct practice in terms of prayer, ritual, and sacrifice, not faith or dogma. But over time, as the republic grew into an empire, the Romans adopted a kind of cover-your-ass spirituality where they adopted any and every foreign god and religion. They didn't meet a god they didn't like."

James frowned, trying to dredge up relevant details from a philosophy class on Roman philosophers that he'd taken. "So, when the legions brought back mystery cults from the eastern provinces, the emperor was deified. Philosophy began to displace religious worship, which had hardened into rote formalism. Gibbons says it best in *The History of the Decline and Fall of the Roman Empire*: 'The various modes of worship which prevailed in the Roman world were all considered by the people ... '"

"'... as equally true; by the philosopher, as equally false; and by the magistrate, as equally useful.' Sounds like the First World today," finished Stryver. He reached for some biscotti, which he waved around as he spoke. "And in the end, Christianity replaced them all. Not bad for a splinter Jewish mystery cult."

"I'm still waiting for the nuclear-bomb metaphor."

"Don't you get how explosively radical Jesus' teachings were? Can't you see it? What His followers were going on and on about when they talked about the 'Good News'? Pagan gods didn't demand a personal relationship with individual people or tell them to treat their neighbors as themselves.

"It wasn't a part of anyone's creed to be a Good Samaritan. Some acted out of innate altruism, but that wasn't what the gods asked of them. There was no need to examine conscience or to try to improve ethical or moral behavior—"

"Wait! Marcus Aurelius extols service and duty in his *Meditations*...."

"Written almost two hundred years *after* Christ and inspired by the stiff-upper-lip school of virtue that rewarded the right person with happiness based on a Spock-like lack of emotion. Not exactly the stuff of hope for your typical downtrodden slave from the outer bum-fuck province of Dacia, eh?" Stryver paused.

"There was also no imperative to forgive. None. Not once let alone seventy-seven times seven instances. There was only predatory survival, divine appeasement, and the harshness of laws, both civil and divine. In point of fact, Christ singlehandedly enabled humanity to outmaneuver the law of the jungle."

"Because he extended basic Jewish tenets about the welfare of widows and orphans to include the weak and oppressed of any age and gender and of all peoples," said James.

"Bingo," said Stryver. "Not just those whose foreskins had been removed and who followed all the proper dietary laws, etc. The whole proposal is unnatural. Anti-evolution and survival of the fittest, you might say."

James sat back in his seat and studied Stryver, who appeared quite pleased with himself. He rubbed his chin. "Okay, Christianity was a nuclear bomb, I guess. But that metaphor doesn't really work, does it? Nuclear bombs are more about destruction than the growth that occurs afterwards, if you know what I mean."

He paused and then went on. "Christianity definitely remade the world. That's why there's a B.C. and an A.D. even if the revisionists have turned those into B.C.E. and C.E."

Stryver chuckled and tossed his cognac back in a swift gulp. "Now, now, James. Don't talk like a bigot, an ignorant American post-colonial imperialist. Just because the Common Era has as its foundation the Western world's formerly held beliefs in the primacy of the birth of 'our Lord' doesn't mean you should be so snarky and deliberately exclusionary."

James shook his head and, sighing, said, "Shit."

Stryver poured them more cognac. "Maybe a better metaphor would be that Christianity is a virus. A hot-burning plague like the Black Death. Or Ebola. Well, maybe not Ebola. It kills its hosts too quickly to proliferate."

James halted in the act of picking up his cup and considered this possibility.

"Well, it certainly spread with the swiftness of a pandemic. In only three hundred fifty years, it became the official religion of the Roman Empire, having captured the heart of the Emperor Constantine. Elira would probably have something to say about that, wouldn't she?" he asked.

"Oh, absolutely," said Stryver. "She never misses a chance to crow about one of her heroic warrior ancestors, Constantine being one of the greatest."

Stryver ate his biscotti with apparent relish and then asked around a mouthful, "You haven't happened to see her in the past few weeks, have you?"

James returned casual with casual. Looking down to select his own Italian cookie, he said, "I thought you said you always knew how to find her. Or that she's never gone for long."

Now Stryver sounded more confident. "That's true. And she hasn't been gone long."

James, who'd wondered what had become of his bloodthirsty sprite following Duka's capture, looked around the espresso bar and what he could see of her bookstore, dark and empty this evening. Whatever she was doing, Mirjeta had been safe.

"Six weeks isn't long? Aren't you worried about her?"

Stryver shrugged and said, "Six weeks, six months. She's like a cat, our Elira. She'll turn up, a little worse for wandering but starved for attention."

"She doesn't have family in the area, does she? I always got the impression she was a loner, except for you."

Stryver's gaze sharpened on James. "I'm Elira's only family." Then he relaxed and said, "Then again, I'm willing to share her with the right party."

"I'll pass." James held himself still, but he'd almost shuddered. If he were honest with himself, he knew that his response wasn't entirely motivated by disgust.

"You can say that, but Elira gets what Elira wants. You hear what I'm sayin'?" asked Stryver.

James grabbed the cognac and splashed a generous amount into his espresso cup. What he'd drunk already had started to settle in between his eyes, but the sudden urge to get hammered appealed to him.

"I'm Elira's friend, pure and simple. Nothing more, nothing less," he said.

Stryver reached for the cognac, which had drained so low that only a few fingers of the golden-brown liquid caught the warm light of the overhead pendants. He laughed. His eyes gleamed, dark and inscrutable. "Elira's friend? Wherever she is, man, you can bet she doesn't give a shit about your friendship. If she did, would she let you worry about her the way you are?"

ELIRA LEANED AGAINST A black Lexus SUV with tinted windows that was parked across the street from All Souls. Although the bar—a favorite haunt of the Krasniqis and their underlings—stunk as badly as any medieval charnel house, she knew that only Jak and some of his favorite thugs were inside.

Zamir, the sadistic one, had a distinct reek that scorched the delicate membrane inside her nostrils. She'd know precisely when he arrived. On her mp3 player the harsh hip-hop lyrics of Tribunal's Tribunal Axe beat on her eardrums. She closed her eyes and inhaled. It was like breathing super-heated air.

"Where are you, you *qij sëmurë*?" she whispered. *Sick fuck. Right.*

Her soft laugh was mocking. She rubbed the scar over her heart. It ached and burned until she thought she'd go mad with it. To distract herself, she pulled her ear dagger out of her thigh-high dominatrix boots and considered it under the streetlight.

"My precioussss." She laughed again and then whirled, ramming it into the SUV's front tire. Swearing at her impetuous gesture, she yanked it free and tested the blade's edge. It would still do. She would see to it.

The drums beatbeatbeatbeatbeatbeat until her heart thudded along. She closed her eyes again. She chanted, stomping and swaying. When she opened them, a man and woman watched from the opposite sidewalk. Their grins faded. Then their faces disappeared into the collars of their winter coats as they hustled away from All Souls.

Elira smirked and tossed the dagger above her, catching and flinging it several times almost without looking at it. Instead, she watched the couple, who were arm-in-arm and laughing now, as they walked down the block, L.L. Bean and J. Crew from their heads to the faux-wool on their waterproof suede boots.

She'd bet her last bag of heaven dust that they were college students who believed the world revolved on an axis of truth, justice, and the American way. Mirjeta too wanted to believe that world existed. She should know better. But she'd escaped her uncle and his incestuous pedophilia in the chaotic, bloody Balkans to come here, live free, and love.

Elira caught the dagger, squeezing its grip and pressing her thumb between its pommel ears. She could throw it and be on the woman before the man's life bled out on the sidewalk. Neither would see her coming nor have more than a moment to reconcile themselves to regret and loss.

Mirjeta's adamant voice rode roughshod over the angry rap, drowning it out. *I won't become one of them.* I won't. *I won't fight fire with fire.*

Elira swiped the dagger's razor-edge over her forearm, her avid gaze on the dark, welling blood. She lapped at it, tasting its stagnant potency. "Don't worry, my *gjakova*. I'll do it for you."

"AGAINST THE HARSH LIVING conditions of the ancient world, what poor woman or slave wouldn't grasp at the delusion of a personal, loving Father? One who paid back the evildoers of this world in the next? That's another promise Christianity used to seduce the weak and downtrodden: the afterlife."

Stryver had gone back to the espresso machine, and now its ominous hissing threaded through his words. "Come now. The Egyptians, Jews, Greeks—all had an afterlife. Anubis weighed the hearts of the dead with a feather to judge their fate. The idea that what we do in this life has consequences for eternity even drives Hinduism."

Stryver set an espresso before James. "It's a triple to counter the cognac. Trust me. I've got the caffeine-to-alcohol ratio necessary for stimulating intellectual conversation down pat."

He returned to the espresso maker.

"Ah, but did these other belief systems offer up hope to the living that what they suffered at the hands of the unjust would be rewarded in the end?" he asked.

Stryver grabbed his espresso and returned to the table.

"Nice twist, eh? It only adds to the strength of the contagion. Add to that the notion, so very seductive, that an all-powerful, all-seeing, all-knowing God came down to live as one of them—the sparrows of the field—take on their burdens, and die for their sins. What an irresistible pathogen!" He paused to sip his coffee.

"Which leads me to my next bit of evidence that Christianity is a particularly virulent virus. Once its host, the Roman Empire, collapsed and died, Christianity in the form of the Catholic Church became the reigning power in Western Europe."

"But the Roman Empire didn't die in the east. It lasted another thousand years," said James.

"Yes, but in that case, the virus completely transformed the state as well as the church. Remember that Constantine, who thought the Christian God had picked him out to rule, did everything he could to keep divine favor on the healthy half of his empire."

"Well, the Greeks and the rest of the eastern provinces were always more mystical than the hard-headed and prosaic Romans."

"So, you can see why the virus worked differently there. In the Byzantine Empire, the emperor became God's regent, His chosen representative on earth and at the top of the social hierarchy. God remained very active, if distant, in choosing His rulers in Byzantium, where church and state had a symbiotic relationship. It was this ideological 'glue' that kept the Byzantine Empire together as the acid of Islam slowly eroded its borders and the acrimony of religious debate isolated it from the Christian West."

"Sounds like their faith gave the Byzantines great heart. Who wouldn't want that kind of faith? I've seen it in my Special Forces team in Iraq and Afghanistan."

Stryver grinned at James. "Ah, yes, the Byzantines hold a very special place in my affections for their massive, long-lasting shared delusion. It gave them almost superhuman strength as they were embattled on all sides."

"But in the end, they were overcome by the Turks and the backstabbing Catholic Church."

"Who remained a strong host for the Christian virus. Recall your biology? Viruses are very opportunistic. They drill their way into host cells, kill the cell's own DNA, and then use the cell's DNA factory to churn out copies of them. Unless stopped, they keep reproducing until they kill the host. Successful viruses keep jumping to new hosts."

"But Christianity hasn't 'killed' any hosts. You just said it kept the Byzantine Empire alive under incredible circumstances. Some would say it played a major role in the development of Western civilization."

Stryver clicked his tongue and shook his head. "Like all viruses, Christianity mutates, adapting to changing conditions. It hit the ancient world so hard precisely because the human immune system had never been exposed to anything like it before. Think Native Americans and smallpox. The Europeans, who'd lived with smallpox for years and been exposed to similar, but less deadly, pox diseases, didn't die at the same rate. As a group, they had more acquired immunity. But is the surviving host stronger because it was infected or despite the infection?"

"Some might argue both." James looked down at his fingers as they toyed with his empty cup. He had the inexplicable urge to cross himself but feared that he couldn't handle Stryver's reaction. "So, Christ is just the original black rat in this scenario? A Typhoid Mary?"

Stryver leaned forward, forcing James to look at him. "Oh, no. I would never compare Him to vermin. Or an ignorant Irish woman who couldn't put two and two together."

He held James's gaze for a moment and then reached for the last of the cognac.

James pushed his chair back enough to pull his gaze away. "This all begs the question. What's the purpose?"

Stryver, who'd started to pour, stopped. "Come again?"

"What's the purpose for this so-called virus? Why does it exist?"

"Do viruses have to have a reason beyond surviving long enough to reproduce, the basic biological imperative?"

An inexplicable tension rose in James. "No, maybe not." He swallowed and went on. "Yet the Christian 'virus' clearly lives longer than is strictly necessary to reproduce. The Good News was for individuals, not institutions, but you've been using "host" to mean empires and civilizations."

Stryver sat back, the empty cognac bottle dangling from his fingers. "That's what makes Christianity particularly resilient, man. It infected a key agent in Saul of Tarsus, who went from persecuting this heretical sect to promoting it throughout the known world. St. Paul did more than all the other disciples together to ensure that Christianity proliferated and succeeded in the Roman Empire."

He leaned forward. "It was St. Paul who turned faith in Christ from a personal 'infection' into a communal 'disease.' He's the one who made the dregs of the Roman world realize that the meek can inherit the earth if they work together to infect everyone. In short, Christianity is a virus that's mind altering. It hijacks the minds of infected hosts so that they promote it, thereby guaranteeing an endless supply of new hosts."

He finished with a flourish of the bottle before banging it on the table. "Evolutionary biologist Richard Dawkins says faith is analogous to smallpox and more difficult to eradicate."

"G. K. Chesterton said the paradox of Christianity is that it loves the world so much it wants to lay waste to it only to rebuild it into a New Jerusalem." James stopped and then plunged ahead. "Maybe the virus has a symbiotic relationship with its host, conferring benefits to make the host a healthier organism. Maybe"—here his voice grew stronger—"maybe Christianity aids human evolution ... and that's the reason it exists. To change humanity over time into something better. Instead of a virus, perhaps Christianity is a different microbe: yeast."

"Turning humanity from water into wine?" Stryver laughed and then tilted his head to study James. "Are you a believer? Is that why I sense some unhappy vibes emanating from you? Geez, man, I thought we could have this discussion because you're an intellectual who understands the rules of the game. A little inquiry into the origins of your faith shouldn't be a problem if you're confident in what you believe."

James compressed his lips and began crumbling the remnants of his cookie on the plate in front of him. "Let's just say I believe, but lately some doubts have begun to creep in. My dad always says the one non-Christian belief he's tempted to subscribe to is reincarnation because the whole damn human race is so stubbornly set on doing evil that it surely needs more than one lifetime to let the Good News sink in. You've just made it clear that the love of Christ has been working on the human heart for centuries. Yet from all I can see, most people are still as hardhearted and bloodthirsty as the day Cain killed Abel."

Stryver jerked and knocked his espresso cup to the floor where it shattered. With a small cry, he slid from his seat to gather the pieces.

"Sorry!" James started to drop to his knees to help, but Stryver waved him away. "No, no. It's not a big deal."

James studied the back of Stryver's neck as he bent over the mess. On any other person, it would have looked vulnerable. Stryver's neck, its skin oddly wrinkled and speckled, didn't. James felt ice razor down his spine. He looked at his watch. It was late. He should have left an hour ago. Mirjeta was all alone this evening at his apartment. After six weeks, she no longer had a friendly security detail outside their door, just an occasional drive-by.

Stryver sat back on his heels and laid his hands on his knees. "You may be right about the human race in general, but at least you know you can count on your friends and family, right?"

ELIRA STOOD UNDER THE window to James's apartment and pulled her earbuds out. Jak had left All Soul's an hour ago, and she'd taken the opportunity to ride Eddie for a little intelligence briefing. In the midst of begging her not to stop, he'd panted out that he'd overheard Jak setting up a rendezvous with Zamir over the phone. Afterwards, as she'd tugged her skirt straight, he'd said around the cigarette dangling from his lips that Jak had promised to bring him a sweet piece of Albanian ass later that evening.

"No offense, darlin', but I could do with something a little hotter than you. Never had pussy so cold in my life." He'd laughed.

In response, she'd kicked his head, knocking him out. Her own laugh had held little mirth. "None taken." Then she'd left Eddie in the storeroom with his Levi's around his ankles.

Now she waited, the engraving on her dagger hilt biting into her palm, for the two men whose blood she'd craved for longer than she'd ever craved any debtor's blood. And she'd been without blood—real, life-sustaining blood—since she'd killed that last sex trafficker in March. Since James Goodman, a righteous man, had endangered his own life to donate his blood to save hers.

Fading into the shadows, she turned to look at the street. "Come, *derra*, time to settle your debt."

Even in the frosty air, her breath left no trace.

Eleven

LORETTA WALKER HATED TRAVELING WITHOUT HER HUSBAND WYATT, although Lord knew that she'd had to do it often enough in the past ten years, which of course only made her more aggrieved with him. The fool man had always threatened to drive fifty miles outside of Charleston and leave her to see if she could make her way home without him. It was a game that they'd played. She'd pretended to get all flustered and upset only to assure him that she'd never, never in a million years on God's green Earth be able to manage without him—especially if she had to rely on the kindness of strangers.

"You know, Wyatt, what people are like these days. Not a one of them has the fear of the Lord in them, not like in the old days. If my mama were here, she'd faint just thinking about how rude and uncharitable people are. Why, just the other day Ava stopped to get directions at the Shell station on Mount Pleasant Street. When she had trouble understanding the clerk's directions, he rolled his eyes and turned away from her. He ignored her to wait on other customers while she waited patiently for several minutes. Then he sighed and rolled his eyes as he turned back to her. Well, of course, Ava asked him where his manners were. He responded by calling her a nasty name and telling her to get lost—which she already was, by the way!"

And Wyatt would pretend that she meant it, that she couldn't handle all the details of planning, packing, navigating, and driving. But they both knew that she'd raised three boys while he'd been gone to Vietnam and afterwards, when he hadn't been himself with the nightmares and the drugs. But she didn't like to remember that about him.

What's past is past, she always said. *Ain't no use in crying over what can't be changed.*

Maybe she'd only pretended to have that conversation with him. Ava, after all, hardly spoke to her after that last meeting, the one in the church basement when she'd announced her intention to go to D.C. and invited any of the other mothers who wanted to come with her to sign up. In fact, come to think of it, probably the only thing that Ava had said to her in the last four months was that she'd pray for her, Loretta, to reconsider what she was doing.

Of course, Loretta had turned the other cheek and found someone else to share coffee with after service. It had been challenging, but the Lord had fortified her to harden her heart against Ava's pernicious wiles. As a result, Loretta knew what she had to do as a spiritual warrior: she'd spent an entire week on her knees after supper supplicating the Lord to redeem Ava from the delusions with which the Father of Lies had ensnared her. Ava deserved Loretta's efforts. Not only had she been Loretta's oldest friend, she too had lost a child.

But the ways of the Lord are mysterious, and Ava still hadn't asked for forgiveness. Thinking about Ava on this chilly February morning, Loretta sniffed and snuggled into her fleece jacket, the one with the huge red rose blooms that Sawyer had given her before he shipped out to Iraq this last time.

It smelled like him. She'd snuck into his room and dug through his duffel for some of that fancy designer cologne that he'd liked to wear for his lady friends and sprayed it all along the front. Though she'd not been able to find the exact print for the ladies in her group, she'd found a similar fleece and a McCall's pattern to make them jackets. Sylvia, her lieutenant, had insisted on making a matching red beret upon which she'd pinned her Samuel's 101st Airborne Division flash. All of the mothers in their group wore one of the four highest military decorations: the Medal of Honor, the Distinguished Service Cross, the Silver Medal or Bronze Star Medal, though most had more than one medal or commendation. Loretta and Sylvia had a Purple Heart each. They had, some said, the largest fruit salad of any single congregation in the Southeast.

Loretta stared at the stained glass in the sanctuary of the church near the Motel 6 where they'd stayed overnight. Had she forgotten anything? Footsteps sounded behind her.

"There you are, hon. I knew you'd be in here talkin' to the Lord."

It was Sylvia, a veritable sprite who always managed to look as though she'd just come from a curl and set at the salon.

"I brought you some of Mama's rubber cookies."

She held out a napkin-wrapped bundle. Over her shoulder hung an ever-present tote bag, which was almost bigger than she was. In that tote, Sylvia had so many numerous and mysterious pockets that her granddaughter Jane Ann said that it was like the magical witch's bag that her favorite character from Harry Potter carried. Loretta kept her thoughts to herself, but she suspected that that book series bordered on the satanic—even if C.S. Lewis had also written about magic. Narnia had been a Christian parable. Harry Potter wasn't.

"I've got a surprise for you." Loretta patted her mouth with the napkin after swallowing the last of the cookie flavored with sorghum-molasses and spice. "I realized what we should call ourselves last night."

Sylvia, who was easily distracted, rifled through her tote as she said, "Ooh! What do you think about this?"

She held up a nubby knitted sack. "It's called a bobble cocoon. I thought, you know, the babies would be almost swaddled in it."

Loretta took the cocoon. "How sweet! They're perfect for the Healing Hearts Ministry." She dropped the sack in her lap and looked at Sylvia. "In fact, darlin', we should call Deacon Butler and see if we left anything undone."

Sylvia rested her hands on Loretta's shoulders and held her gaze. "Loretta, hon, we're only going to be gone a few days. The ministries will go on without us—they always do. Isn't that the way of it? Always work to do in the Lord's fields and never enough laborers."

She waited until Loretta nodded before she said, "Now, what is it you realized we should call ourselves?"

Loretta let her gaze drop to her fingers, which had begun to trace the sack's knitted stitches. If she weren't so anxious, she'd be able to figure out the pattern. Sylvia dropped a hand onto hers, holding them still.

Loretta looked up at her friend's cherubic face, surrounded by white strands as fine as lace. When she spoke, tears thickened her speech. "It's just that I don't know if we're going to make any difference, Sylvia. When I serve food at the shelter, I see what good

I can do in the world. It's right there every time I give Roy Hastings more ham and sweet-potato pie."

Sylvia sat next to her on the pew. "And you can't be sure what we're doin' is right, can you?"

Loretta shook her head, her eyes pricking. "That's not it. I'm sure as sure in my heart what I feel is right and true. But I know not everyone agrees with me. It's just so hard to face that sometimes."

Sylvia gripped her hands. "Now you listen to me, Loretta Walker. Didn't the Lord say 'I know your deeds, that you are neither cold nor hot. I wish you were either one or the other! So, because you are lukewarm—neither hot nor cold—I am about to spit you out of my mouth'? He's talkin' to you and me. He wants us to be passionate about Him! So now, out with it! What should we call ourselves?"

Loretta closed her eyes, took a deep breath, and then looked at Sylvia. "Code Red. We should call ourselves Code Red. Somebody has to acknowledge all the blood being spilled, blood that rightly belongs to the Lord."

"DID YOU KNOW THAT cats have transmitted a personality-altering parasite to half the people on earth?"

Elira started at the sound of purring next to her ear but managed to keep her dagger in her hand. She swiveled to glare at Zophiel, who sat cross legged on the stoop of James's apartment building.

“Get the hell out of here, Zophie! It’s not safe to be here, you stupid, stupid child.”

Zophiel ignored her to gaze down on the long-haired white cat that she stroked. “*Toxoplasma gondii.* Causes toxoplasmosis, which can be deadly to those with weak immune systems. If a pregnant mother passes it on to her baby, it can get very sick, sometimes years later.”

Elira exhaled her breath. The harsh sound rattled the quiet night. “How did you find me?”

Now Zophiel looked at her. Her almond-shaped eyes dominated her heart-shaped face, its luminous skin surrounded by pale hair. A column of moonlight made her look ethereal against the deep blue of night. Sadness radiated through her features.

“I don’t need anything to find you. I know what’s here.” She leaned forward and touched a delicate fingertip to Elira’s scar.

Agony jabbed Elira’s breast, answered by a fierce burning in the fresh cut on her forearm. The cat’s purr rumbled through the dark around them, soothing the hurt to a dull throb.

“Why are you here?” Elira forced through numb lips. She wanted to add *Shouldn’t you be in bed getting a good night’s sleep for school?* But the question stuck in her throat.

Zophiel leaned back and stroked the cat again.

“Women infected with *Toxoplasma gondii* tend to be warm, outgoing, and attentive to others. Men on the other hand,“ she grinned, her pearly teeth dazzling, “tend to be less intelligent and a bit boring. But everyone infected is more likely to feel guilty and insecure. None of them looks or seems ill.”

Elira closed her eyes and prayed that Jak and Zamir wouldn't arrive while this odd creature sat discussing parasites. On the heels of this prayer, her feet and fingers prickled.

Shaking them to return circulation such as it was, she asked, "Does anything you talk about make sense?" The words hissed and spat like sparks hitting water, falling between them.

"Everything I say, dear Elira, makes sense if you'll only pay attention. Now, where was I?"

Zophiel paused and touched her index finger to her chin, screwing her face into concentration. "Oh, yes, I wanted to tell you about this wacky parasitologist who published a paper a few years ago on *Toxoplasma gondii*. He says it manipulates its host's behavior for its own benefit."

She leaned in closer. "Here's the really wild part. He thinks if enough people are infected, this parasite can alter whole cultures."

She leaned back and beamed.

Elira groaned. "I give up. Why're you telling me this?"

Zophiel rolled her eyes and sighed. When Elira glared at her, she continued, "Actually, other researchers noticed a link between *Toxoplasma* infection and schizophrenia, neuroses, and suicide. They think that when people are infected with parasites like *Toxoplasma*, their immune systems ramp up, releasing something called cytokines to activate immune cells. Cytokines can cross the blood-brain barrier, and high levels of them cause depression."

She paused, tilting her head. "Do you think infected people are aware of this parasite and its influence?"

Elira only half heard her. Her sharp hearing had detected the scuffle of shoe leather on asphalt, and her nose told her something rank approached.

"Whatever, Zophie. You'd better run. Something wicked this way comes." She smirked at her quote. The Scottish play had always been one of her favorites.

Zophiel turned serious eyes on her. "Did you love him?" Her soft words crucified Elira, who whimpered. "Why did you take up your burden again?"

She traced the MacNeil tattoo, riven by an angry red line across its circular design. Her touch burned to the bone. She looked at Elira again, her pupils so large that Elira longed to fall into their cool depths. They made her realize how parched and raw her spirit was.

"I'm rather handy with ink. Let me make it whole again. Better than new."

Behind her, Jak and Zamir materialized between two parked cars, the moonlight deepening the shadows of their eye sockets and carving the planes of their faces into death's heads. They paused on the sidewalk. The barrel of a handgun glinted in Jak's hand, but the wicked gleam in Zamir's came from his switchblade. The stench fogging the air around them made Elira gag.

Turning back, she hissed at Zophiel to flee, but the young woman and her cat had disappeared.

FOR MOST OF THE drive to the Islamic Center of Washington, Loretta stared at a portrait of Sawyer in his dress blues, taken during boot camp on Parris Island almost twenty years before. He looked so young, despite the close-shaven head and stern, unyielding features. Even so, she could scarcely believe how he'd been transformed in twelve short weeks from a gregarious puppy into the hard, confident young man in the photo.

She raised the sleeve of the India company t-shirt that he'd given her on Family Day, the day before he graduated from recruit training, and wiped her nose and cheeks.

"Ain't nothin' like a newly minted Marine," Sylvia said from the driver's seat of the full-size van that they'd rented to transport the thirteen Code Red mothers and their supplies.

She sat on a thick cushion so that she could see over the steering wheel, like a child who'd snuck into her daddy's car to twist the wheel and honk the horn. Loretta kept expecting to hear her make driving noises.

"Ain't nothin' like a broken and forgotten Marine," Loretta answered, shoving the photo into her handbag. "Anger at what was done to him eats at me like acid, but it's the sympathy for the Devil's own that won't give me rest."

Sylvia tutted. "The Good Lord told us we must forgive only those who ask sincerely for forgiveness."

Loretta looked out the passenger window, but her eyes wouldn't focus. A small, sharp pain pierced the space between her eyebrows.

"Yes, but even if they never ask me to forgive them, you know I'm not supposed to seek revenge or treat them with anything but kindness. Do right by them. Aren't we going to aggravate them? Cause more problems?"

Sylvia sighed so heavily it shook her tiny body.

"So we're back to that again, are we? Look, love, we're not told to be doormats. Jesus tells us in Luke to buy a sword. He wasn't advocatin' violence and war but lettin' us know we have a right to defend ourselves when the unrighteous persecute us. Despite all that talk about sheep, we ain't sheep, darlin'."

"Is that what we're doing? Defending ourselves? Are you sure?"

"What else can we do? Hm?" Sylvia addressed the women in the seats behind them. "Dolores, Betty. What country do we live in?"

The two women, their conversation interrupted, looked at each other.

"The U.S.," Betty said as Dolores answered, "America." They sounded puzzled.

"There!" Sylvia gestured with her right hand.

The van swerved as she did, sending Loretta's heart thumping. Sylvia gripped the wheel again, bringing it back into the lane and speaking as if nothing had happened.

"As Americans, we defend ourselves with free speech. Not with a sword but with words. We're not maliciously provokin' anybody."

"Maybe not. But we're stirrin' up a hornets' nest, and that's for sure. Just because we have a right to do it doesn't mean we should. What difference will it make anyway?"

"Look, love." Sylvia glared at her, transformed into a ferocious pixie.

Loretta remembered then that Sylvia's son Grady had killed two of his captors before they could behead him. She shivered, feeling suddenly feverish, as her friend continued.

"Not only is it our right to protest against the turban heads, it's our duty. If anyone gets their panties in a twist over what we do, tough cookies."

They didn't speak for the remainder of the drive until they'd arrived at the parking garage where a cadre of veterans waited to escort them. After everyone had lined up to accept bags and totes, Sylvia grabbed the handle on a sturdy plastic red wagon that she'd borrowed from her grandchildren and then turned to Loretta.

"You want to know what difference this will make?" she asked. "A day's comin' in the not-too-distant future when the Lord will separate the goats from the sheep—and don't you go gettin' smart on me and remind me I said we're not sheep. You know what I mean. We're just helpin' out by markin' the goats for Him. Kinda like the Hebrews did during Passover so the Angel of Death would pass over them, only in reverse."

When the Code Red mothers arrived outside the center, they stood and stared at the large building with its Turkish tiles and 160-foot minaret, dedicated by President Eisenhower more than fifty years before. The mosque's key-hole arches, the decorative merlons along its crenellated roofline, and the Arabic lettering over the courtyard looked unutterably exotic to Loretta, who narrowed her eyes and sucked in a steadying breath. These people, these followers of Mohammed, were alien to her.

“Wonder if ol’ Ike would be so quick to extend a welcome if he knew what happened on 9/11,” asked one of their escorts.

“Pretty sure he wouldn’t be so convinced of ‘our common goals’ or that Ali Baba is ‘faithful to the demands of justice and brotherhood,’” said another, quoting from Eisenhower’s dedication speech. Everyone present for the Code Red protest had read through the President’s words, letting their good-natured and trusting sentiment fuel their resentment.

Sylvia pulled her wagon to rest against the wrought-iron fence and stepped next to Loretta, who turned to face the gathered protesters. The early morning sunlight wrapped them in fiery halos, drawing sparks from their medals, those relics of their loved ones who’d been sacrificed to the ideal of defending American freedom—including religious freedom. Even though her eyes hurt, and the pain in her forehead had intensified so much that it made her sick to her stomach, she let her gaze linger on each Code Red member, suddenly certain that she’d been called to testify as John the Baptist had been called. She was a voice crying in the wilderness.

Raising a large poster depicting Mohammed, she shouted to the group as she shook it. “Code Red! Code Red! Blood will have blood!”

Sylvia held fluid-filled balloons in each of her hands. Shrieking “vengeance is mine, I will repay, says the Lord,” she launched first one and then the other over the fence.

Unbidden, the rest of Romans 12:20-21 filtered through Loretta's thoughts.

To the contrary, if your enemy is hungry, feed him; if he is thirsty, give him something to drink; for by so doing you will heap burning coals on his head. Do not be overcome by evil but overcome evil with good.

She shoved the words away.

Pigs' blood splattered on the paving stones in front of the entrance. Pages torn from copies of the Koran fluttered against the robin's-egg-blue sky like white butterflies.

JAK PAUSED ON THE sidewalk in front of the apartment building where his bitch cousin waited, unsuspecting and unprotected. Zamir shifted to step onto the walk, but Jak threw out his hand and caught his younger brother by the upper arm.

"*Prit.*" Wait.

Zamir might be a stupid prick, but he wasn't too stupid to listen to Jak's instincts. It was Jak's instincts that had led them to the U.S. to grow their business, and it had grown faster and larger than Zamir had the mental capacity to wrap his mind around. And Jak's instincts kept them one step ahead of their competitors and law enforcement. The imam trusted him—and that man had eyes as dead and cold as a venomous snake. One day, when they could afford to break free of him, Jak would let Zamir slice the imam open. They'd find a shriveled, black stone between his ribs and maggots eating his entrails.

"A shihni diçka?" Did you see something?

A frigid breeze rustled litter along the street behind them. Shadows moved across the full moon, dimming the previously bright night. All along the block, streetlamps flared out as if someone quenched a row of candle flames.

Low laughter growled, enveloping them. Spikes of fear sprouted down Jak's spine. Zamir whirled, slashing the air. Jak waved the barrel of his gun, but only shadows moved.

"Ju nuk jeni shumë të zgjuar, po ju, derra?" Not very smart, are you, pigs? The husky female voice echoed all around them in the still night. *"Ajo është e imja." She's mine.*

Jak gripped his gun tighter, swallowing. He spat.

"Këto janë fjalët e guximshme nga një lugat." Brave words from a ghost. "Tregojnë veten, magjistare." Show yourself, witch.

"Like this?" came the silky reply in his ear. Something kissed the side of his neck as pain sliced across the backs of his knees, toppling him.

Jak rolled to the side, ignoring the agony in his legs as he fired. Laughter rolled around him like close thunder, its trajectory half a second ahead of his aim as he pumped the trigger.

Zamir screeched and dropped, hard.

Absolute silence fell.

She was toying with them. Bile rose in Jak's throat at the realization.

Pushing himself up onto his forearms, Jak looked over at his brother. Zamir knelt, panting. Even in the dimness, Jak could see sweat glistening on his forehead. He brandished his blade in the general area around him.

"Eja, bushtër. Më lejoni të ndërtoj zemrën tuaj." Come, bitch. Let me carve out your heart.

"Like this?" came the question again.

This time Jak saw her. She knelt in front of Zamir as the moon slid out from behind the darkening clouds, one fist clutching his brother's shirt, the other her dagger—the one that legend and rumor whispered had bitten thousands. She punched it upwards, beneath his ribcage. Zamir's squeal abruptly changed into a gurgling choke as blood spewed from his mouth. Jak watched, horrified, as the lugat leaned forward and kissed his dying brother. After an eternity, Zamir's gasping and struggles faded and ceased. A moment later she shoved his limp corpse off the dagger.

Then she glanced at Jak. Eerie gray eyes glowed wolf like above a mouth wet with his brother's blood. She grinned, and it punched through his gut. He watched as she cut through Zamir's belt and unzipped his pants.

"Zamir nuk është i vetmi që merr trofe, miku im." Zamir isn't the only one who takes trophies, my friend.

Jak shit himself as he tried to crawl away.

He felt her hands on his ankles as she began to pull. His fingertips dug in, scraping against the pavement until they bled. And then she flipped him over.

He struggled. Stupid, he knew, but he wouldn't let her sit on him without a fight.

"*Luftë, derr. Unë në mënyrë të gëzojë atë.*" *Struggle, pig. I enjoy it.*

Her throaty comment maddened him with terror.

It lasted less than fifteen seconds.

After which, she had a knee pressed into his gullet, and a hand pinching his mouth open. And then she shoved Zamir's severed cock into his mouth, letting her knee slide to the side. She watched him for a long time, perhaps more than a minute, as he gagged and choked, his thoughts spinning while pinpricks of light dazzled his darkening vision. At last, she leaned closer, grabbed his face between her hands, and then nibbled and licked his earlobe. The sensation of her bloody mouth sliding over the vulnerable skin under his ear made him tremble, but when she blew on it and laughed, he started to go mad. Then she thrust her cold tongue into his ear cavity several times, laughing more as he bucked and rolled.

Caressing his ear with her open mouth, she whispered, "*Dhe ju nuk jeni i vetmi për të fus një karin poshtë fytin e viktimës tuaj.*" *And you're not the only one to shove a cock down your victim's throat.* "What goes around comes around, eh, my friend?"

He screamed around the suffocating member when he felt her teeth rip through the skin of his belly.

ELIRA VOMITED.

She vomited copious amounts of black, congealing blood, thick chunks of abdominal fat, shredded layers of skin, and lumps of stomach, spleen, kidney, and liver.

It was as putrid as any decaying flesh that she'd ever smelled, scalding her nose and burning her esophagus.

Crawling on her hands and knees away from Jak's ravaged corpse, she continued puking every few feet until there was nothing left but dry heaves wracking her. She waited with her head down and panting, until even those stopped. Weakness washed through her. Her head pounded, and her body ached. Dust and ashes coated her tongue. The scent of a thousand battlefields filled her nose. Grasping the telephone pole that she'd managed to attain, she struggled to pull herself to her feet. Water filled her legs and arms, turning her into an articulated sack.

Around her, the *Lament for the Death of Hugh Allan* swelled on the empty night. She began weeping, her mouth closed against the sobs roiling through her. The tempest claimed her for several minutes.

And then, snarling, Elira swiped the tears away. The lament cut off. She pushed off the pole and shoved her booted foot, heavy and numb, against the sidewalk. Staggering, she threw her arms wide and planted her feet to keep from falling. She must find shelter until this strange feebleness passed. But where?

Tipping her wobbly head, she looked down. She was covered in gore. Swiveling, she saw that she'd left a trail of bloody prints between still-steaming piles of vomitus.

Shaking so hard that her fingers kept fumbling with the laces, she managed to pull a boot from one foot. She stopped as vertigo battered her, but when it had passed, she discovered that she'd remained standing beneath its onslaught. She waited. After sixty increasingly slow breaths, she leaned down with all the care of an ancient gardener stooping to weed and removed the second boot.

Fifteen minutes had passed since she'd killed Jak. Every minute that she remained in the open increased her danger.

As if in response to her worry, the front door to James's apartment building opened. Her heart skittering like a small rodent, Elira dashed between two parked cars and crouched, clutching her boots to her chest.

A hoarse voice abraded the frosty air. "Holy Mother of God!" was followed by the sound of retching.

Closing her eyes, Elira held her breath. And found herself transported back to the battlefield at Culloden—her last battlefield, and the one where Duncan had died.

She'd stood with him, strangely eager to fight again at his side after almost a decade of peace on Barra. Duncan, however, hadn't wanted to leave their sturdy little blackhouse for the uneven, marshy ground of the Drummossie Moor in the northern highlands. He'd grumbled the whole journey there from their western island.

"'T'won't make a bit o' difference, lass. Bonnie Prince Charlie won't win agin' the English no matter how great a quantity of Highlander blood is spilt. And it's all for naught an'way."

"For naught?" she'd scoffed. "These English, they have sold out their Mother Church to take what rightly belongs to her. All these so-called Protestants claim authority which does not rightly belong to them. They make a mockery of all the blood spilt, all the lives given, to defend Christendom against the Mussulman. The Turks laugh at Christian Europe as it tears itself apart."

Duncan had said nothing for a long time.

"Besides," she'd argued, goading him to speak, to agree with her. "The MacNeil has sworn loyalty to the Jacobite cause."

Duncan hadn't looked at her. "Ye've no reason to remind me of my clan's honor."

"Then why cannot you see how necessary it is to heal this breach? We must fight to recover Christendom here in Scotland or we will not stand against the onslaught of the infidel!"

Duncan had stared at her before laughing. It was a bitter sound. "I very much fear, lass, that there is no such kingdom as Christendom, and perhaps there never was. Did Christ not say that He had not come to establish a kingdom on earth? No, I fight neither for a lost cause nor for the blood of my clan. I fight purely for love."

God help her, but jealousy had winged through her like lightning. "Love? Who then do you love so much that you go to war with *claidheamh mor* and bagpipe against an enemy with cannon and light cavalry? Surely you do not speak of me?"

She'd tried to keep her voice light, but he'd heard the tremor in it and placed his hand on her sword arm. When she would have kept her face turned from his, he'd slipped his fingers under her chin and turned her to look at him.

"Hear this: I love ye above all others. This ye know."

He'd waited for her to nod, tears in her eyes, before he'd continued. "But I also love many in my clan, not the least of whom is Rory."

"This I know too," she'd whispered.

"Then ye must know that I would save him by the strength of my arm, and the experience of my days on the battlefields of the continent."

He'd dropped his hand and looked away, angry now.

"Oh, lass! He's as green as new heather and as wobbly as a lamb new born! This battle canna' be won, and ye know it as well as I do! 'Tis suicide to meet the English on such poor ground, tired after a night chasin' their ghosts in the dark."

And Duncan, neither green nor wobbly, had charged with the MacNeil clan across the rough boggy field, six-foot claymore held above his head and bellowing to put the fear of God in the dead, as mini balls and raindrops showered them. It wasn't the artillery that struck the mortal blow, no, nor the bayonet that found its sheath in his side because he'd given Rory his *targe*, his large round shield. It was the bayonet of one of the redcoats moving among the fallen clansmen, nearly two thousand bloody poppies strewn over the churned mud for their Bonnie Prince's final performance in the Jacobite drama.

She'd been unconscious at his side, felled by a blow from a cavalry officer, one that had bitten into the soft flesh between neck and shoulder. If she hadn't flung herself away at the last second, she would have lost her head—and her life. When the English infantryman skewered her, she'd awoken snarling. Wobbly from blood loss, she'd nevertheless snatched the stunned man's musket and dispatched him with his own bayonet. Dropping the corpse, she'd whirled to look for Duncan, only to find him not ten feet away, his life bleeding away into the mud.

Kneeling, she'd lifted his upper body against hers, aware that he had only moments left. He'd raised a trembling finger to her wounded throat before looking at her.

"I would that I died for ye. I would save ye too, love."

And then he was gone, leaving her alone among a wasteland of the dead.

She'd kissed his cooling lips as though she could imbue him with the life that she no longer had herself. He'd always been so warm, so soft. No longer. When her tongue had tasted his blood, she couldn't stop herself. She'd drunk as much as she could summon without the help of his beating heart.

It was the first blood that she'd tasted in more than a decade. Not since she'd put Branilo's relic away in its carved box, buried in the garden behind their blackhouse.

A hoarse voice dragged Elira from her reverie. Whoever had discovered Jak and Zamir had phoned the police and now gave an almost-incoherent account of his discovery.

She slipped to the street and began sidling down the outside of the row of parked cars. By the time that she'd reached the last one at the corner, she'd begun crying again.

"I would that you'd saved me, too," she whispered.

Then she stood up to throw a glance back at the scene of her final carnage before sprinting around the corner. Her feet made soft slapping sounds on the icy pavement as she ran.

Twelve

AS JAMES STOOD LOOKING DOWN ON JAK'S RAVAGED BODY, he knew beyond a doubt that he owed Elira Dukagjini a debt that he could never repay. This went way deeper than friendship and into the realm of family, the link forged from shared trials of blood. The kind of bond that he'd developed over multiple tours with the Silent Ones. Elira had protected Mirjeta when ICE hadn't. When *he* hadn't.

He nudged Jak with his toe, nausea warring with fury in his gut. "Got what you deserved, didn't you, you bastard?"

The wailing sirens drowned out his low voice, which was just as well because Cruncher had pulled up and left his car blocking the street. James waved at his partner and then squatted to peer at the object in Jak's mouth.

Cruncher stopped to examine Zamir's body where it was propped against a fire hydrant. He whistled, long and sharp. "He's missing a vital body part is our friend Zamir. Poetic justice, eh?"

James grunted. A small internal voice chided him for not feeling sicker over what Elira had done to the two Albanians, but he couldn't find it in himself to care more.

Cruncher came to stand next to him. "Sweet Jesus!"

He crouched down and shone his flashlight on the jagged flesh of Jak's midsection, using his pen to move the dead man's clothing away from it.

"He's been ripped open all the way to his backbone." He pivoted, taking in the larger scene. "Whoever did this couldn't stomach the taste, though."

James blinked and studied Jak's gaping abdomen. He hadn't stopped to consider how Elira had done it, but the Albanian Mafioso certainly looked as though a hyena had been tearing at him. He looked around. Vomited body parts splattered the pavement leading up to a nearby telephone pole. Queasiness knifed his stomach. He lifted a hand to his mouth and swallowed hard.

Cruncher stood up. "Well, whoever the killer is, he's one sick fucker, though I suppose he can't be all the way gone or he wouldn't have puked afterwards."

He held out his hand to pull James to his feet. "Is that what I think it is in his mouth?"

"Yup."

"Do you think we have the same perp here as the holding pen in Natick? It never felt right to me, the idea that Prek's last victim chomped through his vitals."

James, the skin on his neck growing taut as a drum, shrugged. "Seems likely."

Cruncher sighed. "Hard to feel sorry for these two pieces of shit. Still, I prefer to lock 'em up for their crimes. Wonder how this is gonna play in the Duka case?"

Shaking his head, he strode off to meet the first boys in blue.

Snatching a glance at the others, James bent over a pile of regurgitated stomach contents. There was no visible connection to Elira, but as the son of a pathologist, James knew that DNA evidence came in many forms—including saliva. It was only a matter of time before someone matched the DNA from the blood sample taken in Natick to what was extracted from this sample. Unless Elira became a suspect, causing them to swab her for DNA, this match would remain in the case file for Jak and Zamir's unsolved murders. James frowned.

For now, he didn't care about that. What he wondered was whether there was more than her DNA in the vomit.

James didn't need to call his father about the results of the latest round of PCR testing three weeks later. First, they confirmed what he already knew: the same individual whose blood was found on the windowsill of the Duka house in Natick had vomited mostly undigested bits of Jak Krasniqi on the sidewalk in front of his apartment. Second, the lab cultured an unknown virus from the sample before using polymerase chain reaction to sequence its genome. Elira was sick, but no one knew with what.

So James called Dr. Wade Alston, a former graduate assistant of his father's and a pathologist at the Center for Disease Control in Atlanta, instead.

He'd forgotten Wade, a lanky southerner with sharp, dark eyes, until Dr. Goodman had mentioned him during a visit in January.

James had told his father about Stryver's depiction of Christianity as a virulent epidemic, knowing that his father would be intrigued rather than offended. After discussing whether the analogy fit well or not, Dr. Goodman had joked that it sounded like a project for Wade, who used PCR to sequence and identify microbial genomes for the CDC. A dedicated skeptic, Wade would love to discover a pathogen to explain religious faith because then he'd be able to inoculate against it.

"Your lab got it right. This genome sequence belongs to an unknown virus, a large, positive-stranded RNA virus. In that, it's like a Coronavirus, but the sequencing is different. I ran it through Genbank and came up empty. Where'd you say you got this again?"

He sounded inordinately excited. "There are traces of blue make-up in the sample for Pete's sake."

"From a crime scene. Listen, Dr. Alston—"

"Call me Wade. We've known each other too long for the 'Dr. Alston' bit."

"Okay, Wade. Can you hazard a guess about how sick someone with this virus would be?"

"Not really, unless you can tell me more about the host. And even then, I've no way of determining what factors figure into the host's immune response, which is what you're really getting at when you ask me how sick the host would be. Some immune systems respond so aggressively to a pathogen they actually damage the host. For example, the Spanish Flu pandemic of 1918 killed mostly young adults whom you'd expect to have the strongest immune systems. And they did. The virus triggered a cytokine storm in them, which means their immune systems basically killed them."

James swiveled his chair around to look out the window, plowing his fingers through his hair at the same time. "How about cannibalism? Is that an aggressive immune response?"

"Cannibalism ... good night, you're not telling me you got the sample from regurgitated human remains?"

"That's one way to describe the source."

Dr. Alston exhaled. "No, James, there's no virus that I'm aware of that causes cannibalism. If there were, we'd have to wonder when the zombie apocalypse would hit. You should try looking into other causes, like drugs. Mescaline, which is derived from the peyote cactus, is highly hallucinogenic and causes aggression. Heroin contaminated with pure mescaline leads to some very bizarre behavior."

"Well, that's a strong possibility. The individual in concern has an observed drug habit." He paused, thinking. "I can't tell you much more due to an ongoing investigation, but I do know she had elevated immune markers following a major traumatic injury last March."

"Unrelated to the trauma itself?"

"Apparently. She checked out of the hospital before further tests could determine why. She appears to be healthy."

"Well, you know as well as I do there's little I can do except confirm that she's a carrier of a novel virus. Whether it's related to her previous symptoms or not, I can't say." He paused. "There *is* one good thing, though."

"What's that?"

"If you're still alive, it's not virulent."

By early April, Elira still hadn't turned up at Jink & Diddle. James found himself haunting Urban Shakespeare rehearsals of *Macbeth*, which were staged in a renovated warehouse close to Boston Harbor. The troupe had chosen to take advantage of the theater's mixed cinderblock and red brick walls, concrete floors, and exposed wires and pipes by setting the play in Victorian Glasgow. On a large blank wall at the side of the open area that functioned as a stage, the Mackintosh Church at Queen's Cross had been recreated through deft shading of the brick, lending industrial-era grittiness to the setting. All the players had adopted Scottish accents and dressed in black leather and grunge designs.

Though he thought that he knew this tale told by an idiot, "full of sound and fury, signifying nothing," James found its lines whispering secrets to his heart.

"Yet do I fear thy nature. It is too full o' th' milk of human kindness to catch the nearest way." In Lady Macbeth's voice he heard echoes of Elira's taunts. *Your father isn't a ghost, is he? Your woman is flesh and blood, isn't she?*

He could easily imagine it was Elira speaking as Lady Macbeth declared how faithfully she'd fulfill a vow to kill her own baby: "I would, while it was smiling in my face, have pluck'd my nipple from his boneless gums, and dash'd the brains out had I so sworn as you have done to this."

"'If we should fail?'" murmured James in unison with Macbeth on his fourth rehearsal.

Lady Macbeth cast a glance toward James, frozen in his front-row seat as she goaded, "We fail? But screw your courage to the sticking place, and we'll not fail."

James squirmed as Lady Macbeth disintegrated into madness, she who'd been so resolutely bloodthirsty: "Nought's had, all's spent, where our desire is got without content; 'tis safer to be that which we destroy than by destruction dwell in doubtful joy."

By the dress rehearsal, he gripped his seat's arms as Macbeth cornered the doctor treating Lady Macbeth's insomnia to demand, "Cure her of that."

"Yes, cure her of that." The serrated words tore from his throat before he wheedled along with Macbeth, "'Canst thou not minister to a mind diseased, pluck from the memory a rooted sorrow, raze out the written troubles of the brain and with some sweet oblivious antidote, cleanse the stuff'd bosom of that perilous stuff which weighs upon the heart?'"

And yet every time the tragedy repeated itself before his eyes. Lady Macbeth took her own life, and Macbeth himself died on the battlefield.

James returned to the Irish pub where Elira had taken him for a pint of Murphy's, but no one had seen her there in months. He even staked out All Souls, ostensibly investigating Jak and Zamir's murders and looking for lower-level Krasniqi kin for the ongoing grand-jury investigation, but Elira never appeared. Worse than that, she never sought him out.

So James grabbed a surly bouncer named Eddie at All Souls, a coarser, heavier version of Sylvester Stallone with a razor cut, a perpetual toothpick in the corner of his mouth, and tattoos on his forearms. After a polite but adamantine request, Eddie confirmed that he'd told Elira about Jak's plans to snatch an Albanian immigrant, "some woman who didn't know her place and thought she could disrespect her roots." James refrained from punching Eddie but made sure that he knew that ICE agents would keep watch over his future activities.

"Any hint you're runnin' on the side for the Krasniqis, and you're busted. We clear?"

Eddie, tugging his jacket into place and glaring, said, "What Krasniqis? Didn't you hear? Some she-demon from the old country, a frickin' nightmare who hunts men like somethin' out of Predator ripped Jak and Zamir apart. Rumor has it she got their baby brother too. Got the whole clan scared shitless and makin' tracks away from the area. Why don't you big bad ICE men keep an eye out for her instead of some crazy bitch who likes rough sex?"

God help him, James shouldn't have snapped. But at least he didn't hit the bouncer, whose Body by Muscle Milk would have collapsed if James had let himself go. No, he did something worse. He spoke the truth.

"Are you really as stupid as you seem? Why the hell do you think I'm here asking about a 'crazy bitch' who knew what Jak was after?"

The blood seeped out of Eddie's face as he spoke.

"Count yourself lucky she didn't rip your cock off and stuff it into your mouth too."

James spent a few days in the office after that, catching up on paperwork before the end of the month. His wedding was only six weeks away, and he'd promised Mirjeta that he'd take off the week before to help her finalize everything. If he was going to do that, he needed to stay on top of the hated administrative tasks as much as possible. He'd just finished reading through the final toxicology reports on Jak and Zamir along with the FBI profiler's report on the unknown killer when Cruncher knocked on his open door.

"You ready to go over the raid on al-Jadar? The State Department's real prickly about what happens when we blow into the domicile of a Saudi princess, slaver or not."

James nodded and waved Cruncher into a seat before drinking the dregs of his morning coffee. No coffee tasted good after four hours on his desk, but the industrial sludge brewed in the office kitchen became a delightful acid that hit his gut like a punch. Setting his cup down on the profiler's report, whose conclusions were of the no-shit-Sherlock variety, James leveled a serious gaze on his partner.

"I've already told Ted and Mike to go easy when they come in through the back. Wouldn't want to terrify either the domestics or the preschooler."

He dug into his side drawer for the bottle of antacids. Their chalky, fruit flavor coated his tongue but did little for his roiling stomach.

Cruncher studied him as he dipped into a bag of M&Ms.

"What's eating you? This doesn't have anything to do with getting married, don't tell me it does. I may come from the heartland, but I ain't fresh from the farm, got me?"

"No, it's not the wedding. I'm not that big a jerk. Mirjeta's the best thing that's ever happened to me." He felt a shadow wing over his face and knew that Cruncher had seen it.

"It's Elira. I haven't seen her since we retook Duka." He shifted in his seat and looked out the window behind Cruncher. "I gave her back that dagger I took off her last year at the first attack and asked her to protect Mirjeta."

Cruncher whistled. "And I chose not to arrest her for taking out those two Krasniqi men down the alley from us." He crushed the M&M bag and leaned forward. "She's managed to entangle us both. Do you think she's the one who killed the Krasniqi brothers? Man, she's not sane." He shuddered. "At least she's on our side."

"For now." James steepled his fingers in front of him. "I've got to find her, do a threat assessment. Get her some help. There's some chance she's got something organic driving her behavior."

He paused, letting his gaze wander, unfocused, above Cruncher's shoulder. *What will I do then?* He cleared his throat and returned his gaze to his partner's intent, knowing one.

"What if we raid al-Jadar's house in the middle of next week? That's school vacation. She's taking the kids to Disney World, which means springing the Filipinos without them getting in the way. Should be easier to get a warrant."

Cruncher waited a moment, sending a shiv of dread through James's chest. Then he nodded. "Yeah, I had that in mind all along. But we'll need a contingency plan."

James swallowed and leaned forward to shift the papers on his desk. "That's easy enough. It's finding a she-demon that's proving hard."

JINK & DIDDLE HAD the air of an abandoned home.

James stood across the street, hands in his jacket pockets, studying the Victorian in the gloom of a rainy April afternoon. Someone, he suspected Stryver, had filed an order with the post office to hold mail for Elira and stopped delivery of her newspapers, so there was no bulging mailbox or scattered, molding newspapers in torn plastic bags.

But there were leaves and other detritus blown from the sidewalk, wrappers, an empty beer can, and a soggily disintegrating McDonald's bag clogging the latticework skirting the porch. Though he suspected that Elira had no tender domestic tendencies that would prompt her to put out pots of pansies or plant bulbs of daffodils and tulips, he doubted that she'd leave litter around her house.

Where was she?

More importantly, in this day and age, how could she disappear so completely?

She'd had a cell phone, but she didn't have a contract with any of the major carriers so he'd been forced to conclude that she used one of the pay-as-you-go phones, buying airtime at any store that sold phone cards. He had no email address for her except the contact address listed on the bookstore's Website, which was a free

Web-based account accessible from any computer with Internet access. Although he'd sent an email to it weeks ago, it remained unanswered. On the off chance that she still checked it, he'd sent another email asking her to meet him here today.

While he was waiting, the young woman who'd slavered over Stryver at the first talk on his Blood Law Theology hurried up the Victorian's porch steps. Her pasty skin glowed in the dim light. She fumbled around in a large messenger bag slung over her shoulder and then taped a flyer onto the entry to Jink & Diddle. After she finished, she pulled out a cell phone, flipping her thick, milkmaid's braid over one shoulder before calling someone. On a hunch, James stepped behind a nearby SUV to be out of casual view. A minute later, the door to the residence opened, and Stryver invited the young woman in.

James waited two minutes before crossing the street and jogging up the steps to read the flyer. It was an announcement for another Blood Law Theology talk that evening. He left, prickles tap dancing down his spine. He didn't believe in coincidence.

He returned at seven but waited outside on the porch, a strange hope seizing him. Elira didn't arrive, however, with the attendees who dribbled into her bookstore. Hunching his shoulders against the chill spring evening, he'd pivoted to enter Stryver's little kingdom when a sweet female voice stopped him. Startled, he turned to look at a teenage girl, fifteen or sixteen he estimated although it was difficult to be more certain in the gloom, standing in the shadows at the corner of the railing.

"What?"

"I asked if you're looking for my friend Elira." She stepped into the warm halo of porch light. "She's not here."

"What makes you think I'm looking for her?"

"I've seen you around with her." She cocked her head, the movement along with the lacy ruff of her rather old-fashioned dress calling to mind a cockatiel. He fancied that wings settled onto her slender back.

He dropped his shoulders. The evening now seemed balmy. "Yes, I'm looking for her. Have you seen her?"

The girl, who had the big, almond eyes that he'd seen on syrupy-sweet figurines while traveling through the Midwest, held his gaze. Even this close, her skin had the same alabaster-porcelain hue, gently rosy along her delicate cheekbones. A mineral scent, something like the sea with sunshine warming it, drifted from her. James looked away. He felt strange. Hollow and wobbly and disoriented as if he'd just awoken from an all-night bender. He placed a palm against the side of the house and prayed for steadiness.

"Not since February. She's gone wandering in the wilderness so to speak." She played with her pendant, something dark that stirred his memory. Then she took his hand. "I'm Zophie. If you're going to the lecture, I'm coming with you." Her small fingers threaded through his, and she beamed at him. James's mouth opened but nothing came out. His mind went blank.

Zophie steered him inside the bookstore and through the front book-lined room, which was lit only by a single floor lamp in the far corner. Shadows loomed, filling James with the surreal sensation that he'd descended into the outer circle of Dante's *Inferno*.

"'Abandon all hope, ye who enter here,'" he murmured and crossed himself, feeling self-conscious.

"Oh, there's no reason to abandon hope. I can always get you out of here."

James peered down at his diminutive guide, whose face was hidden in the gloom. Above them, her gargantuan silhouette disappeared into the darkness, making him shiver.

He laughed at himself and squeezed her warm hand. "Lead on, little Virgil."

A burble escaped her, and an instant later, a sharp snap told him that she was chewing gum.

When they came into the café, Stryver's face swung up. His slow grin unfurled, and his eyes gleamed.

"James, my man! Long time no see. C'mon, sit down front. But be forewarned, friend. I'm moving into dangerous ground in tonight's lecture on Blood Law Theology."

James sat at a café table. Zophie pulled out a chair, flipped it around, and straddled it. Stryver ignored her, just as he appeared to ignore the handful of Acephela students gathered at the other three tables. James glanced around at the stony faces, reminded of the Puritan judges in the movie version of Arthur Miller's *The Crucible*.

"Aren't they all, Stryver?" James asked around a thick tongue. He swallowed, choked a little, and then coughed.

Stryver's eyes narrowed, but he said nothing before gesturing to the hippie chick standing at his elbow. She hustled over to the espresso machine. He rested his hands together on the table before him.

"So, children, let us accept the proposition that Christianity is a virus. Before we move to the next topic, I want to talk about the resistance to it that began even before Christ died." He paused.

"Do you remember the New Testament story where some people tried to trap Jesus with the question about taxes? Christ didn't give them a straight answer. He said, 'Render unto Caesar the things that are Caesar's and unto God the things that are God's.' He didn't identify which is which."

James sat forward, alert. "Are you telling me that Jesus gave humanity a loophole to justify taking blood?"

Behind him, a low hum vibrated among the Acephelites.

Stryver waited until the young woman left an espresso on the table at James's elbow before continuing. "More of a loop to hang ourselves with," he said to James.

"That's why tonight's talk is titled 'Waning Christianity or How a Virus Evolves into Extinction.' Humanity's innate nature, the one that seeks blood for itself, struggled from the start with the Christian virus." He paused and looked at his audience.

"Within just a few years, disputes arose among so-called Christians, all centering on issues that had nothing to do with the fact that Christ had paid an otherwise insurmountable blood debt. No one argued whether or not there was a New Blood Law under which Christians are required to live. Mostly they argued to establish human authority over Christian faith." He sipped his espresso.

"Almost from the beginning, Christianity mutated into innumerable smaller, weaker viruses or heresies in Asia Minor. Was Christ the Son of God? If so, what was his nature, human or divine? If both, how did they work together? And so on. Arianism, Monophysitism, Monothelitism. There never was just one Christian doctrine embraced by all Christians. Even before the crescent of Islam appeared, Christianity had succumbed to tribalism."

James sat back, his hand covering his mouth, studying Stryver, who preened. The Acephelites twittered. After a moment, he let himself speak. "So, humanity's innate 'immunity' was too strong even for the Christian plague?"

Stryver nodded, his eyes gleaming. "Yup. It's a viral bully. Put on a good show, but when the hosts started to fight back, its inherent weakness became apparent."

"And that explains the rest of the history of Christianity?" James's head ached. "The feuds between Rome and Constantinople? The power and greed of the Roman Church, the struggles between pope and kings, the heresies inside and outside the Church, the Protestant Reformation and Counter Reformation?"

"Quite. Christianity has mutated into hundreds, perhaps thousands, of strains, each less effective than the last at changing human behavior. Oh, in theory, the Western world became Christian and acknowledged Christ's blood payment. But most Christians don't even know what they believe, if they ever did. Why should anyone still accept the superstition about the sacred nature of blood?"

Stryver looked around at the Acephelites. "We're not primitive man, ignorant of biology and incapable of even the most basic life-saving medicine. No wonder the fastest growing segment of faith is 'none' for people under thirty."

"What's your degree in again?" James asked. He'd meant it as a joke, but the words clawed their way up his throat. "Anti-theology?"

The Acephelites guffawed.

Zophie, who'd been doodling in a spiral notebook, looked up and fixed a strangely piercing gaze on Stryver. "'For the life of the flesh is in the blood.'"

Stryver, who'd been staring at James, flinched. Then he inched his face in Zophie's direction, gullies squeezing his eyes and mouth tight. He stopped short of looking at her, angling his head instead so that he appeared almost deferential. James looked between them. In the silence, a current sparked and flowed. James thought that he heard Stryver's heart hammering. After an eternal minute, the corner of Zophie's upper lip curled, and she tilted her face back to her doodling.

James sat up and pressed his palms on the table. "You know, Stryver, we might not be ignorant of biology anymore. You won't get any argument from me about the wonders of modern medicine. I know firsthand what it feels like to save a life."

He took a deep breath. "But I also know firsthand what it feels like to lose someone despite all my heroic efforts. And nothing, but nothing, I do will ever bring a dead person back. More to the point, no one has the power to create life."

James turned to address the others listening to his argument. One or two looked intrigued, but hostility glittered in the eyes of the rest. He plunged ahead anyway. "What compels us to progress in our ability to care for ourselves or improve the world we live in?

"Obviously, humanity is driven by more than the biological imperative to procreate. We're driven to create a better world for ourselves and for humanity. Meaning, morality, and ethics matter to us, well most of us." He gestured around at the others listening.

"Then there's hope and optimism. Those are irrational urges that are often at odds with the bare facts of survival and often based on the unseen and ineffable. What's the point to progress if it doesn't address any of the things that matter?"

James stood up, Stryver watching him with an odd stillness.

"No, we might not be ignorant of biology. But we are ignorant about life." He looked down at Zophie, whose fragile pink neck made him feel very protective, and an epiphany lit him. He returned his gaze to his erstwhile lecturer.

"Try this one on, Stryver: maybe the Christian virus is highly adaptive, like the common cold. There's no cure, and the only infallible way to avoid getting sick is to isolate yourself from humanity. Maybe Christianity prevents humans from doing that."

Zophie, her smile radiant, stood up. It was a smile to banish the shadows of hell. She slipped her hand into his. "Time to go."

James didn't move for a handful of seconds. On Stryver's narrow face, a fascinating play of emotions tantalized him. He caught glimpses of anger, scorn, cunning, and sorrow before the other man wiped his expression. The young woman, who'd been busy at the espresso machine, came over and laid her hand on Stryver's shoulder. Her eyes, huge and dark against her ghostly skin, brimmed with poison.

Then James left Jink & Diddle, no closer to discovering where Elira had gone and troubled in his soul about what Stryver might have done to her.

Thirteen

MOST SATURDAYS THE WOMEN IN THE BALM-IN-GILEAD Baptist Church of Charleston hosted the Healing Hearts Ministry, but in the spring of 2010 the Code Red mothers reserved the sanctuary for a much more important event: a city-wide rally against Islam.

Loretta and Sylvia, who wore a white t-shirt with VENGEANCE written in red block letters across the back, hung banners behind the fading peace lilies and handed out pamphlets recruiting for Code Red. Other mothers filled the coffee urn in the church hall and supervised the delivery of coffee cakes, cookies, and Mrs. Hubbard's shoofly pie to a cloth-covered table. Two mothers arranged poster boards covered with photos of Code Red's deceased sons and husbands on easels on either side of the table.

Mrs. Montgomery, her hands clasped at her waist and her lips pressed together, nodded each time a child under ten passed into the nursery where children played polite games of tea or held quiet, controlled Matchbox-car races.

At 10 a.m., the women chatting in the aisles sat down in pews and fell silent. Around the church, Code Red mothers, wearing blood-red t-shirts and black slacks, stood with their hands folded before them, their faces impassive.

Loretta, who stood behind the lectern, let the silence reign for a full five minutes, its heaviness tolling upon her listeners' hearts. Already, the familiar headache had started behind her eyes. Then, after looking around the group, she began.

"Sisters, let us come before the Lord in prayer. Lord, we come before you today with humble hearts, seeking your wisdom and your guidance concerning those who reject Your Son in the name of Islam. Lord, please speak through me. Give me a passion for Jesus and let it ring in my words. In His Name I pray. Amen."

The women murmured, rustling and somber as they gazed at her. Through the eastern windows, golden light diffused through the clear glass into the gloomier interior. Answering heat filled her bosom, radiating outward until she shivered in the cool air.

"Do you know who the largest group of converts to Islam in the U.S. is? Protestants. You heard me, Sisters. Our own sisters and brothers betray Our Lord and Savior more than any other group of Americans. How large *is* the Muslim population? Two percent.

"Before you dismiss that as nothing," she said as the women glanced at each other, shifting in their seats, "consider that sixty percent of Americans believe that Muslims are more discriminated against than Mormons, atheists, and Jews.

"That's right. This tiny minority gets a lot of love and concern from Americans. We've been told since nine-eleven to be careful not to blame the vast majority of innocent Muslims, whose religion is a religion of peace. But is it? What exactly does Islam teach?

"Well, for starters, it teaches that Jesus was nothing but a minor prophet to the Jews. In fact, Islam teaches that God, or Allah, condemns Christians for turning Jesus into God! In the Muslim holy book, the Quran, Allah says"—she looked down to read from her notes—"'Verily, whosoever sets up partners with Allah, then Allah has forbidden Paradise for him, and the Fire will be his abode. And for the wrongdoers there are no helpers. Surely, they have disbelieved who say: Allah is the third of three.'"

Loretta paused to let that sink in. She surveyed her audience again. The rapt, upturned faces glowed in the growing sunlight in the sanctuary. Halos diffused around the hanging lights, blurring her vision.

"Do you understand, Sisters? Muslims condemn us for turning Jesus into God! There is no God but Allah! Believing that Christ paid for our sins on the cross of Calvary condemns us to hell. I find it rather amazing then that American Christians can defend Muslims, who deny the most basic tenets of our faith. What's more, Christians are reviled wherever Muslims govern. Abused. Killed. Churches are burned. Who looks out for their rights? Shouldn't *we* look out for their rights? Shouldn't we let the dead take care of the dead here while we defend the living in other parts of the world?

"For if the Muslims here are peaceful, it's because we live in a civil *Christian* society. Where Islam rules, it rules with a bloody hand. It's time to wake America up. It's time to stop worrying about the tiny minority here and focus on the multitudes beyond our borders. It's time to sound a Code Red. Are you with us? Are you with the mothers and sisters, aunts and daughters, wives and girlfriends of the men who have given their lives to preserve Christian values?"

The room was silent. Loretta's heart thudded and then galloped. Tremors coursed through her so that she had to clutch the lectern to keep from wobbling. After what felt like ten minutes but was probably only thirty seconds, a young woman stood up.

"Even if what you say is true, those verses don't have to be understood literally. The Bible contains many verses that we as Christians know are about spiritual truths rather than literal guides for behavior. No Christian believes that Jesus meant for us to use a sword against our families in Matthew 10:35. Most Muslims *are* peaceful even if they think Christians are going to hell. Shouldn't we seek to win them over with our loving witness?"

Loretta admired the young woman's courage, if not her misguided lack of faith. Still, she was firm. "If Muslims are true to the Quran, they won't be won. For the Quran says"—she looked down again—"O you who believe! Do not take friends from the Jews and the Christians, as they are but friends of each other.

"And if any among you befriends them, then surely, he is one of them. O you who believe! Do not take as friends those who take your religion for a mockery and fun from those who received the Scriptures before you nor the disbelievers.'"

Raising her gaze over her reading glasses, Loretta let sadness creep into her tone. "You must guard against such innocence, child, for the devout Muslim will use it against you. The Quran says that Christians will be the easiest to convert. 'And you will find the nearest in love to the believers those who say: We are Christians.'"

Loretta paused to let her gaze rake the crowd of women. Many leaned forward, silent and intent.

Even as molten pain spread behind her eyes, she hardened her voice to hammer them with the truth. "Why? Why do Muslims seek to convert Christians most of all? Because we are not proud. The Quran says that when we 'listen to what has been sent down to the Messenger,' our eyes will overflow with tears because we'll recognize the truth!

“Then we’ll say: ‘Our Lord! We believe, so write us down among the witnesses.’ *We will reject Christ as the Son of God and our savior.* We will become Judas.”

The young woman remained standing. When she spoke, defiant stubbornness colored her words. “I’m not afraid to witness to Muslims. I’m not worried about what the Quran says. I believe in a living God, not words on paper.”

Several women shouted, “Amen!” and “Here, here!” to her speech. The room darkened as a cloud moved across the sun outside.

“What’s more,” the young woman said with her chin high, “I believe Muslims can be converted.”

“Child, your mistaken trust will cause you to hand over the keys to the kingdom. You and all like you will be the death of our Christian society.” Loretta stopped to catch her breath.

The young woman’s cheeks flared red, and she began to slide past the women in the pew next to her. Several other women followed, but the majority stayed.

It was to them that Loretta directed her remaining pitch. “Sisters, the Quran isn’t just words on paper to Muslims—it’s the Living Word to them! The Quran isn’t just a holy book, it’s God Incarnate! It’s the same as the Catholic communion wafer. Catholics believe it becomes Christ’s body after a priest blesses it. Who is right?

“Blood is being shed *every day* over this. It’s not just some theological debate. You can agree to disagree with Catholics because they also believe Jesus is the Son of God. They won’t behead you for believing the wafer is only a symbol of Christ’s body. Atheists and Jews won’t behead you because they don’t believe in Jesus.

"You *cannot* agree to disagree with Muslims because they reject the resurrected Christ and then kill our brothers and sisters for choosing to believe in Him. So, I ask again, who will join Code Red as we campaign against Islam? Remember what our Lord and Savior said in Matthew: 'He that is not with me is against me!'"

Sylvia, who'd been waiting in the shadows behind her, stepped in and took Loretta's arm, preventing her from collapsing as the fever flared.

HALFWAY AROUND THE WORLD in the Hasan Beg Mosque in Pristina, Kosovo, a young man knelt while awaiting instructions from his imam. Although he'd waited since sundown, and his lower legs had gone numb, he knew that he could kneel for days if it was asked of him. But it wouldn't be. He would be sent on a divine mission instead. He would become a *shahid*, a martyr like those killed in Afghanistan.

A whisper penetrated his reverie, but the young man's training didn't fail him. Pride swelled his chest, yet he kept his gaze on the rug an arm's length away. From the corner of his vision, he saw fine Italian loafers and the cuffs of slacks as the imam stood before him.

"So, you would be a messenger for Allah?"

"Yes, Imam." He kept his head bowed.

Silence fell. A bead of cold sweat popped from the back of the young man's neck and slid down his spine to the waist of his slacks.

"You are not afraid?" The imam's low, silky voice teased his ears.

Although he hadn't moved, the young man would swear that he stood directly above him.

"No, Imam." A legion of sweat drops prickled along his lower back and under his arms.

"Tonight, you will leave for Skopje where you will join my people and travel with them to Piraeus. There you will meet with our brothers from the Foundation for Human Rights and Freedoms and Humanitarian Relief. Together you will sail for Cyprus where you will board the *Mavi Marmara* to sail to Gaza. Do you know why we join with our İHH brothers?"

"To break the *kāfir* blockade of Hamas, Imam."

"Yes." Now the imam gripped his shoulder, which forced the young man to look up into his leader's intense gaze. "The Israelis expect only women and effeminate men to chant and wave slogans. That is what they will find on most of the ships in the Freedom Flotilla. But on the *Mavi Marmara*, they will meet warriors of God ready to die for the freedom of our Muslim brothers in Palestine."

Imam Krasniqi pulled him up to his feet and, clapping his hands on the young man's upper arms, said, "*You* will be one of those warriors of God. As it is said in the Holy Quran, 'Verily, Allah has purchased of the believers their lives and their properties; for the price that theirs shall be Paradise. They fight in Allah's Cause, so they kill and are killed.'

"In the name of Allah, the most gracious, the most merciful, may He protect you and give you success. May He grant that you are in Paradise with seventy-two virgins before the end of May."

Then Imam Krasniqi pulled the young man close and kissed his cheeks before leaving. The young man stood for a moment longer, dazed with the knowledge that he'd been chosen for the righteous struggle with unbelievers.

"As Allah wills," he murmured, visions of virgins filling his thoughts, and left to pack for his final mission on Earth.

"SHILENT SH-SHITTY—OOPS!" JAMES LAUGHED until a hiccup broke it off and he stumbled, catching Cruncher's arm to keep from falling. "I meant 'city.'"

He focused on not slurring. It amazed him how much strength and finesse it took to work his tongue and jaw. "Silent city streets."

He squinted, trying to marshal his critical thinking skills to capture the fuzzy images around him. "Fog presses into hollows where drunks lie passed out. Hey! I d-did it. I composed a haiku. No blood though. Whadaya think?"

He turned toward Cruncher, whose hard grip on his arm and pressed lips penetrated James's own personal fog.

"Too much alliteration," Cruncher grunted. He jerked James upright as he stumbled again.

"I think, Goodman, you shouldn't even walk home by yourself. Even if you don't get beaten and sent to the hospital, you'd break your neck on your stairs. Mirjeta'd kill me if you couldn't walk down the aisle tomorrow."

James laughed, but there was a bitter edge to it that stung his tongue. Even in his stupor, he saw the concern in Cruncher's eyes. "Maybe you should just leave me out here."

Cruncher halted so abruptly that James's hold on his friend's arm tore free, and he staggered forward, though he managed to stay upright. Pivoting, he glanced back to see the other man standing in the phosphorescent glow of a streetlight, his eyes lost in the sharp shadows defining his hawk-like face.

"What?" he mocked and then ruined it with a waiver. "You don't think I should let some psychopath who's seen one too many vampire movies jump me in a dark alley the night before my wedding?"

"James, man, what's wrong? Getting cold feet? I thought we'd already gone over this."

James turned and plunged into the misty darkness ahead. He didn't care whether Cruncher followed or not, but after a minute he sensed his partner's bulk keeping pace at his side.

"Ever get tired of dealing with human trafficking? International drug lords and pimps? How about radical Muslims?" His thoughts sloshed around inside his skull. An image of Elira took shape only to merge with that of Mirjeta.

Almost to himself he said, "I dream about blood and fire cleansing the face of the Earth."

Cruncher sighed but said nothing.

"But then I look down, and there's blood on my hands. And Mirjeta's lying at my feet, wearing a white gown and covered in blood." When he heard what he was saying, James went silent.

“Oh, man.” Cruncher sighed again, shaking his head. “Don’t. Don’t go there. Don’t start thinking you’re gonna turn into one of them. You’re not.”

James didn’t respond. How could he tell Cruncher that he’d gotten it backwards?

“Look, I know this Duka case is dragging. Justice might be slow, but it’s sure. The Feds got the whole American branch of the Krasniqi clan in jail, and they’re working on that whacked imam back in Kosovo. Let it go. You’re marrying a beautiful woman who adores you. If that’s not a gift worth being grateful for, you don’t deserve her.”

“Maybe she doesn’t deserve me,” James said. He didn’t know what he meant by that, so he hurried on. “Hey, man. I don’t know what’s gotten into me. I’m not usually a melancholy drunk. Must be the creepy fog.”

He hunched his shoulders and glanced around them. “Reminds me of a gothic vampire movie where Dracula takes the form of mist and then rolls into his victim’s open bedroom window. I can almost feel him watching me.”

Cruncher barked a laugh and slapped James on the shoulder. He’d clearly decided that his partner’s fancies were no cause for alarm. “This is the most morbid conversation I’ve ever had the night before a wedding!”

He looked ahead and then back at James. “You gonna be all right? ’Cause the lot where I parked is coming up on the right.”

"Go, go!" James shoved Cruncher, whose bulk didn't budge. "If I can't make it another few blocks to my building without a wet nurse, I shouldn't be getting married tomorrow."

Cruncher nodded, and whistling *Get Me to the Church on Time*, strolled down the block to their right. James waited, strangely reluctant to move now that Cruncher's solid, prosaic presence dwindled into the mist on the far side of the streetlight. Jamming his hands into his pockets to keep his posture upright, he ignored the creeping sensation on the back of his neck and began walking.

"Misty summer night," he composed aloud, defying his own nerves.

The image of Mirjeta's brutalized body sprang to life before his mind's eye despite his attempt to stop it. Almost against his will, he heard himself say, "In the dark her white gown glows against liquid red."

A shudder tore through him after he spoke, leaving a cruel, sharp pain behind his left eye and beneath his breastbone. Somewhere a cat yowled. Wind blustered along the street, swirling the mist but not dissipating it. Although it was summer, James felt chilled to his marrow.

Almost as soon as the wind picked up, it died. James thought of Zophie, the girl or perhaps young woman who'd sat next to him during Stryver's last talk. His little Virgil, his guide through hell. The mist retreated to the darkest shadows along the foundations of the nearby buildings. He smiled, feeling better until a thought struck him. Despite Stryver's odd deference to her, Zophie had no business hanging out listening to his twisted lessons on history and theology. A vision of her turning into Elira loomed before him. He couldn't let that happen.

Movement from the corner of his eye snapped him alert. A wrapper kicked up by a cold gust floated off behind him.

Looking around, he realized that he'd walked into an alley that he didn't recognize in his distraction. He couldn't see far in the muffled darkness, but his gut told him that the alley was a dead end. The creeping sensation returned until his senses screamed at him. About fifty feet ahead in the deepest shadows water dripped, reminding him of the sound of blood dripping from the corpse of Jesus Delacruz, who'd been shot in the neck by a sniper in an Afghani village on one of their patrols. James had been forced to listen to it for ten long, godforsaken minutes after he'd hidden inside one of the mud houses.

A presence waited here—something sharp and hungry like Stryver's eyes whenever James sat down to listen to his lectures on blood theology. He slipped his Walther PPK from its holster and slid beside a dumpster. Whoever or whatever it was wouldn't catch him unarmed.

"James."

He whirled, his gun aimed straight at Elira's heart. For several breaths he stood there, his mouth and throat growing dry and his heart pounding.

"We both know that won't harm me," she said at last, stepping forward until he could have touched her with it. "And neither will you."

She wrapped her hand around the muzzle and tugged. He let her have it. She didn't speak while he studied her.

"You look like shit."

"It's good to see you, too." She handed his Walther PPK back. "Never took you for a 007 type. Not suave enough."

"Always preferred beer to martinis too." James reholstered the gun. "Where the hell have you been, *vrasësi im i vogël?*" *My little assassin.*

She shrugged, an eloquent gesture, and turned to lead him out of the alley. James followed, shooting a glance over his shoulder as he turned onto the sidewalk.

Why the hell did he ever go in there in the first place?

"You're getting married tomorrow." It wasn't a question.

It was his turn to shrug. She said nothing for several minutes while they walked. She looked frail, and visible tremors shook her every few seconds. Her hair, always so wild and upright, lay lank against her neck. The scar on her upper lip gleamed against her pale skin. The familiar haunting fragrance of heather and moss infiltrated his nose, reviving his recent wooziness.

"Do you suppose she'll mind if I visit you sometimes?" She kept her eyes downcast, but James heard the uncertainty in her voice.

He touched her forearm. The cold flesh burned. He wanted it to consume him. "No. It doesn't matter if she does anyway."

Her luminous gray eyes swung up, wide and tinged with sadness. She raised icy fingertips to his cheekbones, whispering as she studied him. "Ah, *miku im.*" *My friend.* "I'd hoped he was wrong, but I see he truly knows the human heart. You still burn for Krasniqi blood even though I took so much of it. Perhaps more so *because* I took it."

James pulled from her and, hunching his shoulders, strode away.

"Do you know my father is almost catatonic? I haven't seen him like this in more than a decade. Not since he came home. His friend Jeremy Loring arrived this afternoon as a guest, but now I wish I hadn't invited him. Jeremy got Pop out alive from Pristina. Got some ex-Marines to break him out of Krasniqi's prison and hired a lorry driver to smuggle him to Trieste."

He halted and turned so fast that Elira had to jump, cat like, to avoid running into him.

"As soon as Pop saw Jeremy, he asked for his microscope—the microscope they gave him to identify cells with. Cells from their pubic hair. Cells from their spit. Urine. Shit."

James was crying now, hot tears that scalded his cheeks, snot streaming from his nose into his mouth. It angered him, this show of emotion.

"He's sitting in Jeremy's hotel room looking at the same slides he uses to teach biology. Jeremy has offered to stay, but how can I leave him? How can I go on my honeymoon while Pop relives the torture Krasniqi put him through?"

"James." Elira's hoarse voice made him want to smash his fist into the nearby brick wall. "James, it's not Mirjeta's fault. She isn't to blame for what her uncle did to your father."

His gaze broke before hers did.

"I know that," he said, his own voice hoarse. "I know that," he said again in a weaker voice and covered his face with both hands.

He thought that she'd take his hands and force him to look at her; instead, when she spoke, it was from a distance of fifteen feet and the shadows.

"I envy her, do you know that?" She paused but went on before he could answer. "She told me once that she refused to be like the Krasniqis. And in that moment, I hated her."

Elira swiveled her face toward him; her eerie eyes shone from the darkness that enshrouded her. "Because, you see, I hadn't."

She paused again, her hand flitting to her chest before dropping to her side. "I envy her for being able to leave her past where it belongs. I envy her for not letting her blood define who she is. I envy her for you." Her voice had grown rougher as she spoke until it broke on *you*.

"Do you love her?" Before he could answer, she said, "Forgive her blood, James." Even as she spoke, she faded into the night.

James blinked and realized that he stood on the sidewalk before his building. After a moment, he shook his head to clear it before climbing the front steps.

Blocks behind them, Dr. Aconcio stepped from the black shadows of the alley that James had wandered into, his gaze turned in the direction that his quarry had taken. He raised his hand and licked the blood from his fingers one by one, smiling as he did.

WHEN JAMES AND MIRJETA returned from their honeymoon in Hawaii two weeks later, they found Dr. Goodman drinking coffee with Jeremy at James's old apartment. Something twisted in James's chest, and he had to hurry into the kitchen for a mug before he said something that he regretted.

His father had spent the first three days of their honeymoon evaluating the same slides over and over, shaking his head and muttering that he couldn't isolate the pathogen that infected humanity. James hadn't known this, of course, until the crisis had passed; Jeremy had kept the truth from him, offering excuses about his father's whereabouts each time that he'd called.

The four of them sat and chatted about Hawaii while watching Mirjeta's slideshow of photos. James watched Dr. Goodman more than the slideshow, but he caught nothing, not even a shadow, in his father's face.

Later, when he and Jeremy had a chance to talk, Jeremy warned that it was best to let sleeping dogs lie. So James shook his father's hand, slammed his car door shut, and waved him off, all the while hoping that the heaviness in his chest wasn't foreboding.

Several days passed, and the heaviness turned into fatigue and aches. James began to wonder if he'd picked something up in Hawaii or on the airplane. Traveling was notorious for spreading illness. A slight headache had settled between his eyes when Mirjeta laid a hand on his forearm.

"James."

He couldn't look at her. The sunlight through the window behind her hurt his eyes. "Yes."

Placing her hands on his face, she turned him until he did look at her. "I love you."

For a moment, the headache and body aches lifted. Pulling her into his embrace, James nuzzled the side of her neck and inhaled. Laughing a little, he drew back. "I'd forgotten."

"Did you forget that you love me?"

He studied her face, the lines already growing in the corners of her eyes, the dark brown mole on her neck, the slight dent in the tip of her nose. "Never."

"Your father will be okay. I have faith." She took a deep breath. "You must too."

He wanted to reassure her, but he couldn't. Instead, he buried himself in the mound of work awaiting him, including reviewing his testimony for Duka's indictment, still six months off.

Later that week, he found himself outside Jink & Diddle without a clear memory of how he got there. On the door, a flyer announced the latest lecture on Blood Law Theology, "Islam: A Return to the Original Blood Law."

When he entered the café, a faint stench as of rotting meat permeated the air. James frowned. Stryver hardly acknowledged him, seemingly wrapped up in the young woman from the previous talk, although James was quite certain that his adversary was aware of his presence.

He observed them from the back of the gathering while rubbing his suddenly throbbing temples. Unlike Elira, Stryver's new plaything showed little resentment of her bondage, only brandishing metaphoric claws when anyone or anything appeared to threaten Stryver or his attention toward her.

Neither Elira nor Zophie attended.

As usual, Stryver began with a provocative statement. "If Christianity's a virus, Islam's a fever, raging first in those shut out during the ancient Christian power struggles. Just picture it: six hundred years after Christ, when all of Asia Minor and North Africa had lost the Christology debates, the Byzantines and the Persians tore at each other while the Plague of Justinian killed millions.

"Into this dismal setting came Mohammed, a merchant and shepherd from the backwater of Mecca on the even more dismal Arabian Peninsula. He knew the Torah and the *Mishnah*, part of the Jewish oral tradition. He knew Christianity. He went into a cave to pray and lo, the angel Gabriel appeared to tell him how to rule on the legal debate about Christ's nature.

"That's right children. Islam is a Christian heresy that sprang up outside the Church's authority among pagan tribes who lived in near-constant warfare. Then it burned through the ancient world. Its followers conquered all of the exhausted Persian Empire and half of the Byzantine in just a few centuries."

Stryver looked around the room, appearing to gauge understanding. "Nice huh? Mohammed co-opted another culture's religious narrative and claimed the last word. Spin doctoring at its finest.

"According to Mohammed, Christ isn't divine nor did he pay humanity's blood debt. Christ was simply one in a long line of prophets starting with Abraham and ending with Mohammed, natch. I don't need to say it, but I will: humanity still owes the big-guy-in-the-sky blood. Allah is merciful, but He insists that we submit to the Old Blood Law at sword point.

"Christianity teaches that 'there is neither Jew nor Greek, slave nor free, male nor female, for you are all one in Christ Jesus.' Islam divides the world into two: Darul Islam, the land of believers, and Darul Harb, the land of war. It goes without saying that *we* live in Darul Harb."

Again, Stryver's gaze roamed around his students, whose puzzled faces suggested that they were digesting this unfamiliar description. "Ever wonder why Allah can't be represented? So it's easy to forget Him. No need to keep Him front and center when the rules are clearly defined.

"Mohammed gave power and authority back to Darul Islam to collect the blood owed to Allah. All those who live in Darul Harb must submit. In fact, the quickest way to Paradise for those in Darul Islam is to collect blood from those in Darul Harb. Christians and Jews, however, can never repay the blood they owe for their disbelief, in this world or the next.

"The question this leaves us with is"—Stryver's gaze settled on him, and the headache peaked so that James had to squint—"are you ready to live in a world not dominated by Blood Law Theology and a blood-obsessed deity? Do you owe blood? Does anyone owe you blood? Are you willing to forget all of that debt?"

Images ping-ponged around his aching head: Elira swathed in foggy moonlight, his father muttering and swapping old slides under a compound microscope, grainy photos of Krasniqi shot with a high-powered telephoto lens.

A railroad spike of pain staked him between the eyes, erasing all coherent thought. He stood up, vaguely aware that the dreadlocked young man from his first lecture had also stood up, but he waved him back.

Blindly, he stumbled from the room, barely making the stairs before he vomited. He leaned against the wall, panting, weak and shaky. He shouldn't have come. He should be at home under Mirjeta's loving care.

Fourteen

ON SCREEN AT THE ATLANTA CONVENTION CENTER, four Talib men, their heads and faces covered by scarves, stood above and behind a Christian man, his arms bound behind his back, lying on dusty ground. One of the Talib held a gun. As the video played, English subtitles appeared.

"Victim: For God's sake, I have children (he repeats this sentence many times). I serve your religion. I serve you, my dear brother, ask me first. Let me speak then kill me. Ask me once. I serve you. I have children."

While the second raised a piece of paper, the third Talib came forward and set his foot on the Christian's head on the ground as he struggled to rise and speak. The Talib gunman came forward to stand on his feet. The Talib holding the paper began to read. As he read, the Christian kept imploring them to listen to him.

"In the name of Allah, Peace be on the Leader of all human beings, and the high priest of all holy warriors, Mohammad. Peace be upon him. All praise be to our Creator, Almighty God, who helped and blessed the Holy Warriors of the Alfateh Movement.

"The Holy Warriors of Qenahat belonged to the Afghanistan Islamic Emirates, so we can implement the commandment of Allah on this infidel whose name is Abdul Latif from the Zefareh village of the Enjeel District of Ancient Herat Province, so that he is punished according to his wrong deed. He is punished according to the commandment of Allah as a warning to other infidels.

"(from the Quran) Holy and Almighty Allah says, 'You who joined with pagans, cut their head.' (You are sentenced to be beheaded.) (from the Hadith:) Mohammad (peace be upon him) says, whoever changes his religion, should be executed."

At 1:05 in the video, the third Talib lifted the Christian off the ground, his head disappearing from the camera's view.

The second Talib continued speaking. "Praise and peace ... Allahu Akbar, Allahu Akbar, Allahu Akbar (God is great)."

The Christian, his bare feet bound at the ankles with a red cloth, struggled. He continued pleading, his voice muffled now as the third disguised man pulled his head back to expose his throat.

"Victim: I ate your leftovers, please leave me. I ate your leftovers, please leave me."

At 1:14, blood spurted onto the white sand. Shots rang out as all of the Talib began praising Allah in frantic, almost ecstatic voices. "Allahu Akbar, Allahu Akbar, Allahu Akbar!"

By 1:30, the Christian's head flopped while the Talib butcher sawed through his neck.

"Come to this side."

"Why didn't you behead him from the backside?"

Bright red blood covered the sandy ground under the Christian's shoulders. By 1:58, the Talib had hacked the head from the dead man's body.

"Bring the notice (execution order) and hang it on the wall. Allahu Akbar, Allahu Akbar."

At 2:03, a Talib turned the headless corpse over onto its back so that the Talib holding the head could drop it onto the chest.

All the Taliban again shouted, "Allahu Akbar, Allahu Akbar!"

"Glory and honor to Allah, His messenger, and all believers (Muslims)."

The Talib with the knife swiped it several times on the dead man's clothes. "This is the infidel. This is the infidel."

The video ended at 2:40 as a Talib, holding a bundle of bright orange rope, knelt and adjusted the corpse's legs. After the video finished, the silence in the convention center held the weight of the crypt. Loretta, her stomach cramping, clutched the podium's sides with shaking fingers, and took a deep breath.

She burned. Lord, did she burn. All she could see was Sawyer's naked and headless corpse.

He'd been dragged behind a commandeered Humvee for more than five miles.

Even though the undertaker had washed what was left of him, grains of sand had embedded into his skin, turning it into sandpaper. His head, when it was found, looked like a liquefying cantaloupe and smelled like roadkill despite all the embalming fluids.

Sylvia came and stood beside her, wrapping an arm around her waist. Loretta swallowed the bitterness and fixed her gaze on the women huddled in the rows of chairs before her.

"I have seen worse—far, far worse. I have seen a Muslim boy of twelve behead a Christian man while his father and uncles urged him on. Can you imagine a world where boys become men by slaughtering another man like a cow?"

She paused, feeling their anguish roll over her. One woman wept into a scarf bunched before her face.

"Make no mistake, Sisters. This is Satan's work. Oh, there will be those who preach tolerance in the name of Christianity. Turn the other cheek, they'll say. There will be those who will try to shame us by mentioning the Crusades almost a thousand years ago.

"There will be those who justify this evil by screaming about how we treated Native Americans and black slaves. We're no better, they'll say, so how can we judge? I say we can judge because God tells us to judge!

"We're mothers. We know that one child cannot justify wrongdoing by pointing the finger at his brother and shrieking, 'He did it first! He did it worst!'"

She paused again, again studying the women before her. Most sat erect now, their faces pale but resolved.

"No, we reject that reasoning, just as we must reject those who try to turn us from our Christian duty. Islam is the enemy. We must bring this evil to light. We must be like the prophets. We must raise our voices even when people reject and revile us. We must shout out to the world that the blood of Christian martyrs cries out for justice."

Loretta lifted her voice and shouted, "Justice! Do you hear me? Justice! For every single Christian whose blood soaks the desert of Iraq or the mountains of Afghanistan."

The women sat stunned.

And then Sylvia stepped forward, her free fist pumping. "Code Red! Code Red!"

Throughout the convention center, women rose up, their fists waving.

MIRJETA STEPPED UP ONTO the sagging porch of the two-family Victorian that she hadn't visited in nearly a year, hiked the strap of her violin case higher onto her shoulder, took a breath, and reached for the door to Jink & Diddle. Before she could open it, it swung open. Elira stood, waiting.

Mirjeta, startled even though she'd set out to see Elira, found herself shaking a little. Although Elira's icy-gray eyes had stopped haunting her months ago, she knew what Elira was. Gripping the handle on her case, she fingered the St. Michael medal hanging around her neck, murmured, "*Non timebo mala,*" and stepped past Elira into the bookstore.

Elira's lips quirked, but she remained somber. "Evil's not here right now. I'll let you know if he returns, though, and we'll both get out."

Mirjeta shot Elira a wobbly look and rubbed the medal. "Maybe you shouldn't let him in," she said, her voice almost cracking.

Elira turned away but not before Mirjeta saw a storm cloud churn over her face. She thought she saw fear before the other woman wiped everything from her features and began walking toward the café.

"I'm not sure I have any choice. You know what they say about lying down with dogs."

"No, actually, I don't." Mirjeta stopped. "That's an idiom I haven't heard."

Elira threw a cold smile over her shoulder. "You get up with fleas." She headed back behind the espresso bar and began pulling cups off a shelf.

Mirjeta watched her. There was something different about Elira, but she wasn't sure what. She'd always been deathly white, but she'd been as cut as any fitness model and radiated a feral energy. It had been a terrifying testament to otherworldly strength. Today, she looked emaciated and ill.

"Why are you here?" asked Elira. The cup and saucer that she held rattled until she set it down.

"I find I owe you thanks again." Mirjeta set her violin on the floor in front of the bar. "James confessed he'd started to let his lingering anger against my uncle poison his feelings for me. He says you told him to forgive my blood."

Elira paused in what she was doing and looked at her. "I take it he did, or you wouldn't be here."

Mirjeta nodded and accepted an espresso. "I'm curious why you didn't argue that my uncle owes blood for me. He tried to kidnap me."

Elira ignored her own espresso to grab a chocolate from the tray on the bar. She shrugged. "I could even have told him why your uncle hunts you." She looked up again. "Have *you?*"

Mirjeta looked away. "No. Not yet. And you know why."

Elira ate the candy, nodding. "I'm going to train you in an Israeli self-defense program called Krav Maga."

Mirjeta blinked, taken aback. "What?" Before Elira could answer, she found herself asking, "Why?"

"Now it's my turn: you know why." She held Mirjeta's gaze.

After a moment, Mirjeta nodded. "What can I do for you in return?"

Elira blinked several times before barking out a laugh. "That, *motër të vogël*, is the heart of the problem, isn't it? *Quid pro quo, tit for tat.* Blood for blood. Let me do this for you with nothing in return."

At Elira's *little sister*, Mirjeta stepped forward and laid her hand on Elira's forearm. She kept it there despite the chill of Elira's skin.

"Then let us play together. The sign outside says *seisúns*. What instrument do you play?"

Elira didn't speak for a moment, just stared at Mirjeta's fingers. Then she cleared her throat and looked up. "The fiddle."

Mirjeta laughed, a sound that got a little away from her when she realized that she *could* laugh in Elira's presence—at something Elira had said. She slipped her hand around Elira's and, bending down to pick up her case, led her through the bookstore and to the stairs. James had told her about a large room on the second floor with comfortable seats, music stands, and instruments.

Elira said nothing as she followed, but when they arrived, she went to a case and took out a fiddle whose finish suggested an antique. They rosined their bows and tuned their strings without speaking. When they'd finished, Elira narrowed her eyes, and Mirjeta realized that they stood in mirror opposition to one another. Anxiety bubbled in her stomach, but she squelched it.

"I know something about fiddling. It's mostly taught by ear, which means you have an advantage over me." She paused and breathed, realizing that she'd been holding her breath even as she spoke.

Elira considered this. A slow smile lit her features. "Do you mean that I have a musical skill that exceeds yours?"

For a moment, Mirjeta didn't understand the happy light in Elira's eyes. Then comprehension dawned. "Yes."

Elira continued grinning for several long seconds before tipping her head. "Then I suggest you teach me something first."

Mirjeta nodded back even as she searched her memorized repertoire. She'd gone through several ideas, lightly stroking various measures over the strings, when the appropriate piece started playing itself: David's version of Queen's *Who Wants to Live Forever*.

Closing her eyes, she gave herself over to playing it. She heard Elira breathing as she circled around her, felt Elira's gaze on her fingers, and then she dissolved into the haunting melody. As the aching sweetness the music had drawn from her dissipated into stillness, the sound of weeping replaced it.

Dropping her bow, Mirjeta turned toward the corner where Elira leaned while grasping her fiddle by its neck and covering her face with her bow hand. Mirjeta began to sing softly.

When her weeping had subsided, Elira put her bow on her strings and began to pick out the melody. Mirjeta, stepping closer, began to play again. Together, they spent the afternoon playing until Elira had learned the piece by heart.

Later, after Mirjeta had gone, Elira stood staring out the window, caught somewhere between conscious thinking and an awareness of how sore her chest was. Absently, she rubbed at her scar.

"There you are, my dear. I knew that I would catch you sometime."

Elira started and whirled around. She hissed, baring her teeth. She longed for truly terrifying incisors, not these only-too-human ones. "I'm done with you, old man. You'll get nothing more from me. Our partnership is dissolved."

Dr. Aconcio stood nearly obscured in the late afternoon sunlight streaming across the room. For a wild moment, Elira thought he was the angel of death.

And then he laughed. "Tsk, tsk, my dear. You know better than that. You may have stopped wearing your relic. You have apparently stopped taking blood except for whatever your junior associates freely give you, which as we both know is not at all the same."

He stepped farther into the room, halting in the middle out of the light. He held his cane under the head, waving it like a baton.

She wasn't fooled. He could launch himself on her in an instant.

"If I had a heart, it would be swooning at your chances. Will she save her beloved this time?" He swung his head and sighed. "Ah, the passions of youth. Misspent, all of them. But will you listen?"

The sun dipped below the horizon, and he was nuzzling her neck, his cane holding her hair away from the rapid beating just under the surface of her skin. His fetid breath made her want to choke and struggle, but she wouldn't give him that satisfaction.

"No, Elira, we are far from done. Go and play out your noble drama. 'All the world's a stage and all the men and women merely players. They have their exits and their entrances,' eh?"

He paused to press a soft kiss onto her neck. "When you come home, your thirst for justice will be stronger than ever."

The room slipped into darkness, and he was gone.

Elira shivered. Thin though it was, James Goodman's blood still warmed her heart.

THAT NIGHT, ELIRA SLIPPED out of Jink & Diddle and crossed to Porter Square where a car waited for her. She knew that Dr. Aconcio had seen her leave, but she also knew that he wouldn't follow her. If he had had any idea where she was going, he would never have let her go.

One of her junior law associates drove the three and a half hours to Our Lady of Shkodra Church in Hartsdale, New York, a neat hamlet in Westchester County. Elira stood for a long time in the street gazing at the modern, red-brick building illuminated in the dark of midnight.

Built in 1968, Our Lady of Shkodra lacked an appropriately gothic aesthetic. But its architecture resembled the existing Catholic churches in Shkodër, providing a visual link to her homeland. Still, she hesitated. Her chest, sore earlier, ached and itched and burned. She rubbed and rubbed, but nothing eased it.

A gust of wind blew and subsided. It picked up again as she stood there, uncertain. The wind carried distant voices. Elira pivoted, but she couldn't discern from which direction the voices came.

The wind settled, leaving her uneasy. Screwing her courage to the sticking place as Lady Macbeth had urged her wishy-washy husband, she took a step. The wind immediately picked up again.

She faltered. It stopped.

Shaking her head and muttering, she rushed forward. And the wind roared into a veritable maelstrom, buffeting her efforts to make the top of the stairs. But as she crested them, the wind currents separated into voices, this time all around her. Petrified as a swirling mist engulfed her, Elira clapped her hands over her ears and fell to her knees, hard.

Overhead, the stars disappeared.

The voices flowed over and around her, lifting her hands away from her ears. Elira, who'd closed her eyes, opened them to find herself in the heart of an aurora borealis. She began to pick out groups of voices now, baritones and basses, tenors and countertenors, altos and sopranos. All at once she understood the parts and their complementary colors: phosphorescent glowing of green, purple, aquamarine, and blue. Her chest throbbed in sympathetic union with the voices. Distinct words formed and penetrated her very heart.

"And all flesh shall see it together" sang each section of the heavenly choir, each instance popping around her while tendrils of light caressed her.

The studs over her eyebrow popped out; the ring in her upper lip dropped to the pavement. Handel's "And the Glory of the Lord" from his oratorio *Messiah* wove joyfully around her, beginning as a dance until its cadence slowed to a dramatic finale. As the sections segued into "for the mouth of the Lord hath spoken it," warmth began in the scar over her breast, rising until she felt branded.

And then she stood before the church entrance, the night silent and dark around her.

"You clean up real well."

Elira spun.

Off to her left, closer to the bell tower, the White Goth Girl stood, so brightly luminous that she had no hard edge. She stepped closer and raised a hand to trace over Elira's brow and upper lip.

Then she tapped a forefinger against her pursed lips, squinting as she studied Elira. "Hm. You're missing something." Zophiel smiled, making half-moons of her eyes. "Here, how about your sister's crucifix? Eh?" She dangled the pendant over them.

As Elira bowed to receive it, she saw dark lettering over her breast.

"What does it say, Zophie?" Her own tone surprised—and yet didn't surprise—her.

Zophiel sketched over the words. "*Vincit qui se vincit. He conquers who conquers himself.*" She beamed. "Michael let me pick it myself. I think it complements the MacNeil motto very well."

Her face grew somber. She held her palm up. “Give it to me. I’ll see that it is buried in sanctified ground under the altar.”

Elira, her throat suddenly parched, swallowed. To part forever with Gjergj’s finger bone was nearly unimaginable. But there was just enough imagination left in her to guide her to the leather pouch in her jacket.

Zophiel accepted the relic before whisking it into a pocket of her dress. Then she leaned over and kissed Elira, who was suddenly aware that the White Goth Girl towered over her, on the forehead.

“Go in peace,” said Zophiel.

Fifteen

HUNCHED OVER THE POLISHED BAR of Flaherty's Irish Pub nursing a shot of 21-year-old Lagavulin, James ignored the raw, wet March evening outside.

Mirjeta—37-weeks pregnant and suffering from an aching back, Braxton-Hicks contractions, and a bladder the size of an eyedropper—waited at their apartment. Waited to hear how Ismail Duka's pre-trial hearing had gone, the one where his high-powered lawyer in an expensive Italian suit had papered the bench with motions designed only to slow down the proceedings. Motions that argued that the federal prosecutor was selectively prosecuting Duka in violation of the due process and equal protection clauses of the Fourteenth Amendment. That in fact he'd unfairly targeted a "discrete and insular minority" when he'd indicted Duka on thirteen counts of kidnapping, human trafficking, money laundering, gun running, and selling narcotics. As if being Albanian Muslim should earn Duka a Get-Out-Of-Jail-Free card.

James tossed the remainder of his Scotch, relishing the burn down his throat. It almost dispersed the bitter tang that rose every time he thought about the Krasniqis. His Walther PPK dug into his side, reminding him of other options.

"Shouldn't you be at home right now?"

The husky voice at his ear sent his pulse racing. It shouldn't, but it did. He'd done his best to avoid her over the past nine months, but today he'd found himself at one of her favorite haunts. He gripped his empty tumbler and turned to face Elira, who leaned against the bar at his side.

"After the day I've had, I thought it best to stop here first." He waved at the bartender, who came over with the Lagavulin.

Elira nodded for her own shot and waited until the bartender had left before sitting.

"Duka's pre-trial hearing?" When he grunted, she continued, "He's not the only Krasniqi you've got in custody."

James eyed her. "No. But he's the only one with a lawyer who's not dealing."

She grabbed her shot and sipped. She didn't look at him. "Does it really matter? I heard on the news the Krasniqi finance team has sold out the American branch of the operation. It's only a matter of time before you can extradite Mirjeta's uncle and put him on trial here in the U.S."

"What the hell! Listen to you. You know as well as I do he's still snatching girls in Eastern Europe and selling heroin in the U.S. The longer he's free, the greater his chances at eluding us altogether. If Duka's lawyer is any sign of the caliber of lawyer he's hiring, we're never going to see him in a U.S. prison."

"Really? The lawyer's that good?" Elira studied him.

James held her gaze, searching, but her opaque eyes gave away nothing. He leaned close enough to smell the Lagavulin on her breath. "Don't you know? Hm, Elira?"

When she didn't answer, he said, "Did you know that Mirjeta met Aconcio that first day she came to Jink & Diddle? He's hard to forget, apparently."

Elira dropped her gaze first. "No."

"Why, Elira? Why would Duka's defense attorney visit you?"

She didn't answer.

"Is it because Imam Krasniqi wanted to silence him? Were you hired to kill Duka by Krasniqi?"

Elira whirled and grabbed him by the throat so fast that James saw stars as he choked. "Get this straight, Agent Goodman. Any Krasniqi blood I took went to repay blood owed to *me*."

She let him go. James fell back, panting and bruised, against the bar. She returned to her Scotch.

"Tell me. Would you kill for Mirjeta's uncle?" At his expression, she narrowed her eyes. "I didn't think so."

James swallowed the last of his Scotch and exhaled. "Just what *is* your relationship to Aconcio? Did you know he filed a motion to suppress your testimony of Mirjeta's kidnapping?"

"No, but I'm not surprised." She paused and studied him again. "Look, Aconcio and I go way back. We've been law partners in a manner of speaking."

"Meaning what? Did he feed you information or did you steal it from him?"

She turned back to the bar and her drink.

He studied her profile. She'd changed since his wedding, and he suspected that the changes went deeper than her now more-conservative dress. Even though she still looked like a hip-hip pixie, her black tees and jeans hid most of her pallid and tattooed skin. She hadn't tamed her crazy hair, and she still had scars, but she had stopped wearing eyebrow studs and a lip ring. More striking, she seemed subdued despite the flare of anger a moment before.

"I paid him." Her voice was so low that he almost didn't hear her.

"Paid him?" James sat, stunned. "That's unethical! He can be disbarred for giving you information about his client."

"He didn't represent Duka at the time."

"But he must have represented a Krasniqi." He thought about the Krasniqi brothers and his suspicions about Elira. "Imam Krasniqi?"

"Yes." She tilted her head and looked at him. "Did you receive any helpful information that led you to intercept Duka and the others the night Mirjeta was kidnapped?" At his nod, she said, "Aconcio had a duty to prevent Krasniqi from committing a crime. He didn't shut his door when he reported it. I just happened to be outside in the hallway."

"Ah. Nice arrangement. For you."

She shrugged, but her shoulders remained hunched afterwards. "We're through."

"Since we're clearing the air, what about the Krasniqi brothers?"

"What about them?" Elira waved to the bartender to refill her whisky.

"You get enough details from that phone call?"

She looked over her shoulder at him. "Enough. Enough to dig around in the right places. ICE certainly profited by my sleuthing, wouldn't you say, Agent Goodman? All Souls mean anything to your investigation?"

"Which is why I kept your name out of all this, *Ms. Dukagjini*," he said through clenched teeth. "Why you bothered to tell me how to find the Krasniqi brothers is anybody's guess, but let's be clear. The same person who killed Jak and Zamir left behind blood evidence at the halfway house."

Elira rolled around and leaned on the bar. "And who would that be?"

James felt his anger boil out of control. He grabbed her elbow. "Ha, ha."

Behind them, the bartender cleared his throat. James peered up at a scowl and then removed his hand from Elira. He wiped it down his face and picked up his Scotch.

After the other man left, he asked, "When did you stop using?"

She studied him but didn't dodge the question. "Last February."

"After Jak and Zamir?" he asked quietly.

"Yes."

"Stryver supply you?"

She barked a laugh. "Not hardly. He always complained it dulled my appetites."

"That it? I always got the feeling you two played some cat-and-mouse game over me."

She raised her tumbler in a mock toast. "Oh, we did."

He leaned close and lowered his voice. "Is that why you left him?"

He felt his heartbeat accelerate. She still smelled like something wild and free, but a dark aroma, an earthy decay, underlay the heather scent. It both repulsed and attracted him. Shaking his head, he sat back.

"Among other reasons."

"So, which of you won?"

This time when she studied him, James couldn't return her gaze.

"That remains to be seen." When she put cold fingers on his forearm, he knew that she felt his erratic pulse. "You haven't gone to any more of his Acephela lectures, have you?"

"Not since last June. But I had the Cambridge PD watch Jink & Diddle while he was holding classes there. I thought he was dealing. And I was worried he had a thing for little girls like your friend Zophie." He paused. "He and his girlfriend went backpacking through Eastern Europe last I heard."

"You met Zophie?" Elira's voice sounded strangled. Her hand came to her breast, to the spot where two years before she'd taken a knife for Mirjeta.

James studied her, but her features were unreadable.

"I met her last spring before you returned from wherever you were wandering. She sat in on one of Stryver's lectures, but I haven't seen her since."

"How did he react to Zophie?" she asked in a faint voice.

"He ignored her for most of the lecture, but then she spoke to him. You should've seen him. He couldn't look her in the eyes. I never would've guessed a little girl could make him cower."

Elira gripped his forearm. "Stryver's back. Stay away from him, James. He gathers students like Charles Manson made a family. He's a predator who knows where your weakness is, and he'll find a way to exploit it, trust me."

Although something in her voice sent an ice cube sliding down his throat, James scoffed. "What? He's going to force me to sit through one of his grandiose lessons? And then what?"

Elira shook her head and said nothing. She returned to her drink, which she tossed back. James watched the muscles in her neck undulate. He had an urge to kiss them.

"Elira, what did Stryver do to you?" When she didn't answer, he said, "Let it go. He's out of your life."

When she looked at him, sadness radiated from her expression. "Is he? Sometimes I believe it. Other times, I feel him inside me, inside my head. And then I think it's only a matter of time before I'm his again."

"Listen to me. Forget Stryver." He paused. It had taken him this long to confront her about Jak and Zamir. The next wouldn't be easy to say.

"That blood evidence linking the murders of the Krasniqi brothers?" At her nod, he went on. "It contained an unknown virus."

Her eyes grew more wetly opaque, if possible. "Only goes to show how incompetent pathologists are."

"Please. Just do me a favor." He reached for the index card that he'd carried around in his breast pocket for months. "Let the CDC run some tests on you."

"Maybe I'm a Typhoid Mary."

"Maybe." He held the card out. "Doctor Wade Alston is a former student of my dad's. He's an expert in identifying viruses. I sent him the results of the analysis our forensics lab did, but he needs more blood to run different tests. Plus, he would like to examine you, take a history, that sort of thing."

"Are you afraid I gave it to Mirjeta and the baby?" she asked, no longer looking at him.

"I already asked Dr. Alston to test all of us, including Cruncher." He paused and watched her closely. "That's the funny thing. He found markers for a similar virus in our cardiopulmonary system, but it doesn't appear to cause any symptoms."

"Ah." Before she looked away, James caught the glisten of her eyes. "Tell me, Agent Goodman, will Duka be prosecuted for those murders he committed while trying to escape?"

"After he's tried on the other charges, he'll be arraigned. But the federal prosecutor is already talking a deal with him to get more information about how the Krasniqi mafia operates internationally."

"Then let *me* make a deal with *you*." When she looked at him again, her gaze had honed into twin icy points. "I'll go to Atlanta. Just promise me you'll stay away from Stryver. And don't ever let your guard down where Mirjeta's concerned. Krasniqi will never stop hunting her. This past year has been the eye of the storm."

AFTER ELIRA LEFT, JAMES returned to brooding. It didn't last long.

"Buy me a drink? I've had a terrible day, and you look like just the person to commiserate with."

James looked up to see a statuesque blonde sitting next to him at the bar. There was something familiar about her, despite the fact that he'd never seen her before. She wore a white-leather trench coat and pince-nez sunglasses, reminding him of a popular science-fiction movie from a decade before. Her long white-blond hair fell in a rope-like braid down her back. She exuded a clean scent like rain on mown grass.

"Sorry, I'm not in the habit of buying women I don't know drinks."

She pulled her sunglasses off and stared at him. "You know me."

James felt his jaw drop. "Zophie!" He sat for several moments unable to take in the changes in her. "Wow! You've grown a lot since I last saw you. You're as tall as I am. But are you old enough to drink?"

Zophie looked over her sunglasses at him. "Yes."

James blinked and then signaled the bartender, who came and took Zophie's order for a Guinness.

"So, what happened today?"

Her eyes clouded. "My ward Hitch loves to hear his own voice so much he can't hear or see me at all. I keep trying to reach him, but it's like he's got atherosclerosis of the soul. It's made him deaf and blind. Time's running out, too. He's got esophageal cancer just like his father."

James tried to make heads or tails out of Zophie's words, but he couldn't. The best he could figure was that someone she looked after was dying and was too hardhearted to mend fences.

"Sorry to hear that."

And he was. Sorrow weighed him down. This was just one more piece of evidence that life sucked. Court and trials were just a game, a show. Krasniqi had tortured his father and short of sacrificing his life to pursue revenge, there was nothing James could do to balance the scales. While he played by the rules, the Krasniqis hadn't. And wouldn't. Meanwhile, life went on, the world filled with indifferent or unreliable people as likely to let him down as they were to take care of their own. What had ever possessed him and Mirjeta to have a baby?

"But enough about my troubles." Zophie's voice intruded on his internal litany. "There's always hope, at least when you choose to believe there is. Michael has hope in me. That's why I'm here." She beamed.

He glanced at her. "What does that mean?"

Zophie's tinkling laugh contrasted with the dull roar from the bar behind them, which had filled up since he'd arrived.

"Elira asked me almost the same question once. Here, pick one."

While James had been lost in reverie, she'd gathered a row of filled tumblers. She slid them one at a time down the bar toward him.

"What are they?"

"Ever see *The Matrix*? Loved it. Michael chides me all the time, but what can I say? Movies, books, plays—the best ones are so illuminating."

She picked up the drink nearest to her. It was filled with a reddish liquid. When she spoke, she sounded like Laurence Fishburne as Morpheus. "This is your last chance. After this, there is no turning back. You drink the red drink, you stay in Wonderland, and I show you how deep the rabbit hole goes."

She picked up the middle glass. "You drink the blue one, the story ends. You wake up in your bed and believe whatever you want to believe."

She reached for the last tumbler. "This one is NyQuil. It's for the cold you're going to get after walking home in the rain without an umbrella." She laughed again. "All I'm offering is the truth. Nothing more."

James held her gaze for several moments. "Okay, I'll play."

He picked up the reddish liquid but didn't drink from it. "*The Matrix* is just pop philosophy for the masses. It makes us consider what the nature of reality is and how we look at the world."

He held the drink up, swirling it. "Wonderland. What really lies beneath our everyday perception. A place with its own laws populated with animals and people who don't match up to our constructs for reality and rationality. It's both terrifying and exhilarating."

Zophie nodded. "Alice and Neo wander until they realize they have the power to change their perceptions. Then they can use that power to their advantage."

"Because the underlying law of Wonderland is that they can write and rewrite its laws." James realized that he felt better already. Perhaps ridiculous philosophical bar talk had been the key all along.

He picked up the blue liquid. Curacao? "Ah. Morpheus's escape clause. The unquestioning acceptance of reality despite the splinter in Neo's mind driving him mad."

"A popular drink. Then again, not everyone is bothered by splinters."

"Or they don't have Morpheus guiding them with unerring faith."

"Oh, guides are everywhere. But only those with ears hear."

James wrapped his hand around the NyQuil and ran his thumb over the tumbler's rim. "This I don't get. Morpheus only offered Neo two choices. Truth or willful ignorance."

Zophie laid a hand on his, sending a shock through him. "It's not really a third choice so much as a chaser for the blue drink. It's for those who believe the splinter is a delusion."

James thought about this. He looked over at Zophie, whose *pince-nez* hid her eyes. "Let me guess. They spend their days measuring and marking the boundaries of the Matrix."

"Ignoring Morpheus and collaborating with Agent Smith, who hates humanity."

Zophie's words were still ringing in James's ears when a familiar but unwelcome voice pierced his contemplation.

"If it isn't James, my prize pupil."

James swiveled to look at Jacob Stryver. His mood soured at seeing the foxy beard and glittering brown eyes. An unpleasant smell clung to Stryver, but James couldn't identify it.

"Stryver." He nodded but didn't invite Stryver to sit.

Stryver grinned and sat. "Your girlfriend left you."

"My *wife's* at home," James said through gritted teeth. "I was just chatting with Zophie."

Stryver looked puzzled. "Zophie? I was referring to Elira. I saw her talking to you."

James shot a glance over his shoulder, but the barstool was empty. He looked back at the other man. "What do you want, Stryver?"

"Nothing. Just saw you here and thought I'd say hi." Stryver sipped from his pint glass.

"How's it been going? I miss our repartee. I just got back from hiking through some very back-of-beyond places. Makes you appreciate the finer aspects of American life, including intellectual discourse and decent coffee."

James sighed. "Look, I've had a bad day, and I've already been here too long. I should go."

"Did Elira tell you to avoid me?" Stryver must have seen something in his face because he went on. "Come now. What are you afraid of? That I'll redefine some precious paradigm of yours?"

Stryver's sarcastic remark reminded James of his own observation just minutes before. Despite giving him the creeps, Stryver hadn't done anything to deserve rudeness. James signaled for one last drink. A Guinness this time.

"I've had a lot of time to think about your Blood Law Theology. I think you're right. Blood is the common currency that makes the world go 'round."

"Don't sound so depressed, my friend. It doesn't have to be that way."

"You have no idea what I do for a living, do you?"

"Elira never said. Why?"

"Because from where I sit, it looks like there are only two choices. Civil law or blood law. And civil law isn't very effective against blood law."

"There's a third choice." Stryver leaned forward, his expression intent. "Look, you've overlooked a key point. Blood law is part and parcel with religious belief. Once we jettison religion, we recognize this is the only world we've got. There's powerful incentive for humanity to get along. That's what civil law needs. To rely on reason and science, not blood mythology from the dawn of humanity."

James sensed Zophie behind him. He thought he heard her say, "'All these things I will give you....'"

Ignoring her for the moment, he let himself be pulled into the philosophical debate. "This is an old argument. Ever since the birth of modern science in the seventeenth century, philosophers, theologians, and scientists have argued about the existence of God."

"Darwin and his theory of evolution have more to say than philosophers and theologians, don't you think?"

"What? That there's no evidence for God?"

"But plenty of evidence of delusion about God." Stryver set his empty glass down. "You worry about blood law, but the truth is that as science and reason stamp out irrational religious beliefs, blood law has weakened. As my favorite evolutionary psychologist says, the angels of our better nature are winning."

James rubbed his chin, thinking. For some reason, talking to Stryver had deflated the sense of wellbeing that discussing the underlying metaphors of *The Matrix* had given him.

"This is all well and good in theory. But how does it help me live my life? I've still got to investigate and arrest people who don't give a shit about civil law or science. Hell, most of the world lives under blood law."

"True." Stryver's lips curled in a strange, secretive smile. "Pragmatically speaking, you can't change the world overnight. But we live in a Western society where science and reason have a strong foundation. You can speak out, join organizations that promote secular humanism, and raise your children to think logically and rationally."

"So they grow up with faith in science, unencumbered by myth and superstition?"

"Something like that. Listen, you're a smart, educated guy. Leave the Middle Ages and the religious mumbo-jumbo behind. You can believe in morality and the Golden Rule without believing in a Fairy in the Sky who dispenses justice."

"Why can't I believe in both? Why does it have to be either-or?"

"Really, James? You think rational, logical thinking has room for a delusion about a Sky Fairy? I'd say they're mutually exclusive."

James fell silent, drinking his Guinness and thinking about Stryver's smug assertions. Stryver flagged the bartender down for another beer.

"Did you see that Sherlock Holmes movie, the one with Robert Downey, Jr., that came out on Christmas a year ago?" Zophie spoke at his elbow, startling James.

He laughed to himself. A blond Amazon on one shoulder and a dark, foxy man on the other. It was all too much like a cartoon dilemma. He really should get home. Drunken philosophical debates were best left to college students.

But Zophie continued her story before he could get up.

"There's Sherlock, all sure that Mary Marston is stealing Watson from him, so he filters his observations of her through this pre-existing criminal profile he's imagined for her. He deduces that she's a governess of a young boy based on ink spattered on her earlobe. From there, he figures out she's borrowed her diamond necklace from her employer. He sees a tan line on her ring finger and figures out she's been engaged before. Sherlock then adds up all those facts in seconds and concludes that Mary dumped her first fiancé so she could do better by snagging Watson!

"But that's not the best part. The best part is when Mary looks at him and says, 'He died.' Then she tosses her wine over Sherlock!"

Zophie laughed, remembering. Then she sighed. "So smart, that Sherlock, and he still got it wrong. At least he atones for it later."

Shaking her head, she picked up the tumbler with NyQuil and sniffed it. On his other side, Stryver seemed unaware of Zophie's presence. James frowned and shook his head, which had started buzzing. Something wasn't right, but he didn't know what. When the buzzing faded, Mirjeta filled his thoughts. Swiveling, he gave Stryver a hard look.

"You know, Stryver, my wife's fond of idioms. She'd probably say right about now that the road to hell is paved with good scientific intentions."

He finished his Guinness and stood up. "So, let's see. I have to pick between—what did you call it? A Sky Fairy?—and arrogant assholes like you? The ones who think they get to pick the evidence and define the theories? The ones who lack empathy for the little people? That's how to bring about peace on Earth and good will to all men?"

He glanced at Zophie, who was busy pouring the three liquids together into one tumbler. He looked back at Stryver, who frowned. James leaned forward and grabbed the full tumbler. Before he could reconsider what he was doing, he lifted it and downed the concoction. It slid down his throat, thick and sweet. He swallowed, unable to untangle all the flavors but feeling strangely replete and serene. Turning, he slammed the empty glass down in front of Stryver.

"I'm done being your prize pupil, Stryver. But I'm sure you're lining up recruits to take my place."

Without looking back, James strode from Flaherty's into a rainy March evening. He never saw Zophie block Stryver's exit with a hand on his wrist as she refilled the tumbler with Curacao.

"Ignorant bliss?" Stryver accepted it with a mocking smile. "For me or him?"

MIRJETA HAD JUST FINISHED packing her music player into her suitcase when a rap sounded on her apartment door. Frowning, she looked at her watch. Twenty minutes had passed since she'd called James to tell him it was time to go to Boston Medical Center. He'd promised to hurry, but if he didn't show up soon, she was going to have to get herself there. The rap sounded again. Whoever it was had impeccable timing, but she was going to send him away. Grabbing the bag, she dropped it onto the sofa on her way to the apartment door. She pulled it open to see Elira standing there in a black pea coat, her eyes stormy.

"You didn't check the peephole," hissed Elira, stepping inside.

Mirjeta shivered, absently tapping her St. Michael medal. Despite months of shared fiddling sessions and self-defense lessons, she'd never quelled an initial spurt of fear whenever she saw her "big sister."

Shutting the door, she turned to see Elira sitting on the back of the sofa, watching her. For months, Elira had taught her the basics of Krav Maga: targeted attacks of the body's most vulnerable parts, the eyes, the groin, the solar plexus, and the throat. She'd emphasized over and over *ad nauseam* the necessity of maintaining awareness of her surroundings.

For you, escape is the most important, little sister, she'd said.

She'd disappeared the day after Mirjeta told her that she was pregnant, but Mirjeta suspected that Elira kept watch over her whenever she was alone.

"Don't dismiss me. I know what I'm talking about." Elira looked away as she spoke, her voice thickening. "I haven't taken blood in a year, but lust for it gnaws at the marrow of my bones. If anything happens to you, I can't be sure it won't overwhelm me."

Mirjeta tamped her fear down and stepped forward to lay a hand on Elira's forearm. "I'm sorry. I'm just distracted."

Elira narrowed her eyes, studying Mirjeta. Instead of the expected exhortation to never let her guard down for any reason, she said softly, "You're in labor."

"Yes."

"Then I'll wait here until James comes."

"I planned to get a cab if he's not here in ten minutes."

"Then I'll ride with you to the hospital."

Mirjeta sighed. "That's not necessary."

Elira looked away again. "Perhaps not. But I'd like to."

"Okay."

The next contraction hit her, twisting the word as she dropped onto the sofa next to her bag, an arm across her tightening abdomen. When it was done, she glanced up to see Elira on her knees before her, a strange mix of sadness and yearning twisting her scarred and pierced features.

She let out a shaky laugh. "Whew! That's getting a bit hard to take."

Elira nodded and stood up. "I didn't come to berate you. I camc to say good-bye."

"Good-bye?" Mirjeta surprised herself at the alarm in her voice. "Are you leaving for Atlanta?"

Elira pressed her lips together and nodded again. She reached into her coat and withdrew a slim hardback. "I brought you an anthology of Robert Burns's poetry."

Mirjeta opened the volume to a marked page. Scanning the poem, she smiled and began to read aloud.

"'Hale be your heart! Hale be your fiddle! Lang may your elbuck jink and diddle...'"

"'...To cheer you through the weary widdle o' this wild warl','" finished Elira in a heavy Scots brogue, her gaze far away. "Robbie always had a way with words."

"Thank you." Mirjeta closed the book and slid it into her bag.

"Don't do it." Elira's wistfulness had evaporated, and her eyes were glacial. She loomed over Mirjeta on the couch. Mirjeta's pulse skittered and raced. The baby kicked in sympathy.

"Wh-what?" she asked, her lips numb and her tongue clumsy.

"Don't tour this summer."

Mirjeta squeezed the bag's handle, trying to calm down. She licked her lips, but her tongue was sticky-dry. "I'm committed."

"Get out of it. Make up some story about needing to stay home."

"No." Mirjeta's faint refusal charged the air between them. She cleared her throat and sat up.

"No," she said, her voice louder.

"It's not safe." Elira said in a tone no longer hard but desperate.

Mirjeta took one of Elira's icy hands in hers.

"*Motër*," she said, holding Elira's gaze. In that moment, her heartbeat returned to normal. "This isn't the old country. This is the new world. I'm going to do what I can to make sure it stays that way. That means actively promoting peace with those who don't share my beliefs."

Elira broke her gaze and pulled her hand away. She paced around the small living room like a panther in a cage, muttering and rubbing the scar on her breast. "I can't see it. God help me, I can't see beyond blood for blood...."

"It's what my heart tells me to do. Not my blood."

Elira whirled. "What does your blood urge?"

Mirjeta knew another contraction was on its way. She pushed herself up from the sofa, and, clutching the suitcase handle, took a step toward the door.

"My blood? My blood cries for revenge. For me. For my mother." The contraction hit, forcing her words out in a breathless groan. Something gave way deep in her groin, and bloody fluid showered the floor.

After a minute, she looked up. "But my blood doesn't rule me. Your blood doesn't rule you, either."

"Me?" It was a whisper. "I'm a lost cause."

"If that were true, you'd still be taking blood."

Mirjeta laughed, but there was no humor in the sound. A third contraction followed on the heels of her amniotic sac bursting. She doubled over, panting through it. “You and I aren’t so different.”

Where was James? She needed to call a cab.

Elira shook her head as she pulled out her cell phone. “My story doesn’t end well.” She swiped the screen and lifted it to her ear.

Mirjeta stood up as the pain abated. “As the proverb says, ‘God writes straight with crooked lines.’”

Elira’s gaze locked on hers as she spoke into her phone. “Forget the airport. I need you to take me to the hospital. Put on your sirens.”

She dropped the phone into her coat pocket. “I don’t know about that proverb, but at least I can make sure your story ends well.”

Sixteen

TWO WEEKS AFTER THE BIRTH OF HIS NAMESAKE, James was called to testify at Ismail Duka's trial at the U.S. District Court in Boston. He hated courtrooms, judges, and ties, not necessarily in that order. Added on top of his sleep deprivation and a reluctance to leave his family so severe that it bordered on irrational, the four-hour wait to be called up to the stand had made him more than a little testy. So as Aconcio approached, his Italian loafers gleaming beneath his tailored slacks, James braced himself, buttressing his wits against his emotions.

Aconcio stopped ten feet from him.

"Agent Goodman, you testified that you speak fluent Albanian. That is rather unusual for an Immigration and Customs Enforcement agent, is it not?"

He smiled. James's gut clenched in response.

"I wouldn't know."

"In fact, there are only two ICE agents who speak Albanian, and the other is a second-generation immigrant. Did you learn Albanian for the job?"

"No."

Aconcio's smile widened at James's laconic answer. "How long have you spoken Albanian?"

"About twelve years."

"Where did you learn to speak it?"

James hesitated for half a heartbeat. "My father taught me."

"What is your father's occupation?"

James shifted in his seat. "He teaches biology at the Maine Maritime Academy."

"Is speaking Albanian a requirement for teaching?"

"No."

"Is your father Albanian?"

"No."

The federal prosecutor, Joseph Addison, stood up. "Your Honor, is there any point to this line of questioning?" He never looked at his rival counsel.

Judge Parker turned to Aconcio. "Well, counselor?"

"If Your Honor will allow me some leeway, I think it shall be quite clear what point I am making."

James hoped that the judge found Aconcio's diction as irritating as he did.

"I'll allow it, but get there quickly, understand?"

"Indeed, Your Honor, I shall endeavor to do so." Aconcio pivoted toward James. "Agent Goodman, how is it that your father speaks Albanian?"

"He spent some time in Kosovo." James wanted to squirm, but he grounded his ass in his seat and met Aconcio's gaze.

"When was this, Agent Goodman?"

"1998 to 1999."

"How long was your father there?"

"Thirteen months." James bit out the words.

"Thirteen months." Aconcio paused, appearing to consider. "Did he teach biology in Kosovo?"

"No."

"Was he on vacation?"

"No."

"Why was your father in Kosovo for thirteen months?"

"He worked for the World Health Organization."

"What was his job for WHO?"

"He worked as a pathologist."

"In Kosovo?"

"Yes."

"Is it not true, Agent Goodman, that your father headed a clandestine group that investigated abuses of medical ethics around the world?"

"Yes, it's true." James closed his eyes briefly. This was going nowhere good, and he couldn't head it off.

"Is it not also true that your father was in Kosovo when the Kosovo War broke out in 1998?"

"Yes."

"And then did your father come back to the U.S.?"

"No."

"Why?"

"Because he'd gotten reports of a black market in organs in the Balkans."

"Who did the reports implicate?"

"Reports claimed a splinter group of the Kosovo Liberation Army was taking organs from Serb prisoners."

"Who led this group, Agent Goodman?" Aconcio gave him a wolfish grin.

"Commander Xhemajl Krasniqi." The name was ash on his tongue.

"The same Xhemajl Krasniqi now a respected imam?"

"Yes."

"The same Xhemajl Krasniqi who is Mirjeta Gjakova's uncle?"

"Yes."

"The same Xhemajl Krasniqi who supposedly ordered Ismail Duka to kidnap Mirjeta Gjakova?"

"Yes."

"Did your father find evidence of Commander Krasniqi's involvement in the illegal trade in organs?"

"He did."

"Are you aware that Dr. Goodman's case file at WHO shows that he did *not* have evidence against Commander Krasniqi but found it instead against the group that Commander Krasniqi commanded?"

"That's not true."

Aconcio shot him a smile. "But it is, Agent Goodman. Your Honor, I would like to submit to the court excerpts from the WHO case file which documents the worldwide investigation into medical ethics abuses under Dr. Goodman's leadership. The excerpt details Dr. Goodman's findings about the illegal trade in organs in the Balkans."

James felt his blood run cold at the information. He waited while Judge Parker accepted the exhibit and scanned the relevant pages.

Addison must have felt the same panic as James. He stood. "Your Honor, defense counsel has had more than enough time to get to his point. What Agent Goodman's father did a decade ago has no bearing on the charges against Ismail Duka."

Judge Parker looked up. "Oh, I think I can see where this is going, counselor. You can sit down. I'm going to let this play out a little longer."

Addison, his face dark, sat down.

“Thank you, Your Honor.” Aconcio faced James again. “What happened to your father’s investigation into the illegal organ selling?”

James scowled. He didn’t know how to answer this simply, and too many words would trip him up.

“Agent Goodman, answer the question.” Judge Parker focused on him.

James nodded and cleared his throat. “My father got intel that someone inside WHO was facilitating the transfer of organs. He—“

Aconcio interrupted him. “He suspected someone on his own team, yes?”

“Yes.”

“Did he identify the collaborator?”

“No.”

“Why not?”

“He got a tip from someone he thought was a trusted informant. When he went to meet him, he was ambushed.”

“What do you mean ‘ambushed’?”

“He was knocked unconscious, drugged, and taken to a secure hideout where he was held for six months.”

“His captors tortured him, did they not?”

“Yes, you sonofabitch!”

Judge Parker's gavel slammed against his bench. "Agent Goodman, no more outbursts like that in my court or you'll cool your jets behind bars, got it?"

James sat back in his seat, shooting a glance at Addison as he did. The federal prosecutor, his lips pressed into a thin line, shook his head slightly before glaring at Aconcio's back. "Yes, sir."

Aconcio returned to interrogating him. "Did your father identify his captors?"

"Yes, it was Xhemajl Krasniqi and his KLA command."

"Are you sure about that?"

"Yes!" A deep piercing tic began behind James's right eyeball.

"Well, Agent Goodman, your father was much less certain. His debriefing after his rescue is confused and rather incoherent. In fact, he seems to have suffered delusions as a result of his unfortunate treatment, which WHO doctors describe in the exhibit I supplied to the court."

"'Unfortunate treatment?'" James echoed as Addison said, "Your Honor, is there a question in there somewhere?"

"Counsel, *do* you have a question?" Judge Parker asked Aconcio.

"Yes, I do, Your Honor, and it is this: Agent Goodman, are you aware that it was Xhemajl Krasniqi who alerted an undercover operative about your father's whereabouts as part of a negotiated deal between U.N. forces and the KLA at the end of the Kosovo War?"

"Yes, but that's because Krasniqi was covering his ass—" began James.

Aconcio cut him off. “What is your relationship with Mirjeta Gjakova?”

Heat and ice alternated through James. They’d known this question was inevitable, but he still didn’t want to answer it. “We’re married.”

“Were you married at the time that she was supposedly kidnapped at her uncle’s orders?”

“No.” James wanted to punch him for repeating ‘supposedly.’

“But you knew her.”

It wasn’t a question, but James answered anyway. “Yes.”

“How did you meet her?”

“We were traveling on the same flight from Rome.”

“Was this the same flight from Rome that your father took home after being rescued from his KLA captors?”

“Yes.”

“Are you aware that your wife was running away from her uncle when you met her?” Aconcio’s words hammered against James’s chest. “Agent Goodman?”

“No.”

“Can you speak up? I am having difficulty hearing you.”

“I said, ‘no.’”

“Did you not find it strange that a sixteen-year-old girl who barely spoke English was traveling alone?”

"No."

"Are you aware that Imam Krasniqi supported your wife's education at Julliard?"

Hope stirred in James. "That's not true. She had a merit scholarship."

"One Imam Krasniqi funded. Your Honor, I have here records of Imam Krasniqi's financial support of his niece, Mirjeta Gjakova, while she was a student at Julliard."

The pain behind James's right eye radiated outward through the entire top of his head.

"Agent Goodman, are you aware that Imam Krasniqi had been communicating with his niece for six months prior to the night that Ismail Duka contacted her on his behalf?"

"Yes, if you call stalking her 'communicating'!" shouted James.

Judge Parker banged his gavel hard, but James had already quieted. He threw a helpless look at Addison, who was shaking his bent head and scribbling furiously. Aconcio stood smiling, his sharp teeth just visible beneath his thin lips.

"Is it not true that you wrongly blame him for what happened to your father during the Kosovo War because you need someone to blame? Is it not true that your wife so feared what you'd do if you knew that she was related to the man that you'd sworn revenge against that she lied about being kidnapped?"

"No," said James through clenched teeth. His jaw ached. "No, no, no."

Aconcio paced away and then turned back.

He addressed his comments to Judge Parker. "Mirjeta Gjakova took advantage of her uncle's generosity even after she ran away from Albania as a rebellious teenager in 1999. She was desperate to come to the United States where she hoped to succeed as a classical violinist. Once she found Dr. Goodman and his son James Goodman, she lived in fear that they would discover her blood relationship with Xhemajl Krasniqi.

"Agent Goodman, already convinced of Imam Krasniqi's guilt, allowed his feelings for Mirjeta Gjakova to bias him about Ismail Duka's intentions on the night of March 11, 2009. Your Honor, this prosecution of Ismail Duka for kidnapping is the result of a malicious fraud perpetrated by a young woman trying to protect her own interests."

Addison stood up again. "Your Honor, this is ridiculous! The United States filed charges against Ismail Duka for kidnapping following an eighteen-month Immigrations and Customs Enforcement investigation into the Krasniqi mafia.

"ICE agents, including Agent Goodman, responded to an informant's tip. Not a single agent was aware of the victim's identity before the raid. Defense counsel is drawing on irrelevant and prejudicial background to confuse the facts of this case."

Judge Parker, who had appeared to be reviewing the documents that Aconcio had submitted rather than listening to Addison's objection, looked up. "Indeed, counsel, it appears that the U.S. government acted in good faith."

But then he looked at James. "However, it's less clear whether you, your wife, and father-in-law did as well. I will need some time to review these documents more carefully. Court is adjourned until tomorrow morning."

James said nothing. He was well aware that arguing with a judge would only cause trouble. As he stood, he glanced at Aconcio, whose little smile had returned. He had the sinking feeling that no matter what the outcome of the judge's review Aconcio would enjoy the game—not because he loved to win legal challenges but because he got his rocks off on James's helpless rage.

ELIRA SAT ON THE examining table, gripping its edge until her fingers grew numb and fighting nausea. After several deep breaths, she stood and ripped the johnny over her head before dropping it in a pile on the floor. She felt cold and her head ached, almost as if she were sick.

But she hadn't been sick in so long—she *couldn't* get sick.

And then she thought of Jak and Zamir, and her stomach clenched, hard. Wiping the back of her hand across her mouth, she gazed down at the good doctor's blood staining her skin.

It was brilliant red.

Life-giving red. Life itself.

Whirling, she grabbed her skirt and yanked it on before pulling her camisole over her head. The heavy cotton caught at her crucifix and tore it free from its silver chain. Gasping, she managed to catch the jeweled figure before it landed on the white tile.

Closing her eyes at the close call, she bent over and sucked in a shuddering sigh.

After her nausea and panic settled, she picked up her denim jacket, threw it around her shoulders, and then rammed first one arm and then the other into its sleeves. The crucifix gouged her palm between her tightly curled fingers, but she coaxed them open enough to drop it into the jacket's breast pocket before buttoning it. Then, thrusting her feet into her boots, she tied them with savage tugs.

Dr. Alston had asked her to wait until he could return. He'd intimated that he wanted to continue their liaison under the guise of further testing and research. It had been easy enough to lead him to share what he'd discovered through her usual means of persuasion, but she didn't need to learn more. And she didn't need any more junior law associates. He'd have to find another subject to study somewhere else.

Opening the door to the examining room, she heard Dr. Alston's voice. She ducked her head out. Farther down the hall and to her left, he stood chatting with a shorter, white-haired man in a matching lab coat. Elira darted to the right and around the corner, silent curses pinging in her thoughts at the lack of darkness and shadows in which to hide.

As she passed the corner, she heard him shout. That's when she took off at a dead run down the corridor before punching through the door to the stairs. As she ran, she dialed her driver, a highway patrolman who would make sure that she made it to the Atlanta airport without being caught.

She only slowed down when she entered the main lobby to the CDC research labs. The security guard behind the reception desk eyed her, but she unclipped the visitor's badge from her jacket lapel and tossed it to him.

Though weak and shaking, she draped herself over the counter to sign the visitor's log. The guard's gaze glazed over at the sight of her breasts plumped up on display. Elira caught his eye and smiled, slow and wide, before caressing his fingers as he took the log from her. Behind him, the phone rang and rang while monitors showed a phalanx of researchers entering a bank of elevators. The guard nodded at her without looking at her signature or the badge, waving her through as the next visitor stepped up to the desk.

She made it outside into the Atlanta sunshine before her stomach heaved again. This time, she threw up in the shrubbery not far from the walk. It was an improvement, she thought, on the corporate landscaping.

Two hours later she sat sipping a Coke and reading a magazine while waiting for a flight to New York when a news story on the overhead TV caught her attention. Looking up, she recognized Osama bin Laden's photo in an upper right corner of the screen while the news anchor droned on about the raid by U.S. Navy Seals that had killed him.

"'They that take the sword shall perish with the sword.' Do you really think the world witnesses an Arab Spring where democracy and human rights will replace the Old Blood Law?"

Elira started and nearly dropped her Coke. Zophiel sat next to her, luminous in a white T-shirt and white jeans. Small silver studs spelled *Attitude of Gratitude* on her chest. Sunlight from the overhead windows haloed her white-blond hair, shadowing her face. She made Elira feel small, small and inconsequential.

Zophiel laid a hand on Elira's forearm. Her touch burned. "What's wrong, Elira?"

A wild laugh burst from Elira. She choked it back. "I have a parasite in my heart. Isn't that amazing, Zophie? A parasite."

"But you knew that, didn't you?" chided Zophie. "You know exactly when you got it."

Elira shook her head. "He said it was so embedded that he can't remove it, that it's changed my system so much that I'd die without it anyway." She laughed again. It sounded like a seal barking. "If I thought that were true, I'd let him remove it."

"Would you? 'For dust you are, and unto dust shall you return.'" Zophiel touched her collarbone. "But that's not the only thing inside you, is it?"

Elira swiped under her eyes with her thumb. "No, oh, no. There's a virus in my blood. That's how he found the parasite—while testing my blood, he found antibodies to the parasite. And then he looked at a blood smear under a microscope."

She gulped a breath and a shudder answered. "He found it, curled up like a zygote in the left ventricle. There's some necrosis in its segments, but I don't know if that's a good thing or a bad thing."

Zophiel rubbed her hand along Elira's arm and up over her shoulder. The flesh under the MacNeil tattoo quivered.

"I love the American Museum of Natural History. Just think: thirty-two million specimens from the natural world. So much discovered, preserved, catalogued, dissected, and displayed by naturalists and scientists, but only a small fraction can be displayed at any given time. Skews human understanding of reality a little, eh? Like that old parable about the three blind men groping an elephant.

"One of my favorite dioramas depicts a battle between a giant squid and a sperm whale. You know, most people think the two sea monsters are evenly matched. Makes for a more exciting story that way. But the truth is the squid has no hope against the whale."

Elira snorted. "I imagine the whale isn't so sure about that."

"True, it's hard to see the consequences in the middle of the struggle. But the whale has tenacity, and when the moment is right, she defeats her prey."

LATER, WHEN ELIRA ARRIVED at James and Mirjeta's apartment, it was early evening, and faint stars shone in the denim sky. Elira watched their window from across the street as dusk deepened and the silvered glass dissolved into a golden pane. Mirjeta appeared with a small bundle.

"Infant on shoulder, young mother sings lullabies," she whispered to herself. "Limned against May night."

She jammed her hands into her jacket pockets. She longed to hear Duncan's voice, to feel him inside her head as well as her heart, but he no longer walked with her, no longer spoke to her. She hunched her shoulders and stared at the window, unsure what to do. As she stood trying to decide, a second figure joined Mirjeta within the window's frame. Although he was backlit and his features in shadow, she knew who the bald head belonged to: Dr. Alexander Goodman, James's father. Her uncertainty disappeared.

Five minutes later, Elira knocked on the Goodmans' door, her gaze traveling the bright hallway several times while she waited. The thin mewl of a newborn, followed by murmuring and a man's voice preceded footsteps.

Then the door swung open, and Dr. Goodman stood there, blinking owlishly at her. He was taller than James and a good deal heavier, but his eyes were the same Adriatic blue, and the shape of his mouth, even the smile lines in his cheeks and radiating away from his eyes, were the same. Elira's heart clenched. She fisted her hands and, shoving them inside her pockets, turned away.

"*Prit.*" *Wait*. Dr. Goodman's pleasant voice caught her between the shoulder blades. She halted but didn't turn to him. "Elira? *Jeni Elira Dukagjini*?" *Are you Elira Dukagjini?*

A hot river ran down her spine as she turned back to see that he'd taken a step into the hall. "Yes."

"Come in then. I've wanted to meet you for some time."

He didn't wait for her answer. Elira said nothing but followed him inside. Mirjeta sat on a loveseat in front of the large window through which Elira had watched outside. On one shoulder an infant swaddled in a pale blue blanket tucked a dark head into her neck as her hand pressed against his back. She widened her eyes and snuggled the baby closer but didn't get up.

"Ismail Duka was convicted today." Mirjeta's soft voice stirred the downy hair on her baby's head.

Elira nodded. "I know."

"You ran out on Dr. Alston." It was Dr. Goodman, who'd seated himself in an easy chair next to his daughter-in-law.

Elira felt as though she stood in front of a tribunal. She shrugged, although pain jabbed her upper left back. "I learned everything I needed to know."

"Did you?" He picked up a glass of wine, studying her. "James told me a bit about you. You and I have something in common it seems."

"Really? What's that?"

He leaned forward. "Our enmity toward Krasniqi." The intensity of his voice matched his gaze.

Elira's own gaze darted to Mirjeta, who'd gone white. She looked back at Dr. Goodman and shrugged again. "I'm no longer concerned with Krasniqi. His blood debt to me is paid."

Dr. Goodman leaned back. "Is it? Have you truly taken all the blood he owes you?"

Elira closed her eyes and sucked in a deep breath. Then she met his gaze. "There was a time when I thought I'd never take all the blood owed me. I was wrong though."

"How's that?" He watched her, his gaze too sharp to fit his genial features.

"It wasn't my blood to take."

A key rattled in the apartment door, and then James entered, carrying a takeout bag in one hand and six-pack of bottled beer in the other. He stopped when he saw Elira.

"Elira." His gaze darted toward Mirjeta and Dr. Goodman.

Anger, which she'd thought had died in her, flashed white-hot in her breast. She'd crossed the room and planted her hands beside Mirjeta's head on the loveseat before she knew what she was doing.

Leaning in, she hissed, "Worried I'm going to go on a rampage?"

The baby squirmed and let out a squawk as Mirjeta squeezed him against her. "Elira."

James stood behind the loveseat. When she looked up, she saw the Walther PPK in its holster under his arm. Dark purple shadows under his eyes stood out against his pale face and creases and lines marred his features. He was aging. She was not.

"She has reasons to seek blood from Krasniqi even if I do not. Don't you, *motër të vogël*?"

Elira traced the edge of Mirjeta's jaw. Hunger flared at the feel of silky skin, the spicy warm scent of vanilla and musk, the faint thrumming of pulse along throat, the low susurrus of breath as Mirjeta's chest rose and fell.

"Yes," Mirjeta whispered.

Her honesty pricked Elira. "When will you tell him?"

She kept her gaze on Mirjeta, ignoring James, Dr. Goodman, the baby. She dropped her nose to nuzzle the other woman's neck on the side away from the baby's head.

Mirjeta gulped. Elira felt her neck undulate beneath her lips. "S-soon. I'll tell him soon."

Elira pulled back and looked up at James, whose lips had tightened. Without taking her gaze from his, she dragged her finger down Mirjeta's throat and toward her chest. She pulled the neckline of the nursing blouse down until the tip of her finger rested over Mirjeta's left breast. James didn't move, but tension thickened the air around them.

"I can make her like me. Isn't that what you're afraid of?" He didn't answer, but she felt his gaze boring into her upper back. "Then again, perhaps I should make *you* like me. You're the one whose anger still burns. Burns blue as your eyes. That's what I was supposed to do. Make you a full partner."

She glanced down and watched her finger as it swirled over Mirjeta's warm, unblemished skin and thought of the last time her own breast had flushed with healthy blood. Then she looked at Dr. Goodman, who'd sat silent while she sparred with James. A strange gleam lit his eyes, and he sat forward in his chair, his wineglass loose in his hands. He was a big man, well over six feet tall, and heavy in the way that aging men who were once muscular become. As a young man, he must have been intimidating. What would it be like to feel your own slow decay? To lose your power and charisma? To fade into a living ghost?

"Unë jam Engjëlli i vdekjes, Aleksander." I'm the Angel of Death, Alexander. "Më lejoni t'ju shënojë për të kaluar mbi." Let me mark you to be passed over.

Dr. Goodman never took his gaze from hers as she lifted her wrist to her mouth and scored the tender, thin skin on the inside. It stung, but it was harmless. She ran her thumb across the welling blood and then turned to spread it across Mirjeta's forehead, first horizontally and then vertically. Mirjeta gasped and cringed, but Elira ignored her. Dr. Goodman nodded at her questioning look, and she marked his forehead as well. When she turned back, James had moved between her and Mirjeta.

"James." Elira let all the yearning she felt, all the loneliness and regret of a very long lifetime suffuse her voice.

He staggered a little and closed his eyes. Then, swallowing, he dipped his chin.

Rising to her toes, Elira reached up and drew the sign on his forehead too before stepping back. Now she lost her edge. Her throat thickened. Pressing her lips together, she gestured toward the baby, whom Mirjeta had started nursing.

No one spoke. Elira began to feel lightheaded in the warm apartment. She swayed a little, catching the back of her calf on the coffee table. It was time to go. She'd done all that she could.

"Wait," said Mirjeta. She shared a look with James before returning a steady, knowing gaze to Elira. She lifted the baby. "Please."

Elira's dizziness passed, leaving her mind clear. Dragging her thumb through the congealing blood on her wrist, she leaned forward and blessed the baby.

Her blood, dark and thick, stood out in glistening relief.

Seventeen

THE TEMPERATURE HAD FALLEN A MERE FIVE DEGREES from the daily high to a steamy eighty-five the evening that Mirjeta began her goodwill concert tour at the Callanwolde Fine Arts Center in Atlanta. Even so, premonitory gooseflesh puckered her bare arms and made the hairs on her neck creep as she tuned her violin outside the former home of Coca-Cola scion Howard Candler.

A small, polite crowd sat on blankets and in folding chairs behind the Gothic-Tudor mansion waiting for the concert to begin. Mirjeta scanned the sloping lawn beyond for signs of James, wishing that she'd known back in January that she'd regret accepting the invitation to tour so soon after giving birth.

And, if she were honest, wishing that she'd listened to Elira's plea to beg off. James had been able to travel with her and the baby for this first stop, but they'd had to hire a nanny for the rest of the tour. For some reason, she wanted to see them as she began playing. But they'd disappeared in the deepening shadows of twilight.

She shuffled and turned toward the front of the mansion where an odd sight froze her. A group of middle-aged and elderly women wearing red t-shirts and carrying placards strode beneath the archway covering the long driveway.

Mirjeta's bow arm dropped as she realized that they headed for the platform. They arrayed themselves in an orderly crescent on the strip of lawn between the audience and quartet. Two elderly women led the group, one a tiny woman with white hair like spun sugar and the other a tall and spare Amazon with a no-nonsense glare. The smaller wore a t-shirt with white capital letters spelling out VENGEANCE.

Mirjeta swallowed and lowered her violin. Then she noticed the camera crew from one of the Atlanta TV stations as it set up in the corner of the assembly. Despite advance publicity and a feature spread in the *Atlanta Journal Constitution*, they'd been unable to interest any of the nearly dozen broadcast affiliates in covering their concert. A bead of icy sweat slid down her spine.

"Mirjeta Gjakova?" asked the taller one.

Mirjeta licked her lips. "Yes?" It was faint in her dry throat.

The elfish woman threw something at her. Mirjeta flinched, but a fist-sized, squishy object hit her midsection and burst. A warm liquid soaked her evening gown, which had cost her four hundred dollars after alterations to allow her to breastfeed during intermission. She gasped, drawing air to protest, when several more women pelted her and the members of the quartet.

The remaining red-shirted women began chanting, "Code Red! Code Red! Code Red!"

Violence twisted their grandmotherly visages.

Mirjeta pressed her palm against the chiffon of her gown and raised it. It was covered with blood. She shrieked and almost dropped her violin. At that thought, she glanced at it. Blood dripped from the scroll and along the fingerboard, but none appeared to have made it into the F-Holes. On the patio behind her, the other musicians either moaned or yelled.

She whirled, unable to interpret the fractured tableau around her. The glare from the TV camera punctured her vision, sending brilliant shards into her brain. Dazzled and dizzy, she blinked to focus. When she could see, she found herself face-to-face with the Amazon. The red-shirted gang fell silent.

"You're a vampire, darlin,'" declared the woman in a booming voice.

Startled sounds came from the audience while the Code Red women murmured approval.

"You're a Muslim subversive, not a Catholic. Your uncle is Imam Krasniqi, a Wahhabi extremist in your native Balkans. Right now, as you pretend to ask for 'tolerance' and 'dialogue' and 'peace' here in the U.S., your uncle leads a protest of a thousand Muslims in Pristina.

"Your uncle acts on the orders of Fuad Ramiqi, the Taliban of the Balkans. So much for the Arab Spring. Now we have a Summer of Protest in the Balkans where Saudi money pays for radicals who bully moderate Muslims and terrorize Orthodox and Catholic Christians.

"You." Here she swept the quartet with a wave. "Y'all are what's wrong with this country. Y'all are collaborators with people who only want blood from those who don't submit to their religious law."

Turning her back on Mirjeta and the rest of the quartet, she addressed the stunned concert audience, her mob, and the TV camera. "The only way to deal with vampires is to destroy them, not tolerate them.

"I'd line up all Muslim jihadists, whose only goal in life is to get to Paradise where young virgins of both sexes service their lusts while they sate their gluttony on wine, honey, fruit, and fowl.

"I'd line them up and behead them in front of their mothers, just as they beheaded my son, Sawyer. They live by the law that demands an eye for an eye, so let's give them what they ask for."

Mirjeta started shaking. She opened her mouth, but no words came out. How was it that she'd been able to stand up to a real *lugat*, to defend her faith, when she could do nothing but let this primeval Fury mark her with the very same bloody brush as her uncle?

That night she told James in halting phrases and stumbling words the truth about why she'd fled her uncle more than a decade before.

She told him how her mother, Liridona, had been kidnapped from her home village of Gjakova at the age of sixteen by Xhevdet Krasniqi, the younger twin brother of Xhemajl. Xhevdet took Liridona to Pristina where he raped her before forcing her to convert to Islam and marry him.

When Mirjeta was eight, Liridona, now a widow, escaped with her to the Accursed Mountains. After two years, they settled in Tirana so that Mirjeta, who had learned to play the violin in Pristina, could continue studying.

"I didn't know until I was sixteen." Mirjeta's throat thickened, and then hot tears struck like a thunderclap, her nose streaming. "I didn't know. I didn't know what she went through. She told me when she realized my uncle had found us. She ran away, she risked her life because he'd planned to marry me just as the prophet took a bride at nine."

She looked away, choking out the rest of it. "He had her killed. Raped and tortured first. I found her one afternoon when I came home from practicing at the Academy of Arts. That's when I packed a suitcase and ran. So I am what Loretta Walker said I am. I'm a Muslim apostate and collaborator."

James grabbed her face with both hands, compelling her to look at him. "You are your mother's daughter, Mirjeta: brave, faithful, and compassionate. Nothing more and nothing less."

But she saw the angry anguish in his eyes.

ELIRA HAD WATCHED THE Code Red protest from behind the trunk of a Hightower Oak. After Sylvia the Vengeance had pelted Mirjeta, Elira had sprinted toward the group only to come up short and hard when Loretta thundered, "You're a vampire, darlin'."

She'd stood there, thunderstruck and deaf while the world kept spinning around her. Later, after the police had arrived to lead the protesters away in handcuffs, and the TV station had interviewed Mirjeta, the other musicians, and numerous concertgoers, Elira called her local associate for a ride. She took Elira back to her house in Druid Hills where Elira dutifully drank a bottle of pinot noir with her and then took her to bed.

She undressed the woman, stripping panties and kissing her way down silky thighs while the woman writhed and moaned. Elira felt nothing. Not drunk. Not lust. Not urgent. Not the driving need for the sweetness of blood freely given. Nothing but empty mechanics moved her. She'd felt this way before, once. After Duncan's death, she'd bedded and bitten and swallowed copious amounts of whisky and beer until something deep and weedy had sprouted in her.

At last, when she realized her partner grew restless on her fifteen-hundred-thread-count Egyptian-cotton sheets, Elira rose up to simulate her own release, more tired than she could ever remember being.

"Take me, take me, take me!" commanded the woman, grabbing Elira's hair and pulling her head down for a violent kiss.

Elira pulled away, panting. Her stomach clenched, but she ignored it to grind methodically. Nothing happened. The woman groaned and pinched Elira's nipples hard.

Fury erupted in Elira, and she struck, her teeth crashing into the woman's upper breast. Her partner groaned again, pitching and wrapping her arms so tightly around Elira's head that her face was smashed, and her teeth scraped against an upper rib. Blood flooded her tongue, but it wasn't sweet. Bile rose in her throat instead of cries of ecstasy.

Ripping away, Elira staggered into the bathroom, a funhouse tiled in white marble and walled in mirrors and polished nickel. She collapsed on the floor, puking. The sight of bright red against the sterile floor spiked a headache so fierce her vision blurred. The harsh fluorescent lighting sent stabbing pains through her until she curled into a fetal position, rubbing at her aching scar.

At first her partner soothed her, helping her rinse her mouth and stumble back to the dark bedroom before cleaning the vomit and bringing her chilled spring water followed by Scotch. But when Elira refused to let her press her naked, rank body against her back, the woman clicked her tongue, snatched a pillow from the bed, and stomped out.

Elira didn't see her the next morning, although she'd left money and car keys for Elira along with a petulant letter demanding she not return until she'd gotten over whatever bad attitude had ruined their sport. Elira studied the letter for ten minutes. A yawning ache opened under her scar. She almost wished Zophiel would appear out of thin air and say something odd.

Instead, she wandered around the upscale home decorated in Southern Living style, tracing her fingertips over polished wood, oil paintings, plush cushions, and buttery leather. Was this what her partner had sold herself for? Was it really worth it? An image of James and Mirjeta's tiny two-bedroom with its consignment-shop furnishings filled her.

Plopping down on the divan in the family room, she flipped on the flat-panel TV and began scrolling through the inset onscreen menu while a local channel played news.

A name caught her attention. Turning up the volume, she listened to a Boston lawyer reading Dr. Alexander Goodman's statement to the national media.

"Yesterday in Atlanta, my daughter-in-law, Mirjeta Goodman, was publicly attacked and humiliated by a group of homegrown terrorists calling themselves Code Red. Mirjeta Goodman is in no way responsible for the actions of her uncle, Xhemajl Krasniqi, a radical imam in her native Kosovo.

"I have personally suffered at the hands of Krasniqi. In 1999, while working for the World Health Organization, I was held hostage for six months by the Kosovo Liberation Army. Krasniqi commanded that group. As a Catholic, I fully support Mirjeta's efforts to promote peace, tolerance, and justice. I believe what she's doing is what separates Americans from religious extremists like Krasniqi.

"I urge everyone to reject Code Red's message. If no one listens to them, they won't have any power. As for the Krasniqis of the world, we must hold firm to the rule of law on our own soil and defend against their aggression where we must, but we must learn to separate the guilty from the not guilty or we'll be no better than the bloodiest zealot."

Elira turned the TV off. The mansion closed in around her. Jumping up, she paced through the rooms, looking for something, anything, to distract herself.

She no longer had a purpose. She no longer had any means to amuse, pleasure, satiate, or even muddle herself.

Passing by the counter where her associate had left money and keys, she snatched both up. She headed southwest out of Atlanta on I-85 toward Alabama, enjoying the wind whipping through her hair as she floored it. An image from the HBO TV series *True Blood* filtered through her mind, and she laughed. What would it be like living in Louisiana?

She made it as far as Lanett, Alabama, where she stopped for lunch and gas before her tether pulled her up short. Driving back to Atlanta as a murderer might drive to the police station to turn herself in, she thought of nothing but what surrounded her for the first time in decades. The Georgia sunlight in skies the same color of blue over Lezhë. The heat of the sun on her forearm where it hung out the driver's window. The wind that fingered her hair. The smell of the leather seats and the greasy hamburger and fries that she'd eaten for lunch. She drove aware of everything around her and yet detached from it.

When she turned down the street for the Cathedral of Christ the King in time for the 4 p.m. Mass, her indifference lifted like a window blind snapping up. She parked and walked up the front stairs as one condemned. At the threshold to the vestibule, she stopped.

"I'm not worthy," she whispered.

"Your soul shall be healed," responded Zophiel at her shoulder.

Later, after Mass, Elira called Mirjeta to ask if she could visit her at her hotel. When Mirjeta answered the door, she declined to enter. Instead, she brought Qendresa's crucifix from her jacket pocket and held it up for Mirjeta to see.

"I've carried it with me a long time," she said.

Mirjeta, her eyes brimming with an emotion Elira couldn't name, bent her head and accepted it.

JACOPO ACONCIO PREPARED HIS favorite speech for Ismail Duka's sentencing hearing. He would have liked Elira and James to hear his masterful delivery, one honed on innumerable occasions, but needs must.

"'Your honor, I have unsuccessfully defended Mr. Duka from a prosecution that I believe has been unjust. As you deliberate upon what sentence you would hand down, I ask that you keep in mind that Mr. Duka's actions in kidnapping Mirjeta Gjakova stemmed directly from his Muslim faith and his devotion to his teacher, Imam Krasniqi. If you would indulge me one more time, I would like to quote from Portia's speech from *The Merchant of Venice*, the one describing the quality of mercy."

He waited until Judge Parker nodded, a small smile aimed at him. Aconcio turned toward the courtroom, which was peopled with reporters, Duka's mother, and the federal prosecutor, whose glare promised a satisfying future relationship. Aconcio ignored Addison for the moment and addressed the reporters.

"'The quality of mercy is not strained. It droppeth as the gentle rain from heaven, upon the place beneath. It is twice blessed. It blesseth him that gives and him that takes. It is mightiest in the mightiest; it becomes the throned monarch better than his crown. His sceptre shows the force of temporal power, an attribute to awe and majesty wherein doth sit the dread and fear of kings. But mercy is above this sceptred sway, it is enthroned in the hearts of kings, it is an attribute to God himself. And earthly power dost then become likest God's, where mercy seasons justice.'"

A short silence fell in which the media scribes scribbled his speech. Addison's sigh could be heard throughout the courtroom. Judge Parker shot him a sharp look and then turned to Duka.

"Mr. Duka, are you prepared to allocute?"

Duka stood. "I am, Your Honor."

He shifted so that he half-faced his media audience. "The first thing I'll say is there is no God except Allah and Mohammed is His messenger, peace be upon him. I acted as a dutiful and obedient servant of Allah and my imam's wishes."

He picked up a framed document from the table before him and gestured with it. "Further, while I awaited trial, the Community Church of Boston awarded me the Annual Sacco and Vanzetti Social Justice Award. Recipients are chosen to protest the injustice practiced in the name of modern jurisprudence.

"*Insha'allah*, I will do my best to earn the right to stand among all those worthy people who have been recognized in the past."

"ARE YOU A FAN of *Blade Runner*, greatest movie of all time?"

James started. He'd wandered toward the Back of the Hill to avoid running into anyone. He couldn't stand the thought of speaking to another human being right now.

Judge Parker had sentenced Duka to the least amount of time allowed for kidnapping, ten years. Then he'd added insult to injury by giving Duka "credit for time served" and reducing the sentence further to ninety-one months, or about seven-and-a-half years. With time off for good behavior, Duka could be walking the streets again a year earlier than that.

If he served at all. Aconcio had filed notice of appeal this morning. Addison had filed a counter appeal, if it could be called that, arguing that Parker's sentence was too short and signaling that the U.S. Attorney's Office had no interest in negotiating a deal to short-circuit the appeals process. Meanwhile, Aconcio had responded by requesting that Duka be released on appellate bond.

Was Justice really so blind?

Zophie sat next to him on the grassy field, which Boston's Parks and Recreation Department had designated an "urban wild." It looked like an abandoned lot to him.

"How did you find me?" he asked, letting bitterness color his question. He really wasn't in any mood for her cryptic stories.

She ignored him. "Remember Roy Batty, the replicant played by Rutger Hauer? I love how he misquotes William Blake's *America: A Prophecy*."

As she continued to speak, her voice deepened, sounding remarkably like the actor that she'd mentioned. "'Fiery the angels fell; deep thunder rolled around their shores; burning with the fires of Orc.'" She looked up toward the dark heavens covered in a glowing net of stars.

Before James could gather his thoughts and regain control of his tongue, she murmured as if to herself, "Perhaps I shouldn't like it so much, but I've always been one for finding beauty in the ugliest stories. Good thing Michael doesn't hold it against me."

Then she twisted on her buttocks and, fluffing her short white-blond hair, asked, "Do you think I look a little like Pris?" She frowned. "No, Elira looks more like her."

"Zophie." James managed to interrupt. "What the hell are you talking about?"

She focused on his face, her gaze capturing his for the first time. An almost visible current leapt between them. James's heart began to race. At that moment, if he could have moved, he would have settled for crawling away. As it was, he felt pinned to the earth. She loomed over him.

"I've always loved the scene where Roy saves Deckard just before dying in the rain. And they said replicants didn't have empathy! Love Roy's speech."

Again, her voice changed. "'I've seen things you people wouldn't believe. Attack ships on fire off the shoulder of Orion. I've watched c-beams glitter in the dark near the Tannhäuser Gate. All those ... moments will be lost in time, like tears ... in rain. Time to die.'"

Zophie let her head droop before looking up again. "It was supposed to be much longer, boring and lame. But Rutger Hauer took out what he didn't like and added the last two lines himself. And then, letting the dove go as he dies!" Here her long-fingered hand fell open, and something winged through James's vision.

"That was Rutger's idea too. Brilliant, huh?"

James's lips moved, but no sound came out. His heart continued to race. He briefly wondered if he was in shock or perhaps hallucinating.

Zophie pinned him again with her gaze. “Ever see the director’s cut? I prefer the alternate pastoral ending to the bleaker cityscape released in theaters.” She leaned in. “But it doesn’t matter what I prefer. The question is: which do you prefer?”

Eighteen

ACONCIO SURPRISED HIMSELF WITH how much he missed Elira. He missed her even more than he missed the blood that he took from her, truth be told, though what came from her heart tasted sweeter than his favorite Brachetto d'Acqui from his Piedmont homeland.

He could always slake his needs from a never-ending supply of far-more-willing associates. He'd even created another partner or two since Elira had gone on the lam, but none of them had her potential. None had her deep passion for the Old Law, the Law of Blood. None had her lasting ability to seduce others to her cause. Nearly all succumbed to the anemia of modern Western life, becoming a herd best suited to milquetoast revenge. Those few partners who did burn with bloodlust never survived long enough to maintain him long term, but he'd get by. He always did.

No, Aconcio missed Elira's struggle, her spitting-hissing-fish-hook-claws kittenish insistence that he didn't own her, that she was an independent woman free to make her own terms. It was a delight that never grew old.

He sighed. It had been eighteen months since he had had the power to track her and take what was his—and more than a year since she had vowed that their partnership was dissolved, and he had let her go to pursue her misguided love for James Goodman.

He had not thought that she had it in her to hold out this long. After all, she had returned to him with a renewed sense of vengeance after Duncan's death.

Perhaps it was time to move back to the Balkans or the Mideast. There was the passion he craved, if not the internal conflict. Unfortunately, recruiting there held no challenge.

Turning away from the mass of court officers, lawyers, witnesses, defendants, and reporters who milled around the lobby of the U.S. Court of Appeals for the First Circuit, he swiped through his contacts on his smartphone before pressing a number. His international call was answered after two rings.

"The appeals judge has granted my request to release Duka on bond. You may alert your local associates that he is to be released tomorrow morning. Where he goes from there is, of course, up to you. If you wish to have him remain in the United States, it would be best if he cooperates with the terms of his release."

He smiled to himself. Krasniqi had no intention of wasting any more time or money on the American legal system. "Indeed, it has been a pleasure. Thank you for keeping me on retainer."

As he hung up, he thought of James Goodman, who had responded so well to his deft handling during the trial. His smile broadened. Perhaps he had been too hasty in considering a return to lands ruled by the Old Law. The blood there, though hot, was rather bland. Better to stay here and collect on an investment. He had, after all, cultivated patience and mastered the long game eons ago. If, as he suspected, Krasniqi still had plans for his beloved niece, James would be easy to turn. And then Elira would return to her place as his primary law partner. He laughed. What an unholy trinity they would make!

Turning around, he glimpsed a bailiff wending his way through the crowd toward him.

"Yes?" he asked, stepping forward to meet him.

"Sir, Judge Joseph wants to see you in his chambers."

Pleasure spurted up his spine, making his jaw ache. He made a courtly half-bow. "Of course. Judge Joseph is an old friend."

MIRJETA MISSED JAMES. SHE'D not understood how much he'd fit into her daily life after they'd married, how large his presence would loom in her thoughts. How could she? The only other person who'd ever taken up such a large spot in her psyche had been her mother.

After Liridona's death, she'd had no one with whom she'd shared such an intimate, daily relationship. Certainly not David, who'd had his own apartment. None of the handful of roommates she'd lived with during school had been more than casual friends. They'd all been too busy, too focused on practicing, auditioning, performing. Not even Dr. Goodman or James during their previous friendship had insinuated themselves into her private space, that invisible bubble that she kept herself cocooned inside. How could she have predicted how hard it would be to sleep alone without using him as a bolster? How could she have foreseen how much she'd long for that final talk before falling asleep, the one where they murmured their plans for the future or reminded each other how much they loved one another?

She snuggled baby James closer, stroking his silky head as he nursed. Though he filled a space in her that she hadn't even realized she had, it would never replace the bedrock presence that James had become. Her son snuffled and pressed his head against her breast, clutching and relaxing his fingers in his sleep.

Elira's anguished visage rose before her mind's eye. Had she known all those years ago that she'd lost the ability to bear a child after her rape? Or had she come to a slow understanding of it over time, an understanding that fired her bloodlust with an unquenchable flame?

Mirjeta rubbed her thumb over the baby's forehead and then her hand dropped to her chest where the antique crucifix nestled. She had no doubt that it was a relic of Elira's former life.

After the baby finished nursing, Mirjeta laid him in the portable crib the hotel had provided. Shutting the door to his room, she returned to the living area of her suite. She'd given the nanny, a young woman named Heather Pross, the evening off to sightsee and shop at the Gallery Place, so she had some quiet time to check email and then read before bed.

Most of her messages related to the upcoming semester at NEC, for which she'd opted to return to teaching private lessons. She ignored them to open James's nightly email. They'd spoken only an hour before, but he'd taken to sending her goofy photos of himself from his cell-phone camera and writing her absurd little verses about how pathetic and lonely he was without her and the baby.

Scanning the rest of the unread email, she recognized the name of a former student, Lindona Tare. Lindona, the daughter of Albanian immigrants who lived in Natick, had been a talented, if indifferent, violinist. She'd been far more interested in the shopping mall and reality TV than the hours spent practicing daily required to play with mastery. It had been years since they'd been in touch, but Mirjeta had learned through the Albanian community what had happened to Lindona. After her cousin, a marine stationed in Afghanistan, had been killed, Lindona had done the unimaginable and joined the Army. As a Muslim woman, she'd been ideal for the Cultural Support Team assigned to U.S. Special Forces. Mirjeta remembered how enthusiastic and eager Lindona had been to work with poor Afghani women and children, to show them that Americans brought more than death and devastation.

Opening the message, Mirjeta expected to find a chatty description of Lindona's tour in country or, worse, news of a wound or the loss of a friend. Instead, she read a message that made no sense. She read it three more times before what it said sunk in. And then, with a leaden heart, she clicked on the video icon beneath the message and played the embedded video.

Lindona sat on a chair wearing fatigues, her arms behind her back, presumably tied together. Bruises darkened her face, which was swollen and shiny. Behind her stood four men wearing black hoods and holding automatic weapons in aggressive poses. As the video began to roll, one stepped forward and punched Lindona in the back of the head.

"Mirjeta! Please help me! They say I'm an apostate. They say apostates must die."

The hooded Talib who'd smacked her gestured, cutting off her words. The look of terror on the young woman's battered face punched Mirjeta in the gut. The Talib turned to the camera and began speaking in heavily accented but understandable English.

"In the name of Allah, the most gracious, the most merciful, and the high priest of all holy warriors, Mohammad, peace be upon him. All praise be to our Creator, Almighty God, who has helped and blessed the holy warriors of the Dadullah Front who seek to punish this polytheist apostate whose name is Lindona Tare from the village of Stari Trg in Kosovo according to His commandment which says 'But if they turn renegades, seize them and slay them wherever ye find them.'

"According to traditional Islamic law, Lindona Tare will be given three days to repent and return to Islam. If after three days she does not reaffirm that there is no God but Allah, the utterly just, the requiter, the destroyer, and that Mohammed is His messenger, she will be killed as a just punishment and warning to other apostates."

The video ended on an image of Lidona slumped against a background of black-hooded men.

Mirjeta sat staring at the screen, mind blank.

What could she do? Why did Lindona call *her* name? Why did the Dadullah Front email *her*?

A chill settled in her core.

Dr. Goodman's statement to the press following the attack by those horrible women in Code Red. She had been linked, publicly and irrevocably, with her uncle, who no doubt had ties with fundamentalist Muslim groups around the world.

Lindona's kidnapping and the "warning to other apostates" hadn't been random. It was a warning to shut up, to keep her under her uncle's metaphoric thumb. A video of Lindona recanting her work as a CST member followed by her admitting that she *had* fallen away from Islam but had returned under the guidance of the "holy warriors" would come next. It was only a matter of time before the Dadullah Front promoted its actions on the Internet and through any international media who would notice them.

Well, she wouldn't comply with their threat. She wouldn't wait for them to seize the upper hand and win by cowing her. Death threats and beheadings were the actions of bullies to silence their terrified critics. But she wasn't going to let them win this time. Surely her husband or her father-in-law knew people who could do something for Lindona. Meanwhile, she would do her part here at home: she'd write to some of the journalists covering her goodwill tour.

A thought struck her.

She'd even write to that nasty piece of work who led Code Red, Loretta Walker. That woman knew how to make a fuss. Perhaps it could be put to good use. She would tell her in front of the journalists that even though she'd been born to a Muslim father, she had chosen to become a follower of Christ, which meant that she would do all in her power to show all Muslims what it meant to be Christian. That way, she would speak out against the Dadullah Front *and* Code Red's tactics.

Energized by her decision, Mirjeta stayed up until the baby's two a.m. feeding banging out missives to anyone and everyone that occurred to her. Afterwards, despite thoughts darting around her mind like squirrels, she fell asleep nursing James.

She awoke as if her brain had switched from sleep to full awareness to the certainty that something was wrong. For a dozen shallow breaths, she listened to the dark. The baby, who lay in the crook of her arm murmured and latched on, tugging on her breast in his sleep. Thinking that it was his hungry stirrings and her own full breasts that had awakened her, she felt her heart rate and breathing slow down.

Then she heard it. Scratching from the door to the suite carried across the sitting room and through her open bedroom door. Puzzled and groggy, she looked at the bedside clock. Four a.m. It was too early for the hotel to deliver the morning paper. Who would be outside her door? The memory of Elira visiting her in Atlanta popped before her mind's eye. Could it be her? She'd seemed to have crossed some threshold with that visit, but Mirjeta had no idea what motives writhed in her medieval heart.

The scratching came again, longer and more urgent sounding. Mirjeta eased the baby from her breast, and standing, pulled a robe over her nightgown. Stepping into the sitting area, she glanced toward Heather's door, which was open.

That was it. Heather had forgotten her key card and didn't want to call the room to wake the baby.

Relieved that it wasn't the formidable *lugat* waiting on the other side of the hotel door, Mirjeta hurried to let her truant nanny in, promising herself to scold the college-age girl in the morning at breakfast. She'd opened the door wide enough to see the pale moon of Heather's face in the dim hallway before she glimpsed a man's familiar face.

"Mirjeta—" began Heather, her voice shaking.

At the same instant, Mirjeta snatched Heather's hand and yanked. The man, caught off guard, let go of Heather, who stumbled, knocking Mirjeta into the jamb and thrusting the room door wide.

"Get inside!" hissed Mirjeta, pain blossoming in her upper arm even as the attacker pulled her into the hall toward him. She let him, leveraging the weight of her momentum to punch at his face and throat with her free hand. He bent, exposing his upper back, and she came down with her elbow onto the back of his neck. He clung now to her arm for support, nearly overbalancing her.

Twisting into him, she held onto his arm and lifted her knee repeatedly into his chest before shoving him away. As he staggered, she thrust her heel into his groin. He doubled over, dropping the knife he held. Mirjeta kicked at the back of his knee, and he collapsed onto the floor where she stomped on his head. Panting, she stood over an unconscious Ismail Duka.

Behind her, baby James cried. She whirled and stepped over the threshold only to be yanked back by her hair, a knife at her throat. White-hot pain seared her from her neck to her scalp. Her vision faded to a pinprick and winked out before returning to ugly clarity. Above her, with all the perversity of the upside-down, flat-black eyes that reminded her of her uncle gazed back at her.

AROUND THE WORLD IN Pristina, Imam Krasniqi sat at an outdoor table at the Rings Café in Mother Theresa Square watching Kosovars parading along one of the two major thoroughfares of his city. Many were unemployed and found their only affordable pastime in strolling outside during nice weather. In another few months, even that would be denied to them. As he studied the pedestrians, he frowned. Several Serbs wearing t-shirts proclaiming that *Kosovo is Serbia* loitered along the far side of the square.

When would the *kāfir* accept that Kosovo had ceased to belong to Serbs hundreds of years ago? Although the international community had split over Kosovo's independence, he and his brother imams and the teachers and administrators of every Kosovar *madrasa* would continue to keep Kosovo under Albanian control. It mattered not only for his countrymen but also for the freedom of Palestine. Were they not at heart the same situation? He smirked. Israeli foreign minister Avigdor Lieberman had danced a pretty dance this past June when he said that the independence of Kosovo was a "sensitive issue" and that Israel may follow the lead of Greece and Spain in recognizing it.

Sipping his *macchiato*, Krasniqi shoved aside these amusing thoughts and checked his watch. His appointment was late. He did not appreciate being kept waiting, especially by a young man who had a lot to fear from both the local authorities as well as the Muslim leadership in Pristina. He would require a lot of persuasion at this rate in order to advocate for his young friend. He smiled. He would enjoy all the forms of prostration and kneeling that he would insist upon, the many hours devoted to assuring him of Beqir's gratitude for his help. He imagined Beqir's lanky frame naked, the tight buttocks with the dimple at the base of the spine, and he felt himself grow hard. Soon. The young man must arrive soon, or he would be forced to discipline him.

Just as he swallowed the dregs of his coffee, Beqir appeared on the sidewalk, his gait unsteady but his smile bright. Krasniqi acknowledged him with a brief nod but didn't speak. Beqir wended his way among the café tables and plopped down in the chair opposite Krasniqi.

"You try your luck," Krasniqi said, waving for the bill. "I was about to leave."

Beqir ducked his head and tried to smile. Krasniqi noticed that the young man's gaze darted around the square several times before it came back to land on his own face. He let the smile play at the corners of his lips. Beqir had every reason to be nervous.

Beqir leaned forward, licking his lips, and laid a hand over Krasniqi's where it pressed palm-down on the café table between them. "Please, don't be angry. I had no choice." And he kissed Krasniqi on the mouth.

A moment later, Krasniqi felt a searing pain in his left shoulder. Struggling to break the kiss and turn around, he found Beqir's tongue penetrating his lips while the young man's long fingers clutched at his face. Agony bloomed outward through his chest, and he began coughing and clawing at the table.

Beqir leaned back, bright blood staining his mouth. As Krasniqi's vision dimmed, the young man's hand dropped beneath the table, and then he felt it on his crotch.

"I don't think we'll meet in your Paradise," said Beqir, sounding sad.

Krasniqi gasped, bubbling blood stealing his breath. He clutched at the table, his lips opening and closing, but no words escaped. As he laid there, another man, Radoš Ojdanić, an Orthodox Christian Serb, moved into his field of vision. Radoš smiled and waggled his fingertips before sitting next to Beqir.

A last flare of furious bloodlust swamped Krasniqi at the sight: he'd ordered Radoš's brother Savo tortured and killed six months before.

Whistling as he climbed up the unlit stairs towards the second-floor apartment above Jink & Diddle, Aconcio basked in his satiated state. Practicing law in a busy court left him feeling like a cat that had gotten into the dairy. It remained then for him to sleep it off in a suitably warm and cushioned bed, preferably with a willing companion. The young woman—what was her name? Oh, yes, Althea—her blood grew more piquant every day. She promised to make a fine junior partner, nursing her injustices and injuries as one who feeds the barest spark dry tender until it explodes into conflagration.

When he pushed the bedroom door open, a foul stench assaulted his nostrils, mixed with the fragrant scent of fresh blood. Althea's pale form, splayed on the bed like a dropped marionette, glowed in spectral relief in the night-shrouded room. Her head lay at an odd angle on her shoulders. It had been severed from her body.

Aconcio hissed, raising his cane across his chest, and scanned the darkness.

"Looking for me?" Elira's faint mocking voice drifted toward him from the far corner.

As Aconcio's gaze settled on her, she dipped her chin. Before she could attempt to escape, he soared across the room and landed on her, latching his mouth onto her upper chest. He drew on her hard, his fury ruling him. Elira never struggled.

Her blood burned like sulfuric acid along his tongue, palate, and esophagus all the way to his stomach. Screaming, Aconcio wrenched away, his fingers reflexively going to his lips and cheeks.

"Your little minion also found my blood less than satisfactory." She chuckled, but it sounded as if the effort cost her. "If only you'd asked first, I could have spared you this agony."

"What have you done?" His hoarse voice strained the air between them.

"What I should have done many lifetimes ago, may God forgive me."

"He already has." Zophie stood in the room now, as luminous as a full moon.

Aconcio found the wherewithal to laugh. He ignored his old enemy. "And how will you stop Duka now, my dear?"

He coughed and wiped blood from his lips, torn like tissue paper. "Weak as you are, you will never prevent him from taking her to join her friend. Then the world will see how far her nobility carries her."

He watched, panting, as Elira struggled to her feet, swayed, and then caught herself. After a moment, she tugged her jacket down and stumbled from the room. When she'd gone, he let himself collapse onto the bed next to Althea. He shuddered. He hated to do it, but he turned to her. Her loss would suffice in his extremity.

Zophiel's low voice echoed around the room, making him choke. "It is a far, far better thing she does than she has ever done."

And then he was alone, lapping at carrion.

NINETEEN

AFTER READING MIRJETA'S EMAIL, Loretta thanked her lucky stars that she'd been unable to sleep due to whatever lingering illness she'd contracted in the spring—her doctor could find nothing wrong with her except dehydration.

Restless from a low-grade fever and headache, she'd wandered into her den and started surfing the Internet. She did this often, seeking distraction and drawn like a moth to flame to reports of beheadings, stoning, church burnings, beatings, shootings, and rape by Muslims. She especially found herself drawn to stories of honor killings in Europe and the U.S. What would Wyatt and Sawyer, those two throwbacks from the age of Southern chivalry, have said about fathers and brothers murdering their daughters and sisters because they became too "Western"?

The video that Mirjeta forwarded of the female American soldier, whose pulpy features testified to at least part of her treatment (Loretta had no doubt that she'd been raped), made her weep. But she couldn't pray, like Hamlet's uncle. Though words came to her lips, they didn't engage her heart. She no longer believed that anything that happened on Earth had any consequences after death. So she called Sylvia, who also suffered from insomnia, to have her gather the Code Red troops, and then packed a hasty bag before driving to D.C.

She arrived to chaos. Despite her haste, the media swarmed outside Mirjeta's hotel. Loretta frowned, uncertain that she wanted to wade into the mess without her loyal army. But curiosity got her when she noticed uniformed officers shoving the media back beyond a perimeter. So she parked several blocks away and trotted back, taking advantage of her white hair and sharp elbows to get there. As she neared the jostling mass, she spied several serious men in suits and her heart leaped. Mirjeta had pulled out all the stops for her announcement. Too bad for her. Loretta had every intention of making her own message heard.

But ten minutes later, to her ecstatic horror, a serious man who looked a lot like Tommy Lee Jones from *The Fugitive* beckoned the media into the hotel before waving them into a large conference room. Loretta slipped into the middle of this hungry shiver of sharks, managing to avoid the suited man trying to check press credentials at the door. Once inside the room, she moved against a side wall where she would have the freedom to approach Mirjeta before anyone could draw her away. She stood trembling until James Goodman entered from a door behind the podium. His rumpled clothes and whiskered face told their own story. Mr. Fugitive followed him. Scarcely aware of what she did, Loretta leaned forward and everyone else in the room faded away as Mr. Fugitive stepped up to the microphone and spoke.

"At approximately 4:15 this morning, Mirjeta Goodman was kidnapped by Ismail Duka and an unknown man, possibly Albanian. Her kidnappers lured her outside her hotel room using her nanny, Heather Pross, who had been assaulted and threatened. Ms. Pross and Mrs. Goodman's infant son are safe and secure. Ms. Pross has provided us with a description of the second man and local, state, and federal authorities are coordinating efforts to find them."

Hands flashed up, and voices called out questions. Loretta listened, fascinated, as Mr. Fugitive—who identified himself as Jeremy Loring, an old friend of the Goodman family—acknowledged that Duka had skipped his bond for his recent appeal.

"Tell me, Mr. Goodman," she called in a voice designed to pierce the babble. Faces swiveled toward her, including James's. "Does your wife's kidnapping have anything to do with the Taliban's upcoming execution of Lt. Lindona Tare?"

Shouts broke out from the surrounding reporters as they jostled for position.

James stiffened. Ignoring her, he turned to Loring and said, "Get her the hell out of here!"

Loretta pushed away from the wall and squared her shoulders, her chin lifting from long habit. "I'm here because your wife invited me, Mr. Goodman." She smiled at the angry glare he focused on her.

"Like hell she did!" James took a step toward her, but Loring laid a hand on his forearm and leaned in to say something to him.

Then Loring addressed her. "Mrs. Walker?"

She nodded, no longer surprised when a stranger recognized her.

"Whatever motivated Mrs. Goodman to invite you to her press conference, it no longer matters. The Goodman family is understandably distraught. Now is not the time for your political grandstanding."

"'Grandstanding?'" Loretta felt outrage geyser through her, carrying away any last vestiges of restraint. Her head burned and throbbed.

"I am *not* grandstanding. I am here to make sure justice is recognized. Mirjeta Goodman promoted peace and tolerance here in the U.S. where it's safe *after* she escaped her uncle. Now she's been caught by one of his men. Isn't that the very model of poetic justice?"

Loring opened his mouth, while James clenched his hands. To her disappointment, neither moved toward her. Around them, reporters and cameramen listened and recorded.

Loretta held up a hand to forestall any further speech. "No, gentlemen. I'm not grandstanding. Mirjeta Goodman did. Now she's going to get what she deserves. I suspect it isn't going to be a tea party."

ELIRA HAD CALLED IN a lot of favors, favors that she'd thought to use for different purposes when she'd earned them, to discover where Duka and his Krasniqi companion had taken Mirjeta—though she knew her old law partner well enough to have narrowed the search to the right sources and the right sector. After all, Aconcio had a wicked sense of humor. None of the associates that she'd called upon had been happy that she'd wanted nothing more than information and help, but her power over them had remained strong enough for them to do her will.

As a result, she found herself waiting for a charter flight at the Piedmont Triad International Airport just west of Greensboro, North Carolina—a five-hour drive from Washington, D.C. but less than four hours by air from Boston. She didn't know where Duka and his companion had holed up with Mirjeta while waiting to depart, but she'd seen the flight plan filed for a medically equipped jet to fly to Rome at midnight. Besides the sick patient, one Italian national named Elena Monreale, a private nurse and her personal physician had been listed on the passenger manifest. Given that PTI had a single terminal, it hadn't taken much research to discover where the trio would enter and exit and how much time they'd need to get through security. She had the rest of the day to herself.

Though she hated to admit it, Elira needed it to gather what remained of her waning strength and to finalize her tactics.

A heavy male body dropped into the seat next to her at the sports bar. "You look like shit, Dukagjini."

"That's funny. I feel like shit too." Elira turned and locked gazes with Andrew Cruncher. "But I suspect Mirjeta looks and feels worse."

Andrew signaled the bartender and ordered a soda. "Goodman doesn't look any better."

Elira's heart squeezed hard around the half-dead thing lodged in it. Swallowing, she looked away and drank from her own soda. "You didn't tell him, did you?"

"Now what would I go and do something so stupid for?" Compassion mixed with his exasperation. "He's got his hands full enough as it is. His father had some sort of breakdown when he heard Mirjeta had been taken." He sipped his soda. "I told Jeremy Loring."

She nodded. After James had told her about Loring, she'd done a little poking around in this old-family-friend's background. She'd discovered that Loring's credentials encompassed more than being a photojournalist who managed to get embroiled in all kinds of interesting international situations.

"So, what's the plan?"

She smiled. It felt crooked, but that was the best she could do. After a moment, she bent and pulled her dagger from her boot and laid it onto the bar between them.

"A little overdue persuasion. Duka's been expecting me for some time now, so my work's half done."

Cruncher studied her. Something in his expression got under her skin, but she smiled again and leaned against his arm where it rested on the bar.

"Are you sure that will be enough?"

His low voice jabbed at her, and she sat back, snarling. "Doubt me, Agent Cruncher?"

He shook his head slowly, never taking his eyes from her. "No, I've never doubted you." He paused before asking, "What do you want me to do?"

"You? You'll wait for Duka to wheel Mirjeta out to you in a wheelchair. Then you'll drive like a bat out of hell to get her back to James and their baby. Think you can handle that?"

Ismail Duka arrived at PTI an hour before his partner, a frothing-at-the-mouth radical named Tabesh, who made him not a little nervous. How he'd ever found himself at the mercy of these towel heads, he'd never know. Prek Krasniqi had never been too particular about his religious devotions, and that had been fine by him. He'd asked Prek once what the old man back in Kosovo would say about his drugs and women.

Prek had shrugged and said, "Not much. As long we take our women from Darul Harb and sell our drugs to unbelievers, our little indiscretions don't mean much in the scheme of things." He'd laughed and bowed with his hands together. "We serve Allah's cause when we work to ensnare and destroy *kāfir*."

But Tabesh's gaze burned with the fire of a true believer, and Duka's panic rose as the time to depart neared. It had taken all of his persuasive skills, some lying, and, he suspected, Tabesh's need to keep a close eye on their charge to convince his partner to let him run point at PTI. That explained why he didn't see the *lugat,* who lounged against the bar when he entered desperate for a strong drink or three before he traveled to the land of the fanatics. His hand shook a little as he tossed back a shot of bourbon, his other hand raised to stop the bartender from leaving before he ordered another.

"Aren't you worried your devout friend will smell the whiskey on your breath?"

Duka started at the voice, the one that haunted his nightmares. Twisting his neck a bare minimum to allow his gaze to travel to the end of the bar, he confirmed what his racing heart told him. He licked his lips and fondled his bourbon, sloshing some onto the bar as his blank mind whirled.

The creature got up from its stool and slouched next to him. He watched through unblinking eyes as she signaled the bartender, who brought her what looked like a soda. She turned toward him, a small smile twitching the corners of her mouth.

"You know, it almost seems you're trying to fortify your courage. Perhaps," here her smile widened, making her unnatural eyes gleam, "you fear that your partner will suspect you're an agent of the Americans?"

Duka's heart lurched. "That's not true," he whispered, his gaze never leaving her face.

She patted his hand. That's when he noticed the dagger on the bar between them. He flinched at its engraved symbols. She seemed unaware of his reaction, yet she placed her palm over the dagger's rounded ears and began stroking the top of its pointed blade with the tip of her index finger. He swallowed hard.

"Who's to say what's true, and what isn't? After all, evidence, like travel documents, can be manufactured at need, if one knows the right people." She kept her hard gaze on him. "I always know the right people."

"Why should I believe you?"

She fished inside her jacket and pulled out a key and a smartphone before laying them on the bar. She ignored his question.

"You know, my friend, that American justice is quite malleable. Bigger targets often justify lesser punishments for the guilty who cooperate. In your case, the U.S. Attorney's Office will cut you a deal for information about the links between the Wahhabi radicals in the Balkans and the Taliban. That means you won't be tried for killing the U.S. Marshal and the ICE agent when you escaped Fort Devens. They'll even overlook your bail jump."

Duka licked his parched lips again. "Deals can be manufactured, too."

"Indeed. This is the best I can do under the circumstances." She swiped a finger over her smartphone screen and then slid it along the bar so that he could see the video that played.

Joseph Addison, his expression hard, sat with his hands folded on a table or desk. He addressed the camera, his speech clipped and sure. "I authorize Elira Dukagjini to negotiate an immunity deal on behalf of my office with Ismail Duka. The only restrictions are that Mirjeta Goodman must be returned, safe and unharmed, and that his pending appeal is dropped. This offer is good until midnight, Eastern Standard Time."

When he'd finished speaking, the *lugat* pulled the phone back and dropped it inside an inner pocket.

Duka's hand shook as he raised his bourbon, making him curse mentally. Pulling his gaze away, he forced himself to sip the bourbon and set the glass down.

He sat up and faced her. "My lawyer is good, but the video isn't enough for me to risk my life to free the woman."

She studied him. The hair crept up on the back of his neck under her implacable gaze. Then she picked up the key.

"This key unlocks an airport locker. Inside that locker are formal documents granting you immunity from prosecution. Once Mirjeta Goodman has been delivered to my colleague, he'll text me. Then I'll text the location of the locker."

She leaned forward. "This is the only way out, Duka. You get on that plane, you're a dead man. You run, you're a dead man."

Duka passed his hand over his face, no longer caring that she might see its tremors. He looked at his wrist. Panic filled him. "Why bother making deals? Just ground the plane and take her."

She shook her head. "And risk your twitchy friend's poor nerves? Besides, there's more at stake than one woman's life."

Now it was his turn to study her. After a moment, he asked, "Are you sure you're up to this?"

She curled a corner of her mouth, but the smile didn't reach her eyes. "All I have to do is get my cellphone to the Dadullah Front base. Special Forces will take care of the rest." She drained her soda. "You in or not?"

He sighed.

"Good. Tell your friend you had to file a new flight plan because your name and photo have been plastered all over the news, thereby jeopardizing your mission."

She reached into her jacket and pulled out a packet of papers. "New travel documents showing only Elena Monreale and her personal doctor as passengers."

He took them, frowning. "Wait. What about the woman?"

She said nothing at first, reaching instead for a black bag on the floor behind her. He watched as she pulled something out and then bent over the bar. When she sat up, her pale gray irises had been transformed into dark brown ones. The change in her appearance shocked him.

"Ever notice how much I look like Mirjeta Goodman?"

ON SEPTEMBER 11, ELIRA knelt in the dust in the Qalat District, Zabol Province, with an arm wrapped around the shoulders of a sobbing twelve-year-old Christian boy. She leaned as much against him as he did her.

"'There's a divinity that shapes our ends, rough-hew them how we will,'" she murmured as she smoothed the dusty hair from his forehead.

He quieted though she knew that he didn't understand the *Hamlet* quote. She watched the Talib who circled them as he studied her ear dagger, twisting it in his hands so that the noon sun glinted from its intricate design.

From the corner of her eye, she sensed movement beyond the silent group gathered to watch. Shifting to see what had caused it, she went still. Duncan stood on the rise of the stony hill, his eyes full of love and his body whole.

Elira smiled and kept her gaze trained on Duncan's face even as the Talib, satisfied with his inspection, stepped forward and, grabbing her head, exposed her neck.

The dagger, priceless to those who studied the Ottoman Empire, proved that its worth yet extended beyond the museum.

Twenty

JAMES AND MIRJETA WATCHED ELIRA'S FINAL MOMENTS from the safety of their apartment. Although she gasped once, Mirjeta said nothing, instead clutching his hand while fingering the tarnished and twisted figure nestled between her breasts.

Afterwards, she turned from him, her back a barricade against comfort, took out her violin, and played the *Lament for the Death of Hugh Allan*.

As the haunting music swelled around him, James wandered into the kitchen and pulled out the bottle of 25-year-old Macallan, a gift from Elira after Jamie's birth. He'd poured a couple of fingers of the tawny whisky when the phone rang. He wished that he could ignore it, but he expected an update from Dr. Goodman's doctors. It wasn't the treatment facility, yet when he saw the caller ID, James found himself unable to let it go to voicemail.

"James?" Dr. Alston's soft southern drawl punched him in the gut. "Is this a good time? I've got an update on Elira Dukagjini."

James sipped his Macallan before closing his eyes to let its aroma fill his palate.

Swallowing, he said, "This is the perfect time."

"Well, it doesn't make a lot of sense to me, but that parasite I found in her heart?" He waited for James to murmur *mm-huh* before continuing. "When incubated with virus-free blood, its larvae became fertile much more quickly and reproduced more successfully."

"Let me see if I understand. Somehow the virus is fighting the effects of the parasite?"

"Yup. At the time I examined her, the virus had concentrated in her appendix, which is a part of the immune system. In fact, her immune markers had increased two hundred percent since she was hospitalized two years ago."

"What, exactly, are the symptoms of having this parasite?"

"Hosts are anemic and Vitamin D deficient. Since the parasite consumes blood at all stages of its lifecycle, there's a reasonable chance anyone infected long-term would be driven to seek blood to feed it. 'Brainwashing' to do the parasite's will isn't unheard of in parasitology. *Toxoplasma gondii* eliminates fear in its rat hosts so that they're more easily caught and eaten by cats who then complete the lifecycle by passing the eggs on to more rats in their feces."

James pinched the bridge of his nose. This was beyond incredible. "Are you saying that without the virus, the parasite would have turned Ms. Dukagjini into a vampire?"

Dr. Alston chuckled at James's horror-movie analogy. "That's pretty colorful, but I suppose it's one way to describe it. At any rate, given the significant necrosis in the parasite when I discovered it, Ms. Dukagjini's immune system should be able to combat it thanks to this virus."

He paused. When he continued, the humor had disappeared. "But, James, she could never have done it without your blood, which carried the similar virus that I found."

It took James a moment to connect the dots. "Are you saying I gave her a booster shot?"

"I'm saying you saved her life in more ways than one."

AFTER CODE RED WATCHED in silence as several Talib men wearing *kaffiya* head scarves over their faces executed Mirjeta Goodman, Loretta sent most of them home, except Sylvia and the polite young man who'd shown up at their Labor Day rally. Though Jacob Stryver with his overgrown ginger beard and suspenders put her in mind of an Anabaptist farmer, he'd watched the video with them without any apparent discomfort.

"Mr. Stryver," said Loretta, turning to where he gathered the refreshments from the long table in the church basement. "I can't tell you how I appreciate all your help, you being a stranger and all, especially someone with your background. You must find us Southern ladies old fashioned and rather simple."

He tilted his chin and smiled, his rather small and pointed teeth gleaming. His spicy cologne permeated the air, cocooning her in comforting warmth. "No, ma'am. I find your enthusiasm refreshing. Where I come from, sophisticated urban elites can't be bothered to maintain passion for anything except their wine collection, the environment, and organic food."

Loretta preened at his compliment, though she suspected that he laughed at her, old fool that she was. Still, though she knew he hadn't any interest in her dried-up elderly self, it felt good to have the close attention of a young, potent man.

At the thought, her head throbbed as the perpetual fever flared again. She rubbed her temple, restless at the pain. She needed something to distract her, something very compelling. Sylvia had gone into the kitchen to wash and put away dishes before cleaning it. It would be just her and this handsome stranger.

"Forget that for now. Come and watch the video with me again."

His eyes lit up with a fervor that matched hers. Nodding, he followed her back to the small office she'd been given for Code Red and sat next to her on the loveseat brought from her own parlor.

When the short segment began playing, she forgot all about the young man whose thigh pressed against hers in an overly familiar manner.

Instead, she leaned forward, her attention glued to the action.

"She got what she deserves," she crowed as the Talib executioner sawed at Mirjeta Goodman's neck.

At that moment, a sound caused her to look up to see Mr. Stryver transformed into an ancient man, his dark, glittering eyes now set in a face like ivory crepe paper, his mouth wide. Heat flushed through her as she recognized the mark on his forehead.

She let out a little scream as, hissing, he fell on her.

www.ingramcontent.com/pod-product-compliance
Lightning Source LLC
Chambersburg PA
CBHW060024060826
49398CB00032B/270
* 9 7 9 8 9 8 5 0 7 8 1 0 7 *